TAMESIDE LIBRARI

KT-238-558

3801601916869 1

WITHDRAWN FROM
TAMESIDE LIBRARIES

JACK LUDLOW is the pen-name of writer David Donachie, who was born in Edinburgh in 1944. He has always had an abiding interest in history: from the Roman Republic to medieval warfare as well as the naval history of the eighteenth and nineteenth centuries, which he has drawn on for his many historical adventure novels. David lives in Deal with his partner, the novelist Sarah Grazebrook.

*By Jack Ludlow*

THE LAST ROMAN SERIES

Vengeance

Honour

Triumph

THE REPUBLIC SERIES

The Pillars of Rome

The Sword of Revenge

The Gods of War

THE CONQUEST SERIES

Mercenaries

Warriors

Conquest

THE ROADS TO WAR SERIES

The Burning Sky

A Broken Land

A Bitter Field

THE CRUSADES SERIES

Son of Blood

Soldier of Crusade

Prince of Legend

◦◦◦

Hawkwood

*Written as David Donachie*

THE JOHN PEARCE SERIES

By the Mast Divided • A Shot Rolling Ship

An Awkward Commission • A Flag of Truce • The Admirals' Game

An Ill Wind • Blown Off Course • Enemies at Every Turn

A Sea of Troubles • A Divided Command

The Devil to Pay • The Perils of Command • A Treacherous Coast

# HAWKWOOD

## JACK LUDLOW

Typeset in 10/13.5 pt Sabon by
Allison & Busby Ltd

The paper used for this Allison & Busby publication
has been produced from trees that have been legally
from well-managed and sustainably sourced forests.

Printed and bound by
CPI Group (UK) Ltd, Croydon, CR0 4YY

Allison & Busby Limited
12 Fitzroy Mews
London W1T 6DW
*allisonandbusby.com*

First published in Great Britain by Allison & Busby in 2016.
This paperback edition published by Allison & Busby in 2016.

Copyright © 2016 by DAVID DONACHIE

(WRITING AS JACK LUDLOW)

The moral right of the author is hereby asserted in accordance with
the Copyright, Designs and Patents Act 1988.

*All characters and events in this publication,*
*other than those clearly in the public domain,*
*are fictitious and any resemblance to actual persons,*
*living or dead, is purely coincidental.*

All rights reserved. No part of this publication may be reproduced,
stored in a retrieval system, or transmitted, in any form or by
any means without the prior written permission of the publisher,
nor be otherwise circulated in any form of binding or cover
other than that in which it is published and without a similar
condition being imposed on the subsequent buyer.

A CIP catalogue record for this book is available from
the British Library.

10 9 8 7 6 5 4 3 2 1

ISBN 978-0-7490-1963-1

| Tameside MBC | |
| --- | --- |
| 3801601916869 1 | |
| Askews & Holts | 07-Nov-2016 |
| AF | £7.99 |
| CEN | |

# PROLOGUE

'You're a damned scoundrel, Hawkwood, regardless of how high you think to stand in the eyes of our prince. And a satyr to boot. Don't think I've forgotten how you debauched a great-niece of mine. I should have flogged you for that instead of taking you into my service. You may thank God that your skill with a longbow saved your back.'

No acknowledgement of his Christian name from this noble bastard, or of his being daubed knight by Edward of Woodstock. Worse still, silence on the years of service rendered since the day King Edward landed his army at St Vaast in pursuit of the French crown. The temptation to remind him was there, the desire to argue even stronger, to suggest that when it came to debauching it took more than one to make merry. Yet it would be impolitic to say to the Earl of Oxford that his young and comely relative had been a very willing victim in their couplings; all he could do was cross himself and murmur an incantation for a paramour long departed this life, taken in childbirth.

'May God rest her sweet soul and bless Antiocha, the child of our innocent misdemeanour.'

One of the falcons perched in the tent furiously flapped its wings, as if to question the veracity of that statement and it produced for Hawkwood another glare from his liege lord. Was John de Vere being crusty merely for effect? He had barely said two words to the relative in question and Hawkwood knew him to be far from sentimental as regards the loss of even family members or a close friend. As to the child, she was being raised by the earl's Essex cousins.

Right now the enquiry he had posited was more important than pointing up blue-blooded hypocrisy; he needed to stay on the right side of the earl in the hope that he and his company of archers could remain as paid retainers and perhaps even fighting men. Weeks of talking were coming to a head and it was rumoured the two sovereigns of France and England were close to agreeing the terms of a lasting peace, one brokered by a representative of the papacy.

No one doubted the necessity: Edward's army was exhausted by years of campaigning added to the failure to take Paris. They had been obliged to withdraw from a siege they were too few in number to properly impose. Calais apart, all the most important successes in the English campaign had come in the open field on a well-chosen site that suited a numerically inferior force.

Taking fortresses was hard toil: Calais had held out for just shy of a whole year, while the walls of Paris had proved too lengthy to fully invest, which left starvation as the only possible avenue to success without a high quantity of siege equipment and that, as well as the men with the skills to build such things, was lacking. As short of food as the city inhabitants and with morale plummeting, the time had come for Edward Plantagenet to withdraw to the safer territory of Normandy.

Not that they got there unscathed: as if by divine judgement a great tempest, biblical in its intensity, hit the retreating column, with hail the size of rocks and bolts of lightning falling with an intensity akin to the arrow swarms of Crécy and Poitiers. Many a knight perished as well as a number of soldiers clad in chain mail, lightning literally frying the former in their plate armour and striking down the latter either by the attraction of their metal cowls or the tips of the spears they carried. Such chain mail hoods had been the price of vanity; how was it necessary to still be so garbed with no fighting in prospect?

'Transgressions aside, you have grown to be a good captain,' de Vere growled, bringing his visitor back from unpleasant recollection. 'So know this. You have the right to continue in my service, perhaps as a steward like your older brother, though not, God forbid, anywhere near Castle Hedingham, given your previous offence.'

If it was an offer with some attraction – de Vere owned land all over the southern counties of England – but it was one he could not accept.

'You will recall I was asking not just for myself but also

for my company?' Seeing the hackles rise – a belted earl was not accustomed to being questioned by a man-at-arms, even a captain of archers – Hawkwood added quickly, 'I mean should there be an accord that brings an end to the war.'

'What use does King Edward have of an army if there is concord? What use do I have for a hundred longbowmen, men I'll have to sustain from my own purse?' The shaking of the head was violent enough to move the long greying locks. 'No, if a treaty is agreed they must fend for themselves, as will many.'

'On short commons' was the thought that engendered as well as the memory of what he had faced himself after the Crécy campaign. Success in battle had granted Hawkwood and many others much in the way of booty, enough to contemplate a return to England with the hope of a decent life immediately after the capture of Calais.

Contrary winds had destroyed that prospect, blowing the Earl of Oxford's ship off its course for the shores of southern England, driving them far to the west and the coast of Ireland. There they were stripped of all they possessed by the bare-arsed locals, left with only the clothes on their back and a long trek to find a boat to take them home on a pledge of payment from the earl, which counted as money owed.

True, de Vere had lost more than the men he led, but he came back to England and the landed possessions as well as income he held as a potent magnate. In addition to his rents he still had a claim on unpaid ransoms, and they were substantial, from the French noblemen taken prisoner at Crécy.

When the next call to arms was promulgated, for an assault on Aquitaine under the King's son and heir Edward of Woodstock, a strapped Hawkwood, living from hand to mouth on nefarious schemes and with a writ as a common malefactor hanging over his person, had been left with little choice but to volunteer for a second campaign.

At least that had provided good returns. Called the Festival of Pillage, the young prince and his army had devastated the rich lands of the Languedoc, their endeavours ending in the even greater victory over the French at Poitiers. The English nobility had proceeded to ransom half the captured chivalry of France and pocketed fortunes. This would pale into insignificance against the money that would be needed to get the King of France released, also taken prisoner in the battle.

The evidence of success for John de Vere lay all around this beautiful silken tent, once the property of the French Constable: fine furniture, gold plate off which to eat, ornaments and illuminated manuscripts of great value to fill empty hours, while the lordly stables were packed with the finest mounts, saddlery and gilded accoutrements France could produce. And that was before every man he led offered up one-third of his own gains to his liege lord, de Vere in turn passing a third of the whole to King Edward through his son.

If the men had done well from plunder and sack on the march, stripping the dead of their weapons and possessions as well as purloining the property of a slain French knight, the coin gained had been expended to maintain their needs in wine and pleasure in the failed attempt to invest Paris.

Non-noble fighters were not the kind to accumulate: they were a tribe who regularly faced death and not only in battle. Prey to disease as well as misfortune, they lived for the moment and not the rainy day.

Going home to England, which was being touted as their future, would scarce be attractive to the men Hawkwood led. Nor was it to him personally, even with de Vere's offer. Quite apart from the risk to his person, to accept would be a betrayal of those who trusted him to look to their well-being. They were likely to land on their home soil with little left to sustain them and no occupation of worth to look forward to. Skilful archery would not provide a living; the Welsh and Scottish borders, where many had previously plied their trade, were known to be peaceful.

'I would wish to appeal against this, Your Grace.'

'Then I suggest you do so to Prince Edward, who still believes he owes you his life.'

There was mockery in that; many believed the claim that John Hawkwood had come upon Edward of Woodstock just in time to stop him from being skewered by an enemy lance to be nonsense. In addition the prince, having laid his sword upon Hawkwood's shoulders to dub him with the honour of knighthood, had passed by him several times since without so much as a nod of recognition, which marked the elevation for what it truly was: a piece of flummery from a leader in the first flush of glory, designed to add lustre to his name and no other.

'His Grace has his own companies to maintain. I cannot believe he will seek to add to them.'

'You have my offer, Hawkwood, say aye to it or decline.'

'War does not train a man for collecting rents, Your Grace.'

'You were not born a soldier, Hawkwood, you were sired by a tenant farmer.'

'Nor was I born a villein, though happen I saw service under one.'

Accompanied by a glare, it hit home as it was supposed to. The term for an indentured man tied to his strip of land, when spoken, was close to that of a thief. Hawkwood wanted to make it plain that in denying those who had swollen the de Vere coffers any hope of comfort was something akin to robbery. Judging by the flushed cheeks and furious glare he had struck home.

'I bid Your Grace good day.'

The call that followed, not a shout but just as meaningful, told the Captain of Archers in the Earl of Oxford's division there was no going back.

'While I, Hawkwood, bid you a full if not a fond farewell. Oblige me in this, do not call upon my person again unless you learn humility.'

# CHAPTER ONE

The route back to his own encampment took Hawkwood past the tents of both his sovereign and his prince. Above the former flew the lions of England quartered with the lilies of France, the statement made that Edward, third of that name, was the rightful monarch through his mother Isabella, denied his title by the illegal invocation of the Salic Law barring women from succession. Above the tent of his much-loved eldest son flew the armorial design he had taken from Blind King John of Bohemia, who had perished at Crécy: the three plumed white feathers emerging from a golden crown, above the motto *Ich Dien*.

The thought of seeking aid from either died when Hawkwood counted the number of supplicants waiting for an audience: several dozen and possibly many on the same mission as he. If he declined to join them, he did stop long enough to converse with acquaintances. In an eight-thousand-man army and after four years on campaign he could name most of the prominent fellows among them, captains of companies awaiting the pleasure of their prince.

Such talk confirmed to him that which he dreaded. A treaty of peace was close to a conclusion, the last haggle only the ransom price for the French King Jean, living, hunting and hawking in much comfort outside London. Stalemate had been acknowledged: Edward could not win the crown he claimed and the French lacked the force to evict him from their lands.

Those with whom he spoke were sure that Edward would renounce his claim to the French crown, that he would trade some possessions for others, while hanging on to those he considered most important; his family fief of Normandy, Aquitaine and Calais the most vital. When it came to the ransom demand for King Jean, for the first time in his life Hawkwood heard the word 'million' employed. When he asked for clarification as to what it meant, he could get no more than that it was many times greater than a thousand or even ten times so.

'No man, king or commoner is worth so much, whatever he signifies.'

'The French princes will be paying to buy back both their father and the honour of the lands they rule.'

'You cannot purchase honour, it must be earned,' Hawkwood insisted.

He threw a meaningful glance towards that one-time Bohemian banner, fluttering above the tent: Blind King John had ridden into a battle he knew to be lost, his bridles held by the knights who accompanied and perished with him. There was a monarch who needed no money to secure his name; his death and the manner of it had made him immortal. The fellow for whom he had fought enjoyed no such reputation.

'Jean le Bon should have opened his breast to the knife or the sword if he had a care for the name of his patrimony or his realm. To plead for mercy because of his worth in gold was demeaning.'

That occasioned murmured approval; John of Bohemia, by common consent, had a good and honourable death. The King of France lived still, but surely in ignominy. No minstrels would sing of him as they would of Edward of Woodstock, the man who had beaten his army at Poitiers.

Returning to the farmhouse they had taken over as their billet, he noticed some of his archers trying to sham indifference, looking away, fiddling with their long, unstrung bows or examining weapons, starting conversations with their comrades or one of the horses in the paddock, seeking to mask their curiosity. The truth was in the anxiety of those who watched him closely as he approached, hoping to see in his expression some sign of a good outcome. Ever well versed in dissimulation, their captain kept on his face a bland countenance that was impossible to read.

'Gather you all.'

The men shuffled forward, keen to be to the fore. As

he looked around the faces Hawkwood could not help but recall those that were missing, men who had died on the march as well as those who had fallen in battle – few, it had to be said. They had perished in astounding occasions that would be commemorated in songs and ballads or the chronicles written by scribes both noble and monkish. But it would not be the names of the commonality who would be praised. Kings won renown off the backs of their subjects.

'De Vere will not dent his purse and has no use for our service. He means to leave us to make our own way in the world even to the manner in which we get home.'

The statement induced many an angry growl from those assembled. Hawkwood let it run its course before pronouncing on the alternative, which was not really necessary; the men he was addressing knew as well as he what it would be.

'The possessions of the French are vast and most of their manors lie untouched. Our sovereign and his son have taught us it is possible to live well off the land and that is what those of us who do not wish for England must do. For those of you determined to return to your hearths we will bid a fond farewell and pray to God for your safe passage.'

'To hell with hearths, let us form a free company as others have done.'

This admonition came from Alard the Radish, one of Hawkwood's corporals, so named for his rubicund skin added to a propensity to blush at the mere proximity of a woman or any carnal thought. This would produce flaring red cheeks, set off and made more striking by a thick mop of flaxen hair and an impish grin.

'Freebooters we will be,' called another, Badger Brockston, he of the white streak on one flank of his jet black hair. 'If our own will not see to our prosperity then the land hereabouts must, and who is to say we will not be ourselves lords one day?'

'Temper your ambitions, Brockston,' Hawkwood sighed. 'Settle for food and wine. If it is to be done then we must be properly conjoined, with a scribe-written contract by which each who volunteers must put their mark. The same fellow must be taken on for a fee, to keep a tally of that which we acquire and ensure fair distribution of our spoils.'

'First we must elect a captain,' Alard insisted.

'Then we must have a vote. Who wishes to put their name forward?'

Hawkwood was offered no rivals and nor did he expect any; he had led this company of archers for years now. It would have been strange indeed if others had put themselves up to be leader. The acclamation that he should command them was heartening, only the Badger asking, 'No one has asked if you intend to take that path, John? And it is rumoured King Edward is set to forbid it and insist all his fighting men return home.'

'Home to what, Brockston? I have no wife and no property, with little hope of gaining either in a country flooded with the returned of our ilk. No, whatever our sovereign says I will stay in France and seek what the good Lord sees fit to provide.'

'Happen that wife you hanker after,' Ivor the Axe called, his glee obvious.

'Any woman will do, Ivor, for me and I think for us all.'

As a statement it was simple, yet John Hawkwood knew the position he was being invited to occupy carried with it responsibilities. They would not be part of a paid host as they had up until now, nor under the command of leaders who had steered them to great victories. There would be no marshals scouring the land to find the food to feed them, nor Constables to plan their movements and form them up for battle. They must look to their own needs.

What he had said about written commitments was not an idle point: it was vital that all committed to the cause by contract. There would be a need to engage someone capable of acting as their factotum. A monk would be best if he could find an honest one, which was not likely to be easy, as they tended to be a venal bunch. But they generally had a superior command of Latin and numbers.

In what would be a Free Company every man must have a pair of horses and the proper assembly of the necessary weapons, not just a single mount and their bows and knives. As archers there would be a need to get hold of spears and shields as well as a good supply of arrows, for there would be none from a royal source. The ability to deliver a shower of those would be their primary attraction to any host they offered to join, for his brigade were too few and too singular in their skills to operate as an independent body.

The camps around the hamlet of Brétigny were awash with men considering the same course and not all were English. There were fighters from the lands of the Holy Roman Empire, from Brittany, Hainault, Flanders and Gascony, as well as a dozen other provinces, come to fight for the rewards that could be accrued and scarce caring from whom they needed to be taken. Over the next days, as what came to be called the Treaty of Brétigny was settled, John Hawkwood made his way from farmhouse to manor house, from tented encampments to a band who had sequestered a monastery, throwing out most of the inmates, keeping only enough to see to their needs as servants. He sought out those who styled themselves captain generals and examined each group, now beginning to form into companies of a formidable size.

Finally he settled on one led by a Rhinelander called Albert Sterz, who spoke decent English and had gathered under his banner a large number of individual brigades. Most vitally, it was one well balanced in its various arms, including enough mounted knights to effect a telling charge against a well-mounted enemy, should the need arise.

Hawkwood had many reservations about Sterz on his first meeting; in fact he was unsure if he liked the German, not that affection was paramount. Yet he had to admit the man had a level of organisational skill the Englishman could not match and was not prepared to posture and pretend he did. Hawkwood could command his company and lead them to where they were needed: such placement would often lay outside his present competence.

He was welcomed: Sterz was eager to add English longbowmen to the force he had decided to call the Great Company. Here too there had to be contracts: written obligations from captains of bands to serve for a period and a portion of the spoils acquired, which would be disbursed, once a leader's share had been deducted, amongst those they led.

With an air of command, taller by a full two hands than Hawkwood, the German looked impressive. Much scarred by combat, he had a knobbly forehead and a set of greying eyebrows that hung like curtains over his hooded green eyes. The nose might have been prominent once; now it was near flat to his face, evidence of fighting with fists as well as his sword.

Latin was the language of contracts, English of discourse. His was guttural as that of any German speaker but, with a deep voice and an ability to carry without shouting, he possessed the vital air of leadership, backed up by a ready fist with which to quell disagreement that was needed to impose order. Yet the Great Company could be no tyranny: which direction to march, what places to attack and plunder, to accept or avoid battle had to be discussed and John Hawkwood would be as much part of that as two dozen others of equal merit. All that was needed now was confirmation of a treaty of peace and that came within days.

As a loyal subject of his king, Hawkwood had a letter drawn up to tell Edward of his intentions, though that had to be disguised since part of the treaty insisted that all English fighting men must depart France, not a sanction the king was inclined to enforce; peace was one thing, leaving your enemy to prosper unhindered was another. The fact that he swore fealty said that which was required: I am your liege man and wherever I serve I uphold your crown.

Everyone, from lowly men men-at-arms to the greatest magnates, attended the ceremony in nearby Chartres that closed the Treaty of Brétigny, the masses of the commonality held back by the familia knights who rode into battle with their various aristocratic banners to protect their valued person. Edward Plantagenet and his son, gorgeously clad in silks, embraced the offspring of King Jean as if they had been boon companions all their lives. The French princes, Charles and Philip, would have as soon knifed their counterparts as kiss them on the cheek, of that there was no doubt.

Parts had to be played, amity pushed to the fore. Edward Plantagenet now flew a banner above his pavilion with only his three golden lions, the flag no longer quartered with the lilies of France. He had renounced his claim and knelt in fealty to the absent King Jean for his possessions on the Continent as had all Dukes of Normandy before him. After a mass in the Cathedral of Our Lady a feast had to be consumed, with cups of wine disappearing down willing throats, to be refilled with alacrity until most of the main assembly ended up drunk.

Lesser beings were not to be left behind and the fights that ensued were a commonplace with men well into their cups. The mayhem that followed, as the most rapacious descended on the hitherto untouched hamlet of Brétigny, was only to be expected. If the French princes and nobility, still at their tables eating and drinking, heard the screams of violated women and men being put to the sword for seeking to protect them, they paid it no heed. Their sense of personal honour and their tradition of disdain for the commonality demanded indifference.

At dawn the opposing camps began to break up, the English lords aiming to go home through Calais, leaving behind a smouldering Brétigny and those who declined to be part of the exodus. The French, expected to head back to Paris, instead moved to protect Chartres, well aware that those forming free companies would be tempted by such a wealthy prize. Hawkwood moved his men close to the encampment occupied by Sterz and it was there that the first true gathering of captains came together.

The decision, quickly taken, was to march south into the fertile lands of the province of Beauce, known as the granary of France. The towns were untouched, wealthy, the farmers rich in a countryside groaning with produce and so a temptation to the profitable depredations of the Great Company, two thousand fighting men strong.

Other bands headed west and south-west, taking any road that led to profit, scorching that through which they passed to leave behind diminished populations, ruined crops, unwilling women who would in time bear their bastards as well as a dearth of living men to till the soil. Of all the names they were called, and none of them were favourable, the most common became 'Routiers' and this would soon spread over all of France inducing terror.

# CHAPTER TWO

The thick, leafy overhead canopy cut out so much light that the track seemed to be in near darkness, made more telling by the twin arcs of sunlight ahead and behind that showed the outer limits of this patch of deep woodland. Such gloom rendered ethereal the way the forest edge suddenly came to life. The undergrowth began to move, shapes that grew arms and legs moments before this seeming illusion took proper form.

The missiles came next: catapult-launched stones, not as deadly as arrows or spears but with the power to seriously wound those slow to get their sheilds up, made doubly difficult because of the effect on the more vulnerable mounts.

Horses were rearing and spinning, threatening to unseat their riders; the pack horses were straining on their lead ropes, their noisy reaction to pain and shock adding to the general mayhem. Ahead of the column and behind, a succession of tall mature trees began to fall, slowly at first, until crashing through the leafage of those opposite they thudded into the ground to form a set of formidable barriers to the front and rear of the horse-borne company.

John Hawkwood was as astonished as any man he led but as captain it was incumbent on him to produce a response; he needed a cool head not a panicked one and if he wondered from whom this ambuscade came that would have to wait; it was now a matter of survival. Having registered those falling trees he quickly guessed the aim; first to block any desire for continued forward movement, which left him and his men with retreat as the obvious option. That suggested a killing zone had been set up on this side of the thick trunks, easy targets for slingshot and attack, as men and mounts sought to get around or over them.

'Never do that which your enemy desires.'

This was a watchword Hawkwood had learnt from his royal commanders and it was one he uttered to himself now. Fighting to control his courser and aware that the original assailants had vanished, he risked standing in his stirrups, simultaneously unsheathing and raising his sword to shout, not with force enough to entirely overcome the bellowing and neighing but sufficient to get the attention of those closest to him. Enough men moving in the right direction would drag the remainder with them.

A second salvo of catapult stones came winging out of the woods, only for those firing them to once more dissolve into the greenery. That had to be ignored: certain actions were unthinking in a band of professional fighting men. The youngest of his company, boy recruits picked up on their travels, had been quick to follow the standing command that they dismount in order to gather together the still troubled packhorses, thus freeing their seniors to give battle.

Time did not allow for a leader to think on such matters; action was required. It was the aimed sword at the end of an outstretched arm his men followed, not the roaring voice. Hawkwood drove his mount into the dense foliage that hid the forest floor, a thick tangle of bushes in full summer bloom, behind him young Christopher Gold, his standard-bearer as well as his horn-blowing signaller, who never left the side of his chief.

The human form that rose from within was no more than a pair of white, wild eyes in a face daubed the same colour as the leaves around his head, the branch-strewn clothing of a dun and near invisible hue. There was the glint of a blade and the rider knew where that would be aimed: not at him but at the belly of his horse. Hauling hard on the reins and throwing his own weight to the rear of his saddle he got his mount's hooves high enough to flay, a threat that created its own obstruction to his opponent's intentions.

At the same time he was seeking, by the pressure of his knees, to turn to the left and thus clear the way for his sword arm. It all happened in one movement, seconds that felt an age as if time had decided to stand still. The way he had to extend his reach nearly unseated Hawkwood as he slashed at the man's neck. Had the fellow been less eager to strike he would probably have survived, but with his passions high and yelling unintelligible imprecations, he rushed into the arc of the blow.

Taken between jaw and shoulder the sharp metal sliced through the vital organ that carried his blood, sending forth a spray of bright-red fluid. Hawkwood was not looking at that but at the eyes, now displaying the shock of a man who knew he was about to die. With a weapon both sharp on the edge and pointed at its tip the second blow was a straight jab to the upper chest, waste since it jarred on solid bone, sending a telling jolt up the rider's arm.

Given his men had followed his lead, albeit in piecemeal fashion, the entire forest edge was now a melee of freebooters seeking to get far enough into the trees to kill their assailants. Hawkwood had a fear that more attackers, in numbers of which he had no idea, could come upon their rear – and that might prove calamitous.

Wheeling out onto the track and seeing no movement, he called for his horn carrier to blow a command to rally to the banner, raised high and waved by Gold. It was not swiftly obeyed, yet bit by bit those seeking to penetrate deeper into the forest began to emerge, to form up on the track. Blood dripping from many of their weapons stood as testimony to the act of killing; now they must get ready to continue a fight against an enemy that seemed to have disappeared.

'Alard, dismount your section and string your bows. The rest stay horsed and in position to charge.'

In his band, still a hundred-strong after a year of campaigning but of mixed skills as new recruits joined, forty men slid from their saddles, to ease the required weapon from their packhorses. The stringing was quick through long practice and a sheaf of arrows followed, along with the slung quiver to hold them.

Whoever led their attackers must now be wondering what was coming, for the men he had drawn into this ambuscade were not acting as he would have hoped for and planned. There was no headlong rush to get clear and certainly an utter lack of panic, which had surely been expected. Seeking to put himself in his opponent's shoes Hawkwood tried to work out how he would react.

The original method of assault indicated a body of men not trained to fight in the open and thus not soldiers. There had been no thrown spears and that indicated a lack of weapons. The man he had killed carried only a knife and there was no evidence of even a padded jacket for protection.

'Horsemen to the fore,' he commanded, moving forward himself to lead. 'Alard, I will close the range to a hundred paces then you will deploy.'

He had to bank on his enemy remaining in the cover of the trees, but what if they came out to fight? Surely they would be on foot, in which case cavalry could charge and scatter them. He held his breath as he led his men forward, yet it became increasingly obvious he had guessed right. Whoever had contrived this trap was still hoping for an attempt to get past those tree trunk barriers. Even if carried out with no panic the horses would cause difficulties, leaving them in some disarray and thus vulnerable.

The forest was quiet, which had Hawkwood quietly castigating himself: surely it had been that when he entered this stretch of shaded track and it had not registered. There was an alternative: those awaiting him could have been in position for a very long time, which would allow the forest creatures, most importantly the birds, to settle. The horsemen stopped as he held up his hand, the men on foot slipping by to line up, bows resting on the ground and an arrow to hand ready to be nocked.

'Fire on my command.'

Hawkwood tried to conjure up an image of what was being observed in reverse, from within that screen of trees looking onto what was a deeply shaded trail. They would see and recognise the weapons they were going to face: every boy born made a bow as soon as they grew enough to draw and pretend. Yet would they remark on the length of those about to be employed against them? This far south would they have heard of the great defeats of the French kings by the English and the reasons it had come about?

'Your ruse has failed!' he shouted. 'I grant you a chance to withdraw. Send someone to parley if you agree.'

This was called out in Latin, the only language that might be understood in a land where there seemed to be as many dialects as people. Every district he and his comrades had passed through since heading south from Chartres boasted its own unique patois. Only in the towns and cities was there any semblance of a common tongue and that was so larded with idiom as to be nearly as incomprehensible. If they had a monk in the forest then his words would be understood. If not, matters would take their course.

The act of killing did not overburden John Hawkwood but he was still on the wrong side of those tree trunks with no real knowledge of what he faced in numbers and ability. A guess was just that, and it was incumbent on him to preserve the lives of those who followed his banner. It was a foolish captain who led his men into a fight against unknown odds.

'No reply, John.' The words were called back by Alard the Radish. As one of Hawkwood's corporals and commander of the bowmen he had the right to speak. 'They might have fled.'

'But perhaps not. Better safe.'

The order to fire to the left-hand side of the barrier followed immediately. The bows came up, each of an individual length but taller than the man employing it, the long pull requiring strong muscles in the arm and back. There was no need for another command, each archer was trained to count the right numbers in his head for each act and they knew to fire flat in such circumstances and at the perceived range. Thus the volley was simultaneous as was the reloading and firing of a second salvo. By the time the third was on its way from quiver to bow the first screams began to come out of the woods, caused by those arrows that had missed trees and found flesh.

'Fire to the right,' came the shout.

The archers swung their weapons to obey, sending three salvos into the foliage opposite to again be rewarded with more cries as they struck home. Then it was back leftwards to catch those who had forsaken cover to look to their wounded comrades, the increased volume of pained sounds evidence of their success.

'They're coming out,' Alard cried.

Which they did, seeming hundreds of ragged peasants carrying pitchforks, scythes and knives, goaded into action. The price paid for this folly was high as they ran into a hail of arrows, fired with enough velocity to penetrate the trunk of any body they struck, the points emerging out of their backs. As a charge it was suicidal, yet they were strong in passion, for those who managed to avoid a wound came on.

The drill that followed was carried out smoothly; the archers turned and slipped back through the screen of horsemen, who, with Hawkwood to the fore, immediately closed with these poor unfortunates. The sight of big-chested coursers and thudding hooves coming towards men on foot was too much. Some turned and ran to be followed by the more stalwart, many tripping over their dead or dying comrades, seeking the safety of the trees.

Few managed it and a slaughter ensued, for the archers knew what was required. Out came their bollock knives and in they weighed at the run, to skewer or slit the throat of anyone who appeared to still have breath, while the horsemen pursued and sought to kill those still fleeing. They were strangers in these southlands and an example must be set: the best way to avoid any repeat of what had just happened was to leave none of their assailants alive.

\* \* \*

The main body of the Great Company came across Hawkwood's men working with axes and multiple teams of horses and ropes, seeking to clear the forest track enough to let the main body following get through, not least the dozens of heavily laden carts carrying possessions, booty and the hundreds of artisans and camp followers. They required the full width of the track to pass on and the enclosing forest precluded any detour. To one side lay heaped a pile of bodies, the earth stained with their blood. There they would remain as food for carrion if no one came to bury them.

Albert Sterz was to the fore of the host under a banner many times the size of any he led, the look of disbelief maintained even up to the point where he dismounted to survey the scene and demand an explanation. Hawkwood had learnt, once the contracts were signed and any wooing ceased, that he was naturally irascible, a trait which had been made more forceful by the success of the company. Sterz was behaving in an imperious manner now, as if Hawkwood had been a fool to walk into such an obvious trap as well as fight a battle that yielded many a cadaver but not a sou in coin, only to receive a jaundiced reply.

'This was not an occasion for profit, would that it had been. These dead had nothing of value to plunder lest you consider a scythe or two to be treasure. We have never contested with such a pitiable bunch.'

'Not a knight amongst them?'

'No.'

'Then who are they?' Sterz growled.

'I suspect local peasants who heard of our coming and

were determined to stop us burning their crops. If they were aware of our presence they clearly know nothing of our numbers, assuming my brigade to be the main host.'

The German pinched his much-broken nose as he stood over the pile. 'You should have been able to smell them if you could not see them, for I can scarce stand the stench in which they lived their miserable lives.'

'Then I suggest you clamber back into the saddle. There you will see that the sweat of your mount means you can't even smell your own farts.'

The green eyes flashed; Sterz did not relish being talked to in that way and he stretched his body as if to imply that height alone entitled him to respect, his jaw standing as testimony to his natural obstinacy. The man addressed had no intention of allowing this and had shown already he never would.

'We could neither smell them nor see our assailants,' Hawkwood added, explaining the camouflage, 'but we did fight and overcome them, which is what counts in the end.'

'A great victory, Sir Hawkwood,' was the ironic response, the title just short of an insult. 'Shall we give it a name so those who come after us will know where it occurred? Perhaps call it after the nearest village, if we can find one?'

Such a skirmish did not even warrant a memory. To garnish it with a title would be an insult to the recollection of proper battles in which Hawkwood and his men had fought. The attitude had more to do with the way his inferior talked to him than what had just taken place: while willing to acknowledge the German as a good leader, the Englishman had refused to bow the knee to him. Too many

31

of his fellow captains seemed disposed to do so and that added to the impression Sterz had of his own stature.

'Find me a village and I will torch it,' Hawkwood responded, 'so that the likes of these up ahead know what will be their fate if they seek to halt our progress.'

'Something we are not making, Hawkwood. Your task on this day was to act the constable and find a suitable camping ground for the company. So you might be better employed seeking to remove the obstacles ahead rather than these you are working on, which others can clear.'

The temptation to dispute that arose only from pique; what the German was saying made sense. Much of the day was gone and the company needed a large open space to pitch its tents and tether its horses. It had to be near a river so the ever-thirsty equines could drink and the fighting men could have water with which to cook and some even to bathe.

Hawkwood nodded and called to his men to gather up their tools and remount, leading them away as soon as that was complete. If they wondered why he detoured into the woods before he got close to the fallen tree trunks none asked; the undergrowth was thick but not dense enough to stop a strong courser from barrelling through, the rest in his wake. The route Hawkwood chose took them round the second set of fallen barriers. Finally Ivor the Axe, just to his rear, enquired what was to be done about them.

'Let Sterz see to that. It will be an aid in getting some of the fat off the arses of his Germans.'

'He will get another to do it,' Ivor said, his accent heavily Welsh. 'One of his grovellers.'

'You're likely right, friend,' came the gay reply.

The so-called captain general would have seen his ploy and that would irritate him, which was to the good. Better still, he could say nothing to fault the man who had guyed him: finding a proper place to bivouac took precedence over anything else.

# CHAPTER THREE

If Sterz had acquired pretensions to self-worth since taking command of the Great Company, everyone knew him to be the son of a charcoal burner. This, being the lowest of low occupations, occasioned many a joke at his expense, though never within the range of his hearing. He had a fierce temper that acted as a red mist and could kill before the realisation dawned on him it was not necessary. If he had risen by soldiering, his background made him touchy regarding his dignity and the way he lived reflected that.

His accommodation was no mere tent, more a spacious pavilion which was always set down with what wind blew and to where in mind, so that the odours of two thousand men, of horses, livestock on the hoof and that which was cooking did not intrude on his luxury. The contents of several carts were always on display at each tented encampment, likewise laid out when the company assaulted and took a monastery or citadel and rested under a proper roof.

His other habit, playing the great magnate, was to invite his captains to dine with him and his German secretary, the Benedictine friar Cunradus. This would be served at a great board, minions toiling hard to ensure it groaned under the weight of the food he provided. The serving dishes and goblets were of either silver or gold, the decorated knives made from the finest steel Milan could produce. Few alluded to the fact that it was paid for by all; it was shared property, not personal plunder from their joint exploits.

The profits of the host were pooled and distributed according to rank and ability, with Sterz holding such valuables as a common coffer in case times became hard. Hawkwood's English longbowmen and experienced spearmen were highly regarded and thus well rewarded in comparison to others he now commanded. Foot soldiers tended to be no more than armed peasants and so were the lowest paid, just ahead of the untrained youths who had joined their travelling band to escape rural tedium.

There were, of necessity, those who ranked above them all, such as the mailed and armoured knights. Also paid and fed were the scribes, usually but not exclusively monks, others of that ilk acting as mendicants. There were smiths, farriers, sutlers and armourers as well as camp wives and their urchins. All lived off what the company could garner in booty and provisions from those who lay in their predatory path. If they did not plunder they did not eat and the direction in which they went next was of paramount importance; where could they sack, burn or extort to the greatest level of profit?

If the German used his dinners to play the great man, they were also used to lay out plans for future operations and in this he required to know what forces might be ranged against them. Powerful local magnates or large towns who might raise a substantial body of men were left untroubled, the blows falling on those less able to defend themselves: minor nobility, rich urban-based traders as long as their domicile lacked stout walls, farmers of broad hectares and deep coffers, though the poor were not left untouched either.

Wherever a freebooting company went they left behind them a trail of destruction: ruined buildings, scorched fields, cut-down vines, dead men or those maimed by torture into revealing hidden wealth. Women suffered for their gender and the lust of men who were not inclined to bypass vats of wine or the pleasures of free flesh.

The French crown had tried many times to interdict the Great Company, known to be the largest, in the year since Brétigny but the Paris-based princes had never fielded enough men to put a stop to Sterz leading his host to wherever he sought to go. That accepted, contact was avoided: it was no part of their task to engage in fixed battle with a proper army, in which men might expire or pick up a wound without return, so any hint of a substantial opponent close by had an effect.

Flush from ravishing the Beauce, the general intention was to continue south into country that had never seen or been troubled by any of the free companies. Rich pickings were to be expected in places that were blessed by the sun and had seen no turmoil in decades.

Throughout the eating and boasting Hawkwood ate well but drank sparingly, leaving the pavilion early to do the rounds of his own area and ensure his men were content; such diligence was much appreciated for it was not common amongst captains. This occasioned several stops at campfires to exchange words, jests and memories with people he had fought alongside, Hawkwood never having lost sight of the fact that he had once been an ordinary archer.

He was about to get into his sleeping cot – he kept a fairly humble tent on the grounds that display caused unnecessary envy – when the summons came to return immediately to the pavilion. A call of that kind might presage danger and he thought to order a stand-to, with mounts saddled, only to put it aside; Sterz would have called for that already if danger threatened. Yet he did take his own sword and the boy page Christopher, whom he could send back to undertake that task if there was any danger.

Hawkwood was not the last to enter the pavilion and those who did follow him showed evidence of having overindulged in their leader's hospitality, having probably stayed behind when the less gluttonous had departed. Sterz himself, clad in a fine silk gown that had once graced a senior French bishop and shimmered in the mass of candlelight, said nothing. But seeing in Hawkwood's eye the obvious question, as well as his weapon to hand, he responded with an imperceptible shake of the head. There was a stranger present, a fellow whose clothing was covered in the dust of travel which implied he had ridden to this place and was newly arrived, which in turn suggested he had brought intelligence, something the company paid well to receive as a guarantor of both security and opportunity. Was it a chance for booty or news of a hostile force close by? The next act engendered even deeper curiosity and hinted at something very unusual. Sterz ordered his servants, quick to fill and serve goblets of wine, to their beds – all except the monk, Cunradus.

Sure they were gone, he spoke, and for once it was with deliberate softness, half-turning to introduce the stranger. 'This is Antonio di Valona.'

'What does an Italian want here?' called one of the assembly, with a distinct slur.

Sterz favoured the speaker with a withering look. 'He comes to us with information of the greatest import. He will speak, we will listen.'

A gesture brought di Valona forward. In the increased candlelight Hawkwood noted he had lank and shiny black hair as well as smooth olive skin that had a softness to it. His eyes were dark brown, while the features gave him few years and a comely, near-feminine countenance.

'My Lords—'

'Not many of that rank here, fellow.'

The interruption brought forth guffaws and really annoyed Sterz, obvious by the glare and the hand chop demanding silence. A mumbled apology followed from the transgressors.

'I have come from Avignon.'

'The whore of France!'

'Be silent all of you. Let the man speak.'

'You will know that the Pope has been active in raising the gold to ransom the King of France. Three million livres.'

That got a general murmur as minds settled on the sum. If Hawkwood had been thrown the first time he had heard of a million, he was not in ignorance now; it was a fortune in specie the like of which no man from king to commoner had ever seen, a sum so vast it went beyond imagination.

'Innocent sent cardinals to the Florentine and Milanese bankers with requests for loans on behalf of Paris, pledges provided.'

'Even pledging the whole city and the River Seine with it would not cover such a sum.'

'The task was to raise one-third of the monies and in that they have been successful. The charge now is to get it to where it will, once added to that raised by the French crown, achieve its purpose.'

'They should leave the coward where he is,' called John Thornbury. 'France deserves a better king than Jean le so-called Bon.'

'The route,' Sterz added, in an impatient whisper, 'is one on which we can meet them and relieve them of what they carry.'

The muttering that set up – every one of the dozen men present arrived at a simultaneous conclusion – precluded any further discussion. Sterz waited until it subsided before signalling that di Valona should continue.

'The cardinals and their escorts are making for Pont-

Saint-Esprit in the Comtat Venaissin, their intention to cross the Rhone by the Roman Bridge.'

'There are,' Sterz injected, 'few places to cross the river north of Avignon.'

'When?' asked Hawkwood, which had the virtue of being an important question.

The face spun to respond, the candles showing his eyes had within them the light of intelligence. 'Seven days from now.'

'And before that?'

'Each stop has been pre-planned. They intend to stay one night in Pont-Saint-Esprit before proceeding on, the object being to meet with the princes and the remainder of the ransom money in Orleans.'

'Then should we not get there and bag the lot?' suggested a captain called Francis the Belge, who led a body of Hainault spearmen.

'It's too far off, and besides, we would face an army. From my maps I see us as being three days' forced march from the Rhone.'

Several seconds of silence followed those words from the German, no doubt with many present seeking to divide a million into what would be their own share and having trouble with the calculation. There were men in this pavilion, good fighters but finger counters, who struggled to get beyond the number ten without a monk to aid them.

'Why come to us, fellow? Why not recruit a band to steal it yourself?'

The questioning voice had the languid tones of Aquitaine, so Hawkwood knew without looking it was Roland de

Jonzac speaking. A doughty, fully mailed knight, he had fought alongside Hawkwood at Poitiers under Edward of Woodstock.

'The escort numbers two hundred men, papal-funded levies from the Swiss Confederation, and they are sturdy fighters. It will take a strong body of men to subdue them, a force I cannot muster. I lack the means to pay and even if I had the money, would I not risk getting my throat cut once I set out the purpose?'

'You do not fear that to happen here?' asked Thornbury.

'He has my bounden word it will not,' Sterz insisted.

'Better,' Valona added, with the first hint of a kind of suppressed passion, 'to have part of a loaf as against not even a crumb.'

A mass of detail followed; it seemed this young man had left no stone unturned in his calculations. He pushed for the cardinals to be interdicted at Pont-Saint-Esprit for the very good reason that if they were required to get to where they needed to be, a point to the north where they would be met by a very strong force of French chivalry, the crossing of the Rhone was the one part of their journey they could not alter. Also he was unsure of their route once the river had been crossed and thought it unwise to go beyond the crossing into the heavily populated and fertile papal possessions of the Comtat Venaissin, where news of their presence, of a routier band, would quickly spread.

It was telling that the initial scepticism had subsided, yet Hawkwood wondered at Sterz. He too must have been disbelieving of such a tale at first. What had this young man said to so convince him that he now had utter faith in di Valona's explanation? Did he have other sources of information? If he had, he was not saying and nor would he if asked.

There was not a single captain who exited the pavilion, well after the hourglass had taken them past the midnight hour, without thirsting to go after this fabulous prize and who was sure it was close to being in their grasp. To relieve the cardinals of their coffers would far outstrip anything the company had been able to gain hitherto by a huge margin. Even for a common soldier or archer the monies appropriated would be substantial, perhaps enough to put aside a life of constant movement and fighting along with the risk of dying in some foreign field.

Not immune to such imaginings himself and finding sleep impossible, Hawkwood shunned his cot to pace back and forth outside his tent, sending young Gold back to his slumbers. He had spent hours waiting outside the pavilion already and the lad's duties did not extend to watching his master think. To ensure he got peace Hawkwood set off to stroll through the camp.

It was silent now, the only fires still fully lit those of the sentinels on the periphery. The rest were mere embers kept going with the addition of the odd log so they would be quick to revive in the morning. A piquet was necessary but not to protect against a sudden assault, which was unlikely given they generally knew if there was an enemy in the offing.

Besides, night attacks were notoriously difficult to mount without the noise of a large body of moving men alerting the quarry, especially with a sliver of moon and strong starlight. On an open, sloping field there was little chance of an unseen approach: these men were set to ensure that no locals came crawling in to pilfer from the sleepers, a constant concern.

His walk took him through the endless horse lines, the equines either munching at hay or sleeping, heads dropped but upright. He found and murmured words to his own courser, the favoured horse for fast riding which could still be relied upon in battle. The herd included rouncies to act as packhorses as well as the odd knightly destriers, heavy tilting mounts descended from the stallions of Byzantium able to carry a man in full armour.

If it was a task to feed and care for the needs of over two thousand men and the detritus that followed them then that of these animals was just as important, which meant good pasture, hay and a supply of oats. Without fit horses the company would be unable to operate and if there was the odd callous fellow who treated his mount badly, there were many more who held them in higher regard than their human companions.

Head on chest and deep in thought, Hawkwood came eventually to the riverbank, where the gurgling waters of the stream formed a pleasant background sound. Not yet high summer the watercourse was in good flow, reflecting the overhead light, and for a moment he was back in his Essex homeland, a flat landscape crossed by many a watercourse in which he had, as a youngster, fished and swam. It was beside such as this and after a naked dip that he and Antiocha's mother had first lain together and probably conceived her.

As always when such thoughts occurred he went through the various moods, the ups and downs that had brought him to where he was now. Rarely a man to lie to himself, John Hawkwood was aware that in the life he had lived he had been far from perfect even when very young. It had never occurred to him he had a position to maintain to protect the reputation of his family and nor had he paid any attention to that outside his immediate gaze or given any thought to the worries of his father.

In a country riven with several years of famine, Hawkwood senior had held station enough in life to ensure his own wife and children did not suffer as did the peasantry. The youngest in his brood, he had been much cosseted by his mother, who saw him as a late blessing and treated him with a less strict hand than his older siblings. In his mind's eye he could conjure up his home county easily. The seemingly endless Essex landscape, the searing wind blowing too often over the few hills from the sea to the east, the trips with his eldest brother to Hedingham Castle where he had been steward to the de Vere's and where the little brother had seen at first hand the tempting luxury of aristocratic life.

As a boy he had hankered after such as he played within the motte-and-bailey part of the castle, imagining himself as a Norman warrior defending the high square tower and its valuable possessions against hordes of . . . whom? He had forgotten who those boyhood troublemakers were. Not Saxons, for they in folk memory were held in high regard. Danes and Vikings more like, even if it was hundreds of years since their incursions.

There was his daughter, named after a famous crusader victory outside the walls of Antioch, last seen suckling and wrapped in swaddling clothes, a small pinkish face much wrinkled by concentration until he was shooed away by the wet nurse. There was no image of what she would look like now, well past being a young lady; only that of the funeral he had been obliged to watch from a distance as her mother was interred in a de Vere family vault.

John Hawkwood was over forty summers old now and it was hard to count what he had and how he had come to this place as an unmitigated achievement. There existed a desire to return home to the family manor house in Sible Hedingham, not as the prodigal needing forgiveness but flushed with success. This would be measured in money and he desired it should be of a quantity that would see him ride into the village on a fine palfrey carrying saddlebags full of coin, which would enable him to flaunt his status as a dubbed knight.

Perhaps that could be brought to pass with John le Bon's ransom and he now was prey to such visualisations. But it would not happen without guile and application, so he made a conscious effort to put his mind to what he had heard in the pavilion and how what was required could be achieved.

# Chapter Four

First he reprised the list of facts di Valona had imparted to the assembly. Pont-Saint-Esprit had sound walls but no citadel, which he would have expected with such an important river crossing where the bridge tolls would be lucrative. Not all the town income came from that source, it being a place where travellers took their rest before passing on in either direction. That meant lodging houses and inns, where trade in food and drink would be lively.

The fields around the town were fertile, which was to be expected, bordering as it did a great river in warm climes. This produced abundant annual harvests of food and wine, as well as providing good pasture for horses, cattle, sheep and goats in excess of local needs, which spoke of traders in surplus with full purses untouched by war. Never having even been close to the battle zones of the Anglo–French conflict, Pont-Saint-Esprit looked to be a prize worth taking on its own.

The town was garrisoned by a body of some fifty soldiers, these provided for the local citizens by their ducal overlords and paid for through taxes. Those with property outside the walls might wish to see that protected, but di Valona had assured the assembly Pont-Saint-Esprit had no resident force of mounted men, only militia raised as necessary. The soldiers were static and their duty was to protect the major asset, the bridge, not to range far and wide seeking threats.

The questioning had been extensive, most keenly the need to know how he had come by the information he imparted. His answers told those assembled that a papal court was as full of intrigue and competing interests as any staffed by laymen. Jockeying for position in Avignon was endemic, the ear of the pontiff the prize sought, for in that man lay the very fount of a wealth and power to rival and even surpass an emperor.

Having studied civil law at Bologna, di Valona had come to Avignon to acquire a knowledge of canon law, the very different statutes which covered the activities of the Church. Taken in by an Italian cardinal, the young man had resided comfortably in the suburb of Villeneuve rather than be left, like most itinerant students, to lodge in an overcrowded and stinking Avignon hovel. In doing so he had become something of a trusted confidant of this high churchman, the name of whom he declined to divulge.

He did admit him to be a partisan of the Holy Roman Emperor and, like that German potentate, an advocate of a papal return to Rome and an end to the too strong influence of Paris in Church affairs due to residence in Avignon, imposed not least by a succession of popes from that nation, who ignored both German and Italian claimants.

Being so inclined he was no friend to the French princes seeking to free their father, bankrupting their country in the process. Avignon might not be a direct fief of the Crown of France but it depended upon its goodwill for its continued prosperity and was thus obliged to contribute to that outrageous ransom agreed at Brétigny.

Life in a luxury villa, safe from urban pestilence on the left bank of the Rhone, with fountains in the flower-filled gardens and peacocks roaming free, with good food to eat and wine in abundance to consume, had made for a pleasant life. Hawkwood wondered if others might suspect, as did he, that there could be some other connection with his cardinal for this comely young fellow outside the bounds of mere nationality, one in which an indiscretion in a situation of intimacy had provided an opportunity.

Whatever it was, and it could have been sexual, di Valona had been able to observe the centre of a court fully Byzantine in its scheming. The papacy sat at the hub of the vast web of a faith that provided a stream of steady income, not confined to Peter's pence and tithes. Gold flowed into Avignon from all over Christendom in the form of gifts and bribes, both necessary to procure such things as the annulment of an inconvenient marriage or the legitimisation of children born out of wedlock, many of the latter from prelates supposed to be celibate.

Only the Pope could grant permission for the building of new churches or cathedrals, the holding of festivals or any act of community not already sanctioned. In disputes of title over property that could not be decided in civil law or even by a ruling sovereign – and these would be substantial fiefdoms – the papal word was sought and, win or lose, the price paid was high. When it came to making peace between warring sovereigns it was to the Pope they turned for arbitration which, like all other pleas for intercession, rarely came free.

Most lucrative of all, and it had assumed the proportions of a scandal, was the sale of indulgences: the granting of absolution even for sins unconfessed to those with the money to pay. In a world full of wickedness and the prospect of expiring from disease within a single day – the plague was ravaging Europe in waves – many were prepared to pay vast sums to be guaranteed direct entry into paradise or even just to avoid damnation. Such monies flowed through the hands of venal church divines, a great deal of it sticking to their bejewelled fingers before being passed to the papal vaults.

Hawkwood's reflections were not all on popes, cardinals and their greedy excesses. He could not avoid his thoughts returning to what could come from the ransom money, something that could satisfy all his old and unfulfilled longings. He could see himself as the owner of a decent manor. Such a holding would require a wife but as a man of means he knew fathers would queue to offer their daughters in spite of any reputation he might carry.

In his mind's eye he could envisage a substantial timber-framed, wattle-and-daub dwelling, with a good woman, servants and rosy-cheeked children to complete the scene. There would be horses in the paddock, livestock in the fields and hardy souls to sow and plough what was not pasture, with himself in benign authority. First he and his confrères must get hold of that million in species, though, and an immediate worry surfaced, the cause being the ambuscade of the previous morning.

Those peasants, even if they badly miscalculated the numbers they would face, had known who was coming and on routes way off the pilgrim tracks, which meant news of the Great Company ran well ahead of its actual presence, even to the ignorant. If such a thing happened at Pont-Saint-Esprit, with a quicker-witted populace by far, it could spell disaster. Yet to realise that did not immediately provide a means to avoid such an outcome and that was now the thought dominating his thinking.

He was still by the river when the sky turned to grey. Behind him the camp was stirring as the early risers undertook their duty, getting the fires flaring again, filling the cooking pots with water and small wheeled baking ovens with charcoal. Their comrades, when they rose, would first look to their basic needs before seeing to the horses, a vital task.

By the time he made his way back to his own lines through the men grooming hides, picking hooves and bathing equine noses and arses, he had resolved to have words with Sterz and his notion of a forced march. It seemed to him a bad idea for several reasons, not least that if the Great Company arrived outside Pont-Saint-Esprit they would do so in a state of exhaustion and disarray, but that was not the only one.

He found his captain general surrounded by servants and in the act of dressing prior to the morning Mass, which would be taken when the work needing to be done was complete and before any man broke his fast. Courtesies exchanged he began to outline his objection to forcing the company into an immediate movement, careful to avoid detail, such as where they would be headed.

'But it is not that alone which gives me pause: it is the chance of forfeiting that which we seek.'

For a second time in a dozen hours the German dismissed his servants, as well as his personal confessor, leaving only him and his factotum, Cunradus, speaking as soon as it was safe to do so.

'You do not believe di Valona?'

'I am prepared to, without being certain of his honesty. He seems the type to pass through a closed door. Yet I can see no purpose to his coming to you with a lie unless he seeks to draw the Great Company into a trap, and on whose behalf would he be acting if he were? All those who desire revenge on us are to our rear.'

Sterz nodded slowly; clearly he had considered the same possibility, which was positive, yet what Hawkwood was about to propose was tricky. A policy had been agreed, one Sterz had propounded, and he would not be keen to have it challenged. Added to that was their troubled relationship. Hawkwood often made jokes that tested the man's patience. He was also inclined to dispute with his leader, to ask awkward questions as he examined every proposed move from multiple angles. While he respected it, he refused to just accept that the German's experience gave him the right to favour his own opinions.

'Our plan to force-march the whole company to the

Rhone and take possession of Pont-Saint-Esprit is flawed.'

The response was a skywards look, larded with impatience followed by a frustrated glance at Cunradus.

'Is that all?'

'You heard di Valona describe the walls as sound and in good repair. There are papal levies set to guard them.' A nod. 'Not numerous, I grant you, but we will have to fight to overcome them and they will hold an advantage by being on the ramparts.'

'Perhaps you have a Joshua trumpet, Hawkwood,' Sterz wheezed, his belly heaving at his own jest, which got a wry smile from his fat friar. 'Loud enough to bring the stones tumbling down.'

'If I had I would silence it, but I ask you this, how are we to take Pont-Saint-Esprit without news of such a coup reaching the ears of those cardinals who are heading for the same location? We cannot get across the River Rhone lest we use the very bridge those papal levies are there to protect. Nor can we approach the walls from the riverside, as a host, without being seen before we can deploy and begin to besiege it.'

It was a good thing to pause and let that sink in, but the next point was paramount. 'A messenger will surely be sent to Avignon as soon as we are sighted to say we are about to attack and asking for relief. Is it too much to suggest they might well encounter the party carrying Jean le Bon's ransom money on the way and tell them to turn back?'

'What is it you want, Hawkwood?'

'I want to cancel the notion of a forced march so we can decide on a strategy that will gain the end we desire. Pont-Saint-Esprit is tempting but our real aim is to get our hands on that treasure. I ask that you call another meeting at which I can propose an alternative way to proceed.'

It was Cunradus, well larded and sleek, who spoke, not Sterz. 'You have never hidden the notion that you feel that you are cleverer than any one of us, Hawkwood.'

'I have never said so and I do not believe it to be the case.'

'It is not something in need of words.'

'Cunradus, we can march on Pont-Saint-Esprit, invest it, yet even if we overcome those walls that will not happen in one day, so the odds are high that the true aim will fail. News will get out.'

'We can kill everyone down to the rats in their cellars and that will get us silence,' Sterz snorted.

'Thousands of bodies putrefying in the streets, human and animal. You will have a sky full of scavengers visible five leagues off and if you throw them in the river – well that, according to di Valona, flows on to and past Avignon.'

Hawkwood paused once more; he needed to convince this man, not show him the flaws in his thinking. 'I ask only to put my concerns to the captains assembled, and if a better way to proceed emerges then I will be obliged to agree to it. You will, as usual, have the most powerful voice and if you carry the meeting you will not find me wanting in execution. As for a forced march, we have a week, so half a day will make no difference.'

'It is near time for Mass,' Cunradus said, puffing his full and rosy cheeks. 'Perhaps following on from that it can be considered.'

Sterz, who was looking at the monk, nodded. Hawkwood

reckoned not all the time on soul cleansing would be spent in prayers.

'Can I suggest that if it is agreed we should reconvene after Mass, di Valona be escorted to his own tent and not this one? If he needs to know anything it can be imparted once matters are decided.'

That engendered a few moments of consideration, but finally Cunradus nodded.

An assembly of near twenty captains could be a noisy affair and the taking of the Eucharist did nothing to dent their pride; these were men who had led elements of proper armies and were accustomed to having their views considered. Many recalled what had already been agreed and stated they should not be standing around arguing but should be making ready to depart.

It took time for Hawkwood to be given the floor so he could address the same concerns he had outlined to Sterz, indeed to elaborate upon them. Pont-Saint-Esprit presented a problem by its mere nature. The Great Company was ill-equipped to assault a walled town, given they had no ballistas to batter the walls; nor were the men they led of a type to be keen on assault by ladder in daylight; a cause for casualties. Such an undertaking could not but be full of individual risk.

Added to that, if the company moved as a body and acted in their usual manner, stripping the land as they went, word would precede them and the garrison would be alerted well in advance of their arrival. Despite di Valona's assurances, Hawkwood was not prepared to fully trust his account. Any places he had not seen where the walls had been neglected would be quickly repaired.

In addition the means to repel attackers would be put in place: stones to batter and burst open exposed heads, large urns with which to boil oil or tar that would strip the skin off a man climbing a ladder, poles with hooks to overturn the same – all the panoply of defence these captains had faced in previous encounters. It was possible, with enough time, the soldier would be reinforced before the town could even be invested.

'We could bypass it, Hawkwood,' interjected Thibaut of Douvres, a Norman who led the fully accoutred knights. 'It is, after all, not our true object.'

'Not before messengers go ahead of us,' Hawkwood cut in quickly. 'We will take the bridge, that cannot be prevented, but we cannot close it before word of our presence spreads and I am contending that will happen certainly a full day before we get to those walls, maybe more. Do I then have to say what is likely to occur?'

Looking around the faces as he spoke, he sought to pick out those who might support him. He alighted on that of Roland de Jonzac, who, being the friend he was, looked at Hawkwood, a broad and encouraging smile on his face, which was soon followed by a question.

'You have related to us your objections to what we agreed, John. That does little to convince unless you can propose a solution.'

'I am going to suggest that my company, and we alone, take possession of Pont-Saint-Esprit. The host should follow, but slowly, without setting light to a single peasant hut or stripping a single vine or olive tree. We should pay for anything we need instead of just taking it and no man should suffer a wound or any woman be discomfited.'

'Pay?' called Thornbury, with faux shock, while another captain was sure his gonads would not allow him to pass up carnal opportunity. But these were silly objections made as much in jest as protestation; it was not hard to work out that which was greater, the protestation or suspicion, and it was Sterz who voiced it.

'What is to stop you just bypassing the town?'

There was no need to elaborate; beyond Pont-Saint-Esprit the real prize might just fall into his hands. He could protest his commitment to their shared enterprise as much as he liked. In this pavilion were men accustomed to taking that which they desired. The notion of individual greed overcoming loyalty when faced with a million in specie was not very outlandish.

'Would it suffice to say to you all that I value my life, which would not be worth a clipped groat if I was to seek to cheat you? I do not relish the idea of two thousand souls scouring the country for a sight of me and my company, which you would surely do if I sought to make off with that treasure. It is my intention to try to capture Pont-Saint-Esprit and in a manner that suits our needs.'

'And if you fail?' demanded Francis the Belge.

'Then I would request a Christian burial, given survival will be unlikely. For you, nothing will have altered and you can descend on the town and invest it in the manner previously discussed.'

# CHAPTER FIVE

'God spare me another dispute like that. There was too much clamour and Sterz did little to control it.'

'You got your wish, John, be content.'

Roland de Jonzac was with him, sent along with Francis the Belge to see he kept to his bargain; one was a man who could be called a comrade, but the other, if he knew Hawkwood well from service with King Edward, was not seen to be overfriendly. The Belge also had the task of keeping close to di Valona, brought along to proffer advice but also not fully trusted; at the slightest hint of treachery he was to be killed.

The arguments in the pavilion had seen the hourglass turned twice, this so that everyone could have their say, which occasioned much repetition of the possibilities and potential pitfalls. In addition, what Hawkwood had proposed dealt with the outcome not the progress that would take his company to the walls.

He would have to march well ahead but each day he progressed required the route to be sealed to his rear, this to avoid anyone passing beyond him to carry news of the approach of the main host. Then he would have to reconnoitre the place, to add bones to the description provided by di Valona. On the final day's march would come the most difficult part and that was for he and his company to approach the walls unseen, which could only be done in darkness.

For once Sterz stood aloof until Cunradus suggested the matter be put to the vote, which went Hawkwood's way despite numerous objections and no end of suggestions that he was the wrong man to carry out the plan. It was necessary to remind the assembly he had made the suggestion, that he was no callow youth but a fighting soldier of forty summers who had been at war for over half that time. He had survived the carnage of Blanchetaque, had distinguished himself at Crécy, helped capture fortresses in Aquitaine and led a company of archers at Poitiers.

Normally modest regarding that battle and the aftermath, he reminded them that the man who was now termed the Prince of Wales knighted him in gratitude after the battle. He forbore to mention his own opinion that it was an act carried out to embellish the prestige of the prince, not the man he dubbed with his great sword. In the end none of these things mattered; fear of the loss of that treasure won out and his intentions were confirmed.

'That, I suggest, was a ploy worked out at the morning Mass,' Hawkwood insisted to Jonzac. 'Our captain general agreed with what I had already said to him earlier but did not want to be seen to have his previous proposals overturned, no doubt told by Cunradus to avoid any loss of face. His monk waited till the mood of the room suited a show of hands before calling for it.'

That accepted, it was Cunradus who laid down the detailed plan; how far Hawkwood was to progress on each day and how far behind should be the nearest elements of the main body, with different sections leapfrogging to back up the archers. The route was one normally avoided, the main highway by which pilgrims made their way to Avignon or Rome, with some headed for the distant goals of Bethlehem or Jerusalem, there to pray in the Holy Sepulchre. That would be the disguise of the lead soldiery.

Weapons would be hidden in a waggon and they must appear pious. When stops were made, to rest horses and men, prayers should be said and that should apply when they encountered any of the numerous shrines that lined the roadway. Likewise hospices – frequent on the pilgrim routes – were to be shunned. Such places were rarely as virtuous as their founders had intended. Most had become enterprises designed to provide income for a monastery producing wines and food, so were more set to extract money than to provide spiritual rest.

Others had succumbed to a degree of licentiousness that would only become apparent on occupation, with women forced to take the veil by jealous husbands or greedy families stealing their inheritance. Having not naturally chosen a life of seclusion they were always hungry for company. Hawkwood could command his men in battle; it was much harder to make them bend to his will in temptation.

Di Valona had stated with confidence the time of arrival for the cardinals at Pont-Saint-Esprit, given he knew every place at which they intended to stop on their way from Italy. This meant progress could be measured, a mere four leagues a day, which made possible the interdiction of travellers, traders and pilgrims encountered heading south. Those going north were to be allowed to pass unmolested, just like any tempting objectives passed on the march. The final leg would be designed to bring Hawkwood's company to the walls, it was hoped on a moonless night, with his confrères appearing the next day if the outcome was positive.

The sight of a hundred men walking as a body in prayer was unusual but not unknown. It was quaint that once their purpose had been extracted there were often people prepared to come out of their dwellings to offer them sustenance to ease their travel, added to a request that should they reach the Holy Land a prayer be said in the name of the giver. The supposed leader of this pilgrimage from England being one of the monks who rode with the Great Company, names were listed by him for future supplication.

Each night the men of another command caught up to seal the route and it was necessary that Hawkwood set out at dawn to put a distance between them. Singing psalms as they progressed, frequently stopping to be blessed and confess, they passed for what they claimed to be: seekers of salvation without the means to buy it from a venal papacy, mostly of a different nationality to those whose land they passed through, but of the same faith and circumstance.

Naturally, when resting the main subject of discussion was Pont-Saint-Esprit, di Valona repeating and elaborating on his descriptions of the place and its walls while the man who would be tasked with taking them formulated ways in which they could be overcome. On the night before the last leg Hawkwood would proceed ahead of his own men and Jonzac made an obvious point.

'For all your confidence, I cannot see, John, how you can plan to overcome walls you have not seen with your own eyes?'

'There's truth in that, by damn,' was the trenchant opinion of Francis the Belge.

Hawkwood knew as well as his fellow captains they were right. Description, though comprehensive, could not replace his own experience of assessing defences. Yet certain facts they could guess, like the number of guards who would be on the walls through the hours of darkness. In a body of fifty men there would be those of rank who did not do the duty, though they might be the ones obliged to check their men were awake at their posts or called on to oversee the changes of watch, which had to be split so men could sleep.

Hawkwood reckoned he would have at the most a dozen men to deal with on walls that to be properly defended against a serious threat required perhaps a hundred, and that could only come with help from the citizens. At night they too would be asleep, though there would be a tocsin with which to summon them from their beds in an emergency.

'In these parts it is dark by the seventh hour after noon and not light again till seven after midnight. Twelve hours means, in a normal garrison, three guard changes at least. With such small numbers it is possible the last set will be the same as the first, men made weary from disturbed slumbers.'

There were dwellings along the main road north which could provide cover for an approach, but they would contain dogs and geese, the latter the best alarm system invented by nature. For that reason he reckoned he would need to use the narrow strand along the riverbank, likely to be the least well defended.

'I reckon on a parapet without tubs brimful of water, either.'

That earned a nod of recognition from his peers. Such tubs could, by the tiny ripples on the surface of the water, detect the vibrations of multiple horses' hooves on hard ground.

'Such devices would be saved for approaches that favoured cavalry, would they not, which cannot apply where the walls abut the river?'

The Belge pointed out there were bound to be beacons, fire-filled ironwork baskets attached to the top of the walls to cast a faint light on the ground below, but Hawkwood was sure that men, if they looked at all from castle walls, aimed their gaze out not down if anything drew their attention.

'Are you to go ahead alone?' asked Roland de Jonzac.

'I'll take young Gold. He can return to us if anything goes awry.'

'And if you are intercepted he is too young to be seen as a threat.'

That got a smile from the lad's master and a nod at his Aquitanian friend. 'Even if I told him not to, he would dog my heels, anyway.'

'He's faithful, right enough, I can hear him slithering about ten paces away.'

'He fears I will suffer the fate of his father and be struck by lightning.'

'And how,' the Belge asked, with scant grace, 'does he intend to prevent what will be the will of the Almighty, without even mentioning the weather is clement?'

Jonzac answered for Hawkwood. 'He prays more than any of us, Francis, and not for himself for I have heard him. He sees himself taking a bolt instead of John here, though he's more at risk from a crossbow, carrying the banner.'

Originally taken on out of sympathy, Christopher Gold had become obsessed by the need to display his loyalty to John Hawkwood. The lad would shield his master if he thought him in danger, even when he was angrily told to desist. Too young to be a fully competent fighter, he was improving by the day due to his constant efforts to hone his skills with sword, shield and dagger. He had transferred the pennant he carried to a spear that could be used to ward off enemies.

'Christopher Gold, stop eavesdropping and come sit by the fire.'

The round face, dotted with angry spots, came into

the circle of light made by the blazing logs, the expression concerned. 'Weren't listening, Sir John, on the lives of the saints.'

Hawkwood shook his head slowly; how many times had he told the youngster not to use that title? The same number of times as he had been ignored, for the lad was proud to serve a true knight, a title taken by many to carry with it no real claim. For his master, the reluctance to have it stated was as much to do with avoiding comparison as a degree of modesty. Besides, those who had elevated themselves became jealous of anyone who carried the right and that was never good in a company of mutual dependence.

A wave brought the boy closer, to sit by his master who was now looking at him with benign affection. Fourteen summers now, the lad had such a sunny disposition that he seemed incapable of making enemies. He had been adopted as a page by Hawkwood after the retreat from Paris, a march that had been depressing enough. Not even King Edward, a man who could charm the birds from the trees, could lift the spirits of an army that felt defeated.

Then came the massive thunderstorm that struck the host on the road back to Normandy. Gold's father, an Essex archer like Hawkwood and from close to Sible Hedingham, wearing a chain mail cowl, had been struck and killed, leaving the boy distraught and an orphan. There was no home to go to, so his adoption was necessary to honour his father's memory as well as to keep him alive.

'Well, can I go on alone?'

'It would not please me that you should, Sir John.'

'So you were listening?'

'Only to that bit.'

Jonzac burst out laughing. 'So how should we go about attacking the place?'

The reply was delivered with all the certainty of youth. 'If my master were to ride to their gate and demand that they open it, they would be fools to deny him.'

'And you would be by his side?'

'Proud to be so, sir.'

'Sleep, boy,' Hawkwood ordered, 'me likewise. I will have the watchmen wake us early so we can leave before the camp stirs.'

The face lit up. 'And will we smite the buggers for certain?'

'Just have a care,' Jonzac jested, 'the smites don't bugger you.'

That brought confusion to the corn-blue eyes; Gold, a good-looking boy even with spots, and naïve, had no idea what he was on about and he did not hang about for clarification. Hawkwood was already making his way to the waggon, under which lay his straw-filled paillasse. It was not long before all the youngster could hear was his hearty snores.

As a pair there was no need for subterfuge or excessive piety. A man and a boy, well dressed now in good if not gaudy clothes, riding together, was too common a sight to be remarked upon on a road getting busier as the light grew stronger, increasingly so as they approached the town, the river and the bridge that spanned it. Hawkwood was armed with no more than a sword and his knife, which would be seen as sensible on a pilgrim's way, much open to banditry.

The quality of the mounts might be remarked upon for they were very fine, the property of a prosperous man, as indeed they had at one time been until taken as booty. Likewise the spear borne by Gold, bereft of the Hawkwood pennant, might raise an eyebrow. But then young men were prey to such martial fancies and since anyone they passed was heartily greeted with a cry of 'Godspeed', no suspicions were evident.

The land was as fertile as reported, with rows of vines on the hillsides and wheat and barley waving on the breeze where the land was flat. Orchards abounded too, with apples, pears and apricots, which were fruit-laden if not yet ripe. The figs were, however, and taken if they could be reached as a welcome purgative to a diet that often left men cozened.

With the heat of the day and a slight haze the walls of Pont-Saint-Esprit, at a distance, seemed detached from the earth, a floating fortress impossible to overcome though the truth became plain closer to. All castles look strong from a distance: in John Hawkwood's experience many did not sustain that formidable appearance when properly inspected. It was something to remark upon that citizens who depended on walls to protect them were too often mean when it came to paying to keep them in good repair, there always being a better use for their money than their own security. A full belly beat sound stones for most, until they lamented their girth when those walls were overcome.

'Calais was not like that,' Hawkwood continued.

He was, as was common, relating to Gold some exploit

from his past, going on to describe the double moat and high curtain walls as well as the separate citadel on the northern dunes and what attempts were made to overcome them. This was meat and drink to the youngster who loved to hear of what he called his master's past glories, though Hawkwood remembered Calais as being more mud than grandeur. It also came from a time when the boy had just been weaned, long before he joined his father in France.

'Could there be a richer town in northern France, with it being the gateway for anyone travelling from England to trade or go on pilgrimage? No need to starve there to attend to their walls.'

'Yet it fell, I know, my father told me of it too.'

'After a whole year it fell and with hundreds of children and old folks kicked out to save the fighters. If the French had possessed a fleet it would be holding out yet, but that was destroyed at Sluys and so we starved them out. The burghers came with halters round their necks to plead that Calais be spared.'

'King Edward will keep it?'

That was a sound question given what he had surrendered at the Treaty of Brétigny; to the thinking of many of his army he had given up far too much of that which they had spent years fighting to take for the English Crown.

'It would be a foolish sovereign who gave that up. When we first came to France it was to an open beach in Normandy. It is not a good route of entry to take if you are opposed.'

A gentle tug on the reins brought Hawkwood to a halt, for the proximity to Pont-Saint-Esprit had dissipated the haze so that the walls were now in plain view and earthbound. If much of the stone had darkened with age, there were enough blocks in original colour and well spread to show they were kept in good repair. The halt was short: running close to the town, the road was now becoming crowded and being static in examination could cause comment. Moving on they passed empty carts coming out from their morning deliveries and jostled with full ones yet to enter the gates. The number of what Hawkwood assumed to be pilgrims making their way homewards had increased to create a crowd by the north-west gate.

Beyond that, with a tollbooth and guards, lay the old Roman bridge: an arch of stones that had stood since the time of the Caesars, a way for the legions to march into Gaul as well as a defensible crossing to keep barbarian hordes in check. It was a sobering thought for Hawkwood that he was contemplating the taking of a fortress on which Rome had relied to defend some of its most fertile possessions. If it had fallen at times, it had not done so often and there was a nagging itch that had him wonder at the wisdom of the claims he had made to his fellow captains.

The gates were guarded and entry was not given freely to strangers, though the familiar went through on the nod. Once the *gabelle was* paid for by Hawkwood, a purpose had to be stated and an official in the stone gatehouse chamber consulted where doubt arose. What saved Hawkwood the indignity was his clear prosperity; men dressed in good clothing and with what appeared to be a servant in attendance were not of the type to indulge in thievery. Besides, the place lived off the traveller and anyone who looked to have coin to spend had to be welcomed, not discomfited, although the municipality wished to be paid a small fee for access to underwrite their activities.

Once through the arch – Hawkwood had noted the double walls and the raised portcullis – they came upon crowded narrow alleys that required pressure from their horses to push through. The way was full of inns, their swinging signs giving names and often their particular specialities. Needing one with a stable, Hawkwood turned off the main thoroughfare to find a less crowded area, with substantial gates hiding houses of some size where the quality of the provender was likely to be higher.

That brought him to the Impious Bull.

# CHAPTER SIX

It is in the nature of innkeepers to be garrulous – their trade demands it – and by ordering a deal of food, as well as the best available wines in the establishment, John Hawkwood got the attention he required, not least an offer of free stabling and livery for his horses. They were fed with oats and washed down to both cool them and remove the dust of travel, then brushed so they gleamed even down to their hooves being oiled, all fitting service to a man who looked as if he could afford to pay.

Claiming to be on the way to Avignon, hinting without actually saying so that his business there centred on a case in the papal courts he hoped would be decided his way, Hawkwood quizzed the owner of the tavern about the town, using praise of its beauty, as well as of the man's service, to open his mind.

'I see you indulge your servant, sir, which is a Christian thing to do.'

This was said as Gold rose, having gobbled his food in the way youths do. Since sitting at the board he had remained silent and concentrated on provender of a much better quality than that eaten with the Great Company on the move, his head rarely coming up from his plate. Without his being commanded to do so he would make sure the horses were being well cared for.

'Good in a servant comes from kindness,' Hawkwood replied, not naming his true position of page, now squire and adoptee. 'To do otherwise gives a man more trouble, not less. He's a good lad when not sneaking off to fish.'

That statement from the supposed master got a quizzical look, which was responded to.

'It is a passion with the lad and I must admit to myself being partial to plying the rod. It can be a sport, but there is little to match the consummation of the catch over your own fire, to conclude a day when God has been kind.'

'It is a common pursuit in Pont-Saint-Esprit, sir; how could it not be with such a mighty river on our doorstep? If you could glance over the parapet you would see many seeking their supper.'

Hawkwood feigned surprise. 'It is permitted on the strand?'

'Frowned on, happen, but none bother to curtail it unless the town is threatened and that, sir, is rare. Why, there hasn't been an alarm since I was working as my father's pot boy in this very place.'

That had to be commented on, so many years of toil, seemingly happily undertaken, before Hawkwood returned to the subject he needed to pursue, beginning with an enquiry regarding those walls, the information quickly forthcoming that the town had a garrison.

'I would have thought the men set to guard them might object to people fishing where they have a responsibility to keep it secure.'

'What, and give themselves exertion?' came the querulous reply. 'No, sir. They are not inclined that way, indeed not much disposed to anything, bar ensuring a full belly and ample wine. There's many a belt needs to be loosened in that quarter, with no thought to the cost laid upon us for their presence.'

Hawkwood had to work hard to avoid looking at the fellow's own ample belly, straining at a thick leather belt and heavy buckle, while the man went on to talk of the garrison's numbers and abilities – and there was scant praise regarding the latter.

'I assume you are taxed to pay for it?'

'We are, and I am not alone in seeing it as nought but waste.'

'It would, then, be permitted for me to have a look at the riverbank? I will come back this way and hope to be less pressed for time, which would allow me a chance to test the river.'

'I judge by your garb, sir, that if you fish, you do not do so from necessity.'

He will be assessing me for what he can fleece, Hawkwood surmised. The man before him had a round, vinous face topped with tight curled hair and eyes rendered sunken-looking by the large puffy bags beneath them. The nose was purple which, added to the mottled skin, indicted a serious imbiber, a man who was not one to put aside a flagon till it was emptied. He might be a glutton too, given his waist required that strong belt to stop his belly slipping to his knees.

'I would be a richer man if the clerics of Avignon were less avaricious.'

'In that we share strong opinions, sir.'

That tended to be a safe subject of conversation wherever you went. The excesses of the Church were a common cause for resentment among the laity. It was said no one ever saw a thin priest or friar, still less a bishop on foot and only rarely favouring a palfrey over a coach or a seat in a servant-borne litter. His host made a good fist of an angry growl and a look meant to convey agreement.

'You hinted at a plea before the papal court, sir.'

Posed as a possible question Hawkwood was not going to oblige. 'One so finely balanced that I fear to talk of it lest I affect the outcome, though when I reflect on the bribes I have to pay to even get a hearing my blood boils.'

'If any in Avignon believe in God over Mammon, it is well concealed.'

Hawkwood sat back and looked at the destruction he and Gold had wrought on the meal: an empty pie dish, likewise the soup tureen, the bones of the two pigeons and a chicken now bare of flesh, patting his own lean and tight-muscled stomach to convey satisfaction. A loud belch got an appreciative nod from the innkeeper.

'I am happily content, sir, and I congratulate you on the quality of what you have provided. Now, before you present me with an account I ask that I may leave our horses for the length of the hourglass, perhaps two, while I walk off being in the saddle all morning as well as the contents of my gut.'

'Why, sir, I have yet to calculate the tariff. Feel free to settle on your return and happen your mounts will need a second feeding too. And might I add that should you feel your nether regions have suffered enough for a day, then it would be my pleasure to accommodate you in my humble establishment and to provide for you anything you might require. If you cast your eyes over the wenches serving and one catches your fancy—'

'What a temptation, for I espied a couple that were comely. I must keep going, though, or risk missing my hearing. But now to stretch my legs.'

'I would welcome you on your return from Avignon, sir.'

'Having found such a fine place, where else would I lay my head? You will certainly see me again and I hope as a happy fellow.'

As soon as he left, the innkeeper set a boy to keep an eye on the stables, not that it troubled Hawkwood to see it; indeed it would have engendered surprise if he had not. Trust was to any man in trade an alien concept and this one had good grounds to act that way. He must have been dunned in the past by a plausible stranger passing through the town.

Hawkwood, Gold at his heels, exited the gate hard by the paved road that led to the tollbooth on the bridge and its barrier, stopping for a while to assess the revenues that this must produce, given the traffic was steady and continuous. The trade between both banks of the Rhone was brisk on its own but this was a major route and not only for pilgrims. Messengers must be frequent, not least those carrying communications from Pope Innocent to his bishops and abbots. There would be diplomatic envoys too, those travelling on behalf of Italian bankers, and that was before the flotsam of a polity in constant flux.

The walk along the strand between the wall and river was made slowly and caused no comment, given it was interspersed with many an exchange. Fishermen were ever willing to talk to anyone interested in the subject, to boast of the best and biggest creature to take the hook on their line, of bait and ways to cast and play a catch as well as the foibles of the differing varieties of fish.

In between such conversations Hawkwood had ample time to closely examine the walls on which he hoped to launch an assault, in good repair like those he had seen earlier. The red-tiled roofs of the houses that crowded against the walls were just visible, which meant once over, anyone assaulting would soon be in among the citizenry before they could be alerted and armed.

The approach was dominated by the square tower of the cathedral, which he had just been informed was dedicated to St Saturnin, a man martyred ten centuries past by being dragged along the ground tied to the feet of a bull and much commemorated in place and church names, not least in the tavern he had just vacated.

The height of the church tower was a worry; anyone up there would be able to observe an approach long before the men on the walls, while he would have to cover as much ground as possible while it was still light to be in place for a final advance. He noticed the beacon baskets, which would be lit before dark, calculated the height of the walls at twenty cubits – ladders would have to be made of the right length – as well as the possibility that the strand was full of vegetation growing out of pebbles, which would make it difficult to keep silent when moving.

Close by were spits that stretched out into the river like sandbars, exposed at this time of year. Their presence created noise as the water flowed over and on to the south at a lick. The whole gave Hawkwood much to think about, not least that he would need a special kind of sky, a mix of cloud and moonlight, for what he had in mind to be a success. To that would need to be added a very large dose of luck.

The day was progressing, the time to leave becoming pressing, as none but a fool would set out to travel with darkness approaching. He called to Gold and they made their way back to the tavern to go through the comedy of being presented with an inflated bill, one Hawkwood paid with seeming willingness to a grovelling but very happy innkeeper. Even the youngster knew it to be bloated and he asked why Hawkwood had been so forthcoming.

'Our fat friend will be less happy when I come next to this place, for my first act will be to retrieve what I have just paid him and perhaps a great deal more.'

No assault would be launched that day and, once he had rejoined his men, word was sent back to Sterz to keep him abreast of events. Hawkwood checked that a company as discreet as his own had been sent forward ready to seal the roadway as evening approached, for delay would become impossible; once in place he must proceed quickly to attack.

The lack of traffic from a countryside accustomed to supply the town would be spotted immediately and could raise concerns. Yet another company would be needed on the following day to mask their movements once they left the pilgrim route and they would also be given charge of di Valona who was no soldier and thus a burden: Jonzac and the Belge were in no way prepared to miss the coming action.

The rest of that day and the first half of the next was spent in preparation. Weapons were sharpened, ladders made in short easy-to-carry sections that could be assembled *in situ*. Longer poles had to be fitted with hooks strong enough to bear the weight of buckets, these with a rope attached in a way that could tilt them so the water they contained, taken from the river, could quietly douse some of the fire beacons and plunge the bank into darkness.

The weather augured well, a mixture of cloud and clear sky with the former increasing throughout the day, which would mean long periods of darkness in the coming night. The approach to Pont-Saint-Esprit was to be made in a wide arc to the south of the town, which would bring Hawkwood to the river before the light faded completely. With the Rhone on one side no further guide was needed, and when the cloud did clear that became a silver beacon by which progress was made easy.

Silence was achieved by using the shallows; water

disturbed by feet sounded no different to the normal flow of the river and when it became too illuminated by the light from overhead a halt was called so that static figures became close to invisible at a distance. Weapons, sword blades and spearheads had been blackened with grease and earth to prevent reflection.

The trickiest moment for Hawkwood was the final approach to the narrow, bush-strewn strand, which was carried out in stops and starts, controlled by him – he had gone ahead with just Gold – using a shaded lantern only ever opened to face the southern side. First his men, once they felt stones underfoot, moved with great caution along the walls, their backs hugging them so that to be seen would require that a guard lean right out over the parapet.

One precaution was essential: a spit of gravel led out into the river near the northern corner of the walls. Out onto that, dressed all in black and with his skin likewise made muddy, went Ivor the Axe who for all his name and skill with that weapon was the best archer in the company. The risk had to be taken; he would stand out in the open and alert those on the strand to a man patrolling the walls by a low bird whistle. His bow would be strung but lowered and if any guard was prepared to risk a fall to see what had alerted their interest, his task was to put an arrow through him.

With much caution the buckets were filled by dipping. Hooked on to the poles they were eased aloft to very slowly extinguish the beacons, not rushed in any way to curtail the hissing of suppressed flames and with a sharp eye on Ivor the Axe. By the time they had finished there was practically no light and men could begin to bind together their ladders.

It required six sections to get to the necessary height. Each one lashed to the next, the join stiffened with another stout piece of wood to act as a batten. Throughout all of these activities John Hawkwood could do nothing but signal a message to proceed at each stage, that being determined by the number of times he unshaded his lantern. But that was over now; everything was either ready or it was not.

The last flick of light from that lantern was upon him and once employed it staying open would be the signal to begin the assault. He waited, as still as a nervous mouse, listening for sounds and sure that his imagination might be providing many. The stakes he could not put out of his mind: those cardinals and that treasure was due at some time in the next day and he wanted them to enter a town that they and their escorts had no reason to think presented any danger.

Many years of experience in giving battle allowed him to steady his nerves and give the candle command that would see the ladders raised. The section at the top of each one had been muffled with cloth so as to make no sound on contact, and slowly they were slid up the walls, the sections being counted off until those below them knew they had enough height to clamber through the crenellations by which the defender expected to be able to repel an attack.

It fell to John Hawkwood to be the first up a ladder; his duty as a leader demanded it and both Jonzac and the Belge had claimed the right to be likewise indulged. Ten ladders spaced at the correct width meant ten men would get to the top of the walls near simultaneously, more than enough to overcome what guards would be on this east-facing aspect when most threats would come from the inland flank.

Swords were held tightly and kept to the centre of the ladder, for a clash of metal on stone would mean instant discovery at a time when a man was at his most vulnerable. Rung by rung and slowly, they kept ascending, knowing that they would not be joined until each was three sections ahead of the next, this to avoid creaking wood and possible failure of a joint.

It was odd how every sound seemed magnified; the least rasp, even the gurgling of the water behind and below seemed louder the higher Hawkwood rose. He knew behind him Gold would be champing to follow and could only hope the lad's impatience to be at his master's side would be overcome by the strict instructions he had been given to wait.

When he came abreast of the crenellations, with the ladder top so close to stone he could rest his cheek and cool it, the sky, which had been cloudy, suddenly cleared, a short break of starlight but enough to give him pause. There was no way to issue orders, he could only hope that his confrères would do as he did and quickly drop a rung to stay hidden until it passed.

Hawkwood was holding his breath, which was necessary since he was unsure his exhalation would be soundless. When the cloud cover came back he moved with speed because a glance aloft told him there would be another burst of light following in short order. A hand grasped onto the crown was sufficient to lever him up and through. There he stopped, crouched and hidden by the depth of the blocks just as the light increased again.

A slowly raised head allowed him sight of the parapet. There was a lone guard with his back to him, walking away, but far enough off to make it a risk to attack him. Lowering himself slowly he eased his feet on to the timber floor, hearing a squeak from wood long laid and dry from being much weathered. He froze and pushed himself back as far as he could, his sword ready. If the man came to investigate he would kill him; if he shouted to alert his comrades he would attack.

Neither happened: another one of his company had come up behind the fellow and, creeping along to his rear, cupped his hand around the mouth and drove a dagger into his lower back, ripping it upwards to cause a massive wound, causing so much shock that no sound would emerge. The next swipe across an exposed throat brought silence, while the now inert body was dropped soundlessly onto the parapet.

All along the walls his men were emerging, moving to occupy the corners and prevent too early a discovery. The target was the town gates; once in Hawkwood's hands he would have what he wanted: possession of Pont-Saint-Esprit with no chance for any of the inhabitants to leave and alert any one approaching.

The overcoming of the guards was a secondary concern. Now ropes were coming up that would allow Hawkwood's men to lower themselves into the actual alleyways below without using the stairways normally employed by the sentinels and their superiors. Once he had two-thirds of his men in the streets, going after the guards on the various gates, he could see to matters on the other three stretches of curtain wall. With every one of his company inside the town these, the defenders, would be outnumbered.

He needed to be down there himself, and using his feet and his hands he lowered himself, waiting at the bottom until Gold and a dozen others joined, to then make their way through the streets to the north-west gate, from which the Great Company would approach. Jonzac had the bridge gate and Francis the Belge the one that faced south.

There were two men on each, secure in the knowledge their walls were sound and protected and thus barely alert. So it was shock that rendered them useless more than weaponry and their quick surrender saved their lives. Meanwhile the citizens they were paid to protect lay in their beds asleep, unaware that their town was now in the hands of the men led by a freebooter of whom they had never heard.

# CHAPTER SEVEN

The people of Pont-Saint-Esprit, as well as those who had chosen to rest there for the night, awoke to find the only armed men in their town were those led by Sir John Hawkwood. Each gate was barred and no one was allowed to leave, though the normal morning carts bringing in market produce were given entry. Anyone who baulked at the strange faces found that a sword to their throat generally altered any objections. Once inside, they too would be denied the right to depart until the arrival of the Great Company.

The wardens manning the bridge toll had been replaced by freebooters, under strict orders to be polite to any west-bound traveller, who could continue their journey if bypassing the town or enter as they desired. If they chose the latter they found themselves in a place in a strange state of hiatus; there was none of the normal activities, no bustle of citizens going about their business. They saw few womenfolk or children, for they had been kept indoors for their own safety.

Hawkwood himself was atop the tower above the north-western gate, looking out for the remainder of the company. When they appeared, the signal, a red flag, was hoisted to say that the town was in the right hands. Soon they were marching through the gate below him to take up residence within the walls, crowding into houses quickly vacated, but with strict orders that there was to be no looting or ravaging and especially no burning. Everything to an approaching traveller must look normal.

'We must send some of our men on south, Sterz. If we do not, then I for one would be made suspicious by the lack of fellow travellers.'

Lacking a citadel, the German had been allotted the spacious Bishop's Palace, the unfortunate divine, seen as a man about whom resistance might gather, being left to contemplate his coming fate in the vaults that lay close to the river. Hawkwood, having assured that all was secure, had come to see Sterz there to proffer that advice.

'Allow that I have wit enough to see that for myself.'

The gruff reply was to be expected; the German liked such things to be broached in a way that allowed him to draw the right conclusion, not suggested as if he had been too dim to see the necessity. Hawkwood saw it as politic to allow for that.

'Forgive the tone. I am exercised by what is at stake, too much so, perhaps.'

Sterz nodded. 'They must be trustworthy.'

Cunradus, present as usual, had words to add. 'As long as they are restricted in numbers and kept separate in small bands they will have to be. Their true task should be to close the road back to Avignon so the cardinals, should they suspect anything, elect to retire.'

It was agreed that a string of routiers, with weapons concealed, would make their way over the Rhone in twos and threes and at intervals, to try and replicate what would be the normal level of traffic, some with a cart, others carrying crosses to identify themselves as pilgrims. In each group there was to be a leader who would act as spokesman should they be engaged by strangers, especially clerical ones in bright-red robes.

'As to the town,' Sterz insisted, 'the captains must patrol the streets in person. We cannot have our men forgetting what we are here to secure.'

He had made a valid point to the captain present; it was one thing to say that the company should behave, another thing to ensure that with drink taken such an injunction was obeyed. Every tavern had barrels of wine in their cellars and many of the better houses would have the same. Broached and consumed, any orders issued would lessen by the goblet.

'I will look to my patch,' Hawkwood replied. 'It is up to others to look to theirs. As of now I must partake of some food and rest. It has been a long night and a tiring one, but thank the lord it was a success.'

There was in that statement an invitation for Sterz to issue congratulations for the way he and his company had achieved that which they set out to do, because by any stretch it was outstanding. All he got was a nod, as if it was only to be expected. That was the way of the man; the German was ever stinting at the achievements of others, while expecting paeans to his insight when he managed anything to be remarked upon.

'Why is it that a man like Sterz sees it as demeaning to give praise to another?'

These words were muttered to only one set of ears: his standard-bearer Christopher Gold. Even if he would never admit it, Hawkwood was wounded by the lack of praise. Not really expecting a reply he continued his grumble.

'A leader should never fear that he is diminished by sharing credit, and in that our German, for all his qualities, is sadly lacking.'

'Does he have qualities, Sir John?' the youngster asked. He saw Sterz only as a distant presence, one who would scarcely deign to acknowledge the likes of him.

'He possesses gifts which I will openly admit I lack. We are two thousand strong and there are proud captains who have to be brought to agreement, while they and their men need to be fed and kept happy, and that takes no account of those who cannot fight but attach themselves to us. That is a task I see as beyond me. Mind, I expect his monk has a hand in the running of the host, but still it must be held together and that alone is hard.'

As he walked Hawkwood was back in the Sterz pavilion, not on any specific occasion but an amalgam of many, to hear arguments, sometimes heated, about future plans or of escapades that had failed to lead to the desired result. If all the captains acknowledged that someone must lead, a few, the likes of Jonzac and Thornbury, were careful enough of their pride to show some independence, while the Belge was a pessimist who rarely saw good in any scheme. If he personally sought to use wit to make his views known, others were sharper in their manner of speaking, which always riled the German.

The position of outright leader, while reasonably secure, was ever open to challenge if matters did not go according to plan and the details of the contract were not met. John Hawkwood wondered if Sterz, or more probably Cunradus, thought of him as one to watch when it came to a bid to replace the leader, when nothing could be further from the truth. For a moment he considered bearding that particular problem only to put it aside; neither Sterz nor Cunradus would believe him if he sought to convince them that leadership of the company was of no interest to him. Quite the reverse, it would only arouse suspicion.

'This I am going to enjoy,' he said as he looked up at the sign for the Impious Bull, with its rough-painted image of St Saturnin being dragged along by the beast to his martyrdom. 'We shall break our fast at no cost and then relieve our fat friend of every florin he has accrued from cheating his customers.'

'If he is wise he will offer it up freely.'

Hawkwood grinned at the boy. 'Some of it, Christopher, but he will seek to keep a sum well hidden and that he must surrender. I will give you the honour of slicing open that belly if he seeks to hold out, but I suspect it will not come to that.'

What the pair experienced as they entered was close to a comedy. The innkeeper had no idea who he had previously served but he knew by now the town was in the grip of the freebooters of the Great Company. No doubt he had spent the time since that became known seeking to conceal what he could and there was a game afoot to get it revealed without violence.

The sight of John Hawkwood and young Gold drained the blood from his mottled face and he looked like a man who had involuntarily evacuated his bowels. The hands were soon wringing, the pleas for understanding gabbled out. He was a poor man, ever having to trim his prices to avoid being undercut by rivals, so that often he incurred a loss.

With no more than a look Hawkwood sat down, followed by Gold, and if that tempered the flow of excuses it was insufficient to stop it entirely, even interspersed with commands to his girls to fetch food, the very best, as well as his finest wines, for nothing could be good enough for these kind gentlemen. The game was played and the pair ate and drank in silence with the fat sod ever in attendance to bark at the serving wenches for supposed failures.

Finally Hawkwood had enough. 'Do be silent man! You will upset my belly with your lies.'

'Excellence,' came the protest, with those fat hands clasped tightly under his chin added to a wetting of the eyes.

'You are a rogue,' a furious shake of the jowls, 'who would dun any innocent traveller who comes your way.'

'Never in life.'

'Life,' mused Hawkwood, throwing back his head to look at the smoke-dark beams. 'Is it better to be alive and a beggar or dead with burgeoning coffers?'

'Alive, always life first,' Gold added. 'Unless you have paid out for an indulgence and are sure of paradise.'

'Have you paid the pardoners?'

'Where would a poor man like me get the means to buy an indulgence?'

'It is not only the Church that can issue such favours. It must be an indulgence to let live a ne'er-do-well who swindles by habit. Much better to string him up by his heels, and then slit his throat so he bleeds like a pig.'

Tears welled up, which nearly got a laugh as a reaction. If Hawkwood was playing with the innkeeper the man was unaware of it, for there was nothing jocose in his tone. Pont-Saint-Esprit may have been spared Routier rapine but what such men were capable of was no mystery, even here.

In truth, while guying his host, Hawkwood was ruminating on that very matter: the citizens, as yet unharmed, must be wondering what was afoot. No doubt their imaginings would be replete with fears of a dreadful fate and the whole town, behind closed doors, was probably on its knees in prayer. By repute, the streets should be running with the blood of the menfolk, while no woman or girl, if the attempt to hide them had failed, should still be unsullied.

They would have heard tales of towns being stripped of everything they possessed to be set alight before the freebooters moved on to their next victim, taking with them the gold of the citizens' coffers and the contents of the public and private granaries, as well as the younger females to act as concubines on their journey to the next set of unfortunates.

Nothing of the kind having taken place, the fact raised in Hawkwood's mind an interesting thought: could the company gain as much by consent, perhaps even more, than they could by plunder? He knew himself to be less bloodthirsty than many of his confrères. That did not mean he would not kill – he would as the need arose – but he had always felt that to slay another for the mere pleasure of the act was sinful. Not that he would interfere with others so disposed; to seek to impede when one of the company was inflamed by bloodlust and no doubt stupidly drunk, was to put one's own life at risk to no purpose.

Likewise with women; John Hawkwood was strong on consent, for he drew little pleasure from forced carnality. Experience again had informed him that in any place where the soldier put his feet there were women willing to become their companion rather than being forced to that estate; all it took was a little time to find one.

Here in this very tavern, one of the serving wenches had indicated that any attention paid to her would not be unwelcome, so any rest he took would be preceded by a good bit of rutting. The other thought he had centred on Gold; the boy was shy, but his voice was breaking. The time had come when the stallion had to be led to the mare, so he would have to find another willing partner for it would not serve for his first dip to be a forced one.

'I must be about my business, pig,' he said finally. 'When I return I expect you to be ready for me to inspect everything you own down to the last copper coin. Should you fail to do so, and there will be a thorough search, you will suffer the fate of the pig, your namesake. If you are honest, and I suspect it will be for the first time in your miserable life, you will see old bones.'

The eyes within those puffy bags narrowed and Hawkwood could sense the man calculating what he could get away with.

'Lie and this building will be demolished down to the last standing stone.' Again there was no need to elaborate; with the inn intact he had a chance of future prosperity. A glance was thrown at the particular wench who had caught Hawkwood's eye to get a quiet smile in response. Beside her was a girl the boy's age with a cheeky cast to her manner, so she might serve to pop the cherry.

'We will rest here tonight, so make our chamber ready with all that is required. Come, Gold.'

Sterz had tried to keep secret from the commonality what the company was seeking but that had barely held; how could it with so many having knowledge? He had seen for himself men whispering in a way that indicated they had some information, if not all, but that was enough to set the mill of rumour furiously turning, strong enough to get pumping the blood of every greed-filled heart. Such stupendous wealth would conjure up a vision in the brain of the meanest intelligence.

A strong command had to be issued to keep men off the parapet overlooking the bridge, lest their sheer numbers caused the approaching cardinals, more so their escorting soldiers, to hesitate. Whoever captained the Swiss bodyguards would be a soldier of some experience and a crowded wall would arouse suspicions. That did not stop the men's leaders from endless visits, ascending the steps to peer along the Rhone bridge and beyond, this in between their need to patrol and keep order in their various sections of the town.

There was traffic, of the kind to be expected. A divine with a relic, a bone of St Anthony on his way to Bourges where it would be venerated in the cathedral. Folk by the dozen who were returning from pilgrimage, most from Rome or the Shrine of St Michael at Mount Gargano in Apulia, others with the darkened skin brought on by the heat of Palestine and many eager to rest. Such travellers were taken into guardianship but not harmed.

One papal messenger on his way to Autun was closely questioned, but could reveal nothing about cardinals and ransom money, so as the day wore on frustrations grew. Di Valona was interrogated but could provide no reason as to why that which he had predicted had not come to pass. Gloom descended as the sun dipped and those men sent out as disguised pilgrims drifted back to inform Sterz that they had seen no sign of the large body they had been told to look out for, heavy waggons and litters being escorted by soldiers.

'Perhaps on the morrow,' was the view of Cunradus when the captains gathered in the Bishop's Palace, candlelit now that the light was fading. 'It would not be unheard of for such a body to suffer a day's delay.'

'I am willing to go and seek an answer,' di Valona ventured.

The look that got for all assembled must have told him that he was far from entirely trusted, which to Hawkwood, who had spent some time in his company, did not now make sense. Suspicious as the next, he had come to see that what this young man had said must be true. He could not get his hands on that treasure on his own so had shrewdly found a way to get a decent part of it, with others taking what risks had to be overcome.

Everyone present was aware of the threat posed by those Swiss mercenaries, formidable by reputation: even as paid retainers they were known to adhere to their bond. They would fight to keep safe the ransom money and their clerical charges, perhaps prepared to die to fulfil their task. Hence the need to avoid a fight in the open because that would not be successful without severe loss; for all their abilities the Great Company were not at their best in formal battle against a disciplined enemy and the men most at risk would be the leaders, of necessity to the fore in a fight.

'I will accompany him,' Hawkwood said, in a voice loud enough to carry over the murmuring that di Valona's offer had engendered.

'Ever keen to put yourself forward, are you not?' Sterz sneered. 'You wish for preferment once more.'

For once, Hawkwood, who was ever carful to contain it in favour of a witticism, lost his temper. 'If you wish to do it, say so or agree it is a wise thing. We cannot just sit here and wait.'

'Why not?'

This was demanded by a captain named Baldwin of Gitschtal, German like Sterz but from land further south, bordering Italy. From the look on the face of the captain general he seemed to concur, which forced Hawkwood to respond.

'How long before news of what has happened here spreads? The hospices and taverns on the road to Avignon must be wondering why they have no custom even now. If we have bottled up the road to the west and north do not tell me we can keep that secure for ever. Nor can we keep the route south intact. Those we have held up will be seeking an alternative route by footpath and there are boatmen all along the Rhone who will be only too willing to carry them across for a fee.'

'We must know if what we seek is coming,' said Thornbury softly, 'and we must be prepared to set out from here and fight to take it should it be necessary, whatever that means in terms of risk.'

'We must do everything necessary. To fail to secure the ransom would be a failure hard to suffer. I for one would happily hang up my sword and my spurs and leave this life we live.'

The speaker was Leofrick of Aachen, a seemingly mild-mannered warrior captain until he had the chance to swing that weapon he was so keen to hang up. His speciality was beheading his enemies, which wits insisted was a ploy to find some brains with which to fill his own empty head, for he was often unwise.

'Someone must go with di Valona,' Hawkwood insisted. 'It need not be me.'

Francis the Belge spoke out, for once positive. 'It should be you and I will come too.'

94

Sterz had his jutting chin on his chest and for once Cunradus did not interfere. Hawkwood was wondering if the German thought he should undertake the task himself. Did it fit with his dignity to do so? When he finally spoke it was mere prevarication.

'Whoever goes must leave at first light.'

'No, Sterz, whoever goes must go now.' That brought up the head, to glare at Hawkwood again. 'It is a clear night and my horses are fresh. In darkness we can see campfires three leagues' distant and such a body must have many of them lit wherever they stop. The accommodation for the clerics will not extend to the Swiss.'

'And if we spy such a camp,' Francis added, 'we have no need to approach it to know it is our quarry.'

Hawkwood indicated di Valona. 'He must not be seen, so spying what we think to be our cardinals, we will wait till dawn or when they break camp, then ride ahead of them at enough distance to see their dust.'

'It will be hard to keep our men in check,' came a cry from Baldwin. 'No drinking, no women, no plunder is not an order they are happy to abide by. It has been hard to enforce this day and it will not ease over another.'

'Then tell them what we seek,' Sterz shouted, his patience clearly exhausted. 'That is if they do not know already. If we succeed, they can drink themselves to death in the company of a personal seraglio.'

# CHAPTER EIGHT

How many times had John Hawkwood ridden half asleep in the saddle, willing to let his horse pick its own way, knowing it would not deviate from whatever track he and his companions, plus two squires, were on? This time it was an old Roman road and, since the wind was from the north-east it was well illuminated, the sky a clear mass of stars, almost like a white blanket, bright enough to wash out the light of a newish moon.

Talk between the leading trio was desultory, going from continued speculation as to future good fortune to the near-unthinkable possibility of failure. The blackened landscape ahead showed no sign of that which they sought, numerous campfires, even from the height of a high hill. On those occasions when the mounts required to be walked it was pointless to even look, so the first tinge of dawn saw the positive part of their mood begin to evaporate; by the time the sun rose it was gone.

'We must go all the way to Avignon,' said di Valona. 'Only there can I get positive information on what has gone wrong. Plans must have been changed. Once we know of those alterations then we will find out what must be done.'

'There's sense in that,' Hawkwood muttered to Francis, knowing the Belge shared his gloom. Having been sustained by a vision of gaining part possession of a great fortune, an ebullient mood that had made sleep seem unnecessary, he was now dog-tired and in sore need of a bed. His fellow captain's mind was on more mundane considerations.

'Avignon is two days distant and that is without resting the mounts, as we must.'

'If we fail to sight that which we seek, how else will we learn the truth?' asked the Italian. 'As for horses, we can change them. We will be coming back by the same route.'

'Di Valona's right, Francis. If we keep going till the zenith and still find nothing I suggest we send one of our squires back to Pont-Saint-Esprit. Sterz will be chewing his belt already. Beyond that I doubt I can go on without rest and I know my horse cannot.'

The suggestion got a nod and a raised arm with a finger pointing to a plume of smoke rising lazily into the azure blue sky. 'Would that be a hospice ahead? If it is, then let us rest now.'

'It is part of the Monastery of Mondragon,' di Valona replied. 'I rested there on my way to join the company. The brothers seemed kind and not excessively greedy, but there are no women.'

'We are about to become pilgrims again,' was Hawkwood's weary response. 'And I for one need a few hours abed and no company.'

Two of the monks who ran the resting place were awaiting them as they passed through the gap in the drystone wall that formed a gate. Benedictines, they wore black habits frayed at the edges indicating they were poor lay brothers, a lower order of sanctity. These were the kind of men who worked to support the monastery, growing the food the choir monks would eat and running such establishments as the abbot saw fit to maintain, this obviously being one of them and designed to produce revenue under the guise of aid for pilgrims.

Hospices like these dotted every route in Europe; there were shrines everywhere, towards which the faithful could travel for general absolution as well as their particular needs. Each saint had a purpose: healing afflictions, protecting travellers, ensuring prosperity, all with the added ability to provide blessedness. Here the welcome was excessively fulsome and so grovelling it matched the advent of the three Magi, explained by the lack of anyone preceding them, with many questions asked as to what could have caused the flow of travellers to cease.

Hawkwood, having failed to consider this, was obliged to think quickly and to allude to a miracle that had been observed in Pont-Saint-Esprit, one that had caused pilgrims to delay there in the hope of benefit.

'A young girl, a virgin, had a vision of bloodstained St

Saturnin leading a bull into the cathedral. A resurrection of sorts.'

Having seen much credulity in his travels, he was far from surprised that this tale was swallowed whole and with many a sign of the cross and whispered incantations. In a previous life, between the campaigns of Crécy and Poitiers and on his uppers, Hawkwood had been part of a group seeking to sell relics to the clergy of middle England: small bones, fingers and toes they had acquired from local churchyards, this as a way of making a living when other schemes – and there had been quite a few – had failed.

It had proved unwise to seek to pass on anything large or from too famous a beatified entity, for the very simple reason that such articles would be the province of the larger diocese and wealthier divines. But a hint in a local tavern that a sanctified bone was close usually prompted the local priest to come and investigate the rumour Hawkwood's accomplices had planted. He was the final link, the innocent fellow who would never sell what he possessed, a valued family heirloom, on peril of his immortal soul – only to be persuaded, and such a thing took time, that he would be more blessed in the parting for a good cause than the ownership.

A money gift would ease the transaction and the cleric would go off knowing that once the news spread, his church would be filled to bursting at the next Mass while his neighbouring parishes would lose a portion of their congregations. Even if he proved sceptical, the bishop would be impressed and that evoked the possibility of preferment at some future date; truly the holy were as competitive as the laity.

'If I had a gold noble for every time I have had a priest feel a bone and tell me he could sense its divinity, I would care nowt for what we seek. I'd own more of England than King Edward.'

None present contested Hawkwood's assertion of clerical gullibility; routiers worshipped God as they must and sought salvation with the same fervour as any man living. But experience made a fighting soldier turned freebooter a more rational believer than those who took the cloth, the only exceptions being those divines prepared to wield a sword as well as a crozier. It was also held as a belief that the higher a man climbed in the Church the less credence he placed in that which he preached to the ignorant layman and his lower clerical orders, material comfort engendering scepticism.

'Nothing more proves that than the whore called Avignon.'

This statement, delivered by di Valona, was borne out on arrival at the city not long after Lauds and another night-time ride without sight of fires on fresh mounts, half a day having been spent in rest at the hospice. Now just three, Gold having been sent back to give a second report, they came to the gates and paid their 'charitable donation' to the poor which permitted entry to the papal city, well aware that little of what was raised would go to feed or house the hungry.

If there were exaggerations of the corruption supposed to be endemic in Avignon, it was not far from the utter truth, for the pure were few. You only had to recall the luxury in which di Valona had related he had been a guest to know that the princes of the Church did not live as ordinary mortals.

The city itself, bounded by the Rhone, was packed, noisy and filthy. Many of the streets were so narrow and crowded it was impossible to ride, a sharp eye had to be kept out for those attempting to pilfer as the accumulated dung of thousands of animals sucked at their boots. If it lacked rain, which it commonly did, Avignon stank of the accumulated dirt, the whole made worse to men accustomed to stench by the heat that seemed to keep the piles of ordure that lay everywhere steaming, creating a mass of flies that needed to be constantly swatted away.

The cries of hawkers filled the air as they sought to sell every kind of religious object to the faithful who passed through the papal city in their thousands each year, spending money to eat, drink and sleep, as well as to purchase that which was being sold as an aid to salvation: crucifixes, medallions and phials of holy water.

The supposed spiritual heart of the city – many claimed it had neither – which lay close to the river and its helpful breeze was the massive Papal Palace. The huge building, all near-white stone, had crennelated spires and square towers, the plaza before it packed with even more vendors. There were tumblers, jesters, lute players and money changers hunched over their scales as they weighed coins for value, plus an odd proselytising monk, a madman dressed in rags so worn nothing of his skeletal body was hidden, promising damnation for the sins he could smell on those who passed him by.

Finely decorated litters borne by strong-armed men

sought to make their way through this throng, the occupants screened from view, leaving those who gazed on ornate decoration to wonder if it carried a duke, a cardinal, or a courtesan and it could easily be the last, for if celibacy was preached by the Church it was rarely observed by those holding high office.

Yet even in its apparent wretchedness and odours the city reeked of wealth. Merchants bustled by, each with an armed escort to force a passage. Notaries in their distinctive headgear, rapacious by nature and without whom no plea could succeed, elbowed their way through the human throng followed by clerks carrying bundled scrolls of legal cases. In the alleyways there were numerous traders in gold and silver who operated from the open front window of their dwellings, their enticing shouts adding to the general hubbub.

Vestment makers were more discreet: their offerings were laid out on tables for inspection, small sections of cloth sewn through with valuable metals, others with jewels or pearls; they had a guard, often a blackamoor, with a broadsword ready to cut off the arm of anyone tempted to steal and there was no shortage of such creatures. Numerous beggars existed, as was to be expected, both maimed and whole, seeking alms and invoking the words of Jesus regarding caring for the meek and deprived.

It was a relief to pass through the gatehouse of the Pont Saint-Bénézet and cross to Villeneuve on the opposite bank, a bridge as famous throughout Christendom as much for its construction as a tendency to collapse when the river flooded. Once on the far shore the streets were no longer narrow alleyways but wide thoroughfares lined on both sides with substantial dwellings hidden by high walls and mature trees.

At a crossroads di Valona insisted he would be required to part company while his companions sought somewhere to await his return: a shaded spot with water to both rest and allow all three mounts to drink. This they found at a tree-lined pond outside a substantial Benedictine monastery, which the Italian assured them was not far from his own destination.

'I must arrive on foot, as a mere student would.' That got a raised eyebrow from Hawkwood. 'A dust-covered horse, tired and obviously one ridden some distance will raise questions. It is not the cardinal himself I must guard against but he has many servants. It would not be Avignon if some of them were not in the pay of those he sees as rivals for the papal ear.'

'What a place,' murmured the Belge, with a shake of the head.

'Just like our moving household,' joked Hawkwood, which got him first a look, then a slow smile of acknowledgement.

Di Valona had kept his actual destination to himself; clearly he still wanted to keep the name of his benefactor secret. This was confirmed when he parted and walked away, ignoring several gates until he disappeared into an alleyway, the quick backwards glance to ensure they were not following a good indication of his desire for continued discretion. The two freebooter captains, having unburdened their mounts so they could graze, took cheese, flats of bread and flasks of wine from their saddlebags, bought from the last stop on the way to the city. The two days spent in each other's company had mellowed the unfriendliness originally shown by Francis prior to Saint-Esprit and he and Hawkwood had fallen to talking about their joint service in the armies of England.

That soldiers recount battles in which they have participated would not cause surprise to any man, yet it was interesting they held different memories of one like Crécy given it had been fought on such a contained field, proving, if it needed to be, that one fighting man could see only that before him and not the whole once he was in any way engaged. That applied more to Hawkwood than the Belge, he being an archer and formed up behind the front line for much of the encounter.

As a spearman, Francis had been given a good view of the opening moves, notably the way the Genoese crossbowmen had been obliged to retire only to be slaughtered by their paymasters because, it later transpired, the French nobles suspected treachery.

'That massacre was a blunder.'

Hawkwood nodded: even if he had not witnessed the fact he knew it had affected the end result. Without crossbowmen to give a modicum of cover, any advancing knight was riding into a death trap. The Genoese had been subjected to the fire of English longbowmen and had wilted, while the knights had yet to have that visited upon them.

Silence followed and lasted several seconds; to men who had observed it, the concentrated fire of sixteen hundred bowmen was a wonder, thousands of arrows filling the sky at the same time, the low whine of their passing like the knell of doom for the targets. To those on whom it had rained it was indeed deadly – if not to the armoured knight, to anyone without plate and more especially to their horses.

'Being paid, the Genoese were distrusted.'

'We were paid, Francis.'

'To fight as one, I recall, alongside your lords, which made the difference.'

Hawkwood nodded; it had been the same at Poitiers. The French noblemen fought for their personal glory, not the cause of their King, and in doing so suffered from having an utter lack of coordination in their repeated attacks. Even after the losses in Picardy they still thought that mailed might and sheer numbers could overcome anything and anyone, not realising that Edward of England had two factors that made his army near to invincible: cohesion and those longbows.

The first meant his line generally held, regardless of temptation – though there was the odd fortune-seeking transgressor – so that his enemies found themselves assaulting time after time a solid wall of defenders. English knights, from the highest earl to the lowest sir, joined their men to do battle on foot and in doing so could exert control. With the archers to the rear firing off their salvos, few got to the English line to do individual battle and if they did they lacked the number to force a break.

'I recall the Earl of Northampton yelling at us not to slit valuable French throats,' Hawkwood laughed. 'Not that much attention was given and you lucky spearmen got there first.'

'The nobility make much from their ransoms, Hawkwood, but the likes of us require quick plunder.'

There had been much of that, even for the likes of the archers who arrived as a second wave. The dead were stripped of anything of value. Then the English army fell upon the tents of the French nobles and finally the huge baggage train. There was much pleasure in listing their individual gains as well as regret at valuables missed.

'And now we require news to lift our spirits in the same manner.'

The Belge looked pensive. 'And if it is not that?'

'And what would you have sought if we had caught those cardinals – like me, a life of peace and plenty and a return to where you were raised?'

'I reckoned on the same at first,' Francis responded, the look of doubt on his face now familiar, 'until I realised I would have to have a care where I came to rest. The lands from whence I hail are not far enough off from the places left devastated under Edward. Without an army to protect my possessions, and no wide channel of water to keep freebooters at bay, I might find myself a victim of such as we.'

'You could cross to England. Having served our King a welcome would be assured.'

'For you it is simple.'

Hawkwood answered while declining to say why it was not, his tone wistful. 'It is from where I hail, Francis. It is home.'

The Belge produced a huge yawn. 'While I have travelled so much I can scarce recall that such a place exists.'

'Time to sleep?' Hawkwood suggested, laying his head on his saddle. 'Our Italian could be an age.'

The sun was long past its zenith and they were awake when di Valona returned, his gloomy countenance enough to tell them that any information he had gleaned was not enough to lift his spirits. The cardinals had been delayed; the reasons were unknown, but were thought to relate to the slowness of the bankers in providing the specie, hardly surprising when Hawkwood considered it: no such sum was likely to have been previously raised.

'And what now?'

'The route is unknown, but it cannot now be through Pont-Saint-Esprit. Its occupation by the Great Company cannot be kept secret for weeks on end and it may be that long before the cardinals move.'

'Then we must return and tell our confrères,' was the response of a low-spirited Francis.

'We as freebooters have the ability to move as we like,' Hawkwood insisted. 'I suggest you stay here in Avignon and seek to find any new route they may take. Once you have anything solid, come to us. Trust that we will find another way to intercept the treasure.'

'You will not be staying in Pont-Saint-Esprit?'

'I cannot see why we would but you will have little trouble locating us.' It was unnecessary to say that all he had to do was follow the trail of destruction they would leave in whichever direction the company went. 'Just as you did before.'

'My horse and saddlery?' di Valona enquired, not bothering to answer that point.

'Can you get another?' A slow contemplative nod but no explanation; no doubt his cardinal would oblige with either a mount and equipment, or the means to buy it. 'Then we shall take it back with us and pick up all our own horses left, yours included, at the last hospice.'

The Italian looked skywards. 'If you wish to get clear of Avignon before dark you should go now.'

There was a moment there when doubt hung in the air. Was this handsome young man with his dark-brown eyes and smooth olive skin too keen that they should depart? Would it be better to perhaps silence him rather than just hope he would still act in their common interest? It would have been good to discuss this with his fellow captain, but of course that was impossible.

Di Valona was standing before them and if he was asked to move away so they could talk there could only be one subject to discuss and he would be a fool not to work out what it was. In his place Hawkwood would take to his heels. When he turned to Francis the Belge prior to mounting he could see in his companion's eyes the question on which he was pondering, a point raised not long after they moved and were out of earshot.

'I cannot see that killing him would gain us much.'

'I agree,' Hawkwood concurred, 'and there's no point in dwelling on it. That is till we meet Sterz, who is bound to ask why we let him go.'

That got a rueful laugh. 'Be prepared to be told you are a fool. I am.'

There was a temptation then to enquire as to his feelings regarding the German but it was quickly buried; they might be on better terms than previously but outright trust was likely to be unwise. Besides, having re-crossed the Pont Saint-Bénézet they were once more in the teeming and narrow streets of Avignon proper and that required concentration as well as an eye both on their purses and their saddlebags, no easy task when being constantly jostled.

They got out of the city before the gates were closed for the night, but not before Hawkwood had registered that there was a well-equipped and numerous garrison. If the number he saw at one place were replicated along the entire parapet, then the city was well defended, as it would need to be given the huge treasure that must be locked away in the vaults of the Papal Palace.

As the sun dipped he looked, by habit, back at the actual walls, noting they were formidable and in excellent repair. The vague notion he had been toying with, that there must be ten times as much wealth in Avignon as was being transported by those cardinals and it would be a fine prize to capture, had to be put aside in the face of reality. The place was too strong unless one had an army to invest it and that was one thing the Great Company was not.

'But what a prize, Francis.'

# CHAPTER NINE

If Albert Sterz had not always been a man John Hawkwood admired, even as he appreciated his gifts, he was obliged to do so after he delivered the bad news regarding the ransom money being almost certainly beyond their reach. If he was disappointed, and who would not be, the German hid it well, even managing to make it appear as if he had anticipated the outcome before immediately going on to advocate another way in which the Great Company could flourish.

'We are in possession of a walled town on the edge of a prosperous region. The granaries are full and the supply of food from the countryside can sustain us, which means we have no need to plunder to eat. Under us is a population cowed but as yet not subject to what they have every right to expect. I say that presents an opportunity!'

Cunradus was a master of dissimulation, his smooth, round face rarely betraying the thoughts he was nurturing. Looking at him instead of Sterz, Hawkwood noted the slight flicker of amazement at what was being suggested; the man he normally advised had surprised his factotum as much as anyone else present.

'Within a few days' marching lies Avignon, dripping with wealth.'

'As well as strong, well-manned walls, Captain General.'

Hawkwood mouthed this caveat in a soft voice. The suggestion Sterz had made, even if he had yet to work out the full ramifications, he found intriguing, but not enough to let the man get carried away: he had been to the papal city and knew of what he spoke, while the man who led the company had not.

'If I say my assessment is shallow, only one great gate and a section of wall, I do not reckon it will alter much on greater examination.'

The way that was taken, immediate agreement, came as a second surprise.

'Acknowledged, Hawkwood, and well said. Numerous as we are there can be no taking of cities like Avignon, but I speak more of their hinterlands. Between us and the defences you mention are many towns lacking walls that will pay us ransom to be spared or yield even more in the way of wealth if they refuse.'

Sterz paused to let his confrères mull on that, a smile edging his lips. There were those present who burnt and destroyed for pleasure as much as profit.

'In addition, we hold one of the few bridges linking both sides of the Rhone and can set a charge to cross at whatever level we like. That will allow us to extract inducements if we think a traveller or goods to be of particular value.'

'Are you saying we stay here, Sterz?'

The use of the surname and no title got Leofrick of Aachen a jaundiced look. In private it would have been acceptable. In such an assembly an acknowledgment of his superior position was reckoned to be politic, making the snapped reply more like the normal Sterz.

'It would take a thick skull with poor content to need to ask the question. Certainly we can leave here and go on our way, but to where? Is there a part of France that will yield more than the Comtat Venaissin, full of abbeys, rich estates and on our doorstep? We can ride out from Pont-Saint-Esprit at our leisure, take that which we desire, then retire behind walls that will keep us safe even from an army.'

'Walls, Captain General, that Hawkwood overcame only days past and with scarce a drop of blood spilt.'

Thornbury delivered those words in an even tone that eschewed dispute; it was no more than a reminder.

'Then perhaps he is the man to ensure it does not happen again. Will you take that on, Sir John?'

The title, rarely if ever deployed without sarcasm, was pure flummery and Hawkwood took it as such: he also considered the possibility that Sterz was shifting the problem of security for the company from off his own shoulders. If the walls were overcome a second time it would not be his fault. Hawkwood could say he was flattered and decline, without loss of face, yet the plan Sterz was pushing to be accepted melded with many thoughts mulled over in the months since Brétigny.

The activities of the Great Company were wearing and ever on the edge of problems in the supply of food, shelter from inclement weather and even horses, for the endless movement bore down hard on the equines. Again his mind returned to that ambuscade, an indication that resistance was hardening against the routiers to the point where untrained peasants felt it better to fight and die than succumb.

If losses in fighting men were small in the article of death or wounds, they were greater in the area of desertion and disease. Some, tired of the life, breached their contracts to quit and probably go home, wherever that may be. They usually slipped away in small groups following on from the highly rewarding sack of a rich town or monastery, taking with them more than their allotted share of the spoils.

Little could be done to prevent that, while in a company dedicated to seeking booty it would be hypocritical to protest; nor was it wise to detach others in pursuit, to thus weaken themselves even more. Not that they numbered less as a body, but being reinforced with village and townsfolk – youths eager for adventure – did not fill the gap.

They were not soldiers and it took time to turn them into even a semblance of one; in the meantime they could be as much a liability as an asset. The Great Company was yet formidable, but to John Hawkwood less so now set against its original strength and that would only get worse. So what was being put forward made sense; being static they could regain their previous power.

'I can ensure that Pont-Saint-Esprit provides for us a safe haven, if that is the wish of the assembly.' That got a rare smile from Sterz, not that it lasted long as Hawkwood continued, 'Yet external threats are only one part of what we might face.'

'Who can threaten us?' demanded Baldwin of Gitschtal.

'How many great fortresses have fallen due to treachery from within?'

'If you doubt any one of us, Hawkwood,' Leofrick of Aachen growled, easing a finger width of sword blade from its scabbard, 'speak now so that matters can be settled.'

Given Sterz had already put Leofrick down with a telling insult, John Hawkwood was obliged to avoid doing likewise, even if it was justified. The man's temperamental nature was no mystery; the puzzle lay in the fact that a fellow so stupid could be voted in as a captain by those he led. In the end it was John Thornbury who replied with what was obvious to everyone else.

'I think you will find our comrade speaks of the citizens, Leofrick.'

It took time for that slow brain to make sense of that. The evidence that it eventually did so was in the hand coming off the hilt of his weapon and the blade being allowed to slip back into the leather.

'So far we have visited upon them little harm,' he hissed.

'Which they can scarcely believe!'

Sterz was right to say that, but they had not remained entirely unmolested: old habits could not be entirely eliminated and not all captains had full control of their band. There had been instances of freebooters, men difficult to discipline by the very nature of their service, getting out of hand: stealing, inflicting beatings to those they thought had great wealth hidden and, of course, many rapes. Yet in terms of what the inhabitants of Pont-Saint-Esprit had anticipated it would appear slight.

'I say we must have them support us, not wish us gone, and that requires vigilance from us all and the need to be harsh with our own to maintain the peace.'

The suggestion from Hawkwood was as radical in its way as that advanced by Sterz, this proved by the many incoherent questions that emerged: he was telling his fellow captains that they and their men must adopt a different way of behaving in pursuit of a more enticing goal, and be coerced if need be to do so.

'As well as ensuring their ability to go about their business in peace, if what our captain general proposes is as profitable as he wishes then some of that should be shared with the leading citizens, namely those on whom we will depend to keep the town secure.'

'We have the power to command that,' insisted Baldwin.

'If you believe that, Baldwin, then I happily yield the security of Pont-Saint-Esprit to you, or anyone else who shares your opinion.'

'I cannot command you, Hawkwood,' Sterz interjected, in a tone that indicated he wished he could. 'But I agree with what you say and I now request you take on that responsibility.'

Cunradus was smiling and Hawkwood thought he might well do so. If he had been surprised as anyone else about that which was being proposed, his fertile mind had subjected the possibilities to shrewd examination. Sterz, by asking that question of Hawkwood had completely bypassed whether his proposal was accepted. He looked like a teacher proud of a star pupil.

'I would not wish that my men be denied anything gifted to others.'

Cunradus spoke for the first time. 'You may find profit for what will prove scant effort.'

Hawkwood naturally set up the centre of his operations in the Impious Bull. Sharing his quarters was the serving girl of mature years and a bold eye previously singled out. Named Aalis, and some twenty-four summers in age, she turned out to be a very warm bed mate indeed, grateful because she was relieved of the need to work for a man she detested.

Eudes the fat innkeeper had been obliged to dig up the gold he had sought to hide in his cellar and that now sat in a locked coffer under the Hawkwood bed, while a second chamber, likewise not paid for, acted as an office. It was not long before the owner came to realise he was suffering where others were not.

'You are doing penance for past sins, Eudes.'

'Have I not been penitent long enough, Eminence?'

'No. Now fetch me some wine.'

That at least the man did not have to buy; gifts such as wine and food poured in from citizens seeking the goodwill of his tenant. Dividing the town into its various quarters and appointing men he could trust as a sort of watch, Hawkwood was able to receive complaints. Some required action and that he ensured was a responsibility shared: any penalties had to be agreed in council.

He also had Sterz free and reinstate the bishop, engaging that divine in keeping the peace, for there were villains in Pont-Saint-Esprit as capable of disturbing the peace as any freebooter. He was elderly and rather confused but to ensure clerical compliance the bishop was given a personal bodyguard led by Ivor the Axe, as much to prevent him entering into intrigue as to secure his person.

The walls were inspected and any weaknesses, cracked mortar or stones that had shifted from their seating were listed for repair, the necessary replacements brought in from a local quarry and the town's artisans set to carry out the work. The clearing of the bushes that lined the riverside was paramount, backed up by the construction of two wooden palisades cutting off the strand to both fishing and nocturnal incursion, these patrolled in darkness by men from whichever band had come back from pillaging to take a rest.

Eager to line their purses, every captain kept his men in the field as long as it was possible to do so, Sterz included, rampaging through the papal possessions, sometimes up to the very walls of Avignon itself, there to hurl insults at the Pope and his cardinals. It was that which made possible the keeping of a sort of concord within, for there were transgressions and as a concomitant there had to be punishments, usually with stocks or a flogging, though two of Baldwin's Burgundians had been hanged for the violation of a girl child.

Insults to the guarded walls of Avignon were mere sport; it was plunder they sought and the Comtat Venaissin yielded a great deal. Hawkwood had control of the bridge tolls and was shrewd when it came to assessing how much travellers would pay for passage. Added to that, monies, tithes and Peter's pence meant for Avignon, which had been sent before Pont-Saint-Esprit fell into routier hands, never got beyond the town. The church vaults that once held the bishop were now a repository for a great deal of Pope Innocent's income.

Messengers despatched by him or his officials were frequent in both directions, the Rhone crossing being a major route by which the papacy kept in touch with every diocese to the west and north and they paid heavily to traverse the river. The Hawkwood band had no need of compensation from their mobile confrères; their revenues, added to taxes from traffic through the town gates – every countryman heading to market had to pay – as well as a levy on trade within the town, which had been paid to Avignon previously for defence, was more than sufficient.

It was a happy man who found out his bed mate Aalis was with child, the news delighting both her and the putative father. She was put in the hands of a set of ladies who would care for her every need and if the notion of nuptials was never broached, it was a given that the child, once born, would become John Hawkwood's charge. It would be a test of the bishop's resolve, for if he was still in Pont-Saint-Esprit it was intended the child should be baptised there, which made what followed interesting.

'There is a papal delegation under a truce flag demanding he who commands the men here to come to attend to their presence.'

With Sterz absent Hawkwood knew that meant him, as did Gold who had brought the message. The boy had been given command of the tollbooth and it was good to see the responsibility had him grow in stature and confidence, though his mentor thought that might also have to do with his eager adoption of carnality; he had one of Eudes' very young serving girls to share his bed and by the noises emanating for their chamber it was no soft and romantic meeting of young bodies: more furious, noisy and repetitive rutting.

'They decline to pass through the toll to meet in Pont-Saint-Esprit, Sir John, to treat you as an equal. Should I send them packing?'

'No doubt it would please you to do so.'

'If you saw their garb you would want to strip them and send them naked back from where they came.'

'Gorgeously attired?'

'That does little justice to their magnificence. The leader is certainly a cardinal.'

There had been one such delegation before, clearly from Avignon, carrying an instruction from the Pope for the Great Company to quit Pont-Saint-Esprit forthwith at risk of damnation. Naturally it had been ignored. Next had come an offer of indulgences, a remission of confessed sins, and that too was brushed aside; Hawkwood was curious as to what message could come now.

'It would be churlish not to meet with such an eminence.'

The papal party had stopped on the highest point of the bridge, still mounted, which indicated this was likely to be no parley. Hawkwood came to them on foot, a dozen of his

119

men behind him for security, to look up at the leader, he of the red cardinal's cap. Astride a beautiful white mount and wearing a cloak of heavy material edged with ermine, he had creased dark skin and heavily hooded eyes, this registered only in passing. He did not deign to speak himself; that was left to one of his minions.

'Who is His Eminence addressing?'

Hawkwood gave his name and rank, which seemed to disconcert the divine; he must know the name of Albert Sterz by now and had no doubt anticipated a meeting with the captain general. After a pause, the cardinal produced a thick scroll, bound in a blood-red ribbon, which was handed to the same speaker.

Untying the ribbon, the fellow rolled it open and began to read in a sonorous voice, telling the man before him, as well as every member of the Great Company or anyone who aided them in any way in their blasphemous behaviour, that they were now beyond a state of grace, denied the Eucharist, confession and the last rites. Pope Innocent had excommunicated them all.

'The Pontiff is, however, a merciful man. He orders that you present yourselves to him at his Palace of the Popes before the Feast of Michael and All Saints, where you will do penance for your manifest sins. You must also make reparations to his Holy Estate for that which you have robbed and despoiled in the lands he holds by the Grace of God for Mother Church. That done, Pope Innocent will consider, should he see true repentance, lifting the Bull of Excommunication.'

The scroll was rolled tight again before being cast down

at Hawkwood's feet. Tempted to ask what paupers had paid with their pennies for the cardinal's mount and his clothing, Hawkwood put that aside. Instead he picked up the Papal Bull, looking at the carved and gilded edges around which it was wrapped before tossing it over the stone parapet and into the River Rhone.

'You will burn in hell for that,' said the cardinal, finally addressing Hawkwood directly.

'I daresay you will provide Lucifer with as good a blaze as me.'

'Do you not realise what I have said? You are beyond forgiveness and so are those you lead.'

A man who did not look capable of anything more than a loud whisper surprised Hawkwood to produce a loud call that was strong enough to reach the walls of Pont-Saint-Esprit.

'Within the town, the men you harbour are apostates and thus you may kill them at will and remain free from sin. Be sure that Christ our Saviour will welcome into heaven any citizen who spills the blood of these delinquents. Mother Church has disowned them and so must you on pain that you too, all of you, will suffer anathema.'

Behind him, Hawkwood heard the growls as well as the swords being unsheathed, which caused him to hold up his hand and call out. 'Belay, let it never be said that we bloody a truce flag even from an envoy of Satan.'

The eyes upon him were cold enough to cause a shiver, for the man looked more devil than priest. The mount was spun round in its own length and the cardinal departed, his escort likewise, leaving the man he had addressed with a conundrum.

'Christopher, go to Ivor and tell him to take the bishop to his church. Then I want it carried by crier to the whole town: everyone to assemble for a special Mass. Let the good folk of Pont-Saint-Esprit see us take the Eucharist, which will tell them what credence we put on papal excommunication.'

'Will the bishop agree to officiate?'

There was nothing calm or restrained about Hawkwood's response; he was seething and it showed. 'If he does not, he will find himself in the stocks with my entire brigade ready to throw the filth of the town at him, and perhaps objects more likely to maim the old sod. Happen we will see if he believes in the faith he professes or has the stomach to be a martyr like St Saturnin.'

# CHAPTER TEN

Excommunication was not the only instrument in the papal tool casket even if the Pontiff, finding himself ignored, had brought down anathema on the Great Company not once but twice. The routiers took this as a compliment, a statement of their worth, it being a sanction only previously applied to monarchs who sorely displeased the Holy See.

The reasons were not hard to fathom: the vaults that had once held the bishop were now full of booty, much of it in coin, a great deal of which had come from the bridge tolls collected by Hawkwood. Beyond that on the east bank of the River Rhone the Comtat Venaissin had yielded up a cornucopia of produce and treasure which included everything from ransoms and raided aristocratic coffers to the valuables of manors, cathedrals and monasteries.

Prized crucifixes were mixed with endless church plate, this augmented by gold, pearl and jewel-sewn vestments. Then came the reliquaries, by which the clergy engaged the veneration of their flocks. It was hard to know what troubled them more; the loss of their gold and silver ornaments or some fragment of the bones of a saint or martyr.

The company was able to mock their denial of the sacraments. More worrying was Pope Innocent's next step: the call for a crusade against the free companies – all of them – primarily those harrying papal lands, with remission of sin, as it had been in all previous Crusades, the payment to serve the needs of the church. The countryside around Avignon was now beginning to fill with encampments as the call was answered, which meant raiding that far south had become perilous even if it was seen in Pont-Saint-Esprit as a distant threat. But it could grow, so riding out in search of plunder was put aside in favour of a council where all could discuss the way to react.

'Indulgences and no need to go all the way to Palestine?' mused Hawkwood, as the gathering assembled.

'A potent threat is forming,' was the opinion of Leofrick of Aachen, 'and one we must carefully consider.'

No one bothered to tell the Rhinelander he was stating the obvious: that such was the very purpose of his presence, though many an eye was raised to the rafters of the bishop's audience chamber.

'The question we are gathered to ask and answer is how do we go about countering it?' If Sterz had expected a response to that query, a solution of sorts, he was sorely disappointed. 'As I see it, there are only two alternatives. Do we stay or do we depart?'

'To where, Captain General?' Hawkwood enquired.

Leofrick puffed himself up to respond. 'We have the ability to go anywhere we choose.'

'Then let us go to Avignon,' joked John Thornbury.

Pompous and bereft of sense as ever, Leofrick replied with due bombast. 'If that is here agreed it will not be my brigade found wanting.'

'Why go anywhere?' Hawkwood asked softly. 'We are in possession of a near impregnable fortress and this supposed host gathering against us is yet nothing but talk.'

'A fortress you, Francis and I captured,' Jonzac reminded him. 'And very easily, I recall.'

'Do not forget my men took part as well.'

Roland de Jonzac smiled, for it was a gentle rebuke. 'Granted, but it was not much trouble.'

'Which I have taken steps to ensure cannot happen again, my friend.'

'It is far from just idle gossip,' Cunradus interjected; as the man charged with knowing about such matters, he had a grasp of the threat greater than those of the soldiers. 'According to the travellers I have questioned, lances have already arrived and we are told of many more on the way. In addition it is not just indulgences bringing them to Avignon: Innocent is disbursing gold in great quantities as well.'

'It is about time he coughed up some of that which he squeezed from his flock.'

The point made by Baldwin set off a general babble as the low opinions of the Holy Church were noisily aired.

There was supposed to be a formula to this sort of council: each captain was empowered to speak in turn, usually to advance the feelings of his own brigade, though sometimes there was scant consultation with lesser beings.

If that was the theory it was not the reality: they never proceeded as smoothly as the likes of Cunradus wished. Men such as these could not be so easily corralled and were reluctant to give way to another so constant interruptions were the norm. Sterz, unless he had already formed an opinion and a plan he was determined to impose, tended to stay aloof but not on this occasion: indeed, he appeared to be in serious doubt. The person he needed to answer his questions regarding a possible course was happy to do so.

'When Pont-Saint-Esprit fell to us it had a garrison of some fifty men in total.' Hawkwood paused while this was acknowledged. 'We are far greater in number by a huge factor and I take leave to suggest we are better fighters than those we overcame.'

Growls greeted that assertion; if the freebooters were proud of anything it was their professional skills. That asserted, they were not as strong as they had been on arrival. Raiding could not be carried out without risk, for not all their victims succumbed without a struggle. If deaths had been uncommon they had nevertheless occurred and with plundering success there had been an increase in desertions. That accepted, as a defensive body they had more than enough men to man the walls as well as to launch sorties to disrupt any preparations for assault.

'Which,' Sterz cut in, 'will make taking these walls a bloody affair.'

Hawkwood concurred before he continued, clarifying that the public granaries were full and not just those; every householder in Pont-Saint-Esprit had been allowed to stockpile their own food, the allowance of which, designed to keep them quiescent, they had taken full advantage. If the freebooters had not been as rapacious as first feared that did not induce any feeling of security in the common breast.

He then reminded his confrères that the wells that supplied the city's water lay within the walls, so the supply could neither be cut off nor poisoned by the tipping in of dead animals, the lack of anything to drink being a sure way to overcome even the most potent defence. As well as wheat and oats there was ample livestock grazing the surrounding fields, all of which could be fetched in, while the huge wine vats were maturing the very good pickings of vendange, while there was fruit in abundance too.

'Can we rely on those we hold?' asked Baldwin.

He was clearly looking for a sound reason to depart. He meant the citizens of Pont-Saint-Esprit, who could betray them and make meaningless the stout walls Hawkwood insisted would keep them safe. Three others nodded in encouragement and all present were aware that fortresses more often fell to treachery than assault, a question Cunradus answered. The monk had authority in this: his anathema meant more to a man of his calling than it did to a freebooter.

'The excommunication extended to anyone who gave succour to us. They too are seen as apostates. I think the citizenry of Pont-Saint-Esprit will know of the fate of heretics, which is how they will be seen by those who see themselves on Crusade.'

The list of massacres in the name of religion was known to all, from the Albigensians to Jerusalem itself, where every Jew and Muslim in the city had been slaughtered in the name of God. Hawkwood wanted to move from the thought of such matters to the reality of anyone trying to take the town as well as the pressure on those in the siege lines.

'Have we not all experienced the misery of such a task only to find that after months of fruitless attacks or waiting on short commons, our bellies ravaged with disease, the defenders demand a parley, then terms, before marching out with their weapons and carts loaded with their possessions? The King gets the castle while we get nothing.'

'Not,' Baldwin opined, 'a release likely to be granted to us. Innocent wants us strung up, I'm sure.'

Francis the Belge spoke next. 'A possibility so far in the future as to be an unknown, Baldwin.'

'I do not claim to know the future, do you?'

Such an irascible response set them all against each other. Cunradus, giving Sterz jaundiced looks for his lack of assistance, tried hard to control the debate, only partially successful as those who wished to run from the impending problem argued with the others who thought they could hold out against Innocent and indeed thwart his purpose. Hawkwood was the most vocal progenitor of the latter, only stopping when Sterz shouted for silence.

'What is known, or will be common talk in this host forming to fight us, is how well we have stripped this province of its wealth. Innocent has bleated enough about it to anyone who will listen. He may be content to drive us off his lands, but what if those he is gathering think not of saving their souls, but of lining their purse?'

Certain points do not require explanation. If there was questionable security within the walls of Pont-Saint-Esprit there was none at all out in the open against a superior foe. It took no leap for men who were themselves greedy to see the attraction of a chase designed to strip the Great Company of all that it had acquired, and it did not need to be the whole host in pursuit; any major portion of such an army would be difficult to confront.

Baldwin was still in favour of departure and he took the lead for the others who shared his thinking. 'Which means that if we are to depart we must do so before they are fully formed.'

'Anyone desirous of an immediate departure may of course do so,' Cunradus responded, 'as long as they recall the terms to which they appended their mark.'

That too required no elucidation; the monk was saying you may go but by contract you leave behind you your share of what spoils have been gathered, something no band would accept, regardless of the strength of their leader. One other point was as well made too by their leader: for security they must act as one or not at all.

'To take with us what we have garnered will oblige us to strip out half the carts in the Comtat Venaissin and that means slow progress. Ask yourself this. In possession of such knowledge and able to ride down your enemies what would you do?'

'Take the treasure and take the life of every man who had owned it.'

This piece of obvious sense from Leofrick caused both wonder and agreement, which was naturally followed with the concomitant conclusion. The company had more chance of survival and hanging on to what they had plundered by staying put rather than seeking to flee and slowly Baldwin and his ilk were won round. That accepted there was a great deal to do; the Comtat Venaissin still had much to yield, for in previous outings there had always been left with their victims enough to bring on recovery, a future source of plunder.

That changed; knowing time was short, the brigades went out to create a desert around their stronghold, burning that which they could not carry off as well as manor houses and peasant dwellings. Vines and olive trees were cut down; local notables and high churchmen who had not had the sense to flee to Avignon were hunted down and taken in chains to the vaults of St Saturnin, there to reside as tokens with which to bargain.

Scouting parties were out continually to report on the growing threat, detailing the number of encampments springing up around the papal capital as well as by which banners they were occupied. Such information provided sobering reflection. There were bodies of lances from half of France, many parts of Germany and even a small number from Italy, especially the Papal States surrounding Rome.

Such intelligence gathering remained a constant until the day came when the papal host moved. With Pont-Saint-Esprit no more than three days distant for a marching army, that meant it was time to call in the bands, drive in the livestock and the last supplies, set fire to that which could not be carried in time, drop the portcullis and man the walls.

With all of that inside, plus the Great Company in its entirety, Pont-Saint-Esprit seemed ready to burst. The sounds of lowing and bleating were not confined to the animals; many a citizen saw only a horrible death as their future, either at the hands of their occupiers or those trying to overcome them. The sounds of endless praying mingled with the rasp of metal on stone, as weapons were sharpened in readiness for battle.

The first sign of the enemy was their huge papal banner, with the image of St Michael blazoned upon it, as they approached the eastern end of the Rhone Bridge. Hawkwood was on the walls with his archers, willing them to attempt a quick crossing. He knew, as did his confrères, that the assault would not just come from one direction; the river level was low now, the run of the water slow, and boats would be ferrying soldiers and their horses across the river to the north and south, to surround Pont-Saint-Esprit and cut it off with the aim of bringing on starvation.

'I pray they have enough arrogance to think us supine,' he whispered to Gold, as ever by his side, though now tall enough to need to bend his head slightly to address his captain. 'They will not if they have heard there are English bowmen here.'

'They will fear the Welsh more, John Hawkwood.'

Ivor the Axe called this out, loud enough to be heard by all; he was fiercely proud of the ability of his countrymen with the bow and often given to stating that without the

Welsh having invented it, no Englishman would know of its existence, never mind its quality. As ever, his assertion was hotly disputed.

'Since when did a Welshman have the wit to invent?' called Alard the Radish, to loud agreement from his own kind. 'I have looked in an ear of your countrymen many a time, Ivor, and seen daylight clear on the other side.'

'Not daylight, Alard – divine light, happen. There's naught in an English head but straw, and damp it will be too.'

'Let us set that aside for now,' Hawkwood insisted, for these were well-worn jokes. 'Baldwin's lances need us to give support.'

The men mentioned had occupied the stone tollbooth and had also built a barrier to the open side in order to deny the enemy the bridge. They had with them half a dozen crossbowmen, not reckoned to be any use at all by their longbow comrades given the time needed to reload such a weapon, added to the fact that it required two men to carry it out. In the same minute a man on a longbow could launch a dozen arrows, which, if they could not penetrate armour at long range, were so disruptive it was considered equal.

There was one great difference here: there would be no essaying out from the defence to seek to kill or maim men whose horse had fallen to Hawkwood's archers, whatever their weapon. Baldwin's men were there to hold as long as possible, which would not outlast the crossings being made on other parts of the river, a manoeuvre that would inevitably cut them off.

Attacking across a bridge is difficult, so few men would be able to deploy. If Hawkwood had been in the shoes of whoever commanded on the east bank he would have never attempted it. That it happened he put down to the enemy being French by their banners, high-born and puffed with arrogance. It was the same stupidity as the battles won by King Edward: each Frankish knight looked to his pride instead of common sense. In such minds no mere mortal, and certainly no peasant soldier, could stand against their chivalry.

Six armoured knights lined up abreast of each other and began to advance, slowly as suited their heavy destriers, the mounts also partially protected by the mail slung on their chests. On each lance there flew a coloured pennant and every shield had on it the rider's coat of arms, proof of their chevalier status. Heads were protected by plumed helmets that testified to the owner's wealth by their elaborate and individual designs.

The crown of the bridge was well within range of Hawkwood's men and their captain waited until his enemy was at that point before ordering that they fire. To him what followed had a sweet sound, the swish of a salvo piercing the air, not as loud as Crécy or Poitiers but audible nevertheless. Skills had not been allowed to rust during the occupation of Pont-Saint-Esprit. Outside the walls stood the butts these men had used to keep such a thing sharp and the speed of the reload and fire was as good as it had ever been.

The missiles, each the length of a tall man's arm, fell upon the line of knights, to ricochet off their armour, those that missed doing the same off the stones. It was the horses who suffered, not their riders, from what was plunging fire. That was the aim: to so discomfit the mounts they would become impossible to control, causing their heavily armoured riders to tumble to the ground as the mounts reared and bucked, to lie there like a beached fish as they struggled to rise again.

That was when the crossbow bolts came into action. They fired a projectile that could penetrate armour and that applied to those who had retained their saddle as much as to the others rendered vulnerable by having fallen, four in total after the bolts had done their worst. Foot soldiers with a wall of shields then came forward to seek to rescue them and get them to safety. Several fell to the reloaded crossbows as well as more plunging fire from the ramparts.

'Enough,' Hawkwood called, when the pair still mounted had retired to safety. 'Let's keep our arrows for more pliant flesh.'

'We're not short,' Alard insisted; he had spent the last weeks with wood, fletching and metal headtips to ensure an ample supply.

'Not yet, friend, but who knows how long this siege will last?'

The only other action that day was to cover the withdrawal of Baldwin's men as the sun went down, made necessary as papal troops appeared on the west side of the river. It could never have been held and had been nothing more than a gesture, a way of saying to Pope Innocent, his cardinals and his noble supporters that his remission of sin was necessary. It was going to be applied to the souls of many of those who had come to serve his cause.

As expected, the enemy tried to effect a coup, seeking

to emulate that which John Hawkwood had achieved and overcome the walls by a combination of subterfuge and surprise. The Hawkwood palisades had been torn down as a matter of course. On a moonless night the papal troops crawled along the riverbank, likewise using the sound of the river to seek to mask their movement but it was a watercourse less potent than previously. The attempt was stymied by the dropping of flaring bales of hay, which lit up the whole strand and the men upon it.

Hawkwood, in anticipation, had built platforms that could be slid out from the top of the walls. Onto these he put his best archers who, with such clear targets unable to respond, made merry. With these sitting ducks it was no more difficult than firing at a straw roundel in the butts. The attack was not only driven off; they left behind many bodies of those wounded and killed. The former were despatched by a party of men from Sterz's own brigade of Germans sortieing out, their bodies thrown into the river to float down to Avignon as a message to Pope Innocent to tell him the price of his attack on the Great Company.

# Chapter Eleven

It does not take long for those holding a fortress to discern the mood of those besieging them. It was plain that the papal forces lacked the kind of will and sense of purpose that would come from a unified command. Innocent had gathered a heterogeneous army made up of individual contingents. Given he was no military leader but wished to exert control through his various cardinals, and they competed for his attention, he was in fact commanding something held together only by his promises of redemption.

Attacks were launched against the walls but with none of the purpose Sterz and his captains had previously witnessed, and when the men on the parapet outnumbered or matched their assailants then the use of ladders was futile and generally fatal. The defenders waited in anticipation for the building of siege towers and had set in motion various stratagems to confound them; they prepared in vain. No sign or sound of carpentry or metal forging disturbed the riverside songbirds, creatures so settled that they were never silenced.

The strand was, of course, relatively free from assault in that manner, which meant the main task of Hawkwood and his archers was to deny the Pope the bridge, which would keep his contingents from easily combining. Every attempt to execute joint attacks was thwarted by long and crossbowmen. When darkness fell, the likes of Jonzac, John Thornbury and Francis the Belge would lead out raiding parties to ensure the enemy was denied sleep. Behind them came the archers under Ivor and Alard, to recover as many of their arrows as they could, which was not many given a great deal ended up in the river.

As the weeks passed with a lack of threatening activity, it became possible to move more freely in the streets of Pont-Saint-Esprit, no longer packed with cattle, sheep or hen coops. They were being eaten, though John Hawkwood, ever the jester, had used a small ballista on the ramparts to fire a daily carcass into the papal camp, which stood as an excellent way to let the enemy know that it would be Doomsday before hunger became a weapon.

'But that day will come,' Sterz pronounced at yet another council, 'as sure as God is in his heaven.'

'Winter is upon our foes,' was the gleeful response of Baldwin, no longer so pessimistic. 'We all know how much discomfort that brings on in siege lines.'

'Not the same problem in these parts as it was in Picardy.'

Hawkwood's intervention got several of his confrères nodding, while recalling past discomforts. This far south the weather was rarely truly inclement: if it rained, and it did, the downpours tended to be short and sharp, quickly replaced by watery sunshine of enough heat to dry out the landscape and those in occupation of it. The sign that it was bad elsewhere showed in the run of the river, not in spring spate but flowing strongly enough to create eddies and white water where it ran into obstacles like the pillars of the bridge.

These besiegers would not experience the sustained misery of endless days in which the skies darkened and torrents fell, to turn paths into mud, wash away poorly sited tents, leave men shivering in clothing never dry, as well as covering everything they owned with mould and rust. If the sun came out further north it was to usher in biting daily winds or heavy overnight frosts.

'I say we have stalemate,' Sterz pronounced, 'and that has within it dangers. We still have good stocks of food, but it takes no great wit to see the speed with which it is diminishing. We are becoming victim to our own strength.'

It was, Hawkwood had come to realise, the one factor he had not included in his calculations when advocating that Pont-Saint-Esprit could not be taken, based on a numerical advantage made possible by the inherent superiority of defence over attack. The latter had to seriously outnumber the former to be successful and the Great Company was so powerful Innocent could never raise and sustain the quantity of men needed to overcome them on the ramparts.

But such a potent force had to be fed and for all the excess by which they had begun, it was obvious that the supplies were being consumed at a rate that posited a day when they would be no more – not immediately but in the easily foreseeable future. The wiser citizens had begun to hide food for what they saw as the coming dearth, not that such games would keep them whole. Freebooters would find their hoards and see them starve before they themselves succumbed.

Yet there was danger, if only on the horizon. In essence, if the Pope could just keep his forces in place until spring then he would have created the conditions necessary to force a surrender and such an outcome would be hard to disguise. There were ways of alleviation, like sending out the old and sick, indeed expelling the whole of the citizenry, but that would only bolster the papal cause; they would know the end was near.

Jonzac spoke up, his tone positive. 'Innocent is not without his own difficulties. There are men from Aquitaine in the papal host and I have exchanged words with them.'

'I too,' added Baldwin, 'with my fellow countrymen.'

A high number of the men outside the walls were German-speaking – they owed allegiance to the Holy Roman Emperor Charles IV – while every possible nationality was represented within the Great Company, even Frenchmen. In a lull in fighting, and they were of necessity frequent, communication between enemies was commonplace. Some even came to the walls to trade for food rather than go foraging. If it was frowned upon it was impossible to stop.

'Not all are happy with what was promised,' Jonzac added.

'Will they not stay as long as they are paid?' Leofrick

asked. 'The coffers of Avignon are said to be bottomless.'

'I think some would go who came for faith, not a wage. They were promised remission of sins committed, plus an indulgence against future transgressions. It seems not all read the undertakings fully and relied on their priests to do it for them.'

'When will the faithful learn never to trust the words of a man ordained?'

Again Hawkwood, in saying that, hit a nerve. Pope Innocent had gathered his lances and foot soldiers with the promise that with the indulgences granted they would bypass purgatory and go straight to paradise. Such a blanket act of forgiveness would have repercussions, not least in denting future income for those around the papal throne who had made fortunes from the sale of such undertakings and wished to continue to do so.

Thus, the missive calling the faithful had been cunningly composed. A more careful reading of the details showed complete absolution applied only to those who died in God's service, really the Pope's. It was not, as had been supposed, a universal and total pardon but partial, and many of the men who had flocked to the banner of St Michael only discovered the difference after they deployed. The need to expire in battle was seen as poor recompense in place of their expectations.

The papal host was not yet falling apart; that would be too much to hope for. Yet it was, according to what they could discern, riddled with a degree of discontent. The pontiff must be aware of this for such matters would be constantly brought to his attention. Sitting in his Avignon palace, was Pope Innocent contemplating the possibility that his forces might disintegrate if the siege went on too long?

'Which means,' Sterz concluded, once these matters had been fully aired, 'that if we have difficulties, so does he. The question is, how do we act?'

'You sense it is time to talk, Captain General?' asked Cunradus to a Sterz nod. 'It is worthy of consideration.'

As the council had progressed, aware as he had been previously that Cunradus often inadvertently gave away things he would prefer were kept hidden, Hawkwood had watched him closely. Yes, he had kept his expression bland, except for a kind of false and occasional curiosity. But the very lack of reaction to important points aired was a good indication of him and Sterz having had a prior discussion.

The whole point of this council, he suspected, had been solely to arrive at the present conclusion. There was no intrinsic objection to this: Sterz was the leader and in that post it was incumbent upon him to provide guidance. If it needed a monk to point him in the right direction, so be it. If anything, Hawkwood had a sneaking admiration for Cunradus and his methods, which often got a consensus among his captains without rancour or dispute.

'I sense the time is coming,' Sterz replied, 'though I think it unwise to be the one to move first.'

Three weeks passed and it was not until the Feast Day of St Andrew that a herald arrived from Pope Innocent asking that his emissary, the Marquis of Monferrato, be allowed to enter Pont-Saint-Esprit in order to convey to the apostates his thinking on the present state of the siege.

'With a possible remission of our excommunication,' Sterz pronounced, not that it was necessary: all his captains had heard the exchange between the messenger and their leader. 'It was put in subtle fashion but it was there nevertheless.'

'In essence, he is offering us our lives,' Cunradus added. 'The question must be, is that sufficient?'

'An opening gambit, surely,' growled Francis the Belge, loudly overcoming the babble of talk. 'He must be willing to part with more.'

'Let us listen to his marquis and see,' Hawkwood responded, to general agreement.

He had other concerns that impinged on what was awaited; Aalis had produced a lusty boy child, to be named William. Should the anathema be lifted he could be properly baptised and without any future queries as to its validity, which made him eager to see what the Marquis of Monferrato had to say.

The named nobleman crossed the Rhone Bridge in style, the river beneath him now a torrent of Alpine snowmelt, escorted by a party of lances in fine if peaceful livery. He himself rode his white palfrey, holding reins through which ran gold thread, covered in a cloak bedecked with jewels and trimmed with ermine. The men he encountered when the gate opened to receive him were much less fine in their accoutrements, seeing no need to don finery – indeed most lacked any such garments – in order to receive this high-born Italian.

If anything many lining the road to the bishop's palace wished to demonstrate an opposite appearance: they were ruffians and would so dress, but that could not apply to their captains, who would treat with Monferrato. They took unaccustomed trouble to appear his equal, knowing they had failed when, divested of his cloak, he showed a fitted, waisted jacket with full sleeves and pearls for decoration, legs encased in tight hose and the points on his footwear rising to curl over his toes. This was court dress of the latest fashion; routiers could not match it even with stolen country finery.

Sterz had decided to occupy the bishop's throne, but did not take it himself until his visitor was seated. If the Great Company captains felt they were tyros in what was coming, they nevertheless knew that much of what went on would be by gesture as much as speech. Thus, Sterz waiting to take the throne, while his captains remained standing, was designed to tell Monferrato that they were very willing to listen.

Hawkwood thought if he were tempted to draw an Italian nobleman Monferrato would fit the bill as a sitter. He had dark skin but with a parchment look to it, as though the lines that marked age would never dare to show, for he was no youth and well past being fully grown. Black hair lacking in lustre framed a face dominated by a hooked nose and a set of narrow lips with a downward curve at the edges, the way they twitched the only indication of a reaction to a point made.

Speculation on his Monferrato title, taken from a town and castle overlooking the River Po, might lead all the way back to the ancients, for the topmost families of Italy tended to a long history and had been able to hang onto their lands and grandeur throughout endless changes of governance:

Goths, Byzantium, Lombards, imperial interventions from the north and a rapacious papacy required an ability to always manoeuvre to be on the winning side. The marquis was a scion of such an inheritance, now the Imperial Vicar of Piedmont and Lord of Turin.

'His Holiness requires that you quit his much-loved diocese of Pont-Saint-Esprit, the occupation of which mightily wounds him.' A soft voice, non-threatening, but to be guarded against for all its silkiness. 'In order that this should be so, he offers to lift the double anathema placed upon you and would be willing to let you depart with your arms.'

'No.'

Monferrato was shocked at the lack of diplomacy, unaware that not only the answer but the method of response had been earlier decided upon. None present had ever partaken in this kind of negotiation but it had been agreed that if they lacked experience it was no use hiding it, for to do so would surrender the initiative to the Pope. Best be blunt with no subtle mediation, which reflected the nature of their company.

'You reject this?'

The look of surprise, arched black eyebrows topped by deep-furrowed skin, looked contrived to Hawkwood and he gazed round his confrères to see if they thought the same. Thornbury and Jonzac were smiling and so was Baldwin. The Belge looked as if he was angry at such a paltry opening offer. Leofrick appeared confused, but then he usually did.

'We do.'

'Signor Sterz, the Pope has decided to be magnanimous.'

'Then as his envoy it is your task to return to him and tell him his magnanimity is insufficient.' Sterz stood, which was as good as saying the talking was over and so soon. 'If you have no more, Marquis, I invite you to dine with us before you depart.'

This too was a ploy. In another chamber the great table had been laid in preparation for a feast. The leading citizens, those who had managed to hang on to flagons of fine wine, had been forced, one or two brutally, to give up their precious possessions. Beef had been hung in preparation, mutton slaughtered and birds plucked and stuffed. The servants of the bishop had good livery and were accustomed to serve at such a board and would be especially efficient on pain of punishments unspecified. Thus the Marquis of Monferrato sat down to a banquet to compare with anything served in his own castle, or indeed within a papal palace famed for its gastronomy.

He would notice the quality of the goblets, the value of the gold plates on which his food was served, and while sat by Sterz he could indulge in a private conversation in which the thinking of the Great Company could be put to him without causing public offence. The message of the meal was obvious: we have food in abundance and can wait out your siege. The fine plates, all stolen, did not need to be referred to but they too told a story: we have this booty and we intend to keep it. This is where we stand, what else have you to offer that will tempt us to relinquish this fortress?

'Before you depart, Marquis, I wonder if you would be so good as to visit the vaults.' Again the eyebrows headed towards the hairline; it was indeed a strange request. 'You will know we have incarcerated many a divine and local worthy, all of whom are available to ransom.'

The Italian tried to produce a look of distaste but failed. The adopted expression looked more like greed, for in ransom lay a way of making a great deal of money for little effort. Then concern crossed his parchment countenance; was this villain indicating that he too could be held and ransomed?

'It will do them good, the poor creatures, to know that their cause is not lost,' Sterz added, finding a silken tone to replace his normally harsh German Latin. 'I fear they expect to be hung from the ramparts.'

The prisoners had been well primed. The men who looked after their needs had been told to indulge in confident conversations within earshot, to talk of how much food they had consumed and what was still to come. The captives were well fed too, unlike most men incarcerated. Monferrato was left alone with these plump creatures to discourse with them and hear their appeals for quick succour, in amongst coffers he was assured were full to capacity with coins and valuables. He would also, it was hoped, hear that the Pope's cause was not likely to soon progress, for if they could be well fed as prisoners, the garrison could not be near starvation.

'I will carry your response to His Holiness,' Monferrato said on his return to the bishop's audience chamber, 'but with a heavy heart, for it will sadden him that you choose to remain outside God's Grace.'

'Never mind his heart,' Hawkwood joked, after the marquis had departed. 'As long as he tells Innocent of his heavy belly.'

Days passed before another communication arrived and once more the farrago was replayed as Monferrato raised the papal offer, to then dine sumptuously at the company board once more. In addition to lifting the excommunications His Holiness would allow them to keep that which they had acquired, an offer to tear at his heart but one he was willing to make to break an impasse.

'The prisoners,' Sterz said at the end of another banquet.

'You wish me to visit the vaults once more?'

'No,' the German replied, with a smile. 'I have them on the parapet.'

Taken up to look over the walls and at his own encampment on the east bank, the sight that caught the Italian's eye was a line of unfortunates, each with a noose round their necks, many crying for what they knew was coming, one or two brave enough to face their fate  stony-faced. It was telling that the latter were laity, while too many of the former were clerics who should have had no fear of perdition.

'If we cannot ransom them, they have for us no value so we will dispose of the need to feed them – not that such a thing is a burden.'

Monferrato's chin went to his chest as he absorbed what Sterz was saying, only speaking after a lengthy pause. 'I ask for a delay so that I may consult with His Holiness.'

'To what purpose?'

'To find a compromise that will meet your needs and save the lives and souls of these poor prisoners.'

'I doubt my captains would agree.'

'You command them.'

'No, Marquis; I lead them, but it is a republic.'

'A week?'

'Two days,' Sterz insisted. 'That I can carry in council.'

'Whatever he offers,' Hawkwood insisted, when Monferrato accepted the deadline, 'he has had up those fancy sleeves of his since the very first day. He has no time to get to Avignon and back.'

'Give us credit for having seen that too, Hawkwood.'

'Us being you and Cunradus?'

'I feel no shame for taking his advice.'

John Hawkwood smiled. 'And I none for saying it is wise that you did so.'

The return of the Imperial Vicar brought good news: Pope Innocent would absolve them of their sins. In addition, he would pay the Great Company thirty thousand florins to quit Pont-Saint-Esprit while the Marquis of Monferrato, locked in perennial conflict with the Visconti of Milan, would add sixty thousand florins, no doubt a subvention from the Pope, to take those elements who wished it into his service as mercenaries.

'Each man has a choice,' Hawkwood said, addressing his company when this had been agreed and the contracts drawn up for signature. 'You may take your portion of both our booty and this papal money and depart. Or, if you desire, take service with Monferrato and proceed to Italy.'

'What are you planning, John Hawkwood?' asked Ivor the Axe.

There was vexation in that question; he had never made much of a secret of his desire to return to England once he had garnered enough money to properly set himself up. Now he had a goodly sum, not the full price of his wildest dreams – there was not enough to purchase a manor and a living – but perhaps funds to buy into the wool trade, where if the risks were great so were the profits.

He also had a son he was determined should be brought up an Englishman. But from what he had heard and with what Monferrato was prepared to pay, well, that changed his thinking. Now, with Ivor asking the question, he was obliged to decide.

'Well, I am tempted to return home with a full purse and my William, but I am told that when it comes to wealth, Italy makes the rest of the old empire look like paupers. They have so much gold even our King Edward borrows from them, though I have heard it said he is tardy when it comes to paying them back what is owed.'

'Sounds like that is where we could ply our trade.'

'You have the right of it, Alard. Happen we can make there ten times what we now have, so I am minded to give it a try. Who is with me?'

'Wouldn't let you go on your own, Sir John,' Christopher Gold insisted, his voice deep and now quite the grown man. 'You might not survive.'

Prior to leaving Pont-Saint-Esprit John Hawkwood made arrangements for William to be taken back to Essex, at some cost but worth it. Then there was provision for the boy's mother who would be staying in Pont-Saint-Esprit – she had no desire to reside elsewhere and while properly pleased at the conception was not wedded to the notion of raising the boy. She was found a house, set up as a seamstress and given servants, one male and one female, with pay for a year, making her a good catch for some local swain.

Almost the last act was to sit down to write to his sovereign once more, to tell him of the exploits of the Great Company as well as its success, with a caveat to apologise for breaking the arrangements Edward had made at Brétigny. He was happy to advise his king that he, his ever-loyal subject, was finished with such. He was bound for Italy and he desired to know if there was a way in which he should act there that would not dent the dignity of the English crown.

Many would have scoffed to know that a mere knight dared address an anointed king but Hawkwood had more than one purpose. One day he would return to England and when he did he would be in need of a pardon. He also had a strong desire to be seen as a successful soldier, which might mean a royal appointment. Added to that, he had an equal desire not to be forgotten and what better way to achieve that than the offer he included? He was prepared to act as his liege lord's eyes and ears in a foreign land, putting the interests of England before his own.

# Chapter Twelve

To arrive in northern Italy in springtime was to begin to realise the sheer depth of opportunity the land presented. Everything a human could want, even if not all ripe, was growing in abundance; the buildings, even the common equivalents to an English manor house, were striking and spacious, glorious when it came to those erected for public use. There were soaring cathedrals, with bishops' palaces to rival Avignon. Aristocratic buildings further testified to the wealth of the patrimony in domestic bastions and magnificent castles, the latter almost always perched on precipitous hills.

The Great Company was no more. On leaving Pont-Saint-Esprit, elements had headed west for Spain, notably Jonzac and Francis the Belge. Others had set off for the various regions of France and a high number of the English elected to go home. The residue, with Albert Sterz still acting as leader, took their Monferrato florins and marched down the valley of the Rhone, avoiding Avignon and scrupulously observing that which they had been bribed to leave in peace. Nothing was put to the torch until they were out of papal lands, the first being the outlying districts of Marseille.

Making away along the coast of the Mediterranean they were met by a papal envoy, a Spaniard, Cardinal Egidio Albornoz, who came to them with a formidable reputation. If he worshipped God that did not prevent him from wielding weapons of war, which he had done much of in the Iberian Peninsula fighting for Christianity against the Moors. It was even rumoured he had saved the life of the King of Aragon in the midst of battle, though that monarch's successor was said to want his head on a pike.

'And I can only claim a prince,' Hawkwood joked, with mock misery when he heard of the lifesaving. 'A king, forsooth. I suppose I will have to give way to his superior entitlement.'

Since leaving Spain, Albornoz had been given responsibility for the whole of Italy, from Rome to the Brenner Pass on the borders of the empire. In a short time he had acquired a reputation for dealing with Italian magnates who dared to defy the writ of the papacy which claimed rights both spiritual and temporal, the latter as a holder of huge swathes of land, many towns and no end of subjects.

Yet it soon emerged that if he had tamed many a lesser troublemaker he had failed to rein in the excesses of the chief villains, the Visconti brothers, Galeazzo and Bernabó, who ruled Milan and its rich hinterlands. Greedy, impious and well armed, they seized papal land with impunity and were seen as sworn enemies of the Holy See.

'You wonder that the Pope still believes excommunicating anyone has purpose. As we ignored him so did these Visconti brothers. They even burnt the Pope in effigy on the streets of the city and the population cheered.'

Hawkwood voiced this opinion to his companion: a fellow Englishman, Robert Knowles, who had joined what was now called the White Company. Sterz had elected that they wear bleached surcoats, fly white banners and burnish their breastplates so they shone in the sun.

Having made much by ravaging the Loire Valley before coming south to the Comtat Venaissin, Knowles had been too late to fully profit from the successes of the Great Company but had been impressed with what had been achieved: nothing less than the humbling of Pope Innocent. Electing to serve under Sterz the two Englishmen, along with John Thornbury, had formed an immediate bond based on a genuine liking for each other, past experience in King Edward's army and matching abilities when it came to despoliation.

'Then let us hope we can grant the pair a wicker cage,' Hawkwood essayed, 'though I would ransom them rather than set them to the torch.'

'If they are like their fellows in these parts they will be ready payers.'

A short silence followed, as the trio of freebooter captains contemplated the level of ransom the brothers would fetch. It took little wit to see why Innocent, through the Marquis of Monferrato, had paid for their services. If the Visconti were hated across Piedmont and Lombardy, that did not lead to any number of men willing to stand up to them, to take to the field and check their excesses. It would need an army to tame such villains and since one could not be raised locally, such a force had to be bought.

This was a frequent topic of conversation between men who were now mercenaries: the fact that the Italians were so disinclined to defend their own property. The only conclusion these outsiders could draw was that the various forces controlling their lives were so equal in their rapacity as to make it meaningless to oppose any single one. It was thus left as a conflict between the powerful who were willing, in search of dynastic gains, to take into their service and pay men who made war for a living.

'Riders coming,' called Gold, raising himself in his stirrups to point over the shoulders of the captains. 'Our own.'

'Keen eyes,' said Knowles, peering ahead.

'Young eyes,' Thornbury responded.

Confident in what Gold had seen, Hawkwood spurred his mount to join his captain general and the cardinal at the front of the host, men to whom these riders, scouts sent out ahead of the main body, would report. They had made contact with Sterz before the Englishmen arrived and were engaged in much pointing and animated digression, which was passed on by their leader.

'There's a strong force ahead of us, holding the far side of a bridge over the Ticino,' Sterz informed them. 'The scouts say the river is in spate so there is no way to outflank them.'

154

'Is an attack possible?' mused Albornoz. 'It would not serve to show fear to a Visconti.'

'Across a bridge,' Hawkwood responded negatively, his mind going back to what his archers had denied to the papal army at Pont-Saint-Esprit. 'They are easy to defend.'

'Crossbowmen will decimate anyone who attacks,' Knowles added. 'We know the Visconti have engaged a brigade from Genoa.'

Hawkwood's point was simple, so much so he declined to elaborate. One good way to devastate his archers was by exposing them to the Genoese, who could fire and have time to reload before the English-cum-Welsh archers could close enough to use plunging fire to disrupt them.

'They know we are here,' Sterz said, pointing to the Milanese scouts on a nearby hill. Obviously they had followed the men from the White Company.

'They will have known for a long time,' acknowledged Albornoz with a growl. 'Is there a soul in Italy that cannot be bribed?'

In a land of shifting allegiances, or none at all, information was of value, such as how many men made up the White Company, what the brigades comprised of in terms of weapons, as well as where they were headed and at what pace: material that allowed their enemies to choose where to block their progress, as they were doing this day and had done twice before already. Well sited they were issuing an invitation to attack them, and that, Hawkwood wanted to make plain, was unwise.

'If you ask among those who served King Edward or his son, you will find they never fought a battle on ground chosen by their enemies.'

'So we let them block the road to Milan time after time?'

'Cardinal, there is more than one road to Milan. Let us find one they cannot block and meet them in battle where we choose.'

A sound policy, it was easier to put into words than to achieve. The only time the White Company came into contact with the Milanese it led to a reverse, for that one criterion had not been met: the ground suited the Visconti. Thus it was the mercenaries who were caught on an ill-chosen battlefield, and the need to retreat inflicted great loss in what was a very bloody pursuit.

It also dented a great deal of pride. After marching in total some forty leagues over nearly two months they were back in Romagnano, their base and the place from where they had set out on the campaign, obliged to go into winter quarters and seek to replace lost numbers. They also had to plan for the following year.

Sterz proved an able captain in the spring campaign. He set off from Romagnano having let it be known he was intent on following the same route as the previous year. Within half a day, the German then abandoned much of his baggage train and moved to get his troops over the River Ticino before the way could once more be blocked.

Prey to misleading intelligence, the Visconti troops were wrong-footed and that allowed the mercenary army to get to their heartlands and wreak havoc up to a couple of leagues from Milan itself in a raid that had to be merciless. The White Company were out on a limb, a hard-riding column following a narrow line of advance, open to an outflanking movement if the Milanese could organise themselves to execute such a manoeuvre.

In their favour was the foot-bound nature of the bulk of the Visconti levies, armed citizens of Milan, added to their fears that what was happening might be a feint, for part of the Sterz tactics – to keep his movements hidden – was to terrorise the population into submissive immobility. Men worthy of ransom were taken in their hundreds, their homes and fields spared the torch only if they agreed to pay handsomely, though their livestock was forfeit.

The florins gained were added to their stipend for service so it was a happy company that concluded the incursion, only the cardinal being cast down; he wanted to take Milan itself, sure God would aid their cause as he had in the weeks of campaigning. Men like Sterz, Hawkwood, Knowles and Thornbury knew better. The Visconti city was walled and garrisoned and they were not equipped for such a battle.

Yet the result proved positive in an unexpected manner. Stung by the raid the brothers saw the need to nullify this threat, for in a new season the marauding might be repeated up to their very walls. Determined to forestall such an eventuality they marched on Novara which, once captured, would expose the base of the White Company at Romagnano. But now it was the turn of the papal mercenaries, forewarned, to choose the place at which to fight and they too elected to defend a bridge over the River Terdoppio.

'Though we must, if we can, tempt them to cross,' Sterz insisted. 'If they do not, we risk another stalemate.'

Hawkwood, after musing for a short while responded.

'Archery can control the flow. We deploy back from the bridge and let them cross at our pleasure.'

'Against crossbows,' asked Albornoz. 'You never tire of telling of the threat they pose. How do you intend to deal with the shortcomings in the range of your bowmen?'

'Straw,' Hawkwood replied.

This engendered a look of deep scepticism, but his thinking was sound and based on his long experience, not least the first real fight he had been engaged in at the ford of Blanchetaque under King Edward. Too junior then to affect what turned out to be a bloody fight, he had seen a way to blunt the power of the crossbow.

'Bales of it tightly bound in canvas, lined on the inside with timber, behind which my archers will stand. The crossbow bolts will not penetrate both, but the Genoese will be mystified as to why, given straw is all they will see – that and no damage to their targets.'

'Obliging them to close their range,' essayed Knowles.

'And in doing so, they will come under the kind of concentrated fire that broke the French.'

There were many more men able to employ that weapon than there had been when they departed Brétigny. If it was a skill, the use of such a weapon could be taught and Hawkwood and his corporals had spent the winter fashioning bows and training many of the White Company to a proficiency in their use. On the east bank of the bridge, set back a hundred paces and almost hidden from view, he could now deploy three hundred bowmen.

'We want them to continue their effort, to keep attacking,' Sterz added, clearly worried such a sight might deter them.

'They must do so,' Hawkwood insisted, 'or face us ravaging their lands once more.'

Egidio Albornoz was not quite satisfied and he responded with a malicious gleam in his eye. 'Beat them here and we can act as we wish. We can make a misery of their lives so the citizens of Milan are willing to offer up their tyrants. I will drag them in chains to Rome.'

It was politic to indulge the cardinal in this fantasy – he was the source of the pay they received – but none believed it was remotely possible. They might be strangers to northern Italy but it had become plain that those who held power did not surrender it lightly. When he termed the Visconti tyrants, Albornoz had named them with accuracy. Such men were far from easy to topple.

'He still dreams of taking possession of Milan,' Sterz said, once Albornoz had departed.

'Then he needs to find and pay a hundred thousand men,' Knowles responded. 'And even if you combined every free company from here to Calais such numbers do not exist.'

It had been a long time since John Hawkwood had participated in what would be a proper battle and some of the men he now led, recruits taken in while travelling, had never undergone the experience. There is a difference in being foot-bound and static as against being mounted and mobile, where the element to guard against is being surprised and that could be nullified with efficient scouting. Every time the White Company had faced the Milanese it had been them defending a blocking position. Now that was reversed.

If the nerves of the leaders were strung taut that was even more evident in the men they led. Hawkwood had placed his defensive wall as an invitation for the enemy to seek to cross and they must be beguiled into doing so in strength. The holding of that obstacle and total denial of access would only lead to another stalemate, at worst to a Milanese withdrawal, neither of which would achieve the purpose as set out by Albornoz.

For all his bellicosity and fantasising, the cardinal must know in his heart that the downfall of the Visconti was a goal too far. The aim could only be to tame their impudence by inflicting such a check on their ambition that they chose caution instead of action. They must be persuaded that papal territory was sacrosanct and the authority of the Pontiff absolute. If either was defied, then the consequence would be a powerful army in the field against them and a cost to their purse and their pride that could be nothing less than agonising.

Prior to what was coming courage had to be bolstered and Hawkwood set about the task. 'The men we will fight are made up of citizen levies, the dregs of Milan's gutters, only leavened with a few men of parts hardened to battle. If you feel fear, and it would be a fool man who did not, keep in your mind that it will be in their thoughts likewise.'

The Milanese were deploying, trumpets and horns blowing, drums and cymbals crashing, great banners waving and a mass of bodies moving to whatever arrangement had been laid down by the constable of the host.

'The racket is to test your nerves. Pay it no heed.'

One or two of his younger men were glancing backwards to fix the location of their horses. The shields and swords they all employed were laid by their side and for some that too was uncomfortable. Flight was in their minds.

'Feel naked as babes, I shouldn't wonder,' joked Alard the Radish, as he and his captain took a last walk along the defence.

Christopher Gold brought up their rear with the Hawkwood banner fluttering high, argent on a chevron sable, decorated with three shell escallops to denote a pilgrimage. Alard's face had not taken well to the Italian sun and was now more a fiery red than ever, which somehow matched his present mood.

'I have been round afore and checked they all have their bollock knives and told 'em to be ready to use them, for when the horsemen get across, we must get amongst them and slice away. Told 'em not to mind the damned great swords swinging round their heads. Drained the blood from their faces that did.'

'When they do,' Hawkwood replied, 'ensure they employ their bows. They will find that a longbow arrow at close range is as deadly as a Genoese bolt. But it is they we must deal with first.'

'Devils they are, too. Do you recall Blanchetaque?'

'I do, which is why I have us behind our walls of straw and timber.'

'Will they be humbugged?'

Hawkwood produced a wry grin. 'Depend upon it.'

The change in the note of the trumpets heralded a messenger, as was common, come to give the White Company the option to withdraw and yield the field. It was left to the cardinal to refuse, which he enjoyed, using the occasion to load the returnee with endless oaths promising damnation to anyone opposed to Mother Church.

'A mother that does not provide milk but sucks it from

the poor,' was the opinion of Ivor the Axe, close enough to hear the loud curses.

'You'll pray to God afore this day is out,' crowed Badger Brockston.

'I am doing so now, Badger, but there's no priest to dun me for a coin to provide aid in seeking salvation.'

The clatter of hooves as the messenger re-crossed the bridge was drowned out by a huge cry from the entire Visconti host, no doubt orchestrated by their leaders. Then a line of interlocked shields began to move forward to the beating of a drum.

'Show your heads, my merries!' Hawkwood yelled, which had his archers standing up to peer over the barrier, the tips of their weapons visible, even more so as they were raised in jeer. Their captain had the call, which would come when those shields parted and the tips of crossbows appeared in the gaps.

'Just come as far as the riverbank,' Hawkwood hissed, before shouting to get down as what was anticipated occurred. Within seconds the thud of loosed bolts, their velocity tempered by passing through packed straw, hit the line of timber battens on the inner side, none penetrating.

That caused a raucous cheer as the bowmen stood again to gesture with rude intent at what was once more a closed line of enemy shields, held for the time it took to get the crossbow rewound on its windlass, loaded and ready for another volley. It was a manoeuvre carried out three times and on each occasion, no doubt because of the poor result, the line came ever closer to the river's edge.

Behind them Hawkwood could see the mounted element

of the Milanese forces struggling to keep their excited horses from running away with them; horses reacted to the noise of trumpets as much as men and they also picked up on human excitement. They had been ready to move for a long time and both riders and mounts were looking to become more and more frustrated.

'Stand ready.'

That meant with heads bowed and safe, yet with an arrow already strung. The last set of crossbow bolts loosed doing no damage, these men stood to their full height and drew back. The command to loose came from Hawkwood and the first three hundred arrows winged forth into the sky, to be followed within a blink by another salvo. Landing among the shield carriers, the first broke them up enough for the second to get through to the partially unprotected Genoese, caught standing and furiously winding the catapult gut. The infantry began to scatter, so the third and fourth rounds did real damage to what became a melee and one slowly inching away from danger, not towards it.

The nobles on their horses had no more sense than their French counterparts when the Genoese and their commoners faltered. With yells and lowered lances they headed for the bridge as Hawkwood changed the focus of his defence to that narrow causeway. He reckoned not to stop them but to merely throw them into disarray, so the fire was deliberately ragged. It would be the task of his confrères to come from behind his barrier, get amongst them and cut them to pieces.

Whoever commanded the Milanese host, even if he could see what was about to occur, lacked the will or the ability to call off the attack, never easy when it came to horsemen committed to a charge. Foot soldiers were now crowding the approach to the bridge, anyway, dying in droves as Hawkwood's archers concentrated on their packed humanity, which meant even if the riders had wished to withdraw it would have been impossible.

Then Sterz had his horns sounded and he led forward his own cavalry to hit the disorganised Milanese hard. So the slaughter began, to create for the enemy, both horsed and on foot, a field soaked with their blood. If they were armoured knights and survived, their lot was to sit in sorry captivity, wondering how much they would be forced to pay for their liberty.

The arrival of envoys from Milan to talk of treaty was not welcomed by the White Company. Surely it took more than one setback to dent the power of the Visconti, and to the freebooters it smacked of Brétigny over again; lords and masters making a peace that suited them but not the men on whom they relied, which could mean for the mercenaries a cessation of employment.

It was not a defeat that brought the Milanese envoys to Romagnano to treat for a truce; the plague had swept through the valleys of the Rivers Po and Ticino to arrive in their city and more than decimate the population. Rumours came too of how the brothers who ruled dealt with the affliction: harshly in the extreme, sealing the houses of anyone sick and waiting till all indoors perished.

Yet such a curse was not to be stopped and inexorably the plague moved on, threatening to catch up with the negotiations between the papacy and Milan, the peril hastening a conclusion which allowed Albornoz to depart for Avignon to report to the Pontiff, albeit leaving behind assurances of future employment. He left a mercenary company calculating the cost of the battle just fought, which had been bloody and expensive, doubly so since there were very few men coming out from France to make up the losses. Then the plague struck Romagnano, sweeping through the lines and carrying off a high proportion of their strength.

No respecter of rank, captains were as prone to the disease as the lowest groom and several succumbed. Hawkwood lost men he had served with since his first enlistment, forced to bury them in mass graves with scant ceremony, all the while thanking God that he had not been afflicted. By the time the plague abated – in truth passed on to the west – several hundred of the White Company had perished, too many of them fighting men, so it was a much reduced force that watched as an embassy from Pisa arrived, seeking their services.

The city at the mouth of the River Arno was locked in rivalry, one close to confrontation, with inland and upriver Florence which, coveting the port, had declared war. The Florentines were arrogant, dishonest thieves, the company was told. Would these men becoming available be prepared to take up the cause of Pisa and humble their opponents? The fee would be forty thousand florins for six months' service.

'How far away is Tuscany?' Gold asked.

'Ask how rich it is, not how far,' was Hawkwood's reply.

# CHAPTER THIRTEEN

There was no hurried progress from Romagnano to Pisa, even if their new employers required they act in haste. Luckily, the mere news that the White Company was on its way put a check on the more numerous Florentines, who had already inflicted a severe defeat on the forces of Pisa. Indeed, it was that and the knowledge of their limited resources with which to alter matters that had brought the envoys north to Piedmont.

Florence would not be easy to contain; the largest Tuscan city was rich – an attraction in itself, of course, to a mercenary army – but that implied too an ability to defend itself. With numbers depleted by death and disease, more lances were required and then there was the state of the company. Wear and tear had affected both the horses they rode and the equipment needed to satisfy the Pisan contract.

That document had been composed with great care. Pisa intended to get for its florins what it felt it needed in the number of lances. Monies would be paid in instalments after regular inspections to ensure the original standards were maintained in what was a flexible force. The term 'lance' when hired in Italy did not refer to one mounted man but three; the leader a soldier, the second an archer, the last a fighting page, all with long lances. They could act defensively as a unit or gather to form an attacking body.

The host included a small body of armoured knights, who operated as shock troops in attack as well as men who could blunt their own kind in defence. In the case of the bowmen, they could combine to provide a deadly riposte to anyone seeking to drive the mercenaries from a position. Each 'lance' must have the requisite mounts and equipment, which entitled them to eighteen florins per lunar month.

In the month it took to get from Piedmont to Tuscany the word had gone out to anyone looking to be part of a successful company and many had been drawn in from other bands tempted by the offer of regular pay and massive plunder, though not all arrived fully equipped. Sterz and his surviving captains, in this situation, acted as bankers, using their accumulated profits to buy horses, saddlery, lances, swords, shields, knives and arrows, while ensuring the men they chose had food to eat and wine to drink.

If the original men in Hawkwood's brigade knew well what he required, new recruits did not and integration took time, so it was late spring before the White Company, now four thousand strong, arrived outside the walls of Pisa. Determined on a fitting ceremony their employers insisted that their mercenary force, as well as their own two thousand-strong militia, parade before the citizens, so that they would know their taxes and forced loans were being well used, the message being promulgated that with Florence humbled, extra trade would flow through their wharves in a quantity to enrich them all.

Vanity had the brigades polishing metal and oiling leather, grooming their mounts until their coats shone. Pisa had previously fielded its own citizens to fight, so there was a gilded captain general's baton for the man who would lead their mercenary forces and this was presented to Albert Sterz in the main Piazza dei Cavalieri, named for the winged horse that decorated the military banner of the city. He then led those he commanded through the streets, the host showered with flowers and cheered to the heavens, this mixed with curses for those they were being employed to chastise. The White Company was now fully ready for battle.

To march up the road that followed the valley of the River Arno as full summer approached was to appreciate the advantage of proximity to the sea. There a cooling breeze could usually be relied upon to temper the baking heat, which became near to intolerable once they reached the valley in which Florence sat, cut off from any wind-borne succour to be like an enervating furnace.

The company was never to know if it was the heat or the news of their imminent arrival that made progress so untroubled; no forces emerged from the city to seek to check them. Fanning out to take the high ground, the first act was to fire the crops in the fields, thus creating a pall of smoke that with little wind sank down towards the river to, it was hoped, choke the inhabitants.

Hawkwood was in command of the next ploy, for every man he led, whatever they were termed, carried a longbow. Combined they fired arrows over the walls into the streets and squares to make it dangerous for the citizens merely to pass from one place to another, with particular attention being paid to those locations leading to and from the city markets.

Sterz kept his main encampment in the hills but set up a satellite as close to the walls as crossbow bolts would allow. Effigies of the leading Florentines were paraded, accompanied by endless rude gestures and bared arses to insult those on the ramparts. A mint was created, silver melted to manufacture coins showing the floral arms of Florence being trampled under the hooves of Pisa, these fired over the walls to reduce morale.

A gibbet was set up on which they hung a donkey, a symbol of cowardice. Two more were killed along with a dog, these nailed in darkness to the city gates bearing in large script the names of those who commanded the Florentine defenders. In radiating circles crops were burnt, olive trees and vines cut down for a full league around, homes torched – but only after their contents had been looted. Trees were left standing since they cast good shade for the company to rest from the midday sun in, as well as being handy for stringing up anyone who dared to resist them.

If it looked like success there was one frustrated captain in the company, for Hawkwood, if he approved of the tactics, could not get from Sterz any idea of the strategy. Was the intention to scale the walls with ladders, to try to take Florence, though that was risky against well-defended ramparts without siege equipment like towers and trebuchets, which they did not possess and lacked the skill to construct? The notion that they might send for the necessary artisans fell on deaf ears or elicited the airy declaration from the German that it might be a notion to consider at some indeterminate time.

'They would not be easy to move once built,' was provided as an excuse.

'Forgive me if I seem confused, Captain General. Where else would we be taking them when our object is to subdue Florence?'

In the end the matter was decided by that endemic problem, hunger. The burning had been excessive and given the crops were far from ripe this led to a dearth. Added to that they were running out of animals to slaughter. The distance from Pisa was just too great to keep supplied a besieging army of six thousand men so, after weeks of demonstrations outside the walls, Sterz decided enough had been achieved for this season and began to withdraw.

The road he chose was not one that took them straight to the coast; there were rich pickings on another route. They made their way via a town called Volterra, which having suffered in its environs paid a handsome bribe in florins to persuade the White Company to move on, keeping safe the town itself.

Thus they rode back into Pisa in seeming triumph, displaying all the spoils of their raid, for it could not be called war, a point made by Hawkwood with some vehemence: the walls of Florence were intact and the city, which drew its food from a large hinterland as well as Sicilian imports and had faced famine in the past, possessed the means to store enough grain to ride out a crisis like that which they had just faced.

If there were frustrations it was pleasing to John Hawkwood on his return to Pisa to find that his communication to King Edward's court had evoked a response, and a positive one, no doubt composed by a scribe but surely at the royal bidding for it had appended to it the appropriate seal. The King had, according to the letter, been delighted to hear from Sir John Hawkwood, His Majesty's most loyal and well-beloved servant, a man whose fame had broken both time and distance. His exploits were known and much admired.

There was a lot of two-way pilgrim traffic between Calais and Italy, some of it by road, but for the wealthy travel by ship was much more preferable. Ports like Pisa and Genoa were prime destinations for those wishing to see something of the country before visiting Rome as well as points of departure for those returning home. Always keen to hear of how matters progressed in England, Hawkwood was happy to welcome those passing through whichever place he was in, which meant he was never in ignorance of matters at home. Likewise it would be such voices that carried news of his activities.

The letter went on to say that should he come across any matter that he felt would impact on his liege lord, then the King would in gratitude receive news of it, knowing full well that he had the affection of a man who had rendered him and his son Edward, Prince of Wales, such sterling service in time past.

If that raised his spirits the recent actions of the White Company did not. Robert Knowles, kept in ignorance of the letter – Hawkwood saw it as a private matter between him and his sovereign – having heard his friend issue a string of curses at what he saw as a waste of time and effort, much repeated since they had departed Florence, sought to balm his anger.

'You can make your disgust known, John. We are on our way to a council at which Sterz will have to listen.'

'He is too full of pomp for that now, Rob, and many of our confrères are blinded by his performance, even Thornbury. Our German sees himself as quite the consul deserving of a triumph. I think he sleeps with that damned golden baton they gave him. If he does, it would be better up his arse than in his hand for all the good it does. If I was Pisa, with what we have achieved I would hold back on payment.'

'Please say that softly, I would not wish you to be giving them any hint of such a notion.'

'Sterz is treating them as if they are fools. Yes, they are impressed by what he has displayed as booty. No doubt they care not what we extracted as ransom for Volterra as a bribe, but the scales will fall when matters are properly assessed. How long before it occurs to them that Florence, resupplied, is as strong as it was the day we first set out?'

A look around the council of captains and the self-satisfied expressions of most of those attending and drinking, when these matters were raised, was enough to tell John Hawkwood that Sterz was not alone in his fantasy of success.

'We have done well enough, have we not?' Sterz insisted. 'We have lost few men, lined our coffers, our paymasters are happy and talk of an extension tour contract while we have time to refresh ourselves before the next assault.'

'I am glad to hear there is to be one, Captain General. When is it to be?'

'When I . . .' That brought on a pause; being singular would cause offence by implying an imperious attitude. 'When we see it as appropriate.'

'And the plan is?'

If John Hawkwood was unaware of losing the room by his hectoring tone, a large chamber in a house given over to the company, Robert Knowles, able to observe, could sense it. The majority of their peers were flushed with success and that was layered with arrogance. Were they not the men who had so recently humbled the Visconti? Had they not made merry with Florence and seen the enemy cower within their walls? It was time to take their pleasure and enjoy the fruits of success. Hawkwood was failing in his attempt to persuade them it was nothing of the sort.

Almost alone amongst the company captains, Hawkwood was not attracted to idleness, either for himself or his men. Yes, they should be allowed time to take their pleasures and spend their share of whatever spoils had been gained, but he knew that too long inactive the discipline of his brigade, of which he was proud, would suffer. He was now looking, he surmised, at a whole six months before Sterz intended to stir again, this in a city full of temptations of the flagon and the flesh.

The men of the White Company were not saints and the Hawkwood Brigade was little different, even if the captain kept them under a firm hand. If anything, they stood as the opposite, being used to taking what they needed without bothering to ask. Too long in Pisa and the mercenaries would become a menace to the citizens not an asset and that he was not prepared to tolerate. There were still a couple of months in which they could be vigorous and he could not fathom why they were not.

'Then if it offends no one,' he said finally, 'I prefer to be active rather than seek the relief others crave. Comfort your whores and your bellies if you wish but I will keep the field.'

'Is there a woman who will have you, Hawkwood?' joked Baldwin. 'And is there enough in your sack to make for pleasure?'

The South German was very drunk; he had to be to make such a crass remark to John Hawkwood. Normally he would never have cared about such a slur, indeed in another's mouth and the right circumstances he would have laughed. Not here and not now, with his evident frustration at the company's inactivity. The sword was out of the scabbard in a blink and he was moving to close and kill a man inebriated and slow to react. What saved Baldwin was distance, Thornbury and numbers: he was far enough away from Hawkwood to allow others to check the Englishman's progress, which was done with caution, given the look of blind fury in the eyes.

It was the voice of John Thornbury that calmed the wrath once he was restrained, a quietly repeated insistence that Baldwin was not worth the consequences, which would be severe. A captain who slew another in fury could not stay with the company, for there was a necessary stricture against such an act. Heavy breathing slowed to become even, the tension in the body relaxed and the sword was slowly replaced.

'You take offence too easily, Hawkwood,' Sterz growled, slapping his gilded baton in a hand. 'You know it is forbidden to draw a weapon in such a gathering.'

'That is true, Captain General, so perhaps it is best that I remove myself from temptation to take offence again. I seek permission to act independently as I see fit?'

The way he had spat out Sterz's title did not go unnoticed, for it singularly lacked respect in its delivery. The German flushed angrily, waving his baton again as he nodded.

When Hawkwood rode out of Pisa he did so ahead of his brigade, taking with him only Gold and others he held as being close to him, Alard and Ivor the Axe, well aware that what he was seeking carried with it a serious risk. The Florentines, with the White Company back in Pisa, would no longer be confined. So the route he took was circuitous to avoid both them and any fighting, keeping a number of leagues between himself and the city in a search for that which he sought. It was a long ride, with nights spent in the open under the stars, comfortable enough in late summer.

Fertile Tuscany was dotted with innumerable small towns, villages and individual fortified dwellings and it was the very first that Hawkwood reckoned he needed, something he explained to his companions.

'If we are not to assault the walls of Florence how are we

to earn our fees, which are being paid to us to subdue them so they cannot threaten Pisa?'

Alard responded, the flames of their nightly fire lighting up his ruddy features.

'I've had words with some in the levies that marched to the walls with us. Not that I claim to get every word they utter, with their heathen tongue, but they reckoned to be bent on capture of the city, with enough slaughter to hold Florence till doomsday, and who's to say our paymasters don't see that as just reward?'

'Pipe-dreaming,' opined Ivor. 'Can't be done without siege towers.'

'You're right, Ivor, and we would need many more men. That only leaves hunger. To starve them out means we have to deny them this year's harvest and don't think what we set fire to already will serve. We have ridden through enough ripening fields on our jaunt to tell us the truth. Harvest the crops and they can last for the whole of next year and for that we would need another contract. Well I can tell you, if I was a Pisan senator I'd look with care afore doing that given what has been so far achieved. That is why we are out here.'

'We can't beat them on our own,' Gold scoffed.

The reply was enigmatic, 'We'll see about that, for I have another notion, which as of now I will not share. Now let's get our heads down, Alard on first watch.'

Hawkwood found what he sought ten leagues from Florence: a small town called Figline, walled, but those in poor repair. Able in such a small number to freely pass through the gates, he discovered it had several advantages, not least that a proportion of its population originated from Pisa and still held a residual loyalty to the place of their birth. More important for his purpose, Figline stood in the most fertile part of the Florentine hinterlands.

From its walls he looked out on endless fields of waving wheat nearing ripeness, groaning orchards and, on the slopes, vines laden with grapes. It lay on elevated ground in rolling, hilly countryside, yet the land was well watered, fed by endless streams from the distant mountains and under near constant sunshine. Such places were part of the bread basket that no great city could do without.

With repair, Figline would become a defendable town the enemy could not just leave in Pisan possession, for from such a base any enemy could cause massive damage. Hawkwood was calculating that it could be so vital to their future survival they would have to come out from behind their walls and fight to retake it. No need to scale walls if the enemy could be beaten in the open.

'All 'cepting we ain't a company, John,' Alard pointed out, 'or had you failed to notice? Right of this moment we is not even a brigade.'

'Which is why Gold is saddling his horse to ride back to Pisa to fetch the rest of our men. I will ask Knowles to join with us, Thornbury too. Once we have Figline, Sterz will have to stir to hold it. Then hopefully he can bring on a proper battle when they exit to fight, as I say they must.'

Hawkwood's own brigade responded with cheering speed, for he had both their respect and their loyalty which he was adamant came from the application of his benevolent

177

control. Some of his fellow captains scoffed at his methods, seeming indifferent as far as their own men were concerned. As long as they fought well their leaders were happy to oversee them with a slack hand. Hawkwood insisted on more: if his being strict was carried out without much of a rod, it held nevertheless, for wit and humour were more often employed than open chastisement. Not that he eschewed more draconian punishments if they were needed; his lances knew he had the will to string up any man who transgressed enough to warrant such a fate.

As soon as the brigade arrived, just over four hundred strong, he put them to ladder building, this carried out with noisy ostentation so as to alarm the citizens of Figline. They knew that in parts of the defences no elevation would be required; boots were all that was necessary to surmount the rubble of a fallen wall. The ride around the town on the day following was made noisily and close, so those same nervous inhabitants could look at what they would face once an assault started – and none could doubt it was coming – while messengers sent to Florence, and they must have been, did not bring the relief the fearful prayed for.

It was a feint; while waiting in Figline for his men, Hawkwood had made contact with the Pisans living within and promised them the town would be theirs to rule. They now snuck out to make contact in darkness, to confirm that at an agreed hour they would throw open the town gates to allow the mercenaries entry, away from where the areas of fallen masonry were being defended.

The time was fixed halfway between Lauds and Matins, when the first grey light of morning would touch what stonework still stood, with the Hawkwood brigade moving forward in darkness and silence to lie in the cornfields and wait. Their captain was to the front, as was common, and it was his standing up, brought on by a whistle from up ahead, that had them moving forward towards a set of gates that swung open before them.

Just inside lay the bodies of men who had been set to man it, their throats cut by their Pisan-born neighbours: easy it was claimed, for they were not soldiers, just citizens set to defend their hearths, as were those guarding the gaps in the walls. What followed was a deliberate tactic; outright terror of the kind Hawkwood rarely indulged in. His men were let loose to do as they wished within Figline, which made up for being denied Pisa, the aim of their captain to force into flight those Florentines who resided there. If treachery could have Figline fall once, it could do so again and it was wise to drive such folk away.

'Christopher, back to Pisa once more, to tell our captain general of what I have done. Advise him and gently, for he is more than proud, that he needs to fetch the host to Figline. Our Florentine friends will be forced to act when they hear it is in our hands. Let him know also, I will be out raiding and lining all of our pockets until he arrives.'

# Chapter Fourteen

What ensued was something of a race; would Sterz move quickly enough to ward off what must come? Would the commander of the Florentine forces act with a speed that had not been evident hitherto? Hawkwood, with scouts out, was soon made aware that his enemies had left the city and were marching to cross a bridge spanning the River Arno at Incisa, just over a league distant from Figline. They could move from there to confront him at will, which had him lighting hundreds of fires at night, hoping to fool them into thinking the whole of the White Company, as well as the Pisan levies, were present.

Sense demanded he go out personally on a dawn reconnaissance to assess what he would face, which inevitably brought him and his party close enough on a hill to grant them a long look at the Florentine encampment, with enough smoke rising in the air from their fires to tell him he was seriously outnumbered and would need the rest of the White Company just to hold Figline. If battle did follow – with Sterz present, that was not for him to decide.

'We need to know more,' was his glum conclusion; Sterz would want as much information as could be garnered before such a choice could be made. 'I cannot see their numbers or how they are deployed at this distance.'

'They will scarce let us approach closer,' Gold replied. 'Who and what we are is too obvious.'

He was addressing a man with his chin on his chest, deep in thought. There was a ploy he had once seen used by Prince Edward in Aquitaine and he was wondering if it might be worth a try now. Within his brigade he mustered twenty bannered knights, some his fellow countrymen, come to Italy in order to both underline their status and to seek plunder and pay. Then there was the possibility of the kind of glorious exploit that would lead to the composition of a stirring tale of prowess, to be spread far and wide by minstrels, fame in posterity of as much value to some as gold.

One such was a truly bellicose Scottish fellow, the youngest son of a Caledonian Earl of Atholl, albeit he was an experienced soldier and doughty fighter. Called Murdoch of Calvine, he had protruding blue eyes, flaming red hair and a temper to match, added to a very high opinion of himself. He might thus be suited for that which was required so Hawkwood returned to Figline to fetch him, requesting that he ride out with him fully armed, this while he and his party changed in to less conspicuously military clothing.

Calvine appeared in his plate armour, lance in hand, sword and mace swinging from his belt, only lacking his plumed helmet to be fully ready to fight. This was only to be expected from a man who always seemed in search of one and that applied to his own confrères as much as it did to the enemy. Within the White Company lines he was held to be a touchy menace. Saying nothing of what he wanted Hawkwood headed out again to a spot where the group could once more observe their enemies.

'Sir Murdoch, yonder sit the knights of Florence. I know you to be eager for combat and renown. It would please me if you were to go forth, seek out one of their number and issue a challenge on behalf of the White Company.'

The reply was typical: Calvine displayed anger and aggression where none was necessary; Hawkwood had barely raised his voice. 'Aye, but will they accept, the dogs? I will not be made a poltroon by denial.'

'I suspect if you term one of them a stinking dog he will have no choice. The way to say it so they will understand is *cane puzzolente*. I suggest no arbitrary contest but a formal duel of the kind that makes reputations.'

The bright-blue eyes narrowed. 'I sense I will be doing what you ask for a purpose.'

Hawkwood was not much given to the blush but he reddened now: his aim was no mystery to this fellow. 'It is for a good cause.'

'The cause for which I care, sir, is my own honour.'

'Which cannot but be enhanced by a bout of single

combat, one I'm sure will grow in the telling as the recounting of it makes its way back to your homeland.'

'The offer?'

There had to be one to make a contest worthwhile. 'Withdrawal from Figline if you lose. The Florentines to return to the city if you win.'

Calvine reflected on that for a moment. With peace between King Edward and the Scots – they had been defeated at Neville's Cross and King David taken prisoner – there was no fighting at home. Hawkwood knew that it was for that reason this Scottish knight had come so far, to a land where there was opportunity for a younger son who would inherit little. Stuffed with pride he wanted nothing more than to be the subject of a heroic ballad, but that did not preclude a desire to return home with a purse full of gold.

'Ensure that the story is related, sir.' He called over his shoulder, having spurred his destrier. 'I would want my name known.'

The Scotsman trotted towards the Florentine piquet, his squire behind him with his Gryphon banner; a suitable beast Hawkwood thought, for it was as snappish a creature as the man using it as identification. He was too far off to hear clearly what message he imparted to a sentinel, no more than indistinct words but it had an effect as another bannered knight, accompanied by a soldier bearing his standard, came in a short time to confront Calvine in an exchange again lost in the air. That was short and the knight soon reversed his course as did Calvine.

'My man's name is Allesandro Farnese and he is a nephew to the captain general of the Florentine host, so a worthy opponent. He addressed me as Englishman, even after I gave him my name and patrimony, for which he will pay. We are to meet inside their lines at sext.'

'We will have to accompany you, Sir Murdoch, disguised as common men, for if we do not how can we chronicle your victory?'

It was again typical of the man in that he took victory for granted, even if his next act was to demand that the priest who administered the host be sent for so he could be shriven. No man, however arrogant, wanted to enter the lists with an uncleansed soul.

The party who followed Calvine towards the appointed hour looked a sorry lot when it came to grandeur. Hawkwood had fetched along disguises: for himself monastic clothing, a worn black Benedictine habit allowing him a cowl with which to hide his features. Gold was dressed as close as he could to that worn by Calvine's squire, while the rest of the party came as mere foot soldiers of the lowest kind, in padded jackets. But all were men who had sharp eyes and the ability to make and recall mental maps.

They found the Farnese nephew bareheaded and waiting at the perimeter of the encampment as Calvine approached, he too now with a banner-carrying squire. The device was six blue fleur-de-lys on argent, which fluttered as he spun his horse to lead his challenger within the lines, followed by Hawkwood et al., progressing through a city of tents until they came to the open ground on which stood the pavilion of the captain general. Above that flew the Farnese flag as well as the arms of Florence.

Horns blew and a crowd of spectators gathered to

witness their man crush this upstart representing Pisa, a number of them German mercenaries. Hawkwood was aware they had recruited such a brigade: big men from Swabia, broad-chested, flaxen-haired, wearing mail and leaning on the long axes they customarily used in battle. Assessed they looked to be formidable opponents.

The Florentine militias lacked the same build, being slighter in their physique, but they were in a majority of the gathered host, which tempered the assessment of the whole. Their champion had arranged for a marshal to oversee the contest, so men under his instruction were busy placing flag makers at either end of the site, of the kind used to range arrow fire on a field of battle.

Hawkwood stayed close to Calvine, which would be normal given his guise as a confessor, but the others were free to mingle and wander as names and titles were exchanged, the rules of single combat – known by heart to everyone – being read out regardless. The last act, having crossed themselves, was for the two knights to don their plumed helmets and trot to their respective places, there to receive lances, which were quickly couched.

On what had to be an oration platform in front of the pavilion, a place from which to harangue and cajole their forces, stood a knot of richly dressed men, clearly the leaders of the host. They would see this contest in the same light as Sir Murdoch Calvine: a fight in which the honour of Florence was at stake with a worthy reward to be gained.

The Farnese nephew was an unknown quantity; Calvine was not and some in the crowd, particularly the Germans, had seen his ruddy face, his square build and the scars of battle, on flesh as well as his dented armour. They perhaps calculated his age and reckoned their man was not a match. Wagers were being laid on the outcome until the buzz of excitement rose. The marshal raised his flag and held it in suspension long enough to energise the Florentine levies who began calling for their champion; those who did not had bet against him.

The flag dropped and the horses, heavy destriers, began to move in the manner of the breed, slow at first, barely gathering anything that could seriously be called speed. With such mounts added to the short distance between the combatants, they met at no great pace, which allowed each to manoeuvre the point of their lance, seeking to deceive their opponent. Looking through narrow visors made calculation difficult but it was vital to assess where the lance point was aimed so as to move a shield to deflect it.

The crash as they made contact, accompanied by yelling that came close to drowning out the sound, nearly unseated both. The fighting lances splintered on contact, both men having got their shields in the right place; they passed each other, seeking to stay seated while at the same time controlling their mount until they reached the opposite end, where another lance awaited and the attempt was repeated.

The next joust showed Calvine's experience. Trotting to close, he dropped his lance to a point that threatened the Farnese horse, but it was a bluff. As the younger man moved to counter that, Calvine's lance came up sharply to get over the top of his lowered shield and strike the breast armour. Caught between breastplate and shoulder guard, looking for a second like a pinned fly, the Farnese nephew was lifted from his saddle to a huge groan from the crowd, his weight with armour making the eventual drop to the ground both heavy and damaging.

Calvine came off his horse in a way that made time seem to stand still, so slow was the action due to the constraints of his armour. Nor was he any quicker as, mace in hand and held aloft, he approached an opponent still struggling to get to his feet and with no weapon ready to defend himself. There could only be one outcome even if the victim still had on his helm. A blow from a mace would crush the metal and that would likewise implode his skull.

The cry to stop needed no translation. The man Hawkwood took to be the captain general leapt from the oration platform to rush forward and get between the still recumbent nephew and the man set on despatching him. The shouted *riscatto* had Calvine hold his mace, still high in his hand, in abeyance, even if the word was probably strange. The next entreaties, delivered with heaving breath and loudly, were in Latin, the common language of Europe for those with any education. It was numerical, a price in ransom florins to spare the young man's life.

There was ritual to this too; it was not for an uncle, however elevated, to plead – that fell to the defeated. It was an indication to Hawkwood of the folly of this kind of honour that the younger Farnese hesitated, until his uncle commanded him to beseech his opponent for mercy. The face of the fiery Scot was not visible, but Hawkwood did wonder if, with his temperament, he could be dissuaded from slaughter by what came next, the figure of three thousand florins for a life?

Money obviously mattered to Murdoch Calvine as much as honour and the mace was dropped. Around the arena, those who had thought the older man a better prospect were collecting their winnings in a way that showed they cared not a whit if Farnese lived or died. Eventually Calvine removed his helmet and verbally agreed to spare his opponent. When, on the way back to Figline, Hawkwood congratulated Calvine, his response was to be irritated.

'If I had known his quality I would never have sullied my lance. He was a mewling dropkin not worthy of my time.'

'But worth three thousand florins.'

'Och, it is a poltroon who cares for silver.'

Hawkwood declined to admit he was that very thing. They stayed to see the preparations being made for a Florentine withdrawal; they waited in vain. The enemy was going nowhere.

'So much for knightly honour,' was Hawkwood's jaundiced opinion.

'What does it mean, a lack of horses?'

This enquiry arose when, riding back to Figline, Hawkwood began to assess what had been gleaned by his party. There were horses within the Florentine encampment but too few in number for what should be present, enough to mount the commanders but not enough for a fighting force known to have cavalry. The response was slow, it sounding like a question to which their captain already had an answer but eventually Gold provided one.

'The Florentine cavalry cannot be with the main host.'

'Are we sure they have any?' Alard asked.

His captain slowly shook his head. 'It would be a poor host without cavalry and Pisa lost to them when they had a strong force. They must be around for Farnese would be near to useless in battle if he cannot quickly call them in.'

'They have been there,' Gold insisted. 'I saw peasants clearing up the dung of a substantial herd.'

'So where have they gone?' was Hawkwood's next question.

To find an answer required more reconnaissance, this time at night, which established that the senior Farnese had spread out his mounted forces along the banks of the River Arno, the only conclusion to be reached being that he feared that the White Company, and he must assume their presence, might avoid his position at Incisa and try to bypass him to cross the river and attack a city short on defence.

'Where in the name of the devil is Sterz?' was the next cry from Hawkwood once he was back in Figline.

Men sent back along the road to Pisa saw no sign of the main body but Robert Knowles arrived with his brigade of three hundred lances, which gave Hawkwood, to whom he was happy to defer, a total force of seven hundred, all mounted. He also brought the depressing news that the main body was yet to stir. Either Sterz did not believe what he had been told or he did not care, which frustrated Hawkwood.

'We can defeat them if we have the numbers. But how soon will it be before they discover how weak we truly are and attack us? Campfires will only fool Farnese for so long, indeed I'm surprised he has yet to see it as a bluff.'

'They have chosen the field, John, and you are forever telling us how vital that is. They may wish to be attacked there, sure they can defend it.'

Another two days would have had Hawkwood tearing out his hair if he had not shaved his head for the heat. The only thing that calmed him was the fact that the Florentines had not made any move to advance. That calm was soon shattered when a messenger from one of his scouting parties informed him that a body of five hundred horsemen were manoeuvring to the north of Figline, no more than a league distant.

'Go back and ensure they never escape your sight. Robert, I need your thoughts.'

'It might be best to abandon Figline and fall back on Pisa.'

'I swear such a move would break my heart. I have drawn out the Florentines, which should have been carried out by another.' The name of Sterz did not need to be mentioned and nor was it possible to underestimate the Hawkwood fury. 'We have here a chance to earn our fee and more and that German swine who calls himself captain general seems unwilling to stir.'

Hawkwood had been pacing as he was complaining. He suddenly stopped and looked quizzically at his fellow captain. 'How many horsemen do we reckon Florence can muster?'

Knowles smiled; he knew well his friend's capacity to ask questions to which he already knew the answer. It was a way of clarifying his thoughts.

'The host is eight thousand in number, we are told. A quarter of that would have to be mounted.'

'And a quarter of those are wandering about to the north of Figline, not close enough to threaten and as yet showing no signs of doing so. Added to that we have some idea of the whereabouts of the remainder and they are strung out along the river.'

'I can see the way your mind is working, but we are seven hundred strong.'

'All mounted, Robert. Farnese has made poor use of his cavalry and they could be too far away to intervene if anything threatens his main body; certainly those we have just been told about would be useless to him.'

'You wish to attack him at Incisa, and it could be six thousand men?'

There was a smile and a nod to indicate that clever Robert had discerned his thinking. 'Six thousand foot-bound men, Robert, think on that.'

'Move towards him and he will know you are coming and prepare his defence.'

'How close would we have to get to come upon his lines at a gallop?'

'Let's start with a slow trot and that would need half a league.'

'When we rode out the first time, we saw no evidence that Farnese had put out a screen to warn of any approach. They would have to be mounted, so he has sacrificed that so he can make sure he is not outflanked with the river at its summer level. The waters are low and at places surely it could be forded.'

'Yet he had crossed it with his main host and has the bridge to his rear.'

'I see him as vulnerable. Do you not?'

'Please know I am not minded to disagree, but I sense nothing I or anyone else says is going to sway you from what you are contemplating.'

'I cannot command you, Robert, you are captain of your own brigade.'

'Did you not tell me of Calvine and his damned honour? If I am not a mad fellow such as he is, I still have some sense of that. I would not want it said that I let you and your men ride to their deaths while I stood back.'

'You are a good friend.'

'It may be that I am a great fool.'

Hawkwood was prepared to abandon Figline, it being no use to him if the Florentines could not be driven off. So he had his waggons loaded and his camp followers and non-combatants made ready for a swift withdrawal. The notion of a complete defeat was not sought, but at least seven hundred mounted, experienced fighters could inflict on the enemy a blow that would keep them too fearful to advance. This would give time for the rest of the White Company to come up for a full-scale battle, if Sterz could be persuaded to take the field.

The move forward was done slowly and in groups, half a league at a time, so as not to raise a telltale dust cloud, a real risk on the dry autumn ground. Added to that contingents were sent by different routes, arching out to the flanks mainly to ensure there was no enemy closing in to get to their rear. In Figline those left behind had the task of keeping alight the night fires that indicated a powerful but stationary force.

Hawkwood could not be certain, but by the lack of response he reckoned he got, over two days, to where he wanted to be without the movement being detected. Now he had to decide to continue or desist, for that remained in the balance. Such thoughts troubled him through a night in which the stars seemed to carpet the heavens, with the regular flashes of heavenly bodies scooting across the sky, his mood swinging from confidence to doubt, as would that of any man with such a weight on his mind.

The hint of grey and a stirring camp, there were no fires, obliged him to decide. He would launch one all-out charge with every man he possessed, but they would be abjured to listen for a horn blowing the retreat. He had to hope the main Florentine camp was still bereft of cavalry so there could be no real pursuit. He could do damage, but with minimal risk if he got clear.

Mass had to be said, given men needed to confess their sins in preparation for possible death, but he made sure the priests were brief. With the horses watered and fed they walked them for a while until that was digested. Finally, the lances were mounted and moving as the sun rose, lighting the way ahead as the two brigades trotted towards the River Arno, which ran behind the rear of the Florentine encampment. That trot turned into a canter when the camp came in sight. Closer to, Hawkwood raised his sword to order the charge.

Ahead of them was confusion. Men hitherto wandering about were running to form lines of defence, with trumpets blowing mightily but to little avail. The Hawkwood and Knowles brigades came thundering down the valley slope to smash into groups of soldiers in total disarray, sweeping them aside as well as killing and maiming those who sought to stand in their way. They faced a fragile front which, when it collapsed, impacted on the men yet to join the fight.

Reluctance to engage turned to panic as the Florentines sought to save themselves, and that transferred itself to the Germans who had assembled in an orderly way; alone they could not prevail and, since the alternative was to die, no welcome fate to men recruited with money, they too began to break apart. The attackers poured through the tents, slashing at the guy ropes to bring them down, but only if there was no human flesh to harm. The Florentine army was quickly broken and running for the bridge that crossed the Arno, one that was too narrow to allow passage to all.

A goodly number of their leaders, if not all, had got mounted and away first – the Farnese standard could be seen on the far bank – which must have contributed to the flight of the rest, even if others were vainly trying get their men to turn and fight. That lasted until the futility of that became evident and they sought to save their lives by surrender. If your senior commanders are running, so must you, yet with a bridge blocked by struggling and pleading humanity the only recourse for the rest was to try the river. If it was flowing slowly at this time of year it was deep by the bridge, so it still had enough force to drown as well as carry the bodies of some of the dead down toward the sea.

Many would snag on obstacles like fallen trees and sandbanks, to be fished out and searched for anything of value, their naked cadavers probably thrown back into the river to continue their journey. A dead body in the Arno was a common enough occurrence yet the sheer number heading towards the sea told a different story and enough had passed on unmolested for their livery to identify them as Florentines.

Pisa thus had a strong inkling of Hawkwood's stunning victory before he and his men, carrying the Florentine standards and dragging in waggons full of booty and prisoners, rode through the city gates to the raucous cheers of their grateful paymasters.

# CHAPTER FIFTEEN

If there was initial exuberance at this triumph, there was, in sober reflection, a question to answer. If less than one-fifth of the strength of the White Company could inflict such a defeat on Pisa's enemies, what could have been achieved had the whole host been present to follow up on the initial success? Florence had lost a battle and badly; they had been checked, but many had survived and were now securely back behind their walls.

Surely there had existed a chance for total subjugation. That naturally led to enquiries as to why the main body had sat idle in Pisa, not just torpid in their presence but difficult in their conduct. The city fathers, the elected *Signoria* had seen in their chambers endless supplicants complaining about the behaviour of mercenaries who plagued the citizenry, not it seemed the city's enemies.

John Hawkwood was received by his fellow captains with a degree of reserve – only Thornbury was open in his praise, his deprecating claims that luck and Florentine stupidity had played as much a part at Incisa as any skill taken as mere flummery, as was his insistence that without the backing of Robert Knowles and his three hundred lances his truncated campaign would have failed.

He was more closely questioned regarding the ransoms he had garnered, for many a Florentine noble had been captured. They were now harassing their relatives to come up with the means to buy their freedom, selling land and possessions to meet the cost. Unlike that which he had taken from the Florentine encampment, and that had produced a stunning bounty for the company, these were not shared but taken as personal profit. The sums gained were remarked on with what sounded like commendation, but seemed just as much prompted by jealousy.

All the captains, Albert Sterz certainly being one, sensed a shifting of the balance of authority: not all had been happy to be stuck in Pisa. If not acting against Florence they should at least have been out plundering bountiful Tuscany and equalling Hawkwood in his acquisitions. Added to that, the contract was coming to an end; would the Pisans renew it and where would that leave the mercenaries if they did not?

The White Company leaders naturally mixed with the leading citizens of the city and many conversations were about mercenary transgressions – women being troubled so much that many were sent away to other towns for safety, taverns being wrecked by drunken mobs, their owners badly beaten as well as the citizens being subjected to rude public behaviour.

Since that victory, expressions of disquiet as to the way the company was operating, up until Incisa mere gentle hints, had become openly expressed dissatisfaction. Meanwhile unbeknown to Hawkwood, Robert Knowles and John Thornbury were quietly canvassing their confrères, and in particular two of his fellow countrymen, to make a case for change. One was Andrew Beaumont, who liked to claim himself a bastard of Prince Edward of Woodstock, the other William Brise, another of those men who had fought in the English army under both Edwards.

Was the way the White Company had been run hitherto a success? Had a certain person grown too big for his bleached surcoat and that damned baton? Was the right man in place to ensure more Pisan florins came their way with a renewed contract? If it was insidious it was effective and Robert Knowles, being wily, made sure that when the question was publicly raised, it was done by another.

'Who is satisfied with the way we have acted?' Brise, ever a man to walk towards confrontation, did not wait for his confrères to reply, adding, 'Our paymasters certainly are not, if what they say to me represents the mood.'

That set up a buzz of mumbled opinion. Sterz tried to sound unconcerned in his response, yet those he was addressing must have noticed the tightened grip he took on his baton, or the way he laid it across his chest so that the symbol of command was very evident.

'I have been negotiating for weeks and have sensed no inclination not to renew.'

Looking around those he led must have induced concern. He barked that the chamber be cleared of anyone not part of the discussion. As usual that meant servants, but also scribes and some of the men appointed as marshals come to witness the deliberations, hitherto not a problem. Once they had shuffled out and the chamber door was banged shut, Sterz indicated that his factotum, Cunradus, should address the assembly, which he did in a barely audible voice.

'The game we play is a delicate one. To extract from the Pisans enough to keep us in their service without acting so forcibly that we do ourselves out of employment. That happened against the Visconti, did it not?'

'Hardly honourable,' Hawkwood said.

Sterz barked his reply. 'Since when was honour the basis of our trade?'

'We are sustained by profit,' was the opinion of Andrew Beaumont: handsome, well set up and some ten years younger than his contemporaries.

Hawkwood produced a frown. 'I would contend that much is to be gained by acting with honest intent. Will Pisa continue to drain its treasury to support a campaign that is never-ending?'

'What choice do they have?' Cunradus hissed. 'With our help they have so fired Florence that it will become a fight to the death. Given they lack the means to fend off that, who will do it for them if not us?'

Robert Knowles spoke up, but without much thrust; he seemed to be musing more than challenging. 'There is much to be gained in this region, I would propose, by being seen to have fulfilled any contract signed. It would be a poor notion to entirely disdain the advantage of a good reputation.'

'Ferocity is our reputation.'

The number of shaking heads must have told Sterz his declaration was not going to carry the room. It was his fellow German, Baldwin, who by trying to bring matters to a head and very likely aid him, inadvertently stuck in the spike.

'We are ever boasting that we are a republic not a tyranny.'

'Are you demanding a vote for captain general?' asked Beaumont, quietly.

Did Baldwin realise he had gone too far in using the word republic? It certainly looked that way as his reply was somewhat stammered. 'Why no. We have not required such a thing since coming to Italy. What we did on arriving in Pisa was mere show.'

Brise was the man to respond; he had taken part in the election mentioned by Baldwin, as had everyone and all had known it was meaningless; no one then would have stood against Sterz.

'A month ago I would have scoffed at any who said there was a requirement for it. Now we need to know our future and I for one think that the person dealing with Pisa should be the one best qualified to get for us a good result. That has to be the man who stands highest in their regard.'

Baldwin was not looking at Hawkwood, his eyes were on Sterz, but no one in the chamber had any doubt who

Brise meant. Sterz acted as if he had been stung; he was being told the man who had humbled Florence already stood a better chance of renewal. The work Knowles and Thornbury had been doing to undermine Sterz paid off in a sort of mumbled agreement which, if it was not unanimous, was so strong that there was no alternative but to proceed.

'I wish to retain my post,' Sterz growled. 'And I have a right to it. So I stand to remain your captain general.'

He accompanied that statement with a ferocious look designed to intimidate any waverers. It was a stupid ploy, for if these men were inclined to indulge his fantasies when the florins were pouring in, they were less willing to do so when that same flow was threatened. Nor were they the type to be silenced by an angry visage.

Andrew Beaumont immediately proposed John Hawkwood.

'On what grounds?' asked Cunradus.

'He will get us better terms than Sterz. He stands high in their esteem and as of this day, from what has been said to me by those who must agree our terms, he who at present commands does not.'

'Ever greedy, Beaumont?'

The younger man was avaricious but he was never one to be embarrassed by it. 'Ever in search of fair reward.'

'And,' Brise chipped in, 'Hawkwood has shown us a leadership sadly missing since we sat outside Florence at the beginning of summer. The people who applauded as we went to that fight would cheerfully see us gone and anywhere, for they are tired of paying for fighting men who trouble them more than their enemies. We have sat on our arse too long.'

'It was Albert who got us to this place,' Baldwin interjected, showing some fraternal loyalty.

'I agree,' Beaumont responded, 'and all power to him. Yet we must ask if he can keep us here? I propose a vote.'

'And I,' Baldwin declared, 'see no need for that.'

'If it is asked for it must be done, that is our creed.'

'Given I suspect what might be the outcome,' Hawkwood said in a soft voice, 'does anyone wish to ask my opinion?'

'Would you be willing to lead the company, John?' asked Robert.

'Am I qualified to do so?'

'Damn your humility, Hawkwood,' Baldwin cried. 'There is not a man present who could not lead us. We act in unison and will ever do so.'

Hawkwood looked to Sterz. 'Do you subscribe to that?'

Hawkwood's softly voiced enquiry left the captain general on the horns of a dilemma. He could hardly say that those he had so far led were incapable of replacing him. Yet the meanest intelligence could discern that to admit the opposite was to virtually surrender his office. There was no lack of brains in Cunradus; he knew when a matter became critical, just as he knew Sterz would want to hang on to that baton. If Hawkwood had the wind behind him, Albert Sterz had a fear of change on his side and that might save him if he acted decisively.

'The only solution is to put forward a candidate to stand against our present captain general and then proceed to an election.'

'I have proposed John Hawkwood,' Beaumont cried.

'Which I second,' added Robert Knowles, with a look

towards his younger colleague that had Hawkwood wondering at collusion.

Called to choose, the hands went up in favour of the Englishman, with fewer for Sterz when his name was called. Slightly stunned, the German took an age to come towards his replacement and proffer his gilded baton. The rest did not hear Hawkwood's response, it being a whisper.

'I pray this is not a poisoned chalice, Sterz.'

'I think you have just been shown it can be.'

'I will depend on your good advice and support. Will I have it?'

The nod was unconvincing.

That the White Company captains had made the right choice was soon apparent; negotiations for an extension of the contract, which had been dragging on, moved to a very satisfactory conclusion once it was the victor of Incisa doing the talking. Pisa was not only anxious to keep the company in its employ, but they were willing to do so for a year on payment of one hundred and forty thousand florins. As captain general, Hawkwood now found himself much better off as well as leading what appeared to be a well-contented company.

If acts upsetting the citizens did not entirely cease they subsided and Hawkwood instituted training on the grounds that men long idle needed to hone their skills, and such activity kept them out of mischief. The turn of the year passed before he was satisfied with progress and he laid out his plans to the men who had now become his chief support.

'It is my aim to get our men away from the city and earning their keep. They are better prepared for fighting now.'

Knowles was sceptical. 'Winter, John, it is January and the weather is cold as well as foul.'

'Movement will be slow,' Thornbury added.

'We have not previously campaigned in these months, it is true, but it will be a shock to our enemies that we do so. Imagine their surprise when we appear outside their walls before the corn is even planted.'

Knowles frowned. 'You will need to carry such a plan with our confrères.'

'Which I shall, and it will be a test of my authority, Robert. If they decline to back me I will have a good indication of my standing.'

'A risk.'

'All is risk and if we never tempted providence we would all be in poverty.'

The plan was supported but against a background of disquiet, though aided by the news filtering in to Pisa. Innocent had died to be replaced by Pope Urban V: another Frenchman and a candidate of Paris still content, it seemed, to reside in Avignon. Like all who had succeeded to the Holy See since the First Crusade, Urban desired to be the progenitor of one of his own, this time by garnering fighters from the free companies troubling Italy. Killing two birds with one stone was the policy.

First there came another excommunication for mercenaries, to be treated with the usual disdain. Next Cardinal Albornoz toured the various city states seeking to drum up support for an alliance to rid Italy of the companies, a proposal received with little enthusiasm. If any city sent their fighters away to defeat the freebooters, would not their neighbours, less committed and never to be trusted, take advantage of their absence? Endemic Italian suspicion of rivals would not allow for that which Urban desired.

Far from willing to relent, the new Pope sent into Italy high-born magnates eager to crusade, their aim, apart from their own personal aggrandisement, to recruit amongst the mercenaries. This came with offers of indulgences and all the panoply of promises a pontiff could dispense. Rumour had it that the ships of Genoa and Venice were waiting to transport them.

'Let them come and find their recruits off a battlefield,' was Hawkwood's opinion.

The time came for him, baton in hand, to lead his mercenary-cum-citizen army out, to further confuse Florence by taking a northern route that would bring them to rich satellite towns such as Prato. His last words on those seeking to recruit his men was harsh.

'Happen when they see what is to be garnered in gold by our service they will drop their crosses and join us.'

Naturally, the brigade he led was to the fore and if those who knew him well could make risible comments about that baton, their man carried it only because he had to, it being the mark of his rank and the symbol of his authority. He now had a personal retinue of bodyguards, scribes, two constables in Knowles and Thornbury, as well as a personal confessor. Far to his rear behind the Pisan levies, now leading no more than his own brigade, was Albert Sterz, now his subordinate. If he appeared an obedient one, he was not happy and made little attempt to disguise the fact.

The route chosen also had the advantage, even at this time of year, of never having suffered from a host passing through, with all that did to the detriment of the citizens in emptied granaries, destroyed stocks and stolen livestock. There was no intention to pause where it was unnecessary so Hawkwood had no expectation of battle prior to reaching the environs of Florence; according to his screen of cavalry the road ahead was clear of any danger.

The force that dented this reverie descended on them from Pistoia, a fortified town Hawkwood intended to bypass. The place was famed for the hardiness of its inhabitants, carrying with them a reputation for bellicosity that went back to ancient times – it was said it had never been subdued. They were inclined to fight even when not under threat and sought no reassurances from those passing by. Assuming they were in danger they came out from their elevated town to take on an army strung out on the march, struggling along in poor weather on muddy tracks, in the mountainous terrain to the west, and they attacked with a ferocity that threw the columns of foot soldiers into disarray.

The effect of these peasants – for there were no knights amongst them as far as Hawkwood could discern – especially on the unprepared Pisan levies, was disastrous as they broke and began to stream back towards their home city. Hawkwood up ahead swung his brigades round to come to their aid, sure that those horsemen to the rear would come forward likewise.

That was a mistaken assumption: the men fleeing blocked the route, making it impossible for people like Sterz to engage, which allowed the whole of the Pistoians to attack the lead columns. Thus they had a fight just to get back and rejoin the main part of the now broken host. Without discipline it would have resulted in a massacre but Hawkwood ensured it did not. With calm determination he formed up his cavalry to mount a charge and break through.

The massed peasant force did what they could to prevent him, but it was hard for a man on foot, poorly armed with what appeared to be mostly farm implements, to withstand mounted mercenaries properly equipped and desperate. Broadswords flashed, maces and axes were swung with gusto, the horses urged on despite their fears, for to slow could be dangerous and to stop was fatal.

The escape was bloody and not without loss, but it would be the number of funerals in Pistoia that would record the result of the day, although what had taken place would be recalled with pride in the annals of the town. Not so in Pisa for the White Company; it was a sorry spectacle as the new captain general led his dispirited men back through the city gates in a torrential downpour that fortunately kept those who might jeer at them within their homes.

It took two months before he could once more lead them out, this time with more care in his dispositions; there would be no more surprises. In effect, his campaign was a repeat of the previous year under Sterz, with much crop burning, albeit more wide ranging. Hawkwood had other plans in train and he waited for the carpenters he had been promised by Pisa, as well as the forged metal components that would need to be fashioned to make proper siege towers.

Erecting once more a straw-and-tinder defensive barrier he was able to move his archers closer to the Florentine walls, ensuring a steady flow of deadly arrows fell within the city. The usual taunts were made – dead donkeys and dogs, the minting of coins as well as raucous entertainments performed below the ramparts, all designed to dent the morale of the defenders who did their best to show that such things were wasted.

Hawkwood knew what would sink that and break their mood: the sign of a siege that was about to be pressed home to the death. And if he was impatient that his towers would be built in good time, he knew that that commodity was on his side. But that turned quickly to dust.

'It is nothing less than treachery.'

Handsome Andrew Beaumont did not even blush. 'We work for reward, John.'

'You would take money from our enemies?'

'Are they enemies? Florence promises to reward us for our support and it does not affect my soul to accept their offer.'

'Pisa has paid you.'

'I have that too. The total exceeds what Pisa would eventually grant us.'

'Sterz?'

'Thinks as I do, and that goes for most.'

'Tell me, Andrew, who took the lead in this? Was it the Florentines who approached you, or did one of your number contact them?'

'To tell the truth, John, I have no idea. But it makes sense to Florence. They know they cannot beat us, especially after what you did to their army at Incisa, and I believe they were told of your future plans. What better way to protect their city than to pay us to defend it?'

'This smacks of Sterz and his anger at being replaced, Beaumont.'

That got a sly smile. 'Am I no longer Andrew?'

'No, you are not. You are to me a mangy dog, and if that offends you enough, let us exit this pavilion and put my words to the test.'

'Why would I do that, John, when I know how well you can fight?'

'Perhaps for royal pride.'

'Ah, that,' was the reply to what was sure sarcasm, followed by raised eyebrows and an expression hinting at confused wonder. 'Such a thing may exist on one side of the blanket, John, but blood honour does not play on the obverse.'

'If an agreement has not been struck, and I do not see how it could be, when will it come to pass?'

'When the contracts are drawn up and the first payment is made. From that moment we cease to act for Pisa and become engaged by Florence.'

'You came to tell me when you could have kept it secret. Why?'

'It was felt you should have a chance to join with us.'

'Under Albert Sterz as captain general?'

'I did think that as a fellow Englishman you should be offered the chance to become part of our new Company of the Star.'

'Does Sterz know you have come to tell me of this?'

For the first time the Beaumont face displayed irritation. 'What do you think?'

'You can depart now. Please ask Robert Knowles, as you pass his tent, if he will join me.'

'I say goodbye, John, not farewell. I hope I do not encounter you on a field of battle, for I might—'

He got no further. Hawkwood cut right across him. 'Be obliged to forfeit your perfidious life!'

The White Company was split asunder. It was not just whole brigades changing sides: each man in the host was free to make a decision for himself, which made it impossible to continue the siege. With his own contingent – they had at least, apart from a handful, remained loyal – and in the company of Robert Knowles who had lost a third of his men and John Thornbury with even less, Hawkwood led the Pisan levies back to their home city, sending ahead a fast courier to warn his paymasters of possible treachery within their own ranks, he having picked up a whisper that part of the Florentine plan was to provoke an uprising in Pisa itself against the revenues being 'wasted' on a mercenary army.

# Chapter Sixteen

To sit in Pisa and do nothing was not an option. The mood of the city was gloomy and far from supportive, which was bound to affect the men who had remained loyal to him and perhaps lead to further desertions. That was made more pressing once information came to him that the Florentines had not only appointed a highly competent general to command their forces, a lord from Ancona called Galeotto Malatesta, but that the enemies he now faced, Sterz and Beaumont included, had been reinforced by the same body of German mercenaries he had encountered at Incisa.

The task was to avoid what had occurred previously from being reversed, this while he had limited time to act to dent Florentine confidence. A general call to arms went out and even scraping the Pisan barrel Hawkwood was now seriously lacking in numbers, with less than a thousand cavalry added to four thousand mostly untrained levies.

'I caught them unawares once, Robert; the trick is to do so again.' Sensing his words begged a question, Hawkwood continued, 'I know it is a risk to seek to repeat Incisa, but perhaps they will think that impossible and therein lies opportunity.'

'The same tactic will scarce work.'

'Then we must contrive something new.'

Hawkwood was not much given to relying on luck only to find he was in receipt of some. It was scarcely believable that Malatesta, just like Farnese, had put out no protective cavalry screen to warn of a Pisan approach, though he had set up camp on the far side of the bridge. This told Hawkwood that in the new general's estimation, he was in no position to do anything other than wait for him to attack and effect a siege. Surreptitious reconnaissance found the enemy host camped once more on the banks of the Arno at Incisa, seemingly in no hurry to cover the ground between.

'If they are reluctant to move, let us give them a nose that bleeds.'

Looking around the faces of those he would rely on to carry out his orders Hawkwood sensed doubt and was obliged himself to admit it was bound to be thus. The consideration that he might explain to them the alternative, which was to wait behind their own walls for what was inevitable, he put aside. It would not raise their morale but perhaps induce more caution than he needed; fail in this endeavour and they would leave Pisa without defence.

Overnight, as usual unable to sleep before a fight, Hawkwood begged that the heavens should cloud over. It might be cool now with a clear sky but in the daytime the August temperature would soar. With what he had planned heat must play upon the strength of his army, especially his cavalry. They were going to be obliged to abandon their horses and try to get to the enemy on foot. To ride down upon them at this time of year would be impossible with the parched state of the ground; it would create a dust cloud visible for miles.

Knowles and Thornbury apart, he had no one to talk to that would ease his concerns. As a precaution he had left behind in Pisa the likes of Alard, Ivor and very reluctantly Christopher Gold. Their task was to guard the house he had been given and more importantly the coffers in the cellar containing the money he had accumulated, including the huge sums gained from the Battle at Incisa. The situation in the city was too febrile to leave it unprotected. Added to that, if he was captured there lay the means by which he could be ransomed.

The grey light brought the customary stirrings until Mass was said. Then on foot, with the waggons containing their equipment and food as well as the very necessary supplies of wine to whet throats bound to become parched, the men marched east. Hawkwood spread them out widely to reduce dust from shuffling feet and stopped often to let them drink and the dust they did create settle.

The river naturally lying in a valley, he was able to get to the top of the hill that framed the western side without being observed, something which he had barely thought possible. Below him, it seemed that half the Florentine army were naked and in the water noisily swimming about, some jumping off the stone arched bridge to splash into the water. They were cooling off on what was now a broiling day, while behind them their camp seemed to lay in somnolent silence with few stirring, again due to the heat.

The far riverbank and bridge by which they would cross the Arno was littered with clothing and weapons so now for the attacking captain general it was a calculation of how quickly his men could descend to the riverbank set against the time it would take for his enemies to get out of the water and to the weapons they needed to fight.

'String your bows.'

The order was passed from man to man along the reverse side of the hill. Hawkwood's archers dropped back several paces in obedience so they would not be observed. Marshals, Pisan and mercenary, were sent along the extended line to give the captain general's command as Hawkwood himself strung a bow. His arrow, fired high, would mark the line at which his archers should stop and fire three quick salvos into the river. Then they were to join with the rest of the host, coming up at the run to their rear.

The object was the bridge. If it could be taken quickly then the Pisan host would hold a position that would nullify Malatesta's numerical advantage. Should things go even better then the attack could continue into the encampment, hopefully sowing the kind of panic that had ensued previously, to set the enemy running in fear of their lives. But another command had to be obeyed and it was paramount that it should be.

With no river to their rear, the Florentines would be able to regroup. Advance yes, but listen for the horn that tells you to halt, for the next task will be to hold that bridge and to do so dispositions would have to be made in limited time to formulate a credible defence.

No one had worn a helmet on the way here; to do so was to fry your own head and it was uncomfortable to don even the padded cap now – metal was worse – the leaders especially, for their helms were already hot, heavy and decorated. That applied even more to the likes of Sir Murdoch Calvine and his confrères, the heavy chain mail they wore making matters near intolerable.

'Worse than Palestine,' was the opinion of one knight who had been on crusade.

Looking left and right Hawkwood made sure all was ready. Every man had been given wine to drink so dust-coated throats were now clear. Then he sensed something that cheered him, an eagerness to be at their enemies brought on by the fact that what was coming their way would be a complete surprise. With deliberate slowness, for effect, he drew his bow and with a telling pause to increase the tension he sent the single arrow on its way, quickly lost to sight against the azure sky.

The movement was immediate; the fighters were on their feet and crossing the crest in silence so that it would be the sight of them that set off the alarm not the sound. Yet several thousand feet cannot move in silence. They sent a tremor through the earth and within seconds the cries from below told of panic at what they saw approaching. The archers had jogged to get abreast of Hawkwood's marker and with practised ease they peppered the river, rewarded with the screams of many of the swimmers who became their victims.

Joined in one mass the Pisan host was running now, the slope aiding their pace, free to yell and help to discomfit those trying to get out of the water. Within the camp horns were blowing, and if they sounded panic-stricken they were in truth noisily summoning all to the defence. Just as the bridge seemed to be within their grasp, the Pisans were assailed by a weapon that had not been anticipated, especially in the numbers that appeared.

Florence, unbeknown to Hawkwood, had recruited a hundred Genoese crossbowmen and they had a discipline lacking in many of Malatesta's men. The first quarrels fired put an immediate check on the forward rush, more with the Pisan levies than the mercenaries. Yet as they continued, separating from the less professional, they became a more concentrated target for the Genoese bolts. The distance to cover, by men who had already tramped a league and half to get to this riverbank, also was taking its toll.

Hawkwood had never ever wanted to take on crossbows in the open; they had a sight advantage in range and if they were less accurate than a longbow that meant little when firing at a mass of advancing bodies. Now they were not really progressing as they had been. No one was running, more were stumbling forward, with as many stopping completely either in confusion or to aid fallen comrades.

Worse, those who had been swimming were now armed, formed up and ready to cross the bridge and engage. A glance downriver showed hundreds of horsemen splashing through the river, using a shallow ford he did not know existed to get to the other bank, and it was obvious once they were across Hawkwood's situation would become unsustainable. The horns blew the retreat and it was only because his motley host was prepared for it that such a command worked.

The mercenaries under Knowles and Thornbury obeyed quickly while maintaining some order as they fell back. The inexperienced Pisan levies only saw themselves being deserted and they panicked and ran. What should have been an orderly retreat quickly turned into a rout, which made it a blessing that those Florentine cavalry did not immediately choose to charge along the riverbank. Instead they continued straight on, which told Hawkwood they would soon have control of his waggons.

Their eagerness to gain that prize gave him the only chance he had to get away without total loss – that and the action of the anointed knights, twenty men under the command of Calvine, whose pride would not allow him to back away, this added to the fact that such heavily accoutred men had the least chance of escape. Forming a line close to the bridge, they presented a barrier that Malatesta's men had to fight their way through to get at the fleeing mass and these stalwarts were not giving ground.

Great broadswords flashing in the sunlight produced founts of blood every time they met poorly protected flesh, while the press of Florentine bodies prevented the Genoese from felling them. Hawkwood, allowing himself a brief backwards glance, could not but admire their stand. This was the kind of knightly resistance that had held the line at

Crécy and Poitiers but soon they would be up against their own kind and in numbers too hard to resist.

Within a blink he was running along with the remainder of his men passing their own waggons in a wide arc, now being looted by Florentines who could have let them be to pursue. This they would not, for the Pisan baggage would become an acquisition of their foot-bound comrades.

They were now streaming up to the hill crest and taking hundreds of prisoners, men wounded as well as those so struck with fear they could only stand and wait to be captured. That no further pursuit followed puzzled Hawkwood until he realised that Malatesta had no need to risk his army; Pisa was now at his mercy.

If it was the same sight from the walls as it had been outside Florence, it was observed from a very different perspective: besieged rather than besieging. There were the same activities: hung donkeys and dogs naming the *Signoria*, the leading citizens who ruled the Commonwealth of Pisa, including Hawkwood, Thornbury and Knowles, as less than excrement. The Florentines staged horse races below the walls to taunt the defenders, minted coins reversing the symbols and indulged in the same kind of revelry that the White Company had employed when besieging their city.

It was galling to see men with whom he had ridden and fought as part of that, while Sterz, Beaumont, Brise and Baldwin seemed to take extra delight in parading with a flying banner every time he appeared on the walls. Even Cunradus was happy to appear on a donkey, as if he wished to display humility in his monk's habit, as well as contempt.

'Yet, *Signor* Agnello, they are no more able to cross these ramparts if they are well manned than we were able to cross theirs. Less, for they will come up against the men I lead.'

'Many of my fellow citizens find such a thing hard to believe and wish to seek terms.'

'Florence looks strong, they have numbers, but it will take ten men to overcome one behind a city wall such as you possess. I can tell you that it is not a task that the men who deserted Pisa will willingly undertake. I am happy to speak to the mob if that will calm their fears.'

'Words will not be enough to quell the discontent and the mob is of no account, even if their voices are loud.'

Hawkwood had to agree. It was no surprise that the majority of Pisans were furious with the way matters had developed but it was the leading citizens who counted. Having dispensed their money, what did they have except abject failure? Yet they were about to compound their situation in Hawkwood's eyes by denying the only men who could mount a defence of their walls the due amount of pay they were entitled to as per the agreed contract.

The men of the *Signoria*, who should have handed over the instalment, were too fearful for their lives to do so, sure their irate citizens would string them up from the quayside cranes. Hawkwood's concern was that with no pay the men he led, even in his own brigade, would desert to Sterz, who could no doubt extract gold from Florence to reward them.

With the *Signoria* unwilling to move, Hawkwood had sought to engage Giovanni Agnello, acknowledged to be the richest man in Pisa, but because of that and his avaricious business methods also the most hated. Added to that he felt slighted: regardless of how many times he had stood to be part of the ruling clique he had always failed to get elected. Hawkwood, who had dealt with him for supplies and found him a hard man with whom to bargain, had in his negotiations been made privy to the man's frustrations.

Naturally he saw himself as better fitted to lead than to follow and was at constant loggerheads with his peers, especially those able to command the vote decried by him as a useless talking shop when what the city needed was the kind of rule imposed by the Visconti: a single brain of the right ability was required and Agnello was convinced he had it.

It was also the case that should Pisa fall, with the huge filled coffers in his cellar he had the most to lose. The solution to both their problems was simple: a coup in which Agnello, who so hankered after supreme power, should have it handed to him by the Commonwealth's captain general. That had been the purpose of bringing him to the ramparts, to underline the dangers and thus leave only one solution.

'When?' asked Agnello, a tremor in his voice, for there was risk in what was being proposed and Hawkwood doubted he was a brave man; he would be torn to shreds if it went awry. 'It must be soon.'

'This very night will serve. I will send my most trusted companions to bring you to the Palace of the *Signoria*. There you will find me waiting. As soon as you arrive my brigade will form up before the palace to protect both it and you. Once power has passed to you, my men will require the terms of the contract.'

'And after?'

'Never fear, Signor Agnello. You will be the ruler of your city and able to act to maintain that position in any way you choose. I will make sure it is so.'

'Proper governance, no more elections and the babble of fools and placemen.'

'Those who have slighted you in the past will be shaking in fear come dawn.'

Agnello looked like what he was: a man who put profit before all, except in his hankering for supremacy. Even in that Hawkwood had no doubt he would use his position to line his purse. With his stooped shoulders and mean-spirited features – hooded eyes, a split nose and thin lips that strained to smile – he was not choice company. One of the regular insults aimed at him was that with all his money he ate poor food, drank cheap sour wine and dressed in clothes bought in the market where the possessions of the dead were sold off.

Those who accompanied Hawkwood to his house when darkness fell were prepared to kill anyone who sought to prevent their passage, which was possible if the conspiracy had been uncovered. In urging Agnello to act, playing on his vanity, Hawkwood had never mentioned his own reserves, less full now because he had been obliged to pitch in much of a ransom money for Calvine and the others knights who had survived at Incisa.

Such a burden fell on every mercenary captain; their adherents expected to be supported if they were taken captive, for few had the funds to buy their freedom. Even if they had enjoyed prosperity in the hands of a freebooter it was not likely to last long. They were men who made their money quickly and spent it in the same fashion. What Hawkwood had left would be forfeit if his former confrères could enter the city, and that might not be all; there was a possibility Sterz, who must hate him mightily for the usurpation of his office, could string him up in the main piazza.

The streets were deserted. If anyone heard the mercenary boots outside their shutters the past behaviour of some of their number now played into Hawkwood's hands, for wisdom dictated they stay indoors. Within the *Signoria* palace it was different; there the men who made decisions on behalf of their citizenry were in deep deliberation, some arguing that surrender was the only option for Pisa, with one or two havering over paying their mercenaries to continue the fight and hold on.

They heard the same studded boots on stone that had disturbed others in their slumbers. The heavy beat and rhythm attested to a purpose not in keeping with political deliberations and they must have wondered why the guards placed to keep them safe had done nothing to prevent entry to what must be strangers.

Had they looked from their chamber into the piazza below they would have seen those men, a dozen of their own citizens, being hustled away in nothing but their shirts, bereft of boots, breeches and weapons. The entry of John Hawkwood, sword in hand, with a strong body of spearmen at his heels, had them cowering away, all demanding to know by what right he had come to this place, to which his reply was brusque.

'Your polity is no more. This *Signoria* is disbanded and Pisa has a new government. Signor Agnello, step forward.'

The merchant did so, the rare smile on his thin lips almost as threatening as the weapons Hawkwood controlled.

'Pisa cannot fight Florence with a talking shop at its centre. The city requires a doge and I am here to ensure it has one and he is the right person.'

'How much are you paying him, pig?' asked one of the council, somewhat braver than his fellows.

'He will pay only what is due and you will be thankful that he does so, for if he did not you would be led along the road to Florence with halters round your necks.'

The speed with which news spread was amazing. From without they could already hear yells and catcalls. A look showed the piazza filling up with irate torch-bearing citizens while before them, mounted and sitting in an unthreatening manner, was a line of Hawkwood's cavalry. The mob could yell as much as they liked but the message was plain. Move forward and you will be cut down.

News of the coup reached Florentine ears quickly enough and caused much reflection. The men they would have to fight had been paid their dues and could not be tempted to desert; Pisa's walls were as formidable as their own but they were seeking to besiege a port, so starvation was not possible for it could always be supplied by sea.

The choice was to invest Pisa for a year or more, to construct siege engines and trebuchets, pay for a massive increase in numbers as well as ships to seek to close off the channels that led to the Mediterranean, which with the time required meant more gold to keep their own mercenaries content.

It took a month before Malatesta was willing to concede he could not prevail and called for a truce. Hawkwood took no part in the talking: that was left to the new Doge of Pisa. Agnello, who had taken to the role as if born to rule and now dressed the part, was well used to hard bargaining and had the patience to wait for the concessions that were eventually forthcoming. In an elaborate ceremony, with Agnello now as glittering in his attire as any prince, a truce was signed that promised peace and amity.

'What of us now, Sir John?' asked Gold, as he watched the gaudily dressed envoys make great play of appending signatures and seals to the document. 'Are we without employment once more?'

'Never fear, lad,' was the reply. 'There is work enough in Italy to see us well provided for many years to come.'

# CHAPTER SEVENTEEN

It had never been Hawkwood's intention to get into conflict with his fellow mercenaries. It seemed perverse that men who fought for profit should so battle with each other, yet circumstances had brought that about and it was about to become increasingly the case. No sooner was peace secured between Pisa and Florence than he received an envoy asking him to attend upon Cardinal Albornoz.

The prelate had been given a huge sum of money by the new Pope Urban to check the continuing ambitions of those Italian states that refused to accept papal hegemony. The first question Hawkwood asked was why he had been chosen, especially given he was now leading a much weakened company.

'You do not see yourself as singular?'

'No, Eminence, I do not,' was the necessary modest response.

'Yet you stayed loyal to your contract with Pisa even when it would have been easy and more profitable to break it?'

It was easy to conjure up a look of humility at the mention of loyalty. Obviously Albornoz had no idea of how strained relations had become between himself and Sterz. Replacing the German as captain general had created a deep animosity, made obvious by the fact that Sterz had negotiated with the Florentines without bothering to include him.

Despite what Beaumont had hinted, Hawkwood doubted that even if he had been tempted to desert Pisa he would have been welcome in the new company. If he had acted honourably and been seen to do so, and such a way of behaving sat well with his own principles, he also had done so without much of an alternative.

'I am bound to point out to you that the Company of the Star is stronger than the men I still lead.'

'Which will matter not. I have the funds by which you can recruit many more.'

Which Hawkwood went on to do and in goodly numbers, even tempting back Andrew Beaumont to his side, necessity being the mother of forgiveness. He led men that matched the abilities of his own brigade, which was far from the case with the rest: quantity hid the lack of quality.

Though there were exceptions the best men generally came from beyond the borders of Italy, especially England, and none matched those who had fought under King Edward and his son against France. Too many of those remained with Sterz and resisted attempts to tempt them away.

If the intentions of Albornoz had been directed mostly at Milan a new threat had arisen in Perugia, suddenly aware of opportunity. There the commune, no doubt witnessing what could be achieved with mercenary armies, had employed the Company of the Star to promote their ambitions.

The cardinal was adamant that his long-term aim of the Holy Father's safe return to Rome, which he had been given a fortune to bring about, could never be accomplished without powers like Milan being brought to heel. If smaller states like Perugia sought aggrandisement it would be ten times more difficult.

The temporal authority of the Pope must hold sway over all of northern Italy while his spiritual power should be acknowledged right down to Apulia, Calabria and Sicily. Thus Hawkwood found himself and the White Company two leagues from Perugia and in formal battle with Sterz and it went badly.

On another blisteringly hot day the two companies fought a bloody and unremitting battle in which no quarter was given. The point came when their captain general knew the White Company could not win and nor, that concluded, could they merely hope to hold the field until stalemate. Sterz had the preponderance of professionals; Hawkwood had too many lances lacking the necessary skills as well as the endurance that went with it.

To call for a retreat hurt badly, though the alternative was worse: ransom at the very least, death at worst, though he did manage to break off the engagement in fairly good order. The next surprise was unnerving; instead of being satisfied with taking the battlefield and giving himself time to regroup, Sterz launched an immediate pursuit. It was then that the dubious make up of his company caused Hawkwood real damage.

The battle had been fought on a dusty plain below a fortified town called San Mariano. Most of the White Company captains led their brigades towards the town in the hope that by occupying the citadel they could break their enemies' desire to continue the fight. Given there could be no real meeting of leaders on the move, it was fragmented and difficult to properly exercise command.

Hawkwood and Knowles argued against entering San Mariano with those they could contact: to do so was to become trapped. Others they failed to persuade, such as Beaumont and Thornbury, were so desirous of even a specious security they would not listen, though perhaps the insistence came as much from the men they led as from their own fears.

Leading half his host beyond San Mariano definitely spared Hawkwood further humiliation. Sterz immediately besieged the citadel, trapping over two thousand men in a castle that had not been set up to withstand being invested. There were no supplies of food, the flow of water could be interrupted and the temperature soared for the few days it took to bring on a plea to be allowed to surrender, days in which men had drunk their own urine as well as the blood of their animals.

'They came out without horses, weapons or armour and were led away like the Israelites.'

Christopher Gold, left as an observer, related the sad tale to a leader seriously downcast. Hawkwood had lost too much to even consider reviving his campaign against Perugia and that was made worse when Sterz, now a hero to that commune, set a high price to ransom the captains and marshals his enemy had led. These were costs Hawkwood was obliged to contribute to: his reputation and standing demanded it. If he got free the likes of Andrew Beaumont, the so-called Bastard of Woodstock now had no men for they were still incarcerated, Thornbury the same.

The German then set out to harry what remained of the White Company in a way that made no sense outside personal animus, not that he participated himself most of the time. Much feted in Perugia, he behaved as he had in Pisa, soaking up the praise and playing the great man. Pursuit was left to his underlings; only rarely did he lead them personally. It made little difference: there was no rest as wherever they headed the Company of the Star followed. The German made it plain he wanted Hawkwood's head on a Perugian gate and was prepared to march over half of Italy to get it.

'I will keep fighting, Eminence, but I cannot in all good faith hold out to you the hope that Perugia will be subdued. I am much reduced since San Mariano and it is only your gold that keeps the men I lead showing any semblance of loyalty.'

Albornoz received this unwelcome opinion in the Bishop's Palace of Bologna, Hawkwood finding himself both surprised and encouraged by his response. He did not indulge in castigation or ask why he had expended so much papal gold to so little purpose. Indeed he did not say a word for quite a long time, instead sitting still, chin on fingertips, his joined hands in sort of a spire to support it.

'Keep clear of the Company of the Star if you can.'

'And Sterz?'

That got Hawkwood an intense look, which left his visitor wondering. Albornoz must know that as long as the German could lord it, with his successes under his belt and the gold of Perugia lining his pockets as well as that of his company, then there was no way to beat him. It implied the cleric was stupid and that was not the case.

'There something must be done,' was the enigmatic response when Albornoz finally spoke. 'I will ponder on it.'

Reporting back to his captains Hawkwood felt it only fair to pass on to them what he thought the cardinal's words meant, namely that the best way to nullify the threat to his aims for a papal return to Italy was to outbid Perugia and buy Sterz with papal gold.

'And if he does?' asked Knowles.

That got a wry smile. 'Then I would best depart for England. Sterz will add my head to his price. But you and Thornbury he will employ if you are willing to serve under him.'

Beaumont was quick to refute that he might do so. 'I came back to your banner because service with him was intolerable. He does not bother with councils now; whatever Emperor Sterz wishes must be obeyed.'

'England is your home too.'

'Not one in which I aspire to live.'

Whatever Albornoz had in mind made little difference to

the present concerns of the White Company. Even pursued they had to live and that could only be done by plundering, which of necessity had to be carried out with haste. It was thus slim pickings, made worse by the continued harrying he was under from a much stronger force. If they took booty it was just as often lost to those pursuing them and that became so relentless as to drive Hawkwood away from Perugia. He headed north, passing between his old stamping grounds of Pisa and Florence until distance obliged Sterz to finally give up.

The remark Hawkwood had made to the young Gold about there being plenty of work for mercenaries in Italy was proven when an offer came from a surprising source, none other than the Visconti brothers of Milan and Pavia. If they had been previously checked and obliged to call a truce with the Imperial Vicar Monferrato, it had not dented their ambitions. Nor did they hold their loss against Hawkwood for they were pragmatists, so the invitation to return to Lombardy was taken with alacrity.

The Visconti had earned the soubriquet of 'the Vipers' from their own heraldic device, the *biscione*, which showed a coiled snake holding a struggling human in its jaws. On entering Milan, hitherto only seen from a distance, Hawkwood and his remaining brigades came into the orbit of the most powerful state in the north of Italy led jointly by a pair who, in their sybaritic way of life allied to cruelty, had no peers.

Galeazzo and Bernabò lived and acted like princes in what was purported to be a republic, being men who had ensured no check on either their way of life or their actions and that included conquest. Their rule came through the office of Imperial Vicars, given to a cardinal uncle, but they had scant regard for the Church. Still, being at peace with the papacy did not prevent them from eyeing parts of rich and fertile Tuscany as a possible area in which to make mischief.

Yet there were other reasons for hiring John Hawkwood: he was what was now being called a *condottiere*, and had a great deal of experience as well as a reputation that had spread throughout Italy and beyond, not least for being more honest than his peers. His employment would gloss over the involvement of a favoured Visconti bastard called Ambrogio, for whom this aim of plunder and possible conquest was to be a gift from his father Bernabò.

The details of this were passed back to England in another of the regular missives Hawkwood sent to his sovereign with passing pilgrims of noble birth, and this time it was of import. Edward was presently lodged in a dispute with the Pope over a marriage for Prince Edmund of Langley, one of his sons, to the widow of the Duke of Burgundy, a woman in possession of a great deal of land bordering northern France. With a Flemish wife and many of his children having been born in Flanders, Edward was eager to have such fiefs under the control of his family.

Such a match would be good for England but it was one that fell very much within the bounds of consanguinity, the proposed nuptials involving close relatives. Normally such a plea was granted without fuss, but Urban V was a child of France and open to the bidding of Paris, for whom the same match represented a setback and a danger.

He was refusing to waive objections to the match.

When advising a monarch care had to be exercised, especially from a simple knight in a far off country and this one had ever been careful to not do much more than list his exploits and add matters he thought might be of concern to a court that had European interests. In this one Hawkwood had to trust Edward Plantagenet to read between the lines of the information he sent.

This would indicate to him that if he wished to put pressure on the Pope to agree to the proposed match, a subject well aired in Italy, then the easiest way to apply it was through an alliance with the Visconti. They were rich, ambitious for aristocratic unions to raise their house, long-standing enemies of the Pope and, with Urban talking of returning to the Eternal City, close enough to Rome to cause trouble in the papal backyard.

As much caution was necessary when it came to his prospective employers. Prickly regarding their relatively lowly status in the European monarchical firmament, any suggestion that they were unfit to aspire to a match with royalty was to invite the kind of blind rage for which they were famed. But they too could be influenced with subtlety, so the mention of a Plantagenet problem, plus the knowledge of a son at present a widower and available, hit fertile ground.

The terms of the Milanese contract were generous, the aims far-reaching and the provision of troops healthy. Hawkwood and Ambrogio Visconti marched out of the city in what was called the Company of Saint George, heading south at the head of ten thousand men, their aim to bring the

Hawkwood skills in raiding to the fractured polity of Siena. It was known as a city state prone to internal disagreements, which meant that organising itself in defence was difficult.

Such a host could not approach without news of their coming running ahead. As soon as the outer regions of the Siena hinterland started to suffer the leading citizens had no doubt they were the target, as they had so often been in past years, for they were seen as vulnerable, though never from a force of this size and power.

The reaction was to get into the city itself and the outlying towns with anything they could move, people included, and then use what forces they possessed to deny the mercenaries what they sought. Siena would burn its own fields, and cut down its own orchards and the mass of vines that covered the Chianti Hills. Yet that was in vain; too much was left to plunder and for a whole year John Hawkwood and Ambrogio Visconti lived off the bounty of the region.

For all the communal efforts the citizens were reluctant to just leave that which they had, nor did they always obey the order to destroy their crops. Siena itself had walls to deter the raiders; that did not apply to the many outlying conurbations who found that no support came from their regional centre when they were attacked, so the spoils were good and the ransoms even better.

Finally Siena sent out the militias to do battle only to see them utterly destroyed and the men who commanded them taken for ransom, which left only one way of driving the mercenaries away from their territory and that was by bribery. Gold would do what patience, self-destruction and sacrifice could not. Forced loans on the already burdened citizenry produced ten thousand florins as well as waggons heaped with armour, much of it gilded and bejewelled, and yet more bearing wine and grain, leaving Siena prostrate.

Such was the destruction and so poor the disguise of the progenitors – the name and fame of Ambrogio Visconti was soon as common as Hawkwood – that the Pope called for the formation of a league to combat all the mercenary companies. The only settlement Pope Urban could achieve – once more his excommunications had been ignored – was an agreement to stop further incursions by mercenaries into Italy and that was more show than reality.

Florence, usually neutral and determinedly secular, was willing to join with the Pope in opposing the Visconti but they too were pragmatic. That did not preclude the provision of an inducement to keep their lands from being ravaged once more by Hawkwood. Six thousand florins was given over to him and Ambrogio to secure several years of peace and it came with all the usual additional supplies and gifts, plus the right to cross Florentine territory as well as recruit within it.

Hawkwood was crossing their land when he heard what had happened to his sworn enemy. 'Dead?'

'Dragged from the palace Perugia gave him as a reward, stripped naked and publicly whipped, then castrated and beheaded.'

The question of why hung in the air, the only known fact being that Sterz had been accused of betrayal, of taking money from elsewhere to turn the Commune of Perugia over to its enemies. Given the reaction as well as the speed and barbarity of its implementation, such an accusation must have been credible.

It was a long time before Hawkwood heard the whole tale; even then it was partial. Somehow his employers had found out Sterz was being bribed – who was the provider he never did know – but that same person had very likely sucked him into a conspiracy, only to betray him to those who extracted their bloody revenge.

When he thought on it, Hawkwood could not put out of his mind the silken contemplations of Cardinal Albornoz. Had that been his solution to the problem the German posed, a man he would not have seen fit to employ as being untrustworthy? If he could not fight him he could pretend to seek his service, then leak his negotiations to Perugia.

'Do you think that is what happened?' asked Gold.

'We'll never know.'

Perugia was much weakened by the murder of Sterz; there was no captain general able to command the two and a half thousand men he had kept in the city so they began to break up into individual brigades. Few stayed loyal to the Company of the Star and when Hawkwood, fresh from his Siennese triumphs and once more leading a powerful force, fell upon the region, Perugia could only send out its own men to fight.

There was no split command now. It was solely Hawkwood who led the Milanese host with Christopher Gold, fully grown and a puissant fighter who had commanded a company of his own, appointed as his constable: in effect the man who would array the White Company forces in any fight.

Ambrogio had gone off to seek his fortune in Naples. Even without him and the men he had taken, Perugia faced a formidable foe. Near a town called Brufa, ever after to be known as the Place of Misery, the Perugian forces were annihilated, leaving well in excess of a thousand dead on the field of battle with half as many maimed. All their commanders were captured and ransomed, the power of their city entirely broken, never to rise again and act as a threat to its neighbours.

Hawkwood returned in triumph to Milan with his spoils and it seemed that the north of Italy was at relative peace. If it had not been a smooth process it was now possible to contemplate that the Pope might really return to Rome. Urban V, unlike most of his predecessors, was a man of simple tastes and one who hated the corruption of Avignon. In Cardinal Albornoz he had found a divine who could add a shrewd military mind to achieving the goal and it was he who could lay claim to bringing such a thing to pass.

Albornoz had played every city state against its rivals, paid mercenaries when necessary and sought to check them when they were a problem. Hawkwood he seemed to trust, but Sterz he had hated so speculation regarding the death of the German freebooter only made sense if the clerical hand was involved. If Albornoz had contrived at murder there was no sign of his conscience being troubled by it as he recruited a temporarily unemployed Hawkwood for a different task.

'His Holiness has already left Avignon and will sail from Marseille to Genoa. I require you to gather a thousand horse to act as his escort to Rome.'

It was the month of May before the papal argosy reached Genoa and there was the White Company on the quayside, breastplates gleaming in the strong sunshine, bleached-white banners waving, waiting to welcome the Pope ashore, confused like the huge assembled crowd when the vessels refused to enter the harbour. A boat had to be sent out to find out what was the problem, naturally fearing the plague. It was Albornoz who was obliged to explain.

'His Holiness has seen your breastplates and banners, Hawkwood, and if he did not know of your presence his concerns were not eased by being told of it. He knows your name from Pont-Saint-Esprit?'

'He fears us?'

'I have reassured him you are here in homage and will cause him no harm.'

'I admit to being a miserable sinner, Cardinal,' was the terse response. 'But the notion I would lay a hand on the Vicar of Christ offends me.'

'Not something you extend to his coffers.'

'They are not spiritual.'

Hawkwood never got to welcome Urban, who still declined to land in the presence of a strong force of mercenaries he was not prepared to trust – what a ransom he would provide! The fleet of the Pope and his cardinals, not to mention several mistresses, sailed south along the coast of Liguria, finally coming ashore at Corneto. A party for Rome awaited him and he was given the keys to Castel Sant'Angelo, not that he proceeded to use them; Rome was seen as too febrile for safety. Instead he was accommodated away from the filth of the Holy City in the castle of Viterbo.

Within weeks Urban was besieged in that castle by the irate citizenry who took exception to so many high church Frenchmen, such as Urban himself, as well as their overbearing actions, obvious opulence and public lack of morality. It took troops from the surrounding city states to rescue Urban, which got a jaundiced response from John Hawkwood.

'Never would have happened had he landed at Genoa.'

The second bit of news from Viterbo brought on less joy. His erstwhile employer, Cardinal Albornoz, had died.

'Was he a good man?' Gold enquired.

'No better than you or I is the way I reckon. But his mind was sharp and his disposition cunning, so happen I must learn from him.'

# CHAPTER EIGHTEEN

Sir John Hawkwood – he was now happy to use the title once his sovereign had acknowledged it – returned to Milan to find that the seed he had sown in writing to the English court had borne fruit, which if not yet fully ripe was well on its way to providing a sweet reward. Envoys had come to Lombardy while he had been away campaigning to propose to Galeazzo Visconti that King Edward's second son, Lionel Duke of Clarence, at present without a wife would, if it was permitted, make suit to the Lord of Pavia's twelve-year-old daughter, Violante.

In effect a proposal of marriage, this presented a massive coup for the Visconti family and no one was keener on the match than Bernabò, the girl's uncle. He had two concerns in his life: to raise the standing of Milan in the Italian hierarchy, and to make the family name one that resounded through Europe and not only because of their fabulous wealth.

Naturally such an alliance did not come without a price; a prince of England must be provided with estates that could support the style of his bloodline, which was normally an occasion for much haggling. Edward's commissioners, however, found themselves pushing at an open door, not realising that the Visconti brother's generosity stemmed not just from eagerness but also from the fact that they were prepared to satisfy financial demands that would have made other polities blench.

Lionel would be in receipt of dozens of fiefdoms across Lombardy, most notably Alba, which together would produce an income of twenty-four thousand florins a year, while the father Galeazzo was willing to make a gift of two hundred thousand from Pavia. In addition, the prince would assume command of all the English mercenaries in Italy, by far the most numerous and, since they were the subjects of his father and were loyal to Edward's crown, ensure that they were put to the service of Milanese interests.

Supposedly a secret, Edward informed Galeazzo that his son would bring with him a strong retinue of fighting men and offered also the prospect of an English army to aid the Milanese in their battles against the Pope and their Italian rivals. Hawkwood, made privy to the proposals, saw it as nothing less than an offer to help the Visconti become so powerful that their rule of all Italy – something that had not existed since the fall of the Western Empire – was in prospect.

Confidences in Italy did not long stay hidden; Pope

Urban had his spies in Milan and Pavia just as his rivals had theirs in Rome, and such a possibility could not but alarm him. Charged with holding intact the temporal power of the papacy such a pact could be terminally inimical to his interests. To ward off such an outcome he sent a papal nuncio to London seeking to stop the match, only to receive an unwelcome proposal of compromise.

'Urban lays aside the consanguinity, agrees to the Langley nuptials with the widow of Burgundy and matters may be altered. If not, face an alliance of England and Milan.'

'I am bound to ask what this means for you, Sir John?'

Christopher Gold's curiosity was natural but his leader suspected the question posed related as much to his recently appointed constable's future as his own.

'We will have a prince of our own blood in need of advice. I do not doubt he deserves his spurs and he will fetch along good fighting men, but Italy is not Picardy or Aquitaine. I fully expect his father to advise Clarence to look to me for help in making sense of what seems from London a chessboard fully cracked and unreadable.'

'You could be at his right hand?'

Hawkwood smiled. 'And I expect you to be that at one remove.' Gold being aware of the supposedly secret parts of the agreement allowed Hawkwood to add what might be possible. 'Imagine all of Italy united, Christopher, and under the control of the man who leads the armies of conquest.'

'The Duke of Clarence?'

'Lionel will be as hungry for power as his brothers, and what a temptation. A conquest to overshadow his father's heir.'

'Am I allowed to say that you have the light of dreams in your eye?'

Hawkwood laughed. 'I would hazard you've seen it before.'

'I have and once or twice noted it preceding near disaster.'

Gold had a serious look on his face as he said that, which had Hawkwood reflecting on how he had matured, while half thinking that he had preferred the callow and blindly faithful youth to the man before him, elevated enough now to question his orders, which any good constable must do.

'Well, I know you will see that coming as quickly as I and have no fear of alerting me.'

If Hawkwood had hoped to lighten Gold's mood by that he was disappointed. 'Never fear, Sir John, I will.'

Prior to the arrival of Prince Lionel all of Piedmont was awash with discussion of the sums and lands expended to ensure the marriage took place. King Edward's commissioners went home laden with fabulous gifts for themselves, their sovereign and Violante's prospective husband and they did so in a daze; where could such a cornucopia come from? If they had stopped to look they would have seen.

Milan stood at an important crossroads from which it fed its products both north and west into France and Germany as well as lands beyond, England included. Its clever and enterprising merchants had created trade routes that rivalled the Silk Road, using the abundance of gifts God had bestowed on the valley of the River Po and Ticino, this enhanced by previous rulers who had created a series of canals to spread the waters around the fertile basin, providing ample irrigation for rich soil while the sun did the rest. These canals had been improved by Galeazzo Visconti, making more abundant what was already an excess.

There were the manufactories, which had existed from Roman times, also improved upon by individual enterprise. If you wanted arms or armour you came to the traders of Lombardy. They had ample Alpine wood to make charcoal, ready supplies of ore in nearby mines and fast-flowing streams to provide the power to turn that base metal into deadly or protective steel.

The citizens with money to spare had, like their Florentine rivals, elevated banking to a level never seen before in the known world; it seemed the Milanese could make money out of merely possessing it in what some were sure was a form of alchemy, but it was really simple. There were few states on the Continent that did not require loans and that came at interest. The accrued sums allowed the Italian bankers to lend more, recover more and grow even richer.

Everyone under the hand of the Visconti was properly taxed and in Bernabò the state had a co-ruler with a passion for the minutiae of collection of monies due which was rivalled only by his addiction to carnality. He had brought his wife to labour sixteen times and fathered dozens of bastards but as much energy was put into proper administration. Bernabò oversaw the tax ledgers personally, plying his abacus with such adeptness it seemed almost musical in its clicking.

No one escaped his attention, from street vendor, prostitute, baker, trader or banker, yet Bernabò was as interested in what the sums accrued were used for, not the mere acquisition. If much of it filled the Visconti private vaults they were also investors in their patrimony. For a family that had achieved power through an imperial appointee they had an abiding desire that their offspring would continue to rule and raise Milan to even greater heights.

Anticipation in Lombardy was not enough to induce speed in the putative bridegroom; a prince of England crossing France when the two nations were at peace was a guest to savour. No member of the royal house or great nobleman was prepared to let such a prize guest pass without feasting him and his six-hundred-strong retinue, five hundred of those soldiers from the best families in England.

In this scion of the Plantagenets they found a trencherman of repute and sound dedication. Lionel loved food and wine almost above all other things but he knew and gave due prominence to his duty as a true knight. Thus he was found in the lists as often as he was found at the board, ever willing to hunt with spear and bow to provide food for his hosts' table. He was a man of strenuous exercise both mounted and on foot, so not a day went by that he did not abide by the Norman creed of practising that which he had been bred to do: fight his father's foes.

John Hawkwood waited with as much impatience as anyone, having received a command from his sovereign to take personal charge of Lionel's escort while he was in Milan. He would have the responsibility to ensure he came to no harm, for it was axiomatic that there were factions in Italy, and not just papal ones, who could see what an alliance with a power such as England might bring down upon them.

Finally, after months of waiting, news was sent ahead to name the day the prince would enter the city. Heralds were sent out to ensure that all were aware so they could be on hand to provide a proper welcome. Not that the population required much in the way of encouragement. It was odd to reflect that a state purporting to be a republic, albeit ruled in something close to a tyranny, was susceptible to, and indeed in awe of the allure of royalty, a station in life its people believed could only be granted by divine approval.

Sir John Hawkwood met Lionel outside the western gates and made the required obeisance, before being raised by his prince to be greeted as a liegeman. Close to, the man appointed captain of his escort saw a face blotched and puffy from overindulgence, while the June sun had not favoured what was the pale complexion of a man russet-haired. There was trace of family likeness to his brother Edward but not the cast of determination in the eye. Yet Lionel bore himself well, albeit with a protruding belly and a propensity to fart.

It was necessary to also meet and acknowledge his cousin, Edward le Despenser. On first impression here was a man to whom Hawkwood took an instant dislike, this for his blatant arrogance and undisguised condescension. He was typical of a certain kind of nobleman, and country of birth had no bearing; anyone below him was commonality and to such people only royalty stood superior in rank.

'I will have to work with him?' Hawkwood groaned to Gold, who had likewise met the man and been treated as nothing. 'He leads Clarence's retinue and no doubt will see himself as the man to command all the English knights if they take the field.'

'Which should fall to you. I am sure King Edward would wish it.'

'Edward is in London, le Despenser is here and it is easy to see Lionel relies on his cousin.'

'I sense they are ready, Sir John,' said Gold, pointing out that everyone was remounting their horses.

Entry into Milan had been delayed as Lionel, Duke of Kilkenny and Clarence as well as a Plantagenet prince, made sure that he and those with him presented the best spectacle possible. Thus any traces of dust had been polished off breastplates, cuirasses and greaves, while fresh surcoats had been fetched from the following waggons as well as new banners unbleached by the sun. The tower enclosing the Porta Ticina was already in sight and as they closed they could see it was fully manned, and as the column moved the trumpeter on the top blew a welcoming and sustained blast, which was the signal that the citizens could begin to cheer.

Hawkwood was third behind his prince – Despenser declined to forfeit his right and even his banner-carrying page took precedence – as they rode through the gate, to emerge from the shades into a crowded route being strewn with flowers. Lionel, bareheaded, knew how to be gracious, how to smile and wave, also to occasionally stop to bend from his saddle and bestow a royal kiss on the cheek of any comely maid he espied.

'What would Violante say to such behaviour?' asked Gold in a whisper.

'She is but fourteen, John, a virgin and, I should think, terrified of what she is being obliged to enter into. She will probably be glad if her new spouse wishes to show favour elsewhere.'

The route took them to the square dominated by the

Palazzo Visconti where the crowd were so packed that the Milanese soldiers had trouble in holding them in check, which had Hawkwood push past a surprised Despenser. He also ordered Gold to follow and take a position on the opposite side of the prince's horse, but not beyond the flank.

'When your sovereign appoints you as responsible for his son's safety,' Hawkwood barked at a furious complaint from Despenser, 'I will gladly give way. Till then I have the duty.'

As if to make amends, Hawkwood peeled off by the gateway that led into the palace courtyard, only following when the entire body of Lionel's escorting knights were inside, there to find Despenser now complaining that his prince had deserved to be met outside the gates and not in the palace, the implication plain: to him the Visconti were below the salt.

Refreshed, the man got first sight of the great feast Galeazzo and Bernabò had arranged, as well as the stupendous gifts that accompanied every one of the eighteen courses. If Despenser tried to hide his amazement, and he did, his royal master did not; he clapped with delight and was quick and frequent to sup from a goblet never allowed to be empty and he consumed his food with equal gusto.

Lionel was presented with hunting dogs by the dozen, all wearing golden collars, multiple raptors under hoods decorated in pearls, gilded armour and plumed helms fantastic in their elaborate fretwork of gold and silver. Fine horses were paraded past the feasting guests, coursers and tilters for jousting, each one gloriously saddled to be followed by surcoats sewn with jewels.

The food was the finest Lombardy could produce, likewise the wines, not freshly pressed but the produce of long-stored harvests, much of the food sealed with gold, which was seen as being healthy. It was a display of magnificence the likes of which no English royal or aristocrat could ever have seen: the wealth required to provide it simply did not exist in chillier northern climes.

'Happen that might dent his damned arrogance,' was Hawkwood's opinion of the Despenser reaction, sat in a place of some honour, given his personal rank as captain general. 'He will scarce dine like this again in his life.'

Another object of his attention was Violante and he noticed her father Galeazzo was keen that she should drink, no doubt out of concern for what was coming. The marriage had to be consummated and that must happen that very evening. Had she been told what to expect or was that down to observation? Lionel's face was bright red and not just from heat, his laugh the hearty bray of the inebriated: he was full of enough wine to make Hawkwood wonder if he would be up to the deed.

The musicians delayed the inevitable, with Lionel in reality meeting his intended for the first time as they performed a rather staged dance and one which was marred by the odd stagger. The prince was not alone in his cups: Galeazzo was close to him in that regard and Despenser, in trying to keep up with his prince and lacking the liver, ended up with his face lying in the plate that had contained a sorbet made possible by Alpine ice.

Finally Violante was led to the bedchamber followed by her father, her uncle Bernabò and various Milanese dignitaries, including the Archbishop of Milan, whose task it would be to witness the deflowering – not visually but by a close ear to the bedchamber door.

Hawkwood had drunk well too and remarked on the length of time these worthies were absent, which could only mean Violante was reluctant or, more likely, Lionel was struggling to meet the requirements of his new estate. That lasted for a seeming eternity until a whispered bulletin passed round the great chamber.

'They heard the scream and entered to see the blood. The deed is done and may God bless the union with a child.'

If Hawkwood had doubted Lionel's liver he had to recant when he came across a prince in robust good health the following morning, to be told that within the day the intention was to proceed to Alba and take possession of the most important of his new fiefs. Hawkwood was obliged to tell his prince he could not accompany him, which did not seem to cause much concern.

'His Excellence Bernabò required that I proceed to secure an important river crossing at Borgoforte, which is under siege by a papal army.'

'How important, Hawkwood?'

'Very, sire. They must be driven away or Mantua is threatened.'

It required a map to show the prince the nature of the threat and Hawkwood had to give him credit for his quick appreciation of the danger to the territories of his new father-in-law.

'I should go, Cousin,' growled Despenser, who looked

a damn sight worse for wear than Lionel Plantagenet and fixed his suffering expression on the captain general. 'Am I not to take command of our English mercenaries?'

'I am happy to yield if required to do so,' Hawkwood lied as he heard confirmed what he had feared: he might end up under this swine's command. 'But I am still under contract to Milan and it will require their word for me to give way to another.'

'A request from you cannot be ignored, Lionel.'

That made the blotched face flush with anger. 'Please be reminded, Cousin, that how we refer to each other in private does not extend to public discourse.'

'Forgive me, Your Grace.'

'I need you in Alba and beyond. My estates need to be properly introduced to their new lord and that requires they observe I have the power to compel. Go about your occasions, Hawkwood, and report to me when you have fulfilled you obligations to Milan.'

'There is a God, Christopher,' was Hawkwood's remark to Gold as they left to gather the men they would need to fight his representative on earth.

The papal army outside Borgoforte outnumbered Hawkwood by a large margin, yet with the cunning that marked him out from his fellow English *condottieri* the superior host was soon seen off. They had set their main encampment on a flood plain that absorbed the waters of the mighty River Po in times of bad weather; by breaking the banks of the waters upstream, Hawkwood washed away their tents and made the ground untenable, so he was able to send word back of a stunning success at the cost of not a single life.

Sent on to Arezzo, hubris caught up with him; riding well ahead of his brigade and thinking his reputation would keep him safe he was attacked at the Porta Buia and captured. That in itself was bad; he would be held for ransom and it would be a large one, yet worse news was to come to him in captivity.

Lionel, it was said from a surfeit of gluttony, had died and the whole edifice of the English–Visconti alliance was thrown into turmoil. Le Despenser and Lionel's knights were sure their master had been poisoned – it was not an unknown way of disposing of rivals in Milanese politics – while Galeazzo, well within his rights in the nature of the marriage contract, demanded back the fiefs he had passed over as gifts.

Hawkwood had to watch from his very comfortable prison – he was given a fine set of apartments that befitted his value – as le Despenser led his retinue, backed up by other English mercenaries, against Galeazzo; yet that had to be put aside as Gold was authorised to sell assets and call in loans to find the hundred thousand florins the papal commander was demanding for his release.

# Chapter Nineteen

Raising the ransom was taking time. If Sir John Hawkwood had made fortunes in the service of his various employers it was not all in easily realisable sums. Many times he had been given properties in lieu of cash and these had to be sold in a way that did not fairly recognise their true value. Added to that he acted as banker to the men he led, lending them sums to buy armour and horses when times were lean and never being seen to press hard for recompense, and then there were the natural expenses of being their captain.

If they got into debt and were hard up for the inability to pay it was to John Hawkwood they appealed and if he met their obligations it was with no certainty that he would be soon recompensed. If they perished it was incumbent upon him to ensure that they had a good burial and that any dependants they had back in England were not left destitute, while in many cases shrines were built to the God it was hoped would ease their way into the afterlife.

Masses had to be said for their souls and priests never performed such services for free. Yes they were sinners, but the Almighty was a forgiving presence. Added to that the Visconti, no doubt having lavished so much on Prince Lionel, had been very tardy in paying his monies and if he had to stand that he could not ask those he led to do likewise.

In the many months of his captivity, as news came in, it seemed to Hawkwood that Edward le Despenser was pursuing a private vendetta, which only served to show his utter ignorance of Italian politics. In cold calculation, for the Visconti to poison an English prince made no sense at all: there was no discernible gain, quite the reverse – with English help, Galeazzo and Bernabò had hoped to break the power of the papacy, which they could not do on their own.

Kept well informed he knew that the Visconti were suffering badly; as was normal they could not find enough men in their own territories to defend it against professional soldiers. Galeazzo did try, sending a force to retake Alba, only to see them crushed and driven back until both Milan and Pavia were in some danger of capture.

Once again stout walls proved their saviour, that and a ruthless attitude to the survival of their population. Many were left to the mercy of the English mercenaries and within the walls of their cities the distribution of food was tightly controlled to avoid speculation. If no one died of starvation when the sieges were finally lifted there was not much skin left on the Lombardy bones.

Finally released on full payment Hawkwood found his personal brigade awaiting. Still nominally in the service of the Visconti he set off aiming to mediate between the two competing forces but with a conundrum: if le Despenser would not back off which side did he support? One, even if he owed him a great deal of money, was his employer. Yet le Despenser represented King Edward, to whom Hawkwood was a liegeman.

It was just as well he found matters, if not settled, no longer so febrile. King Edward had accepted a sworn promise from Galeazzo that he had not poisoned Lionel and le Despenser, in a fit of pique and stupidity, had gone over to the service of the Pope, who was the enemy of his sovereign. Yet there was other business to attend to. Bernabò had taken an army south into Tuscany in an attempt to save from Florence a small but strategically important town.

San Miniato, from its heights, controlled the routes by which goods came to Milan and through there to Europe. Indeed, it stood at a hub of roads that went back to classical times connecting Pisa, Florence and Volterra. By a decision of its *Signoria* it had ceded itself to Florence and that had been overturned by Milan; now Florence was trying to wrest it back and had sent an army to besiege it. Lifting such an investment was difficult; Florence had taken up a strong position that invited attack, but for all Bernabò's eagerness to oblige them Hawkwood counselled caution.

'We cannot just sit here,' was the Visconti response, delivered with the level of bilious rage for which this brother was famed when crossed or questioned, often coming close to an apoplexy. 'We will run out of supplies.'

'Then we must get them to attack us,' was the calm rejoinder. 'I have said it many times, never let your enemy choose the field of battle.'

'How?'

'By invitation.'

What the Florentine army saw was a Milanese army taking up positions that made no military sense, for the soldiers deployed on a flat plain with no cavalry support in sight and two open flanks. Too tempting an offer to refuse, the horns blew and from being drawn up and harangued the Florentines' horse began to advance, to see before them the gratifying sight of their enemy breaking long before contact and fleeing in panic.

Not to follow would have required the patience of a saint and that was not a virtue gifted to men mounted, advancing and excited, especially when behind that fleeing host lay the River Arno, which with no bridge promised much slaughter. The first indication that it would not be so simple came as soon as they found themselves on the low flat ground. This, regularly inundated by the river, proved heavy-going for their steeds, whose hooves began to stick in what was now mud, yet still before them was that tempting objective.

Certainty of success turned to panic as, from their rear, another Milanese army emerged to shut them off from their own support, and if they wondered how this could be – the enemy was both before them and behind them and that was not possible, given their known numbers – there was no time to find out, for all that was left was a reversal: the panicked flight of the Florentines.

Yet to turn and flee over soft ground was impossible; Hawkwood and his men bore down on them and once the archers had dismounted, the slow-moving horsemen found themselves easy targets for a weapon which, fired at close range, could penetrate anything but the best plate armour. For the leaders to continue fighting was to die, to surrender was to live but in poverty, not a possibility offered to the commonality. They perished in droves.

Sir John Hawkwood took great pleasure in parading the army the Florentines thought they could pursue and kill. These were the children of every outlying town, dressed properly and armed by Hawkwood with instruction to take flight as soon as the enemy attacked and draw them into his perfect trap.

'Christopher Gold,' he whooped, 'I care not what they say of me now or in the future. This battle was the perfect thing. If minstrels do not sing of this they do not deserve their lyre.'

Once he had departed, San Miniato reverted to the polity to which it wanted to belong; despite what the Visconti said, the wishes of the citizens could not be gainsaid and a fortress however strong could not be held against their desire to be ruled by Florence and not Milan, which stemmed from the location in Tuscany. A distant ruler would mean constant harassment; one close by might provide the security all Italians craved and rarely now were granted.

That was not the end of Hawkwood's dilemmas; Edward Plantagenet had revived his claim to the French crown on the grounds that the terms of the Treaty of Brétigny had not been met. That was true, but it was the death of 'good' King Jean that prompted the renewed claim.

'To go or to stay, Christopher?'

'Many are leaving, Sir John.'

Called back to the service of their sovereign in his projected French campaign, the English mercenaries were departing Italy, heeding a general call from their king to bolster his army. Edward had always had a residual grip on those who had served him previously and taken to freebooting in peacetime; indeed, it was said by his enemies that he controlled and profited from them. But Hawkwood was singular; he was in constant communication with Edward's court, yet . . . ?

'I have no direct request from King Edward that I do so and I cannot believe it would be left to me to decide.'

'He still has an enemy in Italy. The Pope still refuses to grant leave for his son to marry the widow of Burgundy. Would he not be as well served if you were to act against the pontiff rather than be a mere brigade commander in France?'

If was difficult to know where duty began and self-interest stopped. Gold had made a telling point and Hawkwood's own inclination was to remain in Italy. Of all the English freebooters, he was the most famous, so much so that his mere name carried a potent threat and being captured and ransomed did not much dent that. As an asset to his king that would not carry into France, where he would become merely one of many – lauded he was sure, but not singular.

'We stay.'

And to let the Pope know that all his English troublemakers were not leaving, he rode to Montefiascone, the small but comfortable castle north of Rome, where the Pope had retired to avoid the summer heat. He peppered it with arrows until Urban was driven to make a hasty retreat to the more substantial safety of Viterbo, not that he would be safe there for long.

Hawkwood besieged him and with help from the citizens of Rome, who in the first place hated Urban for being French, and in the second for ignoring their city and staying outside ever since he had returned. Long pressured by his cardinals to return to Avignon, Urban V finally agreed and set out to travel back to France. A certain asthetic nun in Siena called Catherine, famed for her abstinence – in truth, self-starvation enough to bring on visions – and total devotion to Jesus, predicted Urban would die if he left Italy. He was gone in six months.

Hawkwood meanwhile, in a period of relative calm, was busy rebuilding his fortunes. Such was his reputation that the mere mention that he might ravage a territory was enough to have the Italian city states pay him to leave them in peace, and the florins flowed into his coffers to the tune of over two hundred thousand, doubly welcome since Galeazzo Visconti was again being tardy in his payments and he was bearing the cost of the company.

In addition, his support in Pisa, which had lasted since he had elevated Agnello to the dictatorship, was gone and new governance was in place. Agnello had always been a backstop for the White Company, Pisa a place where he could always recoup his losses in equipment as well as secure supplies of food and wine.

He tried to retake it with the aid of a group of exiles but that came to nought; the walls proved too strong for the mercenaries because the attempt at another coup was discovered, which meant they were well manned when the assault was in progress. This led to many casualties as men climbing ladders were either shot by arrow fire, burnt by boiling oil or tipped off them to break bones in such a quantity as to be fatal.

The Visconti were calling again; the new Pope Gregory XI had created yet another league against Milan and, given the assault was coming from the west, it fell to the Lord of Pavia to repulse them and at Asti the Galeazzo heir was to experience his first taste of battle. Tall, handsome and with his mother Bianca's abundant auburn hair, Giangaleazzo Visconti was the hope of his house.

Galeazzo and Bianca sent with their son a pair of counsellors, given instructions that their beloved son was not to be put at risk, something that could hardly be guaranteed in a battle. But his father made sure the White Company was in support and John Hawkwood at hand to give sound advice.

'Which is that we will prevail with a frontal assault on the walls, which are in poor repair and also badly manned.'

'My uncle the Green Count will not give way easily, Sir John. He like you has a reputation he would scarce wish to see tarnished.'

If anything showed the tangle of the politics of Lombardy it was this. Bianca's brother, Amadeus of Savoy, known as the Green Knight for his habit of wearing only that colour in the lists, was defending Asti. Famous throughout Europe, married to the daughter of a king of France, he was one of the most renowned men in Christendom.

While considering how this might affect what was required to be done, Hawkwood forbore to mention that he and Robert Knowles had once taken the Green Count prisoner and ransomed him for the princely sum of one hundred and eighty thousand florins, not that they had yet been paid the full amount; more than half was still outstanding after ten years. The debt was not a secret, but it would be tactless to bring it up.

'Reputation would not serve me if I was weak and it will not serve your mother's brother, puissant as he is. We hold the advantage if we press hard and here you have a chance to win your spurs in style by leading the assault.'

'Leading the assault?' asked one of Giangaleazzo's custodians, his face pinched.

'Of course.'

'I cannot see that as wise, Sir John.'

'It is not only wise, it is necessary. Giangaleazzo is in command. It is incumbent upon a leader to show his men the way.'

'Assault the walls, with, I presume, ladders?'

The response was terse. 'I cannot fly and neither can he.'

The two men sent by the young man's mother angered Hawkwood by the way they moved away to confer without the courtesy of asking his permission to do so, this while the subject of the discussion looked vacantly at the roof of the tent. Much murmuring followed until they broke apart and the one who had asked the question spoke up.

'I fear that is not acceptable, Sir John. We would be failing in the responsibilities we have been given if we were to agree to any action that exposes our charge to harm.'

'I will be with him, exposing myself to harm.'

'Which is your profession.'

'I was under the impression that the Lord of Pavia wanted his son to take up that calling.'

'Truly he would wish it, but not at the loss of his heir.'

'Giangaleazzo, do you concur with this?'

'I am obliged by my parents to listen to the counsellors they have provided for me.'

'So we ask you, Sir John,' came the interjection from the other one, 'to formulate some plan that carries with it less risk.'

'Change my plan?' A pair of nods and again nothing from the object at the centre of the discussion. 'Tell me, what do you know of fighting?'

'I confess to no knowledge at all,' said the one hitherto silent, 'but I think I can speak for both.'

'Then can I tell you the only way to find out is to take part. If your charge is to be the person who holds together his family patrimony he will have to risk his life to gain experience. And given his title, he has to be seen to do so by the men who will rely on his judgement to keep them whole.'

'I fear we must insist on another way to proceed.'

'Do you? A pair of scribblers telling me how to fight? Well, I will say this to your charge.' A really angry Hawkwood turned to face Giangaleazzo. 'Either you overrule this pair of dolts or—'

The young man did not respond himself, he left that to his custodians.

'Only his mother and father can overrule us.'

'Then I leave it to you to tell them that if he is to win his spurs he can do so without my aid.'

Hawkwood was out of the commander's pavilion before anyone could respond. Within hours the White Company had struck its tents, loaded its waggons and was gone and if Hawkwood had any worries about how this would be received in Milan and Pavia it was not apparent.

'Are we still in the employ of the Visconti?'

'We will see, Christopher, wc will see.'

The communication from Pope Gregory XI, another Frenchman, came as a surprise, not least in the way it thanked him for the way he had kept the peace throughout much of Piedmont, which was sophistry of the highest order. Yet it was an olive branch indicating a change of papal policy with the recent transition: Hawkwood was being wooed, and if normally indifferent to such supplications – they came too regularly from other city states seeking the services of the White Company – he saw this as dissimilar.

It was not just the interference of civilians in his decision-making that had made the Visconti less than perfect employers. Once more that came down to money, with two magnates who never seemed to grasp that if they were late in payment he could not apply the same to his men. If they were loyal, and they were exceptionally so by the standards of the trade they followed, they would not march and fight on empty purses and even more strained bellies, and giving property instead of coin was an imperfect way to compensate.

Much of the money he had received from those he had declined to harry was now gone and when he added up what he was owed it ran to a fortune, so his reply to Gregory was simple: make up that missing sum, provide a contract and keep to its terms, and the White Company will enter papal service.

'That's the way of it,' Alard the Radish explained to a recently arrived recruit from England. 'We fight for profit, and outside King Edward we acknowledge no lord and master.'

There was one other request John Hawkwood made to the Pope: a request that his bastard son, at present in London and coming into manhood, be made legitimate, an act that could only be granted by a papal dispensation and only after the expenditure of much gold.

Hawkwood got his for free and once he had secured his supplies set off to beard his one-time employers, leading an attack that took him close enough to the walls of the Lord of Pavia's castle to pick and eat his pears. If he resisted the temptation to jeer at Giangaleazzo Visconti his men did not, even if he was known to be absent.

'It is his mother who will hear this and wonder what business is it of hers to interfere in war.'

# CHAPTER TWENTY

The Lord of Pavia now being *in extremis*, it was left to his brother to come to his aid. As if to mock the White Company they put Giangaleazzo in command, but again he had someone to mind him: his bastard cousin and one-time Hawkwood ally Ambrogio. Meanwhile the White Company had been reinforced with a brigade of Frenchmen, armoured knights under the command of Enguerrand de Coucy, one of the richest men in France and the possessor of a huge and near impregnable donjon that secured the route from the north towards Paris.

As a fifteen-year-old he had fought in the campaign against Edward Prince of Wales and following on from Poitiers and the Treaty of Bretigny had been one of the hostage knights sent to London as a guarantor of the ransom for King Jean. He had impressed Edward Plantagenet enough to allow Enguerrand to marry his daughter Isabella, so he was now also Duke of Bedford in the English peerage.

Of stunning height and build he was imposing also by his manner, which was genial and attractive. It was easy to see how he had charmed Edward and his court, for he charmed everyone with his comely figure, superb conduct and grace of movement. He was said to be a fine dancer, which did not impress Hawkwood.

'I will wait till I see him fight.'

Which he did and that was less impressive: de Coucy suffered from the French aristocratic disease of never granting any ability to his opponents, none of whom were titled enough to be considered worthy. The White Company came face-to-face with the Visconti host but the advantage lay with Hawkwood: he had chosen the field of battle and Ambrogio was no longer present, leaving the command to the inexperienced Giangaleazzo. As such, Hawkwood was prepared to wait for them to commit to the attack.

The Frenchman was not. Just as at all the battles they lost against the two Edwards, de Coucy charged the Milanese lines, which forced Hawkwood to support him and not in an organised way. It was therefore no surprise their attack failed and the horns had to call for a hasty retreat to get the company away from the risk of total destruction. If Enguerrand de Coucy had any regrets, once they retired to a nearby hill where the company and his brigade could regroup, he showed no evidence of it; indeed, he and his surviving knights seemed proud of their conduct and were loudly congratulating each other.

'What do I say to the son-in-law of my sovereign, Christopher?'

'Go and fight somewhere else, lest you wish to pay another ransom.'

'I will seek to tell him of his error, but for all his charm I do not think it will penetrate. His skull is as thick as his breastplate.'

Hawkwood was trying as politely as possible to point out to de Coucy the error of his way of making war when Gold came to fetch him, interrupting the gentle lecture. His constable had spotted that the Milanese were in disarray, too busy sacking the White Company's baggage train to mount a serious defence against a determined charge.

'And it pains me to say, Sir John, the best people to accomplish that are your damned Frenchmen.'

'Please do not call them mine,' Hawkwood responded as he surveyed the scene. 'But you are right. Call de Coucy.'

For once French eagerness and disregard for their foes worked in their favour. Sweeping down from the hill, banners flying on top of their deadly lances, armour flashing in the strong sunlight, they inflicted terror in the enemy ranks and the man in command lacked the skill or the presence to get them to form up for defence.

Hawkwood was not far behind, seeking to capture the scion of the Visconti who would command a ransom to rival the one demanded of King Jean. That very nearly came to pass; Giangaleazzo was unhorsed and had dropped his lance and was without his helmet, but his bodyguard rallied round, getting him remounted so he could flee.

'Well,' Hawkwood opined, 'I failed to teach him anything at Asti but here he has had a sound lesson in warfare.'

It came as no surprise to find later that in writing back to both London and Paris, Enguerrand de Coucy claimed the victory as his.

'Let him do so,' Hawkwood mused, when he was challenged about this by his most faithful followers, Ivor, Alard, Gold and Badger Brockston included, men who had served him for years. 'I have enough glory to spare one encounter.'

'Won't say 'owt to upset Edward Plantagenet, will he now.'

Ever in receipt of ambassadors from somewhere, a Visconti embassy nevertheless came as a surprise, which only went to prove how dire was their situation. Pressed on all sides, with Piacenza besieged and the armies of the papal league under the Green Count pressing right to the heart of their patrimony, their situation looked increasingly bleak and that included leadership: Ambrogio had been killed by peasants, torn limb from limb. His father was both bereft for the loss and without his ability.

It was addressed to the court of the two puissant knights, Hawkwood and the Sire de Coucy, which was not music to the former's ears. As far as he was concerned, even if the Frenchman did not believe it to be true, he was under Hawkwood's command. The offer made was as high as it needed to be, for betrayal came at a high price. Enguerrand was tempted, Hawkwood not.

'It will serve you ill,' he explained to de Coucy, 'if it is seen that you can be at any time bought.'

The story of Sterz was recounted, with the point made that the Perugians had believed he could be treacherous because he had been just that previously with Pisa.

'I am tempted, I have been many times, but when I reflect on that I always draw back. If a contract is broken it is not by me but by those employing me. The Visconti did not pay as they should and now I fight for the Pope. We must send these ambassadors away without anything.'

The next question came with a stinging message from Gregory. The Pope wanted to know why Hawkwood was treating with his enemies instead of pressing the papal cause and finishing off the Visconti for good. They were now outcasts, he was informed, having been stripped of the Vicariate of Milan on which their power rested. God had seen fit to leave them at the mercy of his forces and a soaking dungeon would be their fate.

'And that, sir, is another reason to hold to your contract. Nothing in Italy stays secret.'

Even with the Green Count at the gates of Milan it was disease and the weather that saved the Visconti this time. Amadeus of Savoy fell ill and without firm command of the several contingents a common policy was impossible to implement and that delayed action. The Visconti took advantage of this to score a couple of significant victories. Then the weather turned foul, the rain teeming down to flood the valleys of the Po and the Ticino, making fighting impossible, so the campaign was put on hold as the papal forces withdrew into winter quarters.

Enguerrand de Coucy had experienced enough of Italy, not least because he, like Hawkwood, was as yet unpaid; he had been away from his estates for two years and used that as an excuse to depart, mourned for the loss of his company if not his fighting skills. The Pope was no more forthcoming with what was due than Galeazzo and Bernabò and then the plague struck, spreading out from Siena to ravage the whole of north Italy. Instead of destroying the Visconti, Pope Gregory made peace.

Where the plague struck famine was sure to follow as those needed to till the soil and collect the harvests fell ill. This time the ravages lasted into the winter, with weather that made the situation many times worse. It began with torrential rainstorms that flooded fields, compounded by high winds and eventually snow that on the blast of such tempests created impassable drifts and practically stopped travel.

Italy was in the grip of something biblical in its proportions and those who penned comments on this saw it as a divine punishment for any number of transgressions, not least the way the city states allowed mercenaries to constantly ravage the lands of their neighbours. Such conditions put a check on war but not conspiracy and even if it was not sensed fully at the time, there was a move afoot to unshackle many polities from the grip of an avaricious papacy.

Temporarily, Pope Gregory was cut off from the usual flow of information that Avignon depended on to keep control of its interests. Usually in receipt of a constant stream of mounted messengers, they were no longer able to use the network of post houses and changed horses to cover the distance to the River Rhone in two weeks, this while people in closer proximity to each other could correspond and plan.

Naturally those willing to fight for their freedom knew they needed mercenaries, which meant a stream of visitors to Hawkwood. Offers were made and assessed but it was not just florins that determined the way the captain general thought. He also had to assess the depth of purpose and the determination to sustain a campaign. None wooed him more assiduously than Florence, not least because he insisted his contract with Gregory had expired. Yet the Pope was not willing to lose his most successful *condottiere* and sent John Thornbury to plead the papacy's case.

'Florence has paid the last of my monies this very month.'

'So you have no reason to support them.'

'Except my pension.'

Hawkwood enjoyed the way that discomfited Thornbury. While he respected his fellow mercenary, they were and had been in competition for employment. If the host was considered shrewd he was in the presence of another who had that quality. Thornbury was not going to enquire once his initial surprise had abated. He waited silently, nursing his hot spiced wine for Hawkwood to explain.

'To ensure that I leave them be I am to be in receipt of an annual stipend.' The raised eyebrow asked how much, but it enquired in vain. 'To maintain that, Thornbury, I must surely leave Florence be.'

'They tried to engage your service, Hawkwood, did they not?'

'Most assiduously.'

'I take it by that reply you are as yet not committed.'

'The weather is improving, so I must decide soon.'

'And Avignon?'

'I am no longer in their service.'

'Not what the last messenger from Gregory told me.'

'I have it in writing if you wish to examine it.'

That got a sly smile from Thornbury. Hawkwood had been waving the termination document for months. Avignon denied ever writing it, which left only two conclusions: they were lying or the document had been forged by Hawkwood for his own purposes. For what reason if it was the latter? It had to be better terms.

'Thornbury, you know as well as I do that there are moves afoot to form an anti-papal league.'

'If I were to say that my network of spies pales beside yours it would be nothing but the truth.'

That was acknowledged with a nod as Sampson, Hawkwood's new page, saw to the pewter goblets. The host lifted his to his lips, but sniffed the spiced steam before drinking. Hawkwood paid for information in a way that no other could match bar the Pope himself and his came free from his adherents and officials. With the garnered information the leader of the White Company knew where to lead men next for greatest advantage.

'Say this league is formed, Hawkwood, how long do you think it will hold?'

'The papacy is much hated, nearly as much as we are ourselves.'

The reply was mordant. 'The city states hate us so much they are ever seeking to employ us. Let us put aside such peculiarities and talk of winners and losers.'

'If you wish,' Hawkwood replied, taking a slow sip, for the brew was hot enough to scorch a lip.

'Those who know Gregory talk of his determination. He is not a ditherer like Urban and he sees the many errors of his predecessor. That any attempts to seek accommodation with the likes of Florence and Perugia are wasted. I will not even mention Milan. If he is urged on by others, his cardinals, the Pope is said to require little pushing. He is determined to assert the authority of the papacy in Italy and if that has to be bloody his mind is so set it will not trouble his conscience.'

'And you have been sent to tell me this?'

'It was thought that one of your own would make the case better than a divine.'

'Then they guessed right. Is there anyone less to be trusted than a priest?'

'My view is that any anti-papal league will not hold. Those who propose it hate each other and have spent the last twenty years hiring us to fight their battles. Pay no heed to their blabbing about liberty, all they seek is to embroil their neighbours so deeply against Gregory that they will be weakened enough to fall. They will change sides as soon as it is seen to be advantageous to do so.'

Hawkwood leant forward, smiled and spoke softly. 'What a sorry crew we serve, Thornbury. The offer?'

'You seem sure I have one.'

'Come, friend, you would not have travelled as far as you have without one, but let us save your blushes. I have a little bird that tells me the Pope is willing to pay thirty thousand florins a month for the services of the White Company, is that true?'

'Why do I think I have been played for a dupe?'

The response was expansive. 'Come, if we are not bosom companions, still we are not enemies. If I were to say that I was in two minds and you have settled me on a course would that assuage your pride?'

'If I thought you were truly doubtful and that you have come down on the side I suggest, yes.'

'Then have another goblet of wine to seal a bond.'

'You will contract to the Pope?'

'I will, upon my honour.'

'And Florence, I mean your pension?'

'They will pay for fear of what failure will bring down on their heads if they do not.'

'Then I am empowered to say to you that Perugia is the most feverish location for anti-papal feeling and yet the Church rules. It must be contained and it would please His Holiness if you were to proceed there.'

'To subdue them once more? I am accused of shedding much of their blood.'

'No, they have not yet rebelled, but to ensure they do not a garrison will be imposed upon them.'

Sir John Hawkwood had been instructed by more than one divine, but never had he met one as high-handed as Gérard du Puy. A Benedictine abbot and nephew to Pope Gregory, the man employed wondered if he spoke to him in the manner in which he addressed everyone, which was to treat them as if they were shit upon his shoes. He had more titles than most of the Perugians could count on their fingers but the most paradoxical was his designation of Vicar for the Preservation of the General Peace; no one was less suited to that than he.

Arrogance emanated from him and was evident in his decrees, which were draconian. Any assembly of more than three was banned, chains were used to shut off the city streets at night to prevent clandestine gatherings and after sunset he held the keys to the city gates so as to control unrest even if none was evident. He and his coterie of French clerics occupied a fortress and palace on the city heights, ordinary citizens being barred from entry and leading ones admitted only by permission.

Not satisfied with the citadel overlooking the city he had another one constructed, in order to overawe the citizens, whom he despised. To ensure minimum contact he built a covered walkway by which he could progress from his palace to the duomo without having to soil his thinking and deliberation with exchange; he wanted only to commune with his own and those few grovellers of the local population who would unquestionably do his bidding. The fate of any willing to dispute with him was to be thrown out of the city and barred from re-entry.

Not content with a mercenary garrison, de Puy had brought in from elsewhere to guard his now twin citadels all the very best tools of defence that modern ingenuity could devise. That extended to its construction, with towers from the top of which he could employ arrow fire. There were two types of trebuchet being built to fashion his arsenal – the large for firing heavy enough stones to smash masonry, the smaller to let off showers of pebbles that at the speed they flew could be deadly – but only the smaller ones had reached completion.

Everything, including the extravagance in which he and his cohorts lived, had to be paid for by the population of Perugia and its outlying dependencies. That was before they were charged to provide what could be considered a normal stipend sent regularly to their Holy Father and his extractions and expenditures were so large even Avignon was inclined to question them.

If du Puy was conceited he was not in poor company: such a trait existed within every one of his officials, whose imperiousness matched that of their master and all were French. Whatever excess was committed did not result in redress when brought to du Puy's attention: they behaved as would conquerors, not the custodians they were supposed to be. Nothing demonstrated this more than when a local married woman, to avoid being raped by one of du Puy's nephews newly come from France, threw herself to her death out of a high window. No punishment ensued, indeed the complaint was dismissed with sarcasm.

'The French are not all eunuchs,' du Puy thundered, 'even if you dogs would have it so. We are men and lusty with it.'

The same nephew must have felt he had licence to behave in any manner he desired. Having kidnapped and raped the wife of one of the citizens, he was not reprimanded; he was ordered to return her to her husband, but not for fifty days in which he could do as he pleased. John Hawkwood observed these goings on with a jaundiced eye; he had never had much time for priests and in du Puy he had met what seemed an exemplar of all their worst habits encompassed in a set of vestments. He was being paid to keep the peace and his mere presence seemed to be sufficient to secure that; he had no need to act outside that responsibility.

Setting up his own place of command in the lower town he had little need to commune with the Abbot of Marmoutier and his sybaritic circle. His contact was with the military governor, Gómez Albornoz, nephew of the late cardinal, which had the virtue of sparing him from too much of du Puy's unbearable condescension that always brought him close to felling the arrogant abbot with a blow.

Then came the unrest in Città di Castelli. Informed of this by Christopher Gold, Hawkwood waited to see how Gómez Albornoz, or more precisely Gérard du Puy wanted to react. Minor flare-ups had been commonplace in the surrounding conurbations, hardly surprising given the way the Vicar of the General Peace bore down on those under his thumb with taxes and confiscations. Normally they died down of their own volition: people rioting, once they have looted, normally tire and quickly run out of the desire to continue.

'Which has not happened this time,' Albornoz informed him. 'It has continued for days and, it is sad to reflect, is seemingly aimed not at a lack of privileges or a hatred of assessments but squarely at the Church.'

The temptation to say 'hardly a surprise' had to be held back.

'Abbot du Puy feels that an example must be made for once. The local papal garrison and the city priests have been thrown out of the gates and roughly handled too. It is felt a show of real force must ensue.'

'How many?'

There was no need to explain; Hawkwood wanted to know what Gómez Albornoz thought in regards to numbers.

'Half your company, I suggest, will more than suffice.'

'To subdue a herd of peasants?'

'A herd of rebellious peasants armed with the tools of their needs. The abbot is clear. Those recalcitrant must be seen to be swinging from the bell tower. Let the people of the region know what comes of cursing and manhandling their priests.'

# CHAPTER TWENTY-ONE

Christopher Gold, as constable, was left in command of the remainder of Hawkwood's men. For several days nothing seemed to change but with Hawkwood now some four leagues distant and half the White Company gone, the citizens of Perugia seized the opportunity to back the rebellion at Città di Castelli. A tyrant can impose all sorts of strictures on an assembly, but put-upon citizens will always find a way to circumvent such restrictions and the Perugians were no different.

Having met in secret and determined on revolt when the circumstances were propitious, as they were now, they emerged from their houses on an inky-dark winter night, armed with whatever they could find to employ as a weapon and took over the streets. There was no panic in the citadels. Apart from his own guards, Gérard du Puy had the residue of Hawkwood's company led by Gold, plus a small body of Breton mercenaries under a Gascon knight famed for his barbarity called Bertrand de la Salle.

Albornoz was instructed to restore order by whatever means necessary and thus Hawkwood's men were called out to fulfil their bond and they, along with the other armed contingents, assembled in the main square at first light under the military governor's command. From where they were mustered they could hear the yells and screaming imprecations of the mob, all of which were aimed at filthy thieving priests and an immoral papacy, which had Albornoz construct a barricade of waggons to keep them at bay, which could be pushed aside as easily as it could be defended.

'The task is to take back the streets, which should not be difficult. Once these fools see your weapons they will melt away.'

His confidence in his pronouncement was dented when Christopher Gold asked Albornoz, who was not a military man, how long it would take to get a fast rider to John Hawkwood and seek instructions of what his men should do in this situation.

'You are his constable, you command under me and I tell you what is needed.'

'Even if that were true – and Sir John would never agree to it – I would not order the men I lead to take part in the suppression of this revolt on the command of a man who has never fought a battle, never mind suppressed an uprising.'

'You refuse to obey me?' came the angry reply.

'It means fighting in the streets and alleyways of the city and for that we are not suited. The enemy could include the whole population of Perugia – twenty thousand souls – and be made up of women as well as men, given the way they have been treated.'

'A little high spirits, no more.'

Gold waved a hand towards the noise. 'That is the response to your high spirits.'

'Low pigs.'

'Which we lack the numbers to easily contain. Too many of those you wish to set amongst them will die. A mob is like lava from a volcano and as hard to control. It goes where it wills and the people of Perugia know their byways better than we, which means men being attacked from behind as well as the front by threats that cannot be seen. If, however, Sir John wills it, we will comply.'

'It will require force just to get out of this square, Gold. Have you not noticed that we are cut off from the gates? So your notion of sending a rider to Città di Castelli requires that first we retake one, and even then it could be tomorrow before we get a response.'

That statement was met by a determined look; Gold was not to be moved and it was not from any overt instruction from his leader, it was more a feeling that he knew how Hawkwood would react. The killing of Perugians would not concern him; he had done enough of that in the past. It was the continuation of the rule of the city by Gérard du Puy, for on many a night over food and wine Hawkwood had deplored his excesses and stated that the Pope should remove him, even if he was his own brother. Tellingly, if the White Company was not going to move, neither was Bertrand de la Salle and his Bretons, though he kept his reasons to himself.

'Word will get out, never fear,' was the only opinion the Gascon advanced.

'And until then?' Albornoz demanded.

'Best we stay here in the square,' Gold said. 'Perhaps this turmoil will wear itself out.'

Albornoz would have reacted in an angrier way had not the very same instruction come from the citadel via the du Puy nephew, a smirking popinjay who seemed glad his rapist actions might have set the whole insurrection in motion. The forces in the square were to hold their place. The abbot had seen such spontaneous uprisings before and they had never had the force to keep the flame alight. Soon the protestors would tire and then it would be time for retribution. The ringleaders would be ferreted out and a bloody example made with burnings at the stake as well as crucifixions.

If it was measured in sound, matters were far from settling. The noise was increasing and what had appeared to be hundreds screaming about greedy priests now seemed to number several thousands. The depth of the problem was brought home when those the Perugians would call traitors, du Puy's grovellers, came to say the whole city was alight with fervour. Albornoz finally realised the entire population was up in arms, men and women, threating to cut to pieces anyone who came near their knives, scythes and sharp artisans' tools. Gold had been right: to venture into the streets and alleyways was to invite disaster.

'Yet we cannot stay here, surely?' Albornoz put forward, now asking questions instead of issuing orders.

'The citadel is easy to defend and well stocked with provisions.'

'Withdraw?' The notion clearly shocked him

'Better that than perish here. Those waggons can be moved by peasants as well as soldiers and they will be as soon as it is dark.'

If there was no panic there was relief; the men of the White Company tended to be long-serving and they knew what they might face in seeking to clear a mob: the only way was to kill anything that moved without seeking to discover if they were friend or foe and it could not be done without serious loss.

Every deep doorway could conceal a knife, each arch leading to a courtyard with its fountain would hide dozens of men waiting to emerge in the mood to slay. In the narrower alleys it could be one armed soldier against a person blind with fury. None doubted they would be in such a mood for they too had seen the treatment meted out to them by du Puy and his French acolytes.

Slowly, half the men withdrew into the tunnels that held up the overhead walkway, the rest doing likewise above. The route for both led to the twin fortresses Perugia now possessed: the one built by du Puy and the old citadel, which had stood for a hundred years, both joined by a wooden walkway. There was no safety to be had in holding the outer fortifications so everyone was soon in one of the two forts, able to see the walkway by which they could support each other first emitting smoke, then bursting into flames. Within a glass of sand, it had collapsed.

An attempt to drive back the insurgents led by Christopher Gold – he was acting for reasons of security – using one of the tunnels found the exit blocked by a wall of stones. But those who built the dry stone construct had left gaps through which to fire arrows of a primitive kind, but dangerous nevertheless, forcing him to pull back to safety only to find that was going to be in short supply.

The artisan expert employed by du Puy to construct his engines of war had been seeking to complete his work outside the walls of the city. Approached by the rebellious, he was not fool enough to deny those machines as well as his knowledge about their use to the insurgents or to fail to offer his expertise. He would have been torn apart had he done so.

If they had been built to defend the walls there was nothing to stop the Perugians from breaking them down and dragging the parts inside and up the hill, even if it took hundreds of hands. The biggest problem was the heavy counterweights that made the catapults so effective, this being solved by rolling them on logs, though it was hard toil. Once reassembled the trebuchets were put to immediate use, peppering the fortress with huge boulders and the interior with smaller rocks fired high enough to surmount the ramparts.

Two smaller trebuchets had been built previously and put in place, one in each fortress. So the citizens found their own missiles being returned to them with interest. Their location at the top of the central hill of Perugia increased the range and the houses in the lower town suffered badly, as did any citizens caught in the open when they were fired. Days went by and it was obvious to both sides that the locals could no more overcome the defences than the defenders could essay out and drive them off.

Not that the former were idle; it was an indication of the disrespect in which the papacy was held that a body of knights arrived under the flags of Florence and Siena to assist Perugia. Prior to that, a host of peasants had come in from the countryside with their hoes and shovels and were now busy digging a ditch around the forts so that mining under the walls would be possible. The question for the defenders was simple; where was Hawkwood?

On arrival at Città di Castelli, he had found that what he had been told was not strictly true; the small papal garrison of some sixty men had not been thrown out of the city, they had been slaughtered and the fate of the bishop and his priests was unknown. Leading only half his company and ever cautious, retaking the town from outside looked hazardous and that was rendered more so when the inhabitants came out en masse to drive him off, wielding the weapons that they had taken from the dead.

If he was able to check them and force them to retire it was at the cost of several of his men and that left him outside walls he lacked the strength to overcome, even if they were in poor repair. He tried patience, camping within sight for a few days, uncomfortable in winter, but that only brought him news of the Perugian revolt and how it had evolved. That was an even harder nut to crack than the one he now faced.

Seeking reinforcements he made for the papal stronghold of Viterbo only to find that in bloody revolt as well, with the mercenaries he had hoped to engage having fled. His honour required he attempt a recapture; his honour cost him even more losses, including an old friend, and he was now outside any place of succour in the midst of winter. There was no choice but to return to Perugia and see what could be achieved, in the meantime sending for his fellow captains, the likes of John Thornbury, to bring their brigades to that place.

The Perugians were not fools enough to think there would be no attempt to subdue them. Almost their first act, once they had received the contingents from Florence and Siena, was to destroy the bridge across the Tiber and that was what Hawkwood found when he came within sight of the city. In full winter flood it was unfordable and far from easy to cross by boat.

'Well, we must make camp here on this far bank,' was all he could say.

'It may not be my place to say so, Sir John, but we are very short on provender.'

Hawkwood looked at his squire, Salmon, young and reminiscent of Christopher Gold at the same age. 'Never fear to remind me, lad, but I know as well as you we have a dearth.'

'Am I allowed to ask what the plan is?'

'So you can pass it on?'

The smile took the sting out of the words as Salmon

responded, 'I do get asked of your thinking, sir.'

'Which must leave you in a quandary, since I barely know of it myself.'

The nights were cold with a clear sky that promised a frost but, well wrapped up, Hawkwood went on what had become his usual walk through the tents and blazing fires, stopping to talk to people like Ivor and Alard, grey-haired now and bemoaning the loss of the long-time comrade Badger, who had fallen to a lance outside Viterbo.

'His memory lives,' Hawkwood reminded them.

'Are we becoming too old for this?' asked Ivor.

'Been that for a time,' was Alard's response, 'if my bones have the right of it. But I am damned if I can see another way of goin' about things that won't see me starve.'

'Might happen right here,' the Welshman responded in his sing-song voice.

Hawkwood was quick to jump on any gloom. 'You make it sound as if we're trapped.'

'Ain't we, John, or is it just those poor devils forced to arise and battle that bastard who has preyed on them these last two years?'

'If it eases your mind, I dislike du Puy as much as you.'

'Makes no odds, does it, when he holds the purse.'

'Sleep, who knows what tomorrow will bring.'

'No warmth, that's fer certain.'

That melancholy remark sent Hawkwood wandering again and soon he found himself on the riverbank looking at the rushing waters of the Tiber, hard by the broken bridge. It was not far from this spot that he had slaughtered the Perugian forces and now he wondered if the citizens were about to exact revenge, for he was in a bind.

He could not attack and nor, with half his company inside, could he just depart, which for a mercenary was the wise thing to do. Staying whole long enough to earn the stipend meant more than rescuing a fool like Gérard du Puy. Racking his brain as he must he could not see a solution. Eventually he went to his pavilion and drawing his cot near to the brazier, set himself to sleep, though that did not come easily.

It amused Hawkwood that a papal messenger arrived the next morning, bearing with him a cardinal's hat for Abbot Gérard du Puy. The fellow was invited to take a boat, cross the Tiber and seek to deliver it, an offer he was wise enough to refuse, even when Hawkwood pointed out he might be able to mediate. It was a comment that sparked a thought.

'But who better to do that than I?'

If it was taken as a joke once the word spread, Hawkwood had not meant it as such. His first message was to find out to whom he could talk, the response showing that he was dealing with a better organised foe than he had supposed. The citizens had formed themselves into something like a properly constituted government, with a certain Francisco Molinari appointed as the *podestà*.

In truth that was a relief; it was always better to deal with one administrator than a dozen, as he had been obliged to do originally in Pisa. Not that Molinari saw him alone at the rendezvous by the San Giovanni gate. Stern of face, his original stance was to be brusque and rude. If he had hoped to upset Hawkwood, he had no idea of the man with whom he was dealing, a person who had a temper but knew how to control it.

His offer to mediate was first treated with derision, but Hawkwood was aware of certain facts that, once he established the precise positions of the opposing forces, allowed him to apply pressure to be heard. At the centre of that was the compelling article of food.

'The granaries are within the old citadel, are they not?'

'We do not require them.'

'Signor Molinari, please remind yourself that I have resided in your city for some time. I know where the grain is and where there is none – for instance, anywhere else in the city bar a private family storeroom. We are in midwinter and there is nothing to alleviate that. The fields are now barren and not even planted. It will be six months at least before you can gather the means to feed your rebellion and hot tempers cool on empty bellies.'

He had struck a chord but Molinari was not going to give up easily. There was much airy waving of arms, many recitations of sins committed by the White Company, many of which were carried out by the less disciplined Bretons, though Hawkwood declined to point that out since it would serve no purpose. He knew the man would require time; he needed to talk to those who had put him in place, for he had not been appointed to replace a tyrant.

Two days of talks edged towards compromise. Hawkwood would have sacrificed the newly appointed cardinal but he dare not say so. It was his men he wanted, both unmolested and with their weapons, which he mentioned but not with the same degree of emphasis. The threat he issued, very subtly delivered, was, he knew, an empty one, but as long as the Perugians did not see it as such it could work. The idea that mercenary bands from all over the region would converge to crush the revolt was to Molinari a potent one. Such men would not stand by to see their confrères massacred.

The departure of the White and Breton contingents was agreed. Cardinal du Puy took longer but eventually that too was arranged. He must be allowed to leave with all of his entourage as well as his personal possessions. This required a full inventory of that which he owned set against the property of Perugia and led to a great amount of haggling, with Hawkwood in attendance to remind du Puy that his life was at stake and that certain baubles were worthless to a dead man.

'I do not have to fight to get my men freed, but you! They want to throw you to the mob and your nephew with his too free desires as well. The rest they will only hang.'

Disputes such as these are resolved by necessity; Perugia needed the granaries, Hawkwood was stern with du Puy and eventually matters were settled. The French papal party would leave the citadel on the first day of January. It was a cold and frosty morning that saw du Puy set out on a fine mount that Molinari had insisted belonged to the city – just another of those things that had been fought over.

Hawkwood had brought in twenty fully armed bannered knights to protect du Puy physically, but nothing could stop the citizens who packed the route to the city gate from letting him know their opinions with invective and spittle. At one point they closed in so hard he could hardly make forward progress, while his arrogant nephew was struck on the head with a club, producing a strong flow of blood but little sympathy.

The mules carrying du Puy's possessions suddenly disappeared in the melee that followed, bringing forth a loud complaint that Hawkwood must do something, to which the reply came that he was more interested in keeping the abbot alive than compounding his thefts.

'Keep moving, for if anyone gets their hands on you I cannot save you.'

It was unnecessary to say he might struggle to save himself if the mob went crazy. Behind them came the mercenaries, fully armed and looking determined. That caused the crowds to ease back; no one was fool enough to seek to rob them. Not without difficulty the whole assembly cleared the gates and could make their way north.

Half the White Company was on one side of the Tiber, the rest on the opposite bank so they kept going to the next crossing, hard by a Benedictine abbey, by which time an exhausted group of clerical Frenchmen were near to collapse from expended emotion and fear.

John Hawkwood had one task he needed to perform and that was to ask the newly elevated Cardinal du Puy how he intended to pay the latest instalment of the monies due to the White Company.

'Are you stupid, Hawkwood, or is it you are blind? Did you not see me robbed of everything I possess and, I might add, do nothing to prevent it?'

'Which does not obviate the debt.'

'Well, I don't have it so you must seek it elsewhere.'

'Must I?' Hawkwood replied with a laugh. 'I don't think so. I see payment sitting before me.'

'What are you talking about, dolt?'

'Your ransom, Cardinal du Puy. I count you now as my prisoner and will presently calculate how much I think your holy brother will pay to get you freed.'

'You swine, you will rot in hell.'

There was no more laughter, not even a smile. 'Talk to me like that again and I will hold you in a water-filled pit in the ground until I get my money.'

# CHAPTER TWENTY-TWO

The flame of revolt against the Church spread from Perugia like wildfire. Before spring arrived and eased the threat of famine nearly every part of the huge patrimony of St Peter's, controlled from Avignon, had ejected those who had been set over them, both lay and ecclesiastical: cardinals, bishops, vicars and fortress captains, usually the relatives of high divines, many cruelly treated before expulsion. The Church lost control of over six hundred towns and cities in addition to the loss of over a thousand fortified outposts.

At the centre of this upheaval lay Florence, ever claiming to be independent of both Church and empire. Indeed any overlords whatsoever. It was to that city, happy to be the centre of dissent, that the messengers came bearing flags to tell of their new freedoms, of joyous uprisings, physical ejection and the tearing down of the fortresses their overlords had inhabited in order to keep their power.

The city on the Arno became feverish with what was possible and for once the body called the Eight Saints, men elected to the *Signoria* of Florence and who governed the city, had no trouble at all in raising funds in order to sustain their new-found liberties. The money was used to despatch armed bands to those towns and cities that required assistance, carrying the message that the revolt was not against the Church or God but the venal practices of hated officials.

Even rising against God's Vicar on Earth the citizens in every liberated town still attended Mass, still prayed to the Holy Trinity and their favoured saints and vowed deep allegiance to their religion.

Perugia intended to destroy the citadel which du Puy had sought to defend, seen as a symbol of his tyranny. They had sent for experts in demolition to undertake the work. Yet the men who now ran the city also showed they had a conscience – or perhaps they did not want to be seen as anything like the newly elevated cardinal. The property taken from him as he made his way through that hissing crowd was returned.

Hawkwood now expected to receive his due monies, yet when the inventory was complete there was scarce sufficient in coin and valuables to keep the du Puy retinue in soup, while the cardinal himself maintained that this amounted to the totality of his possessions, which was of course not believed.

Had the men who stole it originally pocketed his money? Had du Puy hidden his money away or, in his depredations, taken care to send out of Perugia the profits of his extortions? Or had he, as he claimed, spent every penny that came his way on maintaining his rule, outside the funds owed to the Pope, which had naturally been passed on to Avignon?

'We could go back and demand it,' was the opinion of Constable Gold. 'The way du Puy lived could not have been sustained on air.'

'Recall we made a promise – you, I, Brise and de la Salle – not to trouble their lands for a period of six months.'

'And we will hold to that.' Gold got a look from Hawkwood then, one that sought to establish if the words spoken had been a question or a statement. Perhaps the nature of it helped form the next remark the younger man made, which was, 'Of course we must.'

'Or find that when we seek to exact money to promise inaction elsewhere, no one will believe it to be true.'

'And what we are owed?'

'The Pope will ransom his brother, he has no choice. I will demand one hundred and thirty thousand florins, which is a high price to pay for such a worthless specimen. But it is also the sum which is due to us as a payment for our services. In truth, Gregory will be getting his brother for free.'

Not wishing to travel with du Puy in tow, Hawkwood sent him under escort to Rimini and into the care of an old enemy, Galeotto Malatesta, who, for a percentage, would hold the cardinal until payment was made. The White Company, still technically in the employ of the papacy, now waited to see how Pope Gregory would react.

For once the Church of Rome was led by a pontiff of a decisive nature and one who was determined to recover the towns and cities he held to be his fiefs. Besides that he still had the power of his office; he was heir to St Peter and not one of the rebels was anything other than a member of his congregation.

The rulers of Florence were summoned to appear before him and they obeyed, doing so because their electors and citizens would not have it otherwise, pleading their case with useless eloquence. Excommunications followed as night follows day, the whole city being put under anathema. Worse for a trading society, all other Italian states were barred from engaging in business with this pariah and the manner in which that was rarely circumvented was testament to the power of religion.

Permission was given to seize Florentine assets and to enslave any citizen of the city resident elsewhere in the whole of Europe. This was too tempting for greedy entities that had happily accepted Florentine money to gain their liberty or so recently sent their flags to the city to join with that of the progenitor of the revolt. If effective, and it looked to be so, Florence would be ruined in a year.

Perugia received special attention as the 'dog that had returned to lick its own vomit from the paving stones'. People were commanded that to sell food to a Perugian was to invite eternal damnation and there too the citizens could also be enslaved. Genoa and Pisa were placed under anathema for seeking to continue their profitable trade with Florence on which their own prosperity depended.

For all the power the office of Pope gave Gregory, it did not return his displaced officials to their positions or bring in the revenues to which Avignon had grown accustomed. That would require force. As his agent to effect a reversal the Pope chose not a soldier – they could not be trusted to stay true – but Prince-Cardinal Robert of Geneva.

If many of his clerical peers were haughty – du Puy being an example – few could match Robert in his manner or his bloodline. He was a direct descendant of Louis VII of France, cousin to the Holy Roman Emperor Charles IV and brother of the Count of Geneva, both sons of the Count of Savoy. In his extended cousinage he straddled every royal house in Europe.

In his prime, Robert was a man certain of his destiny and sure that the glory of God was his to wield as he saw fit; anything he considered right was not to be gainsaid by those of lesser inheritance or intelligence, which in his mind encompassed everyone. Given unlimited licence to spend, his first act was to recruit from southern France eight thousand Breton mercenaries under Jean de Malestroit, a captain noted for his personal brutality, who led a set of mercenaries famed for despoliation and barbarity even among their own community.

Hawkwood was invited to join with them in what Robert saw as a crusade, with all that implied. Anyone who stood against them would be put to the sword and if they survived it would be in a landscape rendered unfit for human existence. No quarter would be given and nor would such a host expend a single florin in their progress. Italy must pay so Italy could once more be subjugated.

Assessing the nature of things put John Hawkwood in a quandary. Still owed a fortune by Avignon he was in a land in which the writ of the Church no longer ran. With that came the utter diminution of their revenues. Without the taxes levied how was he to be paid? Then there were the Bretons who were nothing like those under de la Salle, a small contingent over which he could exercise some control. With Malestroit he would be in the minority and both would be required to obey Robert of Geneva.

Besides those concerns he had worries about the White Company. Long gone was the homogeneity with which they had arrived in Italy. Death from wounds or disease, added to a modicum of desertion, had taken its toll on the numbers. Then there were men leaving with permission, unable to still soldier through age, infirmity or just weariness. These had seriously weakened his English base so the company, through ongoing recruitment, was now made up of many nationalities, which meant the discipline of old on which he had relied was no longer strong.

In a raid that devastated the lands around Bologna – they too having evicted their cardinal-governor and were thus fair game to a papal army – he had encountered too many disputes over booty, including one in which two of his captains were wounded trying to mediate. Even worse, he came across another pair arguing over who should have the body of a young virgin nun, seen as a special trophy – nuns always were.

That she would be ravished was not in doubt, only who would be the perpetrator. That she would suffer was also not in doubt, physically certainly but her spiritual life would probably likewise be destroyed: once a captain was finished with her she would be handed over to their men. Fresh of face and terrified, she was standing, crucifix in hand, praying to God either to be spared or to die, even pleading with Hawkwood for the means to avoid her certain fate.

He argued long and hard but was unable to facilitate a compromise with two intransigent men on whom he knew he would have to depend in future. Hawkwood took out his knife, having kissed her forehead and invoked God, and drove it up and into her heart, despatching her to meet the maker she so clearly worshipped. The contesting pair witnessed a solution that seemed worthy of Solomon. What they did not see was Hawkwood's personal confession and the misery and tears that went with it. That she died with her virginity intact and would surely enter paradise was not sufficient recompense.

Robert of Geneva had his host marching south from his imperial base, presenting such a threat to Pavia that Galeazzo Visconti let him through his lands unmolested, which alarmed a Florence that felt betrayed. If relations with Milan and Pavia had been far from cordial, the Visconti had always stood at the head of resistance to the Pope; now for the sake of their own skin they were prepared to allow the whole of Tuscany to suffer.

With no way to avoid the coming storm, Florence began to extract what it could from papal and ecclesiastical property. The many churches were stripped of anything of value, monasteries too, while what lands they owned were appropriated and sold to raise funds for defence.

Betrayal was likewise in the air; not all those who rebelled seemed sound and every city and town had an element within prepared to back the Church and open its gates to the coming invader. This was made more pressing by the news that Gregory had left Avignon and was returning to Rome, to use the power of his personal office to aid his armies in recovering papal possessions. Advised to make peace with Florence, Gregory responded that he would rather be flayed alive. There would be no compromise: either submit and suffer or stand and die.

'This is not what I want, Christopher.'

Surveying his encampment, John Hawkwood saw unrest where he had once had order. More troubling was the fact that his presence, once enough to quell the most deep-seated dispute, no longer had the same effect. Indeed, he did not feel he was fully in control of the company and neither was his constable.

'If you cannot make them mind you, Sir John,' Gold admitted, 'I am no substitute.'

'This is perhaps the way of our trade and inevitable. How can we ask such ruffians to behave? What I would not give to have back the men I led at Pont-Saint-Esprit.'

Christopher Gold had rarely seen his leader cast down. Hawkwood had always had the ability to be positive even when the situation seemed dire, something that seemed to fire his imagination to create unique ways to win anything from battles to skirmishes, employing tactics that often bemused his own men, never mind his enemies.

'But we must go on with what we have and join with Cardinal Robert and his Bretons. We will break camp in the morning and move to meet them at Cesena.'

One of the few towns to remain loyal to the Pope and situated north of Rimini, Cesena provided a perfect place for Robert to assemble his forces. Romagna was fertile and produced a famous crop of wine once praised by Pliny. The town also had a fortress set on the edge of a cliff which hung over the town dwellings, in which the prince-cardinal could be accommodated in the martial style to which he now aspired. His huge Breton host was encamped in the nearby, well-watered and rolling countryside.

Hawkwood, seeing that area as crowded and wishing to keep his men away from the bellicose Bretons – too great a proximity invited dispute and possibly serious bloodletting – chose to set up camp two leagues distant, in close enough proximity to his titular commander yet distant enough to work on re-imposing a sense of order in his company. Some men were deprived of their ranks, new marshals and corporals taking their place. It was hoped that in time, when they had bedded in, they would earn the respect necessary to exercise proper discipline.

The trouble that arose came almost as if it had been written as a biblical prophecy; a group of unruly Bretons sought a supply of meat in Cesena, but declined to pay for what they demanded. The butcher was unwilling to allow this and brandished his knives and cleavers to ensure no one took what they wanted. Raised voices attracted a crowd, all citizens of Cesena, who had quickly formed a deep detestation for the arrogance of these rogues from Brittany.

Perhaps if the mercenaries had not drawn their weapons it would have been resolved. But the threat of such violence had the locals running for their own arms, to reappear in numbers the Bretons could not hope to overcome. Pride precluded withdrawal and in the ensuing struggle the transgressors, who had demanded free meat, were slaughtered.

Suddenly the whole town was up in arms, with Robert of Geneva watching from the castle as his authority seemed to crumble away.

Once the call went out the remaining Bretons massed closer to the walls, while Hawkwood was summoned to bring the White Company to their support. Waiting outside he sent Gold in to find out what was happening, the news brought on his return heartening, for Hawkwood held that the Bretons, by their high-handed action, probably deserved their fate. If a papal army could only rely on two towns in the whole of north Italy, it made no sense to upset the citizens of one of them.

'A delegation went to the prince-cardinal. They offered to put aside their weapons if he promised no retribution.'

'And?' Hawkwood enquired, gazing from a hilltop into a town that looked very peaceful with the lazily rising smoke of fires. 'Has he agreed?'

'He requires that they surrender their arms to him and provide fifty hostages as a token of their future behaviour. Given that, he granted that the Bretons must remain outside the town and that for trade the vendors will go to them. Added to that they must pay for anything they require.'

'I never had him down for a peaceful solution. Somehow it does not suit the nature I have observed of either our leader or our Bretons.'

'He was said to be all mercy and it shows sagacity. Robert has a bigger task ahead. Cesena barely matters.'

'Muster the men, we will return to our camp. I sense nothing will happen to keep us here. You stay and follow when you are certain there is nothing to concern us.'

The White Company did not get far when an order arrived that they should turn back and take station outside the western gate to the town, Hawkwood to attend upon Robert immediately but discreetly.

'Any notions of what he is about?'

'None, Sir John, but I wonder if it will be as peaceful as you thought.'

Hawkwood took with him no more than a dozen of his own bodyguard. These were familiar faces all the way back to Brétigny and he felt comfortable in their presence. Given one side of the fort formed the outer defence of Cesena, sneaking in through a postern gate presented no difficulty. Soon he was in the presence of the prince-cardinal and what he observed was not the benign presence reported to him by Gold. This was a grandee in the throes of a spitting tantrum and he was demanding retribution.

'The Pope's army and they think they can take up arms against us at will? They must be taught a lesson and so must Italy. Let it be known far and wide what comes of challenging God's will.'

Robert was in a rare passion; there was the smell of drink on his breath and to Hawkwood's mind he had lost sight of reality. He was invoking the will of God when it was his pride that was wounded. He needed to calm down and consider how best to act.

'My Lord, have the population not given in to your every demand? If it is not enough, tell me what is and I will go and ensure they meet your wishes.'

'I want justice, Hawkwood!'

The prince-cardinal was so close, and so venomous was his shout that the Englishman had to use a hand to ward off his expectorated saliva, which was as well for he spat out more.

'No! Blood and justice. Arrange your men outside the western gate and await my orders. Malestroit already has his waiting to get their revenge and he will enter north and south as soon as darkness falls.'

'To frighten the recalcitrant?'

'To chastise them! Let the world see what happens to a rebellious town. A demonic fate will fall upon their heads as it should and I shall pray for their souls to rot.'

'If you let loose the Bretons on the city there will be a massacre.'

'There will be divine retribution. Now do as I command.'

About to argue Hawkwood felt a tug at his sleeve, which was unobserved. Robert had turned away and was fulminating at his own retinue in a like manner to which he had harangued his mercenary general. A low voice with a strong Welsh accent whispered:

'You will not change a mind like that, now will you? Best be far and decide what you will and will not do away from his gaze.'

Hawkwood spun on his heels and left, his mind racing, for he reckoned to have a good notion of what was likely to follow, knowing the Breton reputation and having seen what had happened when Prince Edward let loose his English–Gascon army on the French city of Limoges. That had been an exercise in terror, designed to cow any other municipality that in future thought to stand against him and it had been sickening. By the time he got back to his own lines Hawkwood had decided he wanted no part of what would likely come to Cesena – the level of punishment did not fit the perceived crime.

He made his opinion plain, but now the lack of discipline showed in all its devilish form. The word soon spread of what Robert of Geneva intended and it was obvious that a large number of his men were unwilling to leave the sack of Cesena and the loot that would accrue from it to the Bretons, news of this brought to his pavilion.

'It pains me to say you will face outright mutiny,' Gold advised him. 'Stop those eager to take part and White Company could be no more.'

It was a reluctant commander who was obliged to let every man make his own choice, his only consolation being that he would not partake in what was inevitable. Hawkwood was left with only those around him who held to the previous loyalty. For the rest, they could not wait and once the horns had been sounded they rushed through the gates of Cesena to carry out the wishes of Robert of Geneva.

The slaughter lasted three days and, by the time exhaustion brought it to an end, there was not a living soul in Cesena and the surrounding villages outside those who had raped, pillaged and murdered men, women and children. Many they had also been tortured to find the hidden treasure they were sure existed. Sir John Hawkwood only entered the town when it was over, to kick hard the comatose and blood-soaked bodies of the men he led, drunk from butchery and wine so near insensible to the pain. The White Company must be brought back to its duty and if he felt disgust then that must be hidden.

Only a fear of disease afforded the unfortunates a burial, many bodies being dragged from the town moat and the nearby streams to be thrown into mass graves. If the Pope's prince-cardinal wished to send a message to Italy he succeeded; the news of the annihilation of Cesena spread fast, but the effect was not all that he had hoped. The result was revulsion, not fear. If the Church had been despoiled in what was an interregnum it had still been left with much property and wealth. Enraged citizens all over Tuscany and Lombardy turned on what was left.

Christopher Gold often wondered if it was that disgust which turned Hawkwood against serving the Pope, though he was careful to keep his severance a mystery. All he ever got in response when he sought to find out was that Gregory had yet to pay the White Company. The dishonourable rogue had not even ransomed his own brother.

# CHAPTER TWENTY-THREE

He was owed a fortune in monies; the Pope, like the Visconti, tended to pay John Hawkwood in properties rather than cash. On the face of it this seemed generous, yet it was more of a drag on his finances than an asset. Every gift was in need of substantial repair as well as upkeep and he had his company to maintain as well, though that had shrunk somewhat due to the sudden defection of Thornbury with several hundred lances.

This led to a serious consideration that he might give it all up and return to England, where he owned several properties paid for over the years by money sent back through various Italian bankers. He had even gone so far as to petition King Edward for a pardon, his crime the very freebooting that had made him what wealth he had. In the distorted world of mercenary warfare his sovereign could not be seen to support the likes of Sir John Hawkwood or Robert Knowles in their activities.

If he encouraged the ravaging of the property of the King of France it was supposed to be covert, even if no one was fooled; the Treaty of Brétigny, until Edward himself repudiated it, had expressly forbidden his soldiers to stay in France, an offence in itself to which was added the threat of dire punishment for acts of plunder.

Gratifyingly, no doubt due to his efforts on behalf of the King's late son, he stood in high regard in London. Held up only by the constraints of time and distance, his pardon was soon in his possession and since the Pope was even more behind with payments and the idea of continuing to serve under Robert of Geneva was not one to relish, he began to look for a way to terminate his papal service.

The offer that dissuaded John Hawkwood from leaving Italy surprised everyone and he was no exception. It came from something he had never thought possible: a community of interests between Florence and Milan. Bernabò Visconti had formed an anti-papal league to ward off the attempts of Pope Gregory to reinforce the rule of the Church in Lombardy. Given Florence was fighting the same forces as Milan in Tuscany, neither of the two greatest powers in Italy had anything to fear from each other; if it was far from an alliance, it was an unspoken truce.

As ever, both probed John Hawkwood to see if he would serve their city but it was Milan that won his support. The messengers that came from Bernabò invited the most famous *condottiere* in Italy to take command of his forces, but this time the offer was not just of money: Hawkwood was offered the hand in marriage of Bernabò's natural daughter, Donnina, as a way of binding him to the Milanese cause.

'Too good to be true, Christopher?'

'The Lord of Milan has a large brood and even with their wealth I cannot see a royal hand being offered for one of his bastard children. Such alliances are reserved for the legitimate.'

'So an old freebooter like myself will do?'

'You know I don't mean that, Sir John. As to its advantages, they are obvious.'

Hawkwood did not have to be advised on that; he would be allying himself to the most powerful man in Italy and not just in the way he had previously, by a money bond. If he would not be in receipt of the kind of gifts showered on Prince Lionel, the hand of the Lady Donnina would come with a substantial dowry. It was no secret that in terms of affection, Bernabò did not differentiate between those born within and without wedlock. Even his wife Beatrice treated all the children equally in what was a ménage that occasioned much wonder.

The notion that he, the younger landless son of an Essex tenant farmer, should rise so high was too like a dream, for if John Hawkwood did not lack ambition his aim had never encompassed anything so extraordinary. The title of Captain General of the Host of the Anti- Papal League sounded grand, but he would be more than that, while it did not escape the recipient of such good fortune that perhaps the Lord of Milan wanted him for his political connections in England as much as his sword arm.

'Dammit, Christo, she's only just seen her seventeenth summer.'

'Sir John,' was the sarcastic reply, delivered with a knowing smile, 'please be aware that I am jealous enough already.'

The age difference meant he could be her grandfather, given Antiocha was four times a mother now. Indeed her husband, Sir William Coggeshall, a knight from a prominent Essex family, had come out to serve with him and bring him news of his grandchildren. That presence alone showed how much his stature had already changed back home; wait until news of this new development reached their ears!

Prior to his moving north, the news spread that Edward of England had passed away, his Woodstock heir having predeceased him. The throne was now occupied by the Prince of Wales' ten-year-old son Richard, the second of that name. Ever faithful, Hawkwood, joined by all of his English freebooters, attended a special Mass to pray for the late king's soul.

It was hard to be disconsolate with what was in prospect and when Hawkwood saw his intended bride for the first time it near took his breath away: she was as beautiful as her mother had been when she first attracted Bernabò's wandering eye. It was commonly the case that dynastic unions did not always provide beautiful brides: drawing from a small princely blood pool was more important than comeliness.

But Bernabò, who had favoured many a mistress with his insatiable appetites, never chose badly and Donnina de'

Porri, the mother of five of his natural children had, at one time, been famed throughout Lombardy for her loveliness. Naturally there was nervousness and Hawkwood insisted on meeting the young Donnina with her mother prior to the nuptials, wondering what impression she got of him. Before the seventeen-year-old stood a man coming up fifty-seven. He was also a warrior who wore the scars of his hard service on his face and on his seriously calloused hands.

Where she was slim and graceful, with soft skin, he was stocky and muscular enough to feel a trifle gross. He had the shoulders of a soldier, broad, with limbs made hefty from wielding his sword and hauling on his heavy bowstring. Where her voice was musical his seemed gruff, yet Hawkwood observed no reluctance on her part. She conversed with him easily and without any maidenly shyness, bestowing smiles on him that lifted his spirits.

Donnina's father knew what his putative son-in-law must have: property and revenues enough to keep his daughter in the state in which she had been raised. These were gifted, but that was not all. Sir John Hawkwood was able to write back to his young sovereign and John of Gaunt, his guardian uncle, that his wife had been granted the Castle of Pessano as well as many other valuable properties, the costs to be borne by the state. On the day of the wedding, Donnina would come to him with a dowry of twelve thousand gold ducats.

That was mere icing; the gifts poured in from well-wishers as well as Donnina's mother and Beatrice Visconti. His son-in-law Coggeshall, seated in a positon that acknowledged his relationship to the groom, presented him with a cup of silver, filigreed with gold, while many a noble neighbour and Milanese merchant saw it as politic to gift the newly elevated Hawkwood something of real value. He would remember, but more importantly, so would his father-in-law.

There was one absentee in brother Galeazzo, but he could be forgiven because he was crippled by gout. In truth, Pavia was being run by his son who was proving to be a far better administrator than a soldier, but Giangaleazzo too was missing from both wedding and feast while the lack of any form of gift that would welcome John Hawkwood to the extended Visconti family stood out starkly. If the point was not mentioned it was noted by the bridegroom and put away as an insult not to be forgotten, quickly buried by what was to come.

Hearing his young, coiffed bride answer firmly when asked if she would take him for a husband removed the last residue of concern while the feast that followed the nuptials was near enough a rival to that given to Prince Lionel. It lifted John Hawkwood's heart and he did his part, arranging entertainments at the house he had been given: jousting, jugglers, tumblers and a jester who did not hesitate to make salacious puns about what was about to follow.

The bedchamber, after the raucous nature of the latter part of the day, seemed unnaturally quiet, the only sound being the murmuring and suppressed giggles of the ladies preparing their charge for bed. These girls, none older than Donnina, were her lifelong friends, companions with whom she had been raised, and the talk of conjugality was not something fresh but a subject much raised between them ever since they had come to womanhood.

He found it absurd at his age that he felt so nervous. He had first lain with Antiocha's mother over forty years before when still not much more than a lad. It had been a rare day since that he had not had a bed mate of the likes of Aalis of Pont-Saint-Esprit, and if she had fathered his son she was not the only one. In every place he had laid his head since there had always been someone to warm his mattress, so in terms of experience he was way ahead of his bride.

What Hawkwood did not know was the preparations Donnina's mother had made for this moment, later revealed when they were comfortable together in married estate. She had advised her daughter that while that which came first would be painful, what would follow should be undertaken for pleasure. Donnina was also told that she must ignore any strictures from her confessor about what constituted proper couplings, things which the Church saw as sinful, which was almost anything they could put a name to.

Donnina's friends finished their tasks, curtsied and departed with their secret smiles. She emerged, hair no longer dressed but loose and in a flowing diaphanous garment through which, in the candlelight, he could see indications of her flesh and most certainly her dark nipples and a hint of pubic hair. He had to suppress the urge to rush to take her while suddenly the coat of brocade that he had donned to greet her in modesty felt stifling.

In consideration of her blushes and his much scarred body he blew out most of the candles, leaving only one, sufficient to light them to the side of the bed. There with gentle hands he divested Donnina of her flimsy gown and himself of his coat, before easing her slowly back.

The four days that followed came close to bliss for in his new bride he found no delicate flower, which had Hawkwood wondering how much she took after her parents. Her mother was lusty and her father Bernabò rated as a satyr. She took to carnality with little reserve and an eagerness for experience that surprised him, even with his garnered knowledge. They feasted well, took to their bed frequently and laughed often and long, which had Hawkwood feeling as if the years he carried had dropped away.

'How many of the Church's rules have we broken, sweet one?' he asked on the fourth night.

'Not enough,' came her reply with a throaty laugh.

'It is Sunday.'

'Which will make the sin special, Husband.'

'And the penance?'

She threw him backwards with a surprising degree of strength before straddling him, her intent plain and the notion that it was a sin in the eyes of the Church ignored.

'I look to you for that.'

'Two transgressions at once. Truly you are a fit wife for a freebooter.'

On the fifth day duty called; he was not only the Milanese captain general, he was now bound to the Visconti by marriage, so their enemies and rivals had become his. But first he must secure the properties given to him in the Romagna by the Pope, in one of which he would install his bride, for he had no notion to set up home too close to Bernabò. To act properly he required a degree of independence and Hawkwood's experience of non-military folk was that they interfered, and not to the good.

His property at Cotignola was in poor condition but it was a fief that provided a decent revenue, so it was worth restoration. The coast south of Rimini was a place of salt pans, and given most of the markets for that essential commodity were to the west of him he could extract valuable tolls to allow passage along his roads. Given such revenues it had to be fortified so they could be protected.

Another property at nearby Bagnacavallo already had stout walls in decent repair, though they would have to be strengthened, and it was here he would take up residence. Now he had a wife and she must have somewhere safe to live. Given the accommodation was at present primitive, it was also a place for her to exercise wifely skills and turn into a proper home.

Had the Bretons stayed as a host, life for Hawkwood would have been difficult, but they were as fractious as they were barbaric and in Robert of Geneva they had an overall leader for whom they had scant respect; his manner did not permit that he be loved or held in regard. The prince-cardinal's problem was that in a country in the grip of near anarchy, in which the possibility for plunder was plentiful, groups of his army had begun to ignore the papal cause and split off to seek their fortune.

This led to a very fragmented war as Hawkwood led his men to wherever he could find these Bretons and if he had the numbers, he set out to force a withdrawal; where they outnumbered him it came down to wily manoeuvring to keep them confused and he had any number of fortified places into which he could withdraw. In addition, they too were struggling to be paid by a papacy that had lost the revenues by which such a force could be sustained. This left them low on supplies while their enemies, backed by nearly every town north and east of Rome, suffered no such constraints.

In what would be a war of attrition Hawkwood saw no need to overly expose those he commanded. Aware that the Bretons were moving towards Siena he masked their movements. When they besieged Grosseto he was content to set up a near permanent camp so as to keep their progress under observation. It was there he was called upon by the emaciated Catherine of Siena, come to beg him to return to the service of the Church.

What Hawkwood saw was a strange creature but not a unique one, even if Catherine saw herself as such. The world in which he moved was full of those who were sure they were closer to God than mere mortals and could interpret his wishes in a way that brooked no dissent. In her purity – she drank only water and ate hardly at all, while being given to self-mortification – Catherine sought to persuade Hawkwood that her mission was his. She required him to help broker a peace between Florence and Rome, for both sides were approaching exhaustion and in what way would that serve the Almighty?

That he did not commit himself seemed not to affect Catherine's certainties. Within weeks he received a request from Rome to allow ambassadors to call upon him, which required that he seek for them safe conduct across the territory of Siena, as much under interdiction as most of the Italian cities and likely to string them up without such documents. They too spoke of peace with Milan and Florence and indicated that the famous and feared Sir John Hawkwood was the man to bring it about.

Aware of how such matters could be seen, Hawkwood was careful to keep Bernabò informed. But he also wrote to Florence to tell them what he was being pressured to do, adding he was willing to arbitrate to secure a truce if that was what the Eight Saints who ran the city wished. The rebuff was swift; in effect he was told to stick to his profession of arms and leave such matters to those better qualified to pursue it, given Gregory had previously demanded three million florins in payment for their sins as well as many other draconian disbursements and these he would not soften.

'They are fools,' was the opinion of Christopher Gold. 'They could negotiate and get better terms. Gregory too is on his knees.'

'They are afraid, and not just of Gregory. If they see me negotiating they do not think it is on their behalf but on that of Milan. So see it from where they sit. Bernabò makes peace with the Pope and they then become the place threatened, this time by a combination of Gregory and Bernabò.'

'Talk of strange bedfellows.'

'I don't doubt the Pope would hand Florence over to Milan to bring this folly to an end. No one in Italy trusts their neighbour and certainly they do not trust anyone seen as a rival. They expect to be betrayed.'

'Which I say is what they so often are.'

'Thank the Lord for it, otherwise we would be paupers.'

If the offer of the hand of Donnina had come as a surprise, what came from Florence was close to equalling that. It was nothing less than an invitation for Sir John Hawkwood and those men he saw fit to bring with him to visit Florence, where he would be greeted with all the honour due to his rank. His wife was visiting him when he got the request, come to tell him he was to be a father, which barely seemed to penetrate his thinking.

'I sat outside those damned gates fifteen years ago and have done so many times since. If I had a florin for every arrow I sent over the walls I could buy the place.'

'Are they more important to you than what I carry in my belly, Husband? Arrows?'

The admonition might be gently delivered yet it was firm. John Hawkwood had already found out that Donnina was her own person. She was dutiful but not meek, while her lack of years did not prevent her from checking him when she thought it right to do so. This had happened in the manner of repairs to the mansion that they would call home. He had left behind plans of what he wanted; she had changed them without reference to him and that which she wanted cost twice as much.

'You know I cherish that, Donnina, but Florence and I have a long association.'

'Not one in which you are favoured.'

'This said as you spend the pension they give me on furbelows.'

'You would deny me a fit place to raise our child?'

'My sweet, I would not deny you anything.' As he said that Donnina began to smile, but that was cut short by the addition. 'Because even if I do you would fail to obey me.'

'If I do it is only for the best.'

'And may it ever be so,' he said, taking her hand and kissing her. 'Now you must look to the duty you owe a husband who has been too long parted from you.'

Donnina would not accompany him to Florence, her stated reason being that she saw the city as an enemy of her family and nor did she think they would welcome her presence. What she kept hidden was her real reason which was not to distract him from something he found so precious, for entry into the city he had fought so often would be a moment to savour and not one to share. Fears of being shunned, of being bought off to spare their lands while Florence had held him at arm's length, would fade away, so she went home while he rode into the valley of the Arno.

'How long before they seek to engage your service?'

Hawkwood threw back his head and laughed at Gold's question. 'I daresay not long after the first goblet of wine.'

It took longer than he supposed due to the depth of the welcome. He entered a city decorated with flags and banners, the streets lined with a cheering population, which was mystifying given the miseries he had visited upon them in the last fifteen years. The entire *Signoria* was outside the palace of the Archbishop of Florence to greet him and the celebrations lasted three full days, with endless parades organised by the various guilds as well as a palio in which each had a horse competing in their gaudy colours while an extra mount and rider, both excellent, was included in his.

For years the name of Sir John Hawkwood had been used to frighten Florentine children into going to bed. Now the ogre was in their midst and an object of deep curiosity, as were his famous English bowmen. Everywhere they went, and that included the area of prostitution, his men were followed by the lower orders and being in a benign frame of mind they were happy to engage in many a conversation, for the English and the Florentines had a deep shared interest.

The most famous and profitable export from Florence was cloth and that depended on a regular supply of English wool, the staple of government revenues in Hawkwood's homeland. As much came to Italy as went to Flanders and the artisan quarters of the city of Florence contained the carders, weavers and dyers on which prosperity depended.

The Florentines could not know that the captain general had expressly encouraged these exchanges. From the skilled citizens of the city he would find out that which their leaders would wish to keep hidden, and that was the state of morale outside palaces and banking houses, for there he was exposed to much wooing. He remained immune to the offers hinted at, non-committal so that he did not cause offence, but when he was with those he trusted, he was regaled with tales of grievance.

The war had gone on too long and cost too much; the artisans' trade had halved or worse. The city needed peace and a revival of normal trade, as well as an end to the forced loans and taxations that were ruining their lives.

'They open up all confident and damn Gregory,' said the

Radish, 'but it ain't long afore their true thoughts are aired and the poorer they are the quicker it happens.'

'Ivor?'

'The same, I found.'

Christopher Gold had met a higher class of citizen – merchants, not artisans – but even there he saw their confidence as false, a mask to seduce the English Company to fight on their side and even there doubt existed as to the certainty such an association would prevail.

'They want peace, Sir John.'

'Which is the opposite of what they tell me.' A questioning look. 'Never fear, Christopher, I am no more deceived than you.'

'So?'

'We leave and wish them well. I must go to Bagnacavallo to see my wife and take her the gifts I have received, which I see as much more suited to a wife than a warrior. You take our men back to the encampment at San Quirico and, barring an emergency, I will join you in a few weeks.'

What had become known as the war of the Eight Saints could not go on; everyone was exhausted and the monies expended were taking all parties except Milan close to penury. A conference was called at a town called Sarzana and there, after much deliberation, a sort of peace was agreed – a good one for Milan, but a possibly ruinous one for Bernabò's erstwhile ally Florence.

The world was so dangerous for the papal envoys that they required Sir John Hawkwood and his company to escort them to the conference, and if he was bystander in what followed he was nevertheless an interested one; what transpired might affect his immediate and long-term future.

The Pope was not willing to moderate the terms of his previous demands and the Florentine envoys would have refused to settle if the Visconti had shown them the slightest sign of support. What they got was sweet words and no more, so the matter seemed settled.

'It is far from that,' was Hawkwood's opinion, expressed to his close band of old friends. 'I sense a pause, no more. They will be at each other's throats within the year. For us – well, Milan has us contracted, so let us go and find who Bernabò has in his greedy gaze now.'

# CHAPTER TWENTY-FOUR

Nothing defined Sir John Hawkwood's new status more than the emissary from London, who came to his encampment at Monzambano before he went near the Visconti court, arriving with half a dozen other officials and an armed escort. The object of the embassy was to explore the possibility of a marriage between King Richard II and Caterina, the daughter of Bernabò and Beatrice Visconti. If there was an oddity, it lay in the fact that Hawkwood was busy fighting Beatrice's Scaliger family, who ruled Verona, on behalf of Bernabò.

Charged with presenting this proposal was Geoffrey Chaucer, who had risen from the clerkish role he had occupied previously. Chaucer had met Hawkwood as part of Prince Lionel's retinue and had progressed in the interim to what he was now, a fully-fledged ambassador trusted with the most sensitive of assignments. The reason for the proposal was quickly explained and there was no attempt at subterfuge: matters in the conflict with France had not gone well and had cost much. If that was true for either side the fact was that young King Richard now oversaw an empty treasury.

'It is known that the Visconti sees his legitimate daughters as fit for dukes and counts. We propose a sovereign that must tempt him, for in Richard there is a handsome prince in need of a bride.'

'And a dowry!' Hawkwood exclaimed.

'Of course. He asks that you, known to be a faithful servant of his crown, act to investigate if such a suit would be welcome.'

'I see you wish to proceed cautiously.'

'A rebuff publicly known would do little for King Richard's prestige. He is young and as yet without a reputation to match that of his sire.'

'And a refusal would favour his uncle of Gaunt even less.'

'The Duke of Lancaster had placed much hope in this.'

Within that reply lay a tangled web of the same kind of intrigue that troubled Italy. In producing so many children – even if he had lost several – King Edward had left behind him a set of competing interests and at the heart of that lay the boy king, who would soon come upon his true inheritance as a ruler. Whom would he favour, John of Gaunt, who had acted as his regent, or Gaunt's brother Edmund, the Duke of York? That was beside the point to Hawkwood; what was proposed carried a degree of wisdom.

'It is my duty to do what I can.'

'I thank you, Sir John, on behalf of His Grace our King.'

'Your men are being taken care of?' A nod. 'Then now you must dine with me.'

'And find out the state of affairs in this part of the world, perhaps?'

That got a very loud laugh. 'Such an explanation would take weeks, Mr Chaucer.'

'I learn quickly, Sir John.'

'So I seem to recall.'

The soldier had never quite felt comfortable in Chaucer's presence, even though they had much in common, which got them through the meal that followed. Both had served in King Edward's Crécy campaign and had met, though not intimately mingled, when the previous Plantagenet marriage had been in the process of completion. The man was clever, if anything too much so for the 'old freebooter', able to reference things that never entered the world of a mercenary; poetry, endless allusions to classical history and the writing of the Greeks and Romans, though Hawkwood could hold his own on the military aspects. On his last visit he had spent much of his time in the Visconti library, which housed many a rare book and would no doubt do so again if the opportunity presented itself.

Chaucer was personable enough but with a tendency to wear his erudition on his sleeve. Also, he had about him a slightly sly way of looking when he sensed that something he referred to was a mystery to the listener. Then there were his interrogations, which is what Hawkwood saw them as and he knew he was not alone. The man was forever asking questions about the captain general's past and his recent exploits. It made little difference that he did it to everyone. He seemed to have a facility to remember everything that was said; it was as if he was storing things up for future use, and that could be uncomfortable.

Private reservations had to be put to the side; Hawkwood was needed as an intermediary to broach the prospect of a royal marriage, the man entrusted to test the waters of Bernabò Visconti's feelings on the matter. The ruler of Milan, famed already for his outrageous temper, had not grown mellow with advancing years; indeed he had become worse, the only person who could calm him being his wife.

Added to his rages he had come to a feeling that he need bend the knee to no man and no power; the travails of the papacy, with the whole of northern Italy opposing it rather than just the Visconti, added to the fact that his leadership was acknowledged, swelled a head already too large for much sense to easily prevail.

Besides, and he had kept this from Chaucer, they had a relationship that rested on many uncertainties: the happy estate following his marriage to Donnina had not lasted. As ever, Hawkwood had to argue constantly to get paid what was due to him, as well as explain to a man rarely prepared to listen that to carry out the duties he wanted from the English Company required more lances, which naturally would incur more expense.

Bernabò was always demanding the impossible and would not accept that to go into battle against a superior enemy or overcome city walls without the numbers and equipment required was to risk destruction. As for the Anti-Papal League that seemed in abeyance since the death of Pope Gregory; Bernabò was too busy trying to take power and land away from his neighbours.

It was that temper that persuaded Hawkwood to approach Beatrice first and let her present the subject to Bernabò, for she would do it gently. She engaged her husband enough to agree first to meet Chaucer and then that a return embassy should go back to London with him for further talks.

With his typical swings of mood Bernabò, who at first seemed lukewarm on the marriage proposal, began increasingly to favour it, to the point that he saw it as part of his destiny. He would ask for an English army, with which he could crush every one of his opponents in Lombardy and Tuscany. Wild-eyed sometimes and frequently drunk he would talk in a way that hinted at imperial pretensions.

Meanwhile his captain general, on short commons to his mind, must continue his soldiering and seek ways to nullify Verona, as well as follow his employer's designs on neighbouring Mantua, this on a shoestring. The aim, while still fighting the Scaliger family, was to prick the man who now ruled Mantua, Ludovico Gonzaga, into a reaction that would justify war. The Mantuan tyrant proved too wily to enter the snare.

He was cautious of the strength of Milan, as well as the abilities of Hawkwood, and even if incursions into his territory irked him he responded with no more than written complaints. To these Hawkwood replied with surprised innocence, while listing infractions by Gonzaga's subjects in which he had been deprived of cattle and horses in what became an ongoing and lengthy correspondence, a game in which both men took some pleasure in trying to deceive each other.

The other matter that engaged Hawkwood was the ransoming of his one-time brigade captain, John Thornbury, who had deserted him and ridden off to seek service, as well as personal profit, elsewhere without prior warning when he had been needed. Captured in a running fight he was now a prisoner and where there had once been friendship and trust there was that no more, just a price that must be found for the release of a man seen by John Hawkwood to have betrayed him.

Meanwhile a new pope had been elected, taking the name Urban VI. It was said he had been forced on the College of Cardinals by the population of Rome, who had noisily demanded an Italian pontiff instead of another Frenchman. Since Gregory had changed the rules from a unanimous vote to a majority one, the missing cardinals in Avignon had no chance to interfere, there being enough in the Holy City to grant Urban the mitre.

'He's a peasant,' was Bernabò's verdict on the one time Archbishop of Naples. 'Never even a cardinal. Lord knows what his noble peers will make of him.'

Not a great deal, seemed to be the conclusion, this far from aided by the reported attitude Urban adopted to the men who had elected him. He castigated them for their luxuries and lax morality, even to the point of ordering them to have only one meal a day, to dispose forthwith of their mistresses and to surrender the multiple benefices from which they accumulated their wealth.

Bernabò proved correct on his antecedents: Urban came from the slums of Naples and had crawled up the hierarchy until he had drawn the attention of the woman who became his champion, the Neapolitan Queen Joanna. It was she who had favoured his further progress. Milanese spies took great pleasure in describing him to their master, who was just as eager to tell Hawkwood what he knew.

'They say his temper is uncontrollable.'

'A terrible fault,' was Hawkwood's reply, the irony in his tone completely missed.

'I am told he has even physically attacked some of his cardinals and he regularly tells his Romans of their faults, so they are pelted with rotten fruit in the streets and need armed guards at their residences.'

The news arriving next, that a section of cardinals had declared the election void, set more than Milan buzzing with speculation. In another vote a different man was elevated to the papacy, none other than the Prince-Cardinal Robert of Geneva, who took the name Clement.

'Urban being from the alleyways of Naples makes sense,' Hawkwood opined. 'Clement for Robert of Geneva? The man has not an ounce of compassion in him.'

'Or humility,' was Gold's assessment. 'But who will come out on top? We cannot have two popes.'

'Robert has his Bretons, or what is left of them and they hold the Castel Sant'Angelo. Urban has the people of Rome, but I will favour the man with proper soldiers. For us, Christopher, it means little: we have our own work to do and we must hope two men in the same office will makes things easier.'

If it complicated everything for the Church the effect for Hawkwood was positive. Robert of Geneva – few were prepared to use his papal name – was a scion of France. England being that nation's enemy, they naturally backed Urban, so the document that came to Milan, with the Great Seal of England waxed on the base, appointed Sir John Hawkwood as King Richard's Ambassador to the Holy See, which meant Rome, not Avignon.

Was it that which made so cool the relations between Bernabò and his son-in-law? Hawkwood had no real idea. It could be the proposed marriage negotiations with King Richard, which had come to naught, causing the Visconti dreams to be shattered. Why this would be his captain general's fault could not be fathomed or made sense of, but the Lord of Milan was rarely capable of that these days.

Ever in a court full of rumour and gossip, the complaints Bernabò was now openly making about Hawkwood and his efforts on behalf of Milan reached his ears. The campaign against Verona was not being pressed hard enough. Why was that? Hawkwood was in endless correspondence with Gonzaga. Was he preparing to betray Milan to Mantua and Verona? When could these mercenaries ever be trusted not to change sides for money?

It was likely in one of those ungovernable rages that he issued a decree saying that he would pay a goodly sum in florins to anyone who would kill a member of the English Company, an outburst he might regret in sober reflection but that was not to be trusted. Hawkwood knew the beast within him too well. He had fought against him and for him and his brother, while being often left to wonder which was worse. At the same time he had no faith that his marriage bind would protect him.

'Sir William, take your lances to Bagnacavallo and put my property in a state of defence. I also ask that you protect my wife and daughter as you would look to your own.' He then passed over a rolled parchment to Coggeshall. 'I have written to ask Mantua that you be given safe conduct and that has been here provided.'

'Am I allowed to ask for an explanation, Sir John?'

'Matters in Milan are in an uncertain state. Let us say that I would not wish to have to seek to rescue or pay for the freedom of my family.'

William Coggeshall had been in Milan long enough to know it was a febrile place but the implications of what his father-in-law was saying clearly shocked him. It implied a break.

'Please do as I request, William, and trust that I know of what I speak. All you are required to do is hold Bagnacavallo until I arrive, which will be very shortly after I find it is in any danger.'

Christopher Gold, now Constable General of the English Company, had to be informed of what was about to happen, nothing less than that Hawkwood would detach himself and his company from Milanese service.

'We cannot fight while ever looking over our shoulder. Bernabò wishes for Verona to be crushed but will not provide the money to recruit the necessary lances, while stirring up trouble with the Gonzaga.'

'I have had to, in your absence, buy grain from Mantua.'

'With the funds of the company, and there's the rub. Our men deserve their pay and my pockets are not deep enough to sustain what is being expended. When Bernabò gifted me all those properties in Romagna he saddled me with a bottomless pit. The revenues do not cover the costs. I will keep them, for one is my family home, but to do so I must find a way to earn more for we cannot depend on Milan.'

To explain that to someone like Gold was easy; the person he was worried about was his wife, who would scarce take well the news that he had fallen out with her father to the point of a breach. Heavily with child and already with one infant girl, Donnina still made his heart skip a beat and that brought on hesitation and an attempt at distraction.

'Has Coggeshall seen to his duties?'

'He would not wish to face you, Husband, if he did not.'

'Am I such an ogre that even the husband of my daughter fears me?' Standing over the cradle in which his infant child slept he ran a gentle finger down her soft cheek, which made her stir but not wake. 'Antiocha has four girls I have never seen. I have two sons I know of who were both born to their mothers when I had moved on and I could walk past them with ease, for I do not know them except by letter. Janet here is the first of my children I have gazed on.'

'Then she is blessed.'

'Is she, to have a father so full of years he may not last long enough to give her away as a bride?'

'You are melancholy, Husband.'

He smiled and indicated the cot. 'You do not see me as happy?'

'I sense that there is something you wish to tell me.'

That furrowed his brow; Hawkwood was proud of his ability to mask his feelings, a very necessary attribute when dealing with those he led as well as the men he did business with.

'I am bound to ask why you say that.'

'Allow a wife to see her man better than others. Allow her to ask why William Coggeshall is here with sixty lances and why his men guard the walls of our property with such vigilance. That can only come about because you fear someone and I am enough of a Visconti to guess who that might be.'

'Your father no longer trusts me.'

'My father trusts no one.'

'It may be worse than that. I sent Coggeshall here to ensure he did not seek to use you against me.'

'You think I would oppose you?'

A man does not have to be married to a woman for too long, or spend much time in her intimate company, to quickly see when his words have offended. If Donnina had a beautiful brow it was one that could furrow quickly to produce a look that put Hawkwood on edge. Tempted to remind her of his authority as her husband, which in the eyes of the Church and society was absolute, he refrained. She had a temper that was hereditary and the ability to shift the point of argument to ensure he could never feel he had won.

'I would hope and pray not.'

'You are my husband and the father of my child.' Her hand was on her belly but the second blessing would not be alluded to with childbirth so full of risk. 'When we were married I left the bond I had with my father and entered into one with you and that is made sacrosanct by the vows I took.'

'You would not, then, take Bernabò's part against me?'

'It offends that you should even ask. But I would like to be told of what has occurred.'

Donnina listened in silence to him, but acute observation of the small facial movements around the eyes showed there was a degree of pain in what she was hearing. The notion that her father would welcome the death of her husband was particularly hard to disguise, but it was equally plain she had no illusion about his capability to arrange such a thing. But Hawkwood needed to say more.

'If I were to say to you that trust is essential in such a bond as I have with Milan, you might well laugh. It is not a virtue usually uttered in the same breath as what I do. But I can say to you that I have never deserted a man or his cause who met his pledge, yet this is not the first time your father and I have had disputes over payment. My worry is that now I have you. If he were to act in a way I fear, there is little I could do but give way to anything he demanded of me.'

The slight frown she had worn while listening lifted. 'Why, that sounds like a declaration of love.'

'If you do not know that is the emotion I feel then I am a poor husband, Donnina.'

'Everyone I spoke to before we wed said you were

incapable of love. That you had a warrior's heart and it could not hold such a sentiment.'

'Did you not think to ask me?'

'That would not have been fitting.'

'And now?'

'You hide much, John Hawkwood, for I sense you must, but not from me. I see you as no other does, when we lay together with only the moon to light our talk. If I know little of men, I do know that that is where the real soul of one is revealed.'

# CHAPTER TWENTY-FIVE

Slowly, so as not to cause alarm, Hawkwood withdrew his
lances east into the Romagna, closer to where he and his
family resided, made peaceful overtures to Mantua, then
waited to see how Bernabò would react. With him seemingly
quiescent he could set about the business of raiding and
plundering in Tuscany, allying himself to a German, also a
son-in-law of Bernabò, their combined force a formidable
twelve hundred lances.

For two years their successes were measured in thousands
of florins, though as usual much was expended on keeping
the company whole, while Hawkwood had personal
overheads that needed to be met, such as protecting his
home, which meant a strong garrison permanently based

at Bagnacavallo. Just as much went to support his other properties against anything that might threaten them, which meant his father-in-law.

He was not without information of what was taking place in Lombardy, such as the death of Galeazzo, naturally replaced as ruler by his son Giangaleazzo who, it was reported, had become exceedingly pious, surrounding himself with priests, carrying a rosary everywhere, praying frequently and dressing without show. Such news extended from gossip written by old friends to Donnina, through whispers brought by passing travellers, to downright betrayal of the Visconti family, who like any Italian rulers had many internal enemies though the family were better at suppression than most of their rivals.

When he was home he was plagued by the usual supplicants needing aid, men coming to rejoin his company but in need of funds for equipment and horses. Letters seeking help arrived frequently – for debts or other obligations – and John Hawkwood was heard to wonder if his past generosity in supporting those he had led in battle was wise, given the ongoing cost, but they were not the only petitioners.

Just as often it was conspirators seeking his aid to overthrow the established authorities in whichever commune from which they hailed. Pisa he welcomed since that had at one time been to him a place of refuge, but none of the plotters ever seemed to have enough support to overthrow the individuals who had succeeded Giovanni Agnello; others he always treated with caution, given too many of these schemes were hatched to put into power Guelfs or Ghibellines.

Historical rivals, these factions should have atrophied two hundred years previously when the original cause of the dispute between the papacy and the Holy Roman Empire had been resolved. To John Hawkwood it was typically Italian that it had morphed into factionalism so fluid you could never be sure which side represented what and why; it seemed to have a life of its own set aside from normalcy, yet it could be deadly.

It set fathers against sons, brother against brother, city traders against country landowners, artisans against exploitation by factors, various guilds taking sides and sometimes just sheer bloody-mindedness to keep a dispute alive and extract revenge for slights real or imagined. Every city state and commune down to the smaller towns seemed to be full of folk holding clandestine meetings in which grievances could be aired to eventually grow into an attempt at rebellion.

Most would be nipped in the bud, for if conspiracy came naturally to the people of Italy, suspicion of treachery was its soulmate and guardian. Thus did those who held power protect themselves against usurpers, and the means by which that was achieved held no relation to fair dealing. Everything was permitted: spying was endemic, torture was rife and judicial murder commonplace, while the mood it created affected the whole country.

It was a party of Guelfs who came from Florence to Bagnacavallo with a scheme to overthrow the present Ghibelline *Signoria*, full of promises of rich reward. Donnina, who entertained them as the chatelaine while awaiting Hawkwood's return from raiding, was quick to point out to him that they were not the bankers or large wool and cloth merchants, but landed folk from outside the limits of the city.

Naturally those elected to run Florence favoured those who resided within its walls and not those who grew the food to keep the city fed. Donnina was of the opinion that even if they owned large productive estates, these men could not have access to the funds they claimed and so what they promised, if it ever arrived, would be in some very distant future when they had control of the Florentine Treasury; that was not a proposition she found alluring.

Hawkwood never failed to listen to his clever and beautiful young wife. She had been raised in a Milanese court and had an Italian nose for intrigue, more specifically its chances of success, not great in the orbit of Bernabò given when it came to being suspicious the man was in a league of his own. He had the advantage of being a sole ruler; communes like Florence, run by committee, were more vulnerable.

'So you rate them as exaggerating their support and what they can pay?'

'I do.'

Having been delivered of a second daughter, Donnina had recovered her figure as well as the opportunity to ride, which she enjoyed and of which pregnancy had deprived her. Now she was out with her husband as he toured his outlying properties to ensure those stewards he had left in charge were carrying out their duties properly and not wasting even more of his money.

'Even if they were not,' Donnina added, 'does another rebellion in Florence suit our needs?'

The exploited artisans of Florence, those who washed and carded the wool and worked from dawn till dusk for starvation wages, had recently and spontaneously risen up to take over the city. They held out for six weeks of riot and mayhem in which the houses of the wealthy and those who governed, usually the same people, were ransacked and torched in what was claimed by the downtrodden to be the first genuine republic in Italy since before the Caesars.

The brutality with which it had been put down was harsh even by the standards of the day. The city was stormed by paid mercenaries and taken back with no quarter given, the massacres followed by executions that had lasted a week. Yet it was indicative as to how febrile the polity of it was that a second set of Florentines were looking to overthrow those so soon restored to power, while it transpired they had been part of the combination who had paid to subdue the workers.

'What about your pension, Husband?'

'That has been promised.'

'And to support your expenses?'

'Is there ever money enough for that?' was the mournful response.

His wife knew of the costs of their position as well as he, perhaps better given she oversaw the ledgers. His estates were failing to produce the revenues needed for their upkeep and repair, so were a drain. It seemed the world knew to the florin how much John Hawkwood earned in plunder, pensions and ransoms; no one took into any calculation his outlays, and that was not just in property costs.

First, if no one else was paying his men, he must, or he would not keep them in his service. Promises from those who employed him were just that and, given it was to be disbursed in instalments, it was a rare day that they came when they should, which took no account of the many times it had never arrived at all.

The amounts he had outstanding were huge, not least in ransoms which, if negotiated, were sometimes never paid. If the obligation was met, it rarely came swiftly: those he captured did not have vaults full of silver florins whoever they were, so a ransom was an agreement to pay the sum at whatever date it could be raised by the captive himself or his relatives.

To hold a man till the debt was satisfied would eat away at the final profit, given a prisoner had to be fed and guarded, so it was often better to let them go on a promise of payment by a certain date and the slippage there was commonplace. What it added up to was straightforward: despite the successes he had enjoyed in his career, the Hawkwood coffers were never as full as was supposed.

He had also taken to remitting monies back to England to support a whole host of relatives and to purchase properties, being determined to finally settle there with his family when the time was ripe, which it was not now. John Hawkwood was in his sixties and did not keep active for pleasure; he did so out of necessity.

'Florence pays you, Husband, and that is at present

secure. I suggest it would be unwise to put that under threat given where we are placed at present.'

He had been in this situation before, going from plenty towards dearth and back again many times, which was the way of things in the life he led. But he had, in the past, been immune to concern, with only his own needs about which to worry. That was no longer the case: with a wife and two daughters and his other commitments the requirement for a steady flow of income was altered.

'How much do you think that weavers' rebellion cost Florence?'

'Thousands of ducats.'

'Then ask how much they would pay to avoid another uprising.'

Hawkwood fell silent as he considered what Donnina was suggesting, held until he hauled on his reins, bringing them both to a halt by a stream, where they could dismount and the horses could drink.

'If I were to betray our present callers, it would be necessary to know of their schemes in every detail.'

Donnina came close enough to peck his cheek, her voice low. 'Think like a Visconti, Husband, and also reflect that the people ruling Florence may not like you, but they respect you, pay you a pension and may in future need your services. What is worth more, a bird in the hand or—'

'You're a vixen,' was his response, delivered with a smile.

'About to cub again, John, I think. Another child will not ease the burdens you face, will it? Put your family to the fore.'

Christopher Gold was sent to the Florentine *Signoria*, asking what fee could be extracted to expose a definite conspiracy against them, with enough details but no names to ensure his constable was believed. He returned with an offer of twelve thousand florins, by which time Hawkwood had been made privy to the entire plan of the plotters who claimed a level of support that made their projects much brighter than Donnina had originally supposed; truly Florence was a hotbed of intrigue.

The exposure had to be as clandestine as the conspiracy. Nothing could be placed in writing, certainly by John Hawkwood, for to do so would leave a trail of evidence and that could impact on the future. There had been moments where he wondered if what he was engaged in could be justified, for if he was happy with duplicity when on a field of battle, this seemed less worthy. It was his determined wife who kept him on the chosen path.

'You did not seek these people out, they came to you and in doing so put their heads on the block. If the axe falls it is their own doing, not yours.'

The Florentine envoys never came near his home; he met them instead at Cotignola in a house barren of furniture bar the chairs on which they sat, the only light coming from the logs burning in the huge grate of the hall. The details of the plot were revealed, the leather sacks of coins unloaded from the mules and handed over. There were no pleasantries, no smiles, which meant that Hawkwood's parting remark fell on deaf ears.

'I trust you will recall what Florence owes me.'

\* \* \*

The time came, as it did with all freebooting companies, that a natural division seemed best and on this occasion the parting into two sections was amicable. But since he was static some of Hawkwood's own lances began to drift away and his force was seriously reduced, bringing risks.

'We are too close to Milan, Christopher, and that means too much within the orbit of Bernabò.'

'He has shown little sign of wishing to disturb you.'

'My wife keeps telling me to think like a Visconti. When I do it is a lack of activity that raises my hackles. The Lord of Milan is not much given to forgiveness and making his own daughter a widow will trouble him not. But if not here, where do we go to ply our trade?'

'There are few options. The Accord of Sarzana has held better than you supposed.'

'Aye, I admit to misreading it. Our two popes are concerned more with fighting each other than the recovery of fiefs, though that may alter with Urban's success.'

The accord had held, even if it turned out to be truly unsatisfactory to all concerned, Milan excepted. The papacy was still barred from those places where its representatives had been ejected. Florence, if no longer under papal interdiction, was still saddled with the huge financial penalties first laid out by Pope Gregory. His twin successors were locked in their internecine conflict but that was now in flux.

Urban, with the aid of an Italian *condottiere* who now led the Company of St George, had routed the forces of Clement north of Rome, destroying the Bretons and taking their leaders prisoner. This caused the Breton captain holding the Castel Sant'Angelo to surrender, allowing Urban to take possession of the Vatican.

Clement was checked but not defeated: he went south to Naples, accepting the invitation from the French-born Queen Joanna to afford him sanctuary. In this she misread her subjects, who were all for an Italian pope and especially one who had grown up in Naples. They rose up and drove the one-time Robert of Geneva out of the city, forcing him to take ship and go back to Avignon, while Urban, who had once been favoured by Joanna, saw her aid to his papal rival as an affront; she must be deposed and a new ruler appointed.

The vehicle for this was a magnate by the name of Charles of Durazzo. He was invited to swap a fairly impoverished kingdom on the Dalmatian coast for the fabulous prize of one of the greatest sea-trading cities in Italy. The price he was asked to pay seemed incredible – he would be required to release his most valuable provinces – not least because the recipient would be a nephew of Pope Urban, one Francesco Prignano.

Born into poverty he might have been, but like most popes, Urban was determined his family would gain from his position; the occupants of the Holy See never seemed to take cognisance of how this lowered them in the eyes of the laity.

John Hawkwood might observe this with a jaundiced eye but he was required to look to his own concerns. First he must unburden himself of the cost of the properties his marriage had brought him. These were mortgaged to the

Marquis d'Este, a lord who paid a great deal to get his salt through Cotignola. He agreed to take possession for twenty years for a fee of sixty thousand gold ducats. Now free of encumbrances and with healthy coffers Hawkwood marched south with his family and three hundred men, sending ahead a letter to the *Signoria* of Florence, desiring permission to purchase a house in the city.

'They said no, the ungrateful wretches.'

There was some posturing in that; if John Hawkwood thought Florence owed him a debt of gratitude, they did not see it in the same light. This was a man who had besieged their walls, beaten their army at Incisa, and one whom they had been required to buy off too many times. He had a pension, it was true, but that had not been given freely; it was the cost of having their fields left with wheat to be harvested instead of destroyed by fire.

Another letter outlining his dissatisfaction got a more emollient reply. This informed him he was held in high regard in the city but they did not relish the presence of his company, which made them decline to grant his wish. Had he been a fly on the wall of their deliberations, Hawkwood would have heard the *Signoria* seeking a way out of what they saw as an impasse.

The English Company within the walls and resident was anathema, too dangerous by far, but to upset such a powerful mercenary as John Hawkwood had to be unwise. His fractured relationship with Bernabò Visconti was no mystery yet he was still wedded to the Lord of Milan's natural and much-loved daughter. He might be a friend and as such would be beneficial but it would be foolish to turn him into an enemy. If Milan came calling for his services, as they had in the past, Florence could suffer.

As a compromise he was given permission to purchase a home outside the city, the sequestered property of a fellow who had betrayed Florence in the War of the Eight Saints. The estate of San Donato lay on the road to Prato and was substantial enough to accommodate the family in comfort. In addition it produced any number of crops to help finance its upkeep.

# CHAPTER TWENTY-SIX

If settled in seeming domestic bliss, Hawkwood still had his men and they required employment: fortunately Pope Urban VI was eager to provide it. In a grand ceremony he had actually crowned Charles of Durazzo as King of Naples, which even by the standards of papal excess was astounding given it lay outside his powers. In the same ceremony he deposed Queen Joanna and declared a Holy War against her. The entire power and revenues of the Church were to be at the new monarch's disposal, which allowed for the recruitment of a large army.

The letter from Urban was addressed to the Florentines. It asked that his good and loyal son, John Hawkwood, Knight, be contracted to his service with six hundred lances for a payment of forty thousand florins. By the Accord of Sarzana the fees to pay Hawkwood and the men he would raise would be deducted from that owed to the Pope by the city from the recent war.

In effect Urban was employing the best of the *condottieri* at no expense; his chances of ever getting the three million florins demanded by Gregory were nil. Yet the *Signoria* had no choice but to agree as well as to give permission for Hawkwood to recruit within their own territory to find the extra men needed to get his company up to strength. There were enough lances close by to easily make up the number and some of them were old faces.

'We shall be the White Company once more, Christopher.'

'Are we on the right side, Sir John?' was Gold's question.

Hawkwood laughed for it was a common query, usually answered by where the money lay.

'I daresay Urban is as much of a rascal as those who preceded him and I have no doubt this Durazzo fellow is cut from the same cloth. But Joanna is French and it is rumoured she has asked Paris for support. So we must hold our noses and do that which will please London. Where France takes the field, there we must be to oppose them on behalf of our sovereign, while being blessed with payment for doing so.'

To leave now was so very different from past departures; he was no longer just his own man and if a public display of affection with his wife was not possible in front of his assembled company, no fighting man could object to another embrace and kissing his children. He and Donnina had said their farewells in the grey light of the morning and there were no tears. Her husband was a soldier and she was a warrior's wife.

Daughters were lifted to be kissed and set down again, before the captain general of the Florentine contingent in the papal army mounted his horse – the *Signoria* had bestowed on him the silver and gold baton of their city – and with Salmon and Christopher Gold riding to his rear he led his company out under their billowing white banners.

By the time they joined Durazzo it had been confirmed that Queen Joanna, forty years sovereign of Naples, four times married but yet childless, had conferred the succession of her throne to Louis of Anjou, brother of the King of France and cousin to the antipope, Clement VII. No declaration of hostilities could be clearer.

Durazzo moved with speed, Louis at a leisurely pace, so by the time the French prince arrived outside Naples it had already fallen and Joanna was dead, murdered by Durazzo, her body thrown into the marketplace to be mocked and defiled by her one-time subjects. If John Hawkwood found that distasteful it could not be allowed to interfere with what was necessary.

Observing the army of Louis of Anjou he realised they were preparing to besiege the city but as yet in a state of disorder, so without consulting Durazzo he sortied out as the head of the White Company and launched a furious attack. Not for the first time in his career surprise was his ally. The shocked French broke ranks and fled but not before several of their leading nobles had been captured.

Louis was then faced with the whole of Durazzo's at times formidable army, superior in quality if not in numbers and forced away from Naples. The Frenchman was chased into southern Calabria where his army, short on food and losing men and horses to the climate and disease, ceased to be a force able to give battle. Was it despair that took Louis to meet his maker or illness? It mattered not: without him the men he had led now sought nothing more than a way to get home.

His duty to Florence and Urban completed, and with no great regard for what he had seen of Charles of Durazzo, Hawkwood was free to search for other opportunities. Several bands had begun to coalesce into a huge Company of the Rose, which he joined, and the lands of Campania and the Abruzzi were exposed to the kind of ravages that had so afflicted Tuscany.

As they went on their plundering sprees, John Hawkwood and his fellow captains heard of the trials and tribulations of Urban VI, for there were no triumphs. Durazzo naturally declined to meet his bargain with the papal nephew and Urban decided he alone could chastise his one-time protégé. Coming south to Naples all he achieved was to create a foul stew of his own making. Reckoned now to be completely mad, he ended up torturing and killing six of his own cardinals for a supposed conspiracy to drag him back to Rome and burn him as a heretic.

He also tried to make war on Durazzo, who besieged him so closely that Urban had to be smuggled out of his stronghold to escape back to Genoa by sea. It was there that Hawkwood met him for the very first time, a wild-eyed zealot who saw conspiracy and deceit everywhere while at times frothing enough at the mouth to bite his own lips till they bled.

Yet it was essential that he treat him with the respect due to his office; Hawkwood had been appointed by King Richard as an Ambassador to the Holy See, this time paid, his services seen to be vital to his sovereign's needs. England and Rome had a community of interest in opposing France, plus Avignon and Clement, which outweighed the fact that the man they were relying on was feeble in the head, given to uncontrollable rages and the least sanctified person the new ambassador had ever met.

Such a duty did not drag him from his main occupation, which was plunder. He freely moved between Florence and the provinces of central Italy, sometimes operating on his own, at others with the Company of the Rose, a truly international body made of Englishmen, Italians and Bretons.

Permanently in the saddle he was able to acquire a great deal of money which, not being really safe as specie in coffers, was invested in properties all over the country to join those which came to him from ransoms, all administered in his absence by attorneys.

Sir John Hawkwood was at the height of his standing, the most famous fighter in Italy. He had lived well beyond the allotted span of most of his contemporaries and was happy and fulfilled in his private life, only saddened by the fact that he had lost some close confidantes. Alard the Radish had died of a fever, Ivor the Axe and Christopher Gold had returned to England with the embassy sent by King Richard to Genoa, but with Donnina to support him and growing daughters to tease him he felt the need for male companionship less.

As well as being Captain General of Florence he was the acknowledged envoy of King Richard II, had been gifted a papal standard and given by Urban the title of Duke in Spoleto. His fiefs were now extensive enough to include two important castles held by castellans on his behalf, from which he drew rents and revenues. In addition he still had rights in those properties given to Donnina by her father, for if Bernabò Visconti had fallen out with his son-in-law, he had taken no steps to punish his daughter because of it.

Lombardy was naturally an area of interest, yet it was seen as a distant one. The Lord of Milan was quiet, while he had been in power so long it seemed inconceivable that it should not continue. Yet Bernabò was now in his seventies and such a great age of necessity diminished his abilities. Again it was letters from old friends that kept the Hawkwood household, now home to three daughters and the much longed for infant son, abreast of matters in Milan and Pavia.

Yet the situation was hard to fathom; one set of correspondents warned of a danger to Donnina's father from Giangaleazzo. They insisted the ruler of Pavia was recruiting a large army, binding mercenary captains to his service for years, not months, and in numbers that could only be a threat to all of his neighbours and the nearby provinces of which the closest was Milan.

Others continued to report on his obvious piety and love of peace, calling him the Count of Virtue, the soubriquet by which he was now known. The two different points of view did not make sense. Then Beatrice died and her husband lost the only person who could give him advice, which might have been to guard against his nephew. In any case Bernabò married Donnina's mother not long after, thus making her legitimate in the eyes of the Church.

'Giangaleazzo's as slimy as a slug,' was Hawkwood's opinion, expressed to his wife. 'Bernabò would be a fool to trust him. If it were me I'd cut his gizzard at the first chance I was given. If he's recruiting it can only have one purpose and it's not display.'

'How can you say that when you have read of his deep piety and acts of charity? Besides, you named him a dolt as a soldier and even worse in command, so what is to fear?'

'Donnina, he does not have to be good at soldiering: he only has to employ those who are.'

She sat in his lap and patted his cheek, an indication that she did not agree with him but was not going to take it to an argument. 'So we should expect a begging missive from my father asking you to hurry to his side?'

'Pigs might fly to kiss the moon.'

'Would you not accept to please me?'

'I know you still have love for him, but no.'

'If you had ever seen his kindness you might speak differently.'

The growl was manufactured. 'Bernabò and kindness are two words that seem odd in the same sentence.'

In truth the word that would have applied was dupe. It seemed to those who knew Bernabò well that he had taken no precautions to guard against ambition in his brother's son and it was an indication of his failing powers that he was toppled with such ease. Giangaleazzo arranged to meet him just outside Milan, declining to enter the city yet bringing with him a strong escort, which was as good an indication as any that he had no trust in his uncle.

Bernabò had no designs on Pavia and was quite content with Milan, which he intended one of his bastard sons to rule after his passing. That this did not please Giangaleazzo was hardly surprising but his opposition had been kept completely hidden until he was ready to strike, this with his warm words and false religious posture. At the meeting a poorly protected Bernabò was seized and bundled into a nearby tower as the city was quickly overrun by Giangaleazzo's huge escort.

That Bernabò died so soon afterwards was put down to poisoning, yet such a view, given his age and the shock of his usurpation, could only be speculation. It was rendered more suspicious when his one-time mistress and favourite Donnina de' Porri also died in the custody of Giangaleazzo's guardians. The coincidence was too great.

Giangaleazzo then went after his cousins and that, to John Hawkwood, made sense, though it did not to the woman who had grown up in their company and had lost her mother. The offspring of Donnina senior, no longer bastards, would want only one thing: to avenge their father. Within days a letter arrived from one of them seeking Hawkwood's aid in doing so.

That required calculation; Carlo Visconti had no soldiers and Giangaleazzo had thousands. Much as he was pressed by his wife he had to conclude that to go up against a man so well prepared and with so many armed men at his beck and call was beyond unwise. He could not risk all he had as well as his family on such a tenuous connection; besides there were property matters requiring clarification and the only person who could provide that was the new Lord of Milan.

So it was incumbent upon him to write to Giangaleazzo expressing flowery affection – which would not be believed – and to ask about the continued security of Donnina's dowry possessions. If it stuck in his craw to address this Visconti in an obsequious fashion no other way would serve, just as it was unpleasant and a cause of much domestic disharmony that he found it prudent to pledge fidelity and offered to serve Giangaleazzo for a sum well below that which he would charge any other lord.

'Property is worth more than honour, it seems,' was Donnina's scathing response.

In an atmosphere of domestic chill it was as well the call came from Florence; they wanted the services of their captain general. The *Signoria* had designs on their troubled neighbour Siena. Having never employed mercenaries, that commune too often found itself at the mercy of others, with their less scrupulous neighbours keeping a keen eye on their fractured polity waiting for an opportunity to exploit any differences; this was happening now.

As usual they were virtually defenceless but without the gift of learning from past errors. The amount of produce Hawkwood garnered – virtually everything the land produced, and he even demanded of them carts with which to transport it – eventually forced them to attempt to drive him away by arms. They enjoyed the same lack of success as on previous occasions, left only with the option of ransoming their own captured captains and paying a money indemnity.

While that heartened his hopes for the retention of his wife's possessions, Milan had turned those to dust. Giangaleazzo had seized all of Donnina's properties in Lombardy. Worse, he had declared the marriage of her mother to Bernabò illegal, due to his having had carnal relations with her sister – and it was true, no woman was safe from the old satyr's attentions. Nevertheless, that returned Donnina to a state of illegitimacy. While Hawkwood expected time to produce forgiveness this was nevertheless a setback, so he was glad that another city state called upon his services. Anything was better than the atmosphere in San Donato.

The commission came from Padua asking him to fight on their behalf against Verona and the fee was attractive. This was a conflict between two deeply antagonistic polities that had been at each other's throats for decades and only the destruction of one, it seemed, would bring resolution. Hawkwood, as any mercenary would, waited to see if the terms he had been offered by Francesco Novello, the Lord of Padua, would be bettered by their Veronese enemies. When they were not the contracts were drawn up.

Marching north-east Hawkwood came to Padua with a complement of three hundred archers and six hundred mounted lances, to find waiting for him a force of eight thousand fighting men made up of the Paduan levies plus various smaller mercenary companies. Given what they expected to face it was a formidable force and it departed the city to the roars of the populace, with their lord and Hawkwood in the lead, to move with surprising but pleasant ease in the territory of the enemy.

Destruction was, as usual, the primary tactic so the host burnt and destroyed as it made its way eastwards, meeting no resistance, while the scouts were able to report no forces ahead. This led to the obvious conclusion, this agreed at every meeting, that the Veronese were not going to meet them in battle but were content to rely on their city walls to thwart the offensive.

The analysis was wrong. If they burnt as they went the Paduan army was leaving behind a desert in terms of supply. Then they entered one created by their enemies, who had destroyed their own crops and removed all livestock from the line of Hawkwood's march. Worse, the Veronese forces had let them pass to then swing behind them. This cut the Paduans off from any supply from their own city or region.

Refusing to panic, Hawkwood called a halt, hoping his foes would seek battle. He waited, but in vain. Like any army on the move, what they carried with them was soon consumed, while the horses began to suffer from a lack of fodder. In addition, the wells had been poisoned and a shortage of that for equines was fatal so they began to expire, which at least provided some meat to make up for an utter lack of any other.

'We must fall back and work our way round the enemy.'

Hawkwood's words, which he had cleared with Novello well before, reduced some of the Paduan captains to tears; the mercenaries were more stoic, one asking if there was a plan to go with the captain general's opinion.

'First we must regain our strength and that means eat properly. Therefore my aim is to make our way southwards for the border fortress of Castelbaldo, where we have enough supplies. Once there, we can assess what will serve next.'

'Not all the way to Padua, then?' was the question of Franceso Novello, who had accompanied his host but never interfered in the way it was commanded.

Hawkwood smiled in appreciation of what was clear support, but addressed the room. 'We are heading in a strange direction to get there, My Lord. We have been outmanoeuvred but we are not yet beaten. If the Veronese follow we can give them battle; if not we can possibly resume our advance with a good line of supply, for we will not fall for their stratagems twice.'

It was, of necessity, a forced march and one in which if a man fell behind he was left to fend for himself and that could only be achieved by hiding out and hoping to find food, while escaping the attention of the enemy. For some this was far from an option; they fell from exhaustion and were left to die, and the enemy, in pursuit and too close for comfort, were soon abusing the bodies.

Hawkwood drove his soldiers hard; there was no respite, the only alternative death and a painful one, but at least they got into lands where there was ample water, if few crops. By the time they made Castelbaldo, on the northern bank of the Adige River, it was as a weary army which, if it could eat, found it had little time to decide what was to be done next. The enemy was closing in and in superior numbers.

'We cannot fight here,' Hawkwood pronounced. 'To slow the Veronese down we must take our supplies and cross the Adige, which will force them to detour to do likewise. Once over it is my view we must stand and fight.'

'According to reports,' Novello said softly, 'we are outnumbered near two to one, thanks to what we have lost. I merely say this because once across the river we are going away from any chance of safety.'

'So we invite an attack and at a place we shall choose. To do otherwise is to fail completely.'

The look around the assembly was a hard one; he was asking these men to trust his reputation. Before them they observed a fighting soldier well past his prime, his hair white and his skin sagging on a full, ruddy face. Yet in the eyes was the fierce determination that had got him to his present military eminence.

'Get your soldiers and horses fed and put them to filling the waggons, while I cross the river and reconnoitre the area.'

'You too should eat, Captain General.'

Hawkwood smiled at the Lord of Padua and patted what was a reasonable paunch. 'I carry enough to keep me going for a while yet.'

He found the site he wanted almost directly on the opposite bank of the Adige, near a small village called Castagnaro, which had the virtue of marshes as well as irrigation channels he could employ to tunnel the enemy attack. By reducing the fighting frontage he reduced the effect of their superior numbers. There was little chance for rest – everything had to be fetched over the river by one narrow bridge – and as soon as he had the numbers they were set to dig a ditch across his frontage that would slow any cavalry charge; only then were they permitted to rest.

It was obvious to the densest brain that should they be broken there was nowhere to run and Hawkwood wanted it that way. Let the men he led see that only by standing firm could they prevail. Yet he was not going to rely on them merely being stalwart; he had plans to formulate, well aware that they would only succeed if his enemy reacted to them as he hoped.

After morning Mass the battalions were ordered to eat and drink then arranged to fill the front, longbowmen on one flank, crossbowmen on the other. He had them stood to as soon as the enemy appeared, drums beating and banners waving, their confidence seeming to sweep across the ground to unnerve the defenders. A reserve of fifteen hundred horse was set to the rear next to the priestly cart, a high-wheeled chariot centrally located and easily seen, to which men who were sure they were dying could seek the last rites.

Hawkwood took up his position in the front line where he could be seen by all. His motives were not to boost faith but to control the battle in his own way. As soon as the Veronese were deployed he sent out skirmishers to draw them into a tiring fight. As the enemy pressed, these skirmishers fell back as they had been commanded, drawing on a force that had marched even harder and longer than the Paduans. This brought them to the ditch, which, mounted or on foot, they struggled to cross in proper order.

With the Paduan front still backing away they were drawn on as a mass, pushing toward the centre of the Paduan line until they were exposed to the twin pincers of the bowmen who began what could only be described as an execution. As they fell in on their own comrades to avoid being skewered they turned from disciplined attackers to a rabble.

At that point Hawkwood raised his baton high and called for a general advance of his central battalions, cutting across the front to the left flank and, that collapsing, completely broke any cohesion in the whole Veronese force. Slaughter ensued and within two hours the field was Hawkwood's, if you ignored the piles of dead and twitching wounded.

In the Veronese camp they found the enemy had possessed cannon, new on the battlefield but deadly if they could have been employed. The ground was too soft near the riverbank; indeed it was a wonder they had got them this far, for it must have been exhausting to do so.

'Now, Lord Novello, we can return to Padua or proceed to Verona.'

'I think we can count Verona as no more,' was the reply.

Two days later they were feasting and carousing amidst the general joy and Sir John Hawkwood was the hero of the hour in celebrations that went on for a week. That soured as he waited to be paid, and grew rancorous when excuses were advanced and nothing was forthcoming, this including money to cover ransoms at a time when his own men were wondering when they were to receive their due rewards.

It never came: discord and the need to keep his company intact forced him to depart Padua and beat a retreat to Florence, where he required permission to mortgage not only his family home at San Donato, but several other properties to meet his debts to his soldiers. It had been a military success but a financial disaster.

# CHAPTER TWENTY-SEVEN

The eyes of all Italy were on Lombardy and the so-called Count of Virtue. A man who could come to power by trickery and murder was not likely to be easily satisfied, and it was clear in the first year of his rule that the decrees he promulgated in his territories were no sudden inspiration. They were so complex and far-reaching they must have been deliberated on for years.

If his father and uncle had been talented administrators, Giangaleazzo showed that it was a blood inheritance by surpassing them in every way. Bernabò Visconti had ruled Milan as if it was his private household; Giangaleazzo, from his home in Pavia, surpassed that by applying personal oversight to every town and commune over which he had control. Any person entering or leaving his territories had to be recorded, thus he knew of anyone seeking to avoid their trading dues as well as the level of snooping.

No one could shut off the flow of information, however; everyone knew of the build-up of his military forces and his recruitment of a famous Italian *condottiere*, Jacopo dal Verme. Such people were now a numerous resource, given the locals had learnt their lessons well from the foreign mercenaries, able to apply them with equal or even greater severity.

Everything about Giangaleazzo pointed to overweening ambition to those who feared him most. The Florentine Republic was a state he would most wish to subdue, while it was not too fanciful a notion that the Visconti hankered after a crown. Once his greatest trading rival was under his thumb, the rest of the provinces of northern Italy would have no choice but to bend the knee and accept his hegemony.

The man required to blunt those ambitions was proving very hard to attract. Sir John Hawkwood needed money and without an actual war between Tuscany and Lombardy there was none on the horizon; the rest of the country seemed in a state of either exhaustion or anticipation, waiting to see the way of the wind and ready to jump in whichever direction suited their immediate concerns.

The hinterland around Naples offered the best grounds for plunder and it was there he concentrated his time and efforts, ignoring pleas from Florence that he return, for it was felt his mere presence and his reputation would stay the Visconti hand. Coming up to seventy he was still hale in body and spirit, but he was not to be swayed by supplications unless those who wanted his services were prepared to pay him and handsomely.

'Do I hate Giangaleazzo?' he replied to the latest envoy from Florence, a member of the Salutati family and high in the councils of the city. 'He robbed my wife of legitimacy and stole her properties, castles and fiefs as well as their incomes.'

'Yet it is reported that you offered him your services.'

'Signor Salutati, I sought to ward off his greed and his malice. I will happily send to you a fair copy of the letter I despatched to him after he had usurped his uncle's position and committed murder. There you will see it was but a sop, for I offered to sell my sword arm for less than I now pay one of my marshals.'

'So it means nothing?' Hawkwood laughed and just shook his head. 'I hope you comprehend that in our home city we are concerned.'

'Our home city?'

It did not need to be said that they had barred him from residence within the walls. Yet he was dealing with a fellow who functioned easily in the snakepit of the *Signoria* so he was not to be so easily wrong-footed. The response was as smooth as the best fine wool garments for which the city was famous.

'I hope you believe we now see you as a son of Florence. But the Viper of Milan?'

Hawkwood managed to make his growl sound like he was clearing his throat; he still smarted from that refusal, yet it would be impolitic to rub anyone from the republic up the wrong way when his property and family were so close by and vulnerable.

'I do say this. You are right to fear him, but I also say that sitting and watching a snake will lead to lassitude for he will hoodwink you into a state of sleep. Giangaleazzo does not do anything by chance. He has a plan and he will implement it in his own time and to your detriment. First he will seek to overawe communes that lack the fibre of Florence.'

Salutati gently interrupted, his voice sad. 'Perugia and Pisa have already acknowledged his power. His legates now control their actions.'

Hawkwood sighed. What Giangaleazzo was doing presented no mystery: if his ultimate aim had to be Florence then it did no harm to weaken her first by cutting off the routes by which she could pursue her profitable trades – Pisa, at the mouth of the Arno, being the most obvious.

'And more will follow if you do not act, Signor. But as of now I have needs to see to. You have brought me your concerns, please feel free to return to me when you have a proposal.'

If it was polite, Hawkwood was telling Florence not to trouble him again unless they contemplated action, not aware that he was pushing at an open door. The *Signoria* was already in touch with other communes, places that, if they were only titular republics, adhered to the myth. They were controlled by men who had no desire to be replaced and probably disposed of, for there was no chance the Viper would allow them to remain alive and in their palaces, even for show.

Messengers rode back and forth to set up meetings for more senior embassies at which it was only the final construct that required resolution, plus the agreement that wealthy Florence should pay for the coming war and provide the bulk of the forces. Bologna joined quickly, but nothing showed the depth of the threat better than the fact that Verona and Padua agreed to be part of the grand coalition and act in concert. But Florence could provide more than men: it would deliver Hawkwood.

Given command as captain general of their forces, he first reminded the *Signoria* of how many times he had ravaged their lands and if that induced discomfort it had a purpose. If he could do so, so could Giangaleazzo. Certain things such as moats and outposts must be put in place to protect the Valley of the Arno and thus the city itself.

Satisfied that such matters were in hand he rode north-east to join once more with Francisco Novello, The Lord of Padua, who had been given titular command of the combined army even if no one doubted who would truly lead. The force that marched north in late January in the Year of Our Lord Thirteen Ninety-One looked and was splendid, full of high spirits and comradeship.

Nine thousand horse and five thousand foot soldiers made up the host and in addition there was as a camp following of armed adventurers not paid for by the Florentine League, hoping for plunder. As soon as they appeared close enough to Parma and Ferrara, two city states who had been obliged to acknowledge Visconti as their overlord, they immediately broke that bond.

There was not a commander, captain or marshal who was not convinced that the suppressed people of Lombardy lived under a tyranny and would come to their aid. For that reason there was to be no despoliation, fields were to be respected and everything paid for. It was a command easier to issue than to enforce. The army in general could be controlled; the freebooting adventurers could not and many an offence was down to their actions. They fanned out from the route of march to steal, murder and rape at will, news of which soon spread. The locals did not, when they sought revenge, differentiate between such creatures and the soldiers.

Hawkwood rode at the head of the force with the other leaders, the army strung out behind them on what was an old Roman road, wide enough to only allow four horsemen or six foot soldiers abreast and one waggon. With such numbers the last cohorts were three leagues to the rear of their commanders and such lengthy arrangements allowed the peasantry to strike at will. In addition, the weather, which should have been improving, turned foul and the morale of the host began to suffer from these twin afflictions.

In such conditions supply waggons did not always turn up where and when they should, while at all times, cold and wet, the men had to look out for sudden ambuscades as the natives sought recompense for their losses, where only a blood-soaked and dead enemy would suffice. Once killed they would be stripped and mutilated.

Spirits plummeted as the sheer weight of fear, cold and often hunger sapped the will to continue and desertion became rife, which only added to the problem; men who had left the forces of the league were in hostile country with only one way to subsist. They were forced to take what they needed to survive and since they had set out in high hopes of plunder they indulged freely in that also. Their more loyal comrades thus suffered even more.

'Make camp?'

'No!'

Novello uttered this in a brusque fashion and not in concord. Unlike on the previous campaign with Hawkwood, where he had deferred without demur to the captain general's superior knowledge, he had begun to assert his authority as commander which did not please the other mercenary captains who had taken service. They knew who they trusted and given it was Hawkwood who had made the suggestion it was left to him to respond.

'If we go on as we are the losses in men will render us unfit to give battle and that takes no account of their well-being. A cold and wet army will not fight as it should.'

'The Visconti forces are as exposed to the weather as we.'

'I think, My Lord, that you will find no trace of the enemy. If Giangaleazzo intended they should come and face us; you would. The Lord of Milan has taken the advice of his captains and has kept his men dry and fed.'

Conrad of Landau, brother-in-law to Hawkwood and a *condottiere* he had campaigned with previously, spoke up in support, and he was not alone. Nods indicated he was speaking for the mass.

'We can set up a route of supply back to Padua and also send out patrols to contain those whose actions are cursing our efforts. Then, when the weather improves we move on.'

Giovanni di Barbiano, whose own brother commanded part of the Milanese forces, was vocal in his agreement, which left Novello isolated. If he was not happy he had no choice but to agree, so the next two months were spent in keeping the host intact, no easy task for the foot soldiers, who had been sure they would not be away

369

from their hearths longer than a couple of months.

Hawkwood had no concern for his depleted numbers, now half of his original force; moves had been put in place to engage plentiful reinforcements under the Count of Armagnac, another freebooter, a rare Frenchman who was bringing with him the equipment required to impose a siege. So when the weather turned and the spring sun appeared, the host set off again for a rendezvous with Armagnac that would end, it was hoped, with the fall of Milan.

The Army of the Florentine League marched through the lands of Brescia unmolested and headed for the River Po to rendezvous with the Frenchman, coming to a halt between Pavia and Piacenza. There they waited – and waited – as May turned to June and that became July and with it blistering heat. Scouting parties sought Armagnac in every direction, only to come across the forces of the Visconti massing to engage them in numbers they could not match.

'I have said to you before, have I not, that retreat is not defeat.'

Novello nodded at that; it would not be politic to mention where that lesson had been driven home. The Veronese were allies and it was the man speaking who had defeated them.

'I warned the *Signoria* of Florence,' Hawkwood insisted, 'this would be a long war, not just a single campaign, and for that they are prepared. If we fall back it is not to lose but to regroup, recruit more men and come back when conditions favour us.'

'It is far from glorious.'

'I think, My Lord,' interjected Barbiano, 'that Sir John

has enough glory to withstand criticism.' He might as well have said out loud that Novello did not and the man was visibly stung. 'Better to fight another day than dispose of soldiers' lives to no purpose.'

'The men of Padua will not be found wanting.'

Astorre Manfredi, who commanded the Verona contingent, butted in. 'They will, but they'll suffer for allies to stand alongside them.'

'Enough,' Hawkwood barked; the last thing that would serve was an argument between these two old foes. 'I am with you for my reputation, and based on that, added to my experience, I will insist we fall back.'

Novello went pale; his command title, which was no more than a sop to his pride, had just been overturned and the worst of it was he was isolated. If he wanted to fight Milan he must do so on his own, which would be suicide. He had no choice but to agree and there was no time to waste. Hawkwood insisted they must move at once.

As ever the problem of retreat was compounded by the need to cross and march alongside rivers and these were watercourses fed from the Alpine snowmelt and so always in full flow. If there was one saving grace it lay in the spray that such rushing torrents threw up, which cooled bodies and faces that would otherwise have broiled.

Flight, however tactically astute, is not like advancing. It is enervating and halts were necessary; the host also required a break lasting more than a day to allow for recuperation which was made at the castle of Paterno Fasolaro, and even then immediate rest was not possible. Hawkwood dug his defences well aware that the Milanese were on his heels.

'We are offering battle by doing this,' Novello complained, 'which you said we must avoid.'

He got a wry smile and no more. It was evidence of how close the enemy was that Jacopo dal Verme sent Hawkwood a present, a caged fox, a sign that he was convinced the Englishman and his army were trapped. This arrived in sight of many of the men Hawkwood led, so in a loud voice he pointed out that the animal still lived, opened the cage and let it out. It was in the bushes and hidden in seconds.

'That is what I reckon to gifts from Milan.'

Greeted with laughter and cheers, it was hoped the sound carried but Hawkwood had another ploy. He sent dal Verme a gift in return, a bloodstained glove, a well-known chivalric token that he wished to give combat. The message came back that the challenge was eagerly accepted and the armies would meet the following day. In dal Verme's camp they heard the trumpets blow for the approaching dawn to match their own. First light showed the banners of the Florentine League fluttering in the wind.

Only the rising sun revealed the truth; there was no one to fight, while those fluttering banners were tied to the trees. Hawkwood, having humbugged dal Verme with his tilt at chivalry, had pulled up his tents, loaded his waggons and disappeared in the twelve hours of darkness. He was to say later if dal Verme had listened hard he would have heard his opponent laughing.

Having created a gap it had to be exploited and Hawkwood led his host towards a place where the River Oglio could be forded. Then came the Mincio and once over that water barrier the Florentine League had a clear route back to the Adige and safety, one Hawkwood wished to press on with as soon as they reached the river, a desire countered by the Lord of Padua.

'There is no sign of Milan to our rear,' Novello insisted, 'the men are exhausted and a day of rest will revive them.'

The old freebooter sat with his chin on his chest considering this, watched by the other captains, for it was very likely that Novello had the right of it.

'Conrad, I desire you to send out more patrols. Ride them hard but they are to measure a day's march and no more. If there is no sign of dal Verme I will agree, but if there is . . .'

It was in private that his brother-in-law questioned that decision, but gently.

'I diminished him when first we retreated, Conrad. It will serve no purpose for the future if he feels slighted by me. We will be coming back to fight on these same grounds and that means we need Padua.'

'I would be happier over the Adige.'

'So would I. This is not a place I would choose to make camp. But if we are safe it will serve for one night and make our Lord of Padua feel like a general again.'

With not a sign of pursuit, the tents were set up and the fires lit, prayers said and food consumed before the army settled down for the night. Never a sleeper when deep in thought, Hawkwood was wandering through the lines as he had done on many occasions, thinking of those he used to josh with in times past and missing them.

It took a few seconds to note the rumble, more to discern its meaning and many shouts to seek to wake up those sleeping close enough to hear him, this while he was running as fast as his old legs would carry him to release as many mounts as he could in the time available, which was not much.

The floodwaters, from the broken dam upstream of the Adige, came into the camp as a man-high deluge, sweeping away tents, stacks of weapons, saddles and armour as well as many a struggling soldier. Hawkwood had got mounted on a heavy destrier and faced his horse into the coming flood. He ever thought afterwards that he owed that animal his life.

The first surge having passed it was no longer a torrent but a swirling cataract in which men were struggling to stay on their feet and suffering. In darkness they could not see the tree trunks and debris swept away upstream that came down to kill and maim. Hawkwood had always had a voice to command and now it was at full pitch, making more sense to panicked ears as the sound of the rushing waters subsided.

Pushing his mount through the fast flow he directed everyone towards the high ground, with instructions to grab a horse if they could, for that would lift them well above the level of the water and allow them to rescue others. It was a miracle that so many followed to group, to huddle and curse the Milanese under a warm night sky.

Hawkwood's concern was that dal Verme would follow up this coup by coming upon him and his men, who were without enough weapons to put up even a token fight. With a voice going hoarse from shouting and under the banner saved for him by his squire, Salmon, he ordered them to follow him.

The army that got across the Adige further downriver was a sorry sight, bedraggled, near to weaponless, on horses with no saddles or reins. There was only one choice: to head for Padua and face the derision of the population against such a proud force that in six months had gone from puissance to ridicule.

As the man in whom faith had been placed, Hawkwood took the lead ahead of Novello as they entered the city. If he had been the one to argue for a halt, the Englishman felt the ultimate responsibility, for he had let that argument stand. He was prepared for rotting vegetables, brickbats, even stones, but not for that which he received.

The news of the debacle had run ahead of them, but so too it seemed had the information of how many men his prompt action had saved, many of them sons and brothers; the population of Padua came out to cheer Sir John Hawkwood and throw their hats in the air. Women sought a kiss and their menfolk a hand, freely given in both cases. Even more surprising, when he returned to Florence the city was set *en fête* for his arrival. He had stood high in the estimation of many but never had he risen to such heights of regard.

'Truly, Donnina, if I had known of this I would certainly have lost an army more often.'

# CHAPTER TWENTY-EIGHT

Hawkwood was soon back in the field and riding hard, even if the strain of doing so was beginning to wear out his ageing body. It took a hard look to see how afflicted he was for no word of complaint passed his lips and when it came to making decisions in the field the mind was as sharp as ever, as was his appreciation of what could and could not be done. He came to realise that if Milan was strong, so was Florence, for despite the vicissitudes of the last twenty years both had increased their wealth and areas of land, not diminished them.

The bankers flourished in both, feeding courts all over Europe as well as a strapped and divided papacy with loans. If the odd one went sour and a banking house collapsed there were rich merchants willing to take their place in a game where the rewards were commensurate with the risks, while even in more mundane exchanges – armour and weaponry for Milan, cloth for Florence – trade had increased by multiples.

It was a war short on major engagements, a series of skirmishes and clashes that tended to be indecisive. Hawkwood, by manoeuvre and ambuscade, kept the Visconti Viper from sinking its fangs in and that was sufficient; Florence did not have to beat Milan, it just had to not lose against her.

The day he rode through the gates with Giangaleazzo's own banner was one to savour, a flag he threw from the balcony of the Palazzo Vecchio into the dust where it was abused by the populace, spat on and worse, before being torn to shreds for souvenirs. After a year of fighting and the costs involved, the owner of that banner realised what his great opponent had known since he rode bedraggled into Padua. From that realisation of stalemate the offer of lasting peace was proposed.

Negotiated in Genoa, solemnised in Florence, all the leading figures were there and for the first time since he and de Coucy had nearly taken him captive, Sir John Hawkwood clapped eyes on his enemy. Giangaleazzo still had some vestiges of the handsome youth he had been, with his full head of hair and moustaches, but it was overlaid with the lines of toil. What the Viper observed was a warrior now walking stiffly and it took no great imagination to see that Sir John Hawkwood was not the man he had been, or reported as such, even up till a year ago.

Donnina came along to look upon her cousin and see if there was an ounce of family concern, not surprised when someone with whom she had grown up, albeit of different ages, declined to even acknowledge her. She was on hand to support her husband, the thirty-year age difference between them now fully marked in her continuing beauty against his wrinkled features as he took a place of honour.

The great parchment scrolls were produced, studied and waxed with the appropriate seals and signatures, to bring to an end a conflict that had drained the coffers of the two wealthy communes to no purpose; they stood where they had at the outset.

'Is it truly ended, Husband?'

'My sweet, it is never ended for those here, for they are jealous that one might outstrip the other. They will be at each other again before long but for me, well, I think enough has been done and you know what my mind is set on.'

'I cannot come myself to a decision.'

'And I will not pressure you to do so. I know it is hard to contemplate, but I have lived away from England thirty years now and I hanker to go back before my old bones expire.'

'The climate is cold and wet, you have told me that yourself. Your bones will be better served where we reside.'

'Not always. Who could say that Milan is always warm and Florence ever dry? But I have said you must decide for yourself, as must the girls, but I would like our son John to accompany me.'

That engendered a frown.

'I promise he will be free to return should he wish it, but I should like him to see my birthplace and his grandsire's grave, to look upon London where I spent many years in poverty. And I am assured of an audience with the King and he will attend with me. In addition there is much there by way of inheritance.'

'The return of which would ease our present difficulties.'

'What is in England must stay there and remain a secret between us to those with whom we mix.'

An honoured son of Florence now, Hawkwood was, for all his successes in battle and plunder, burdened with debt. The Lady Donnina had spent most of her time while he was campaigning writing to bankers, agents and past employers, demanding sums of money that were years outstanding. Ransoms were unsettled too, or had passed through so many grasping hands, each demanding a fee, as to be of little value when finally realised, while all the while he had the costs of maintaining that which he owned.

If it was kept hidden and would scarcely have been believed had his situation been made public, Sir John Hawkwood was struggling to meet his obligations. Janet, now fifteen, was betrothed to a knight of Friuli and given away at a ceremony in San Donato, saved from sale once but threatened once more. With the coming of peace the future did not promise much in the way of reward and he had had to sell objects of value to finance Janet's dowry.

The commune had freed him from the forced loans that financed the commune's wars but his other two daughters, growing quickly to marriageable age, required dowries too and he had no notion of where they were to be found.

It was a rueful knight who complained to his wife that prior to coming to Italy he had struggled to grasp what a million was.

'Twice, happen thrice that has passed through my hands, and here I am near a beggar.'

Only the *Signoria* could provide relief and that took months of negotiation, in which time his second daughter, Catherine, was wed to a mercenary captain who had served under her father in the campaign that had nearly seen them both drowned. Conrad Prospergh had won Hawkwood's affection, plus his spurs, for his cool head and outstanding bravery.

In lieu of all his properties, manors, castles and debts outstanding he was granted from Florence future security for himself, his wife and family. Pensions were granted to him and to them in perpetuity, enough to make his children good marriage prospects and to keep his wife in the manner to which her birth and his rank entitled her. With that he could contemplate a thing which he had never experienced for more than a month: inactivity.

It was difficult to know if that caused what followed, but Sir John Hawkwood went to bed one night, having finalised his plans to leave for England, with Donnina only promising she might follow in his footsteps at a later date.

He never woke up from his slumbers.

The funeral was to be as grand as the *Signoria* could make it and executed regardless of expense. He was, after all, the hero of Florence. His body, once washed and mourned over by his family and friends, was placed on a bier laid over the

Baptistery font while the bells of every church in Florence pealed out a mournful cadence.

The arrangements were made to honour him in a way that would mark the debt the city owed to him. On the Saturday of the funeral all shops and business were ordered to close and the bier was taken to the Piazza della Signoria, where it lay with his sword on his chest and his baton in one hand. The entire *Signoria* stood in mourning on the balcony of the Palazzo Vecchio looking down on the packed square filled with bishops, abbots, priests by the hundred, the leaders of the guilds and the men of the Merchant's Court surrounded by the swaying masses of the city.

Sir John's own bodyguard lances stood before eight richly caparisoned warhorses, each with a liveried groom, holding his standards and the plumed and decorated helmets that had adorned him on the battlefield, to then partake in the procession to the duomo where a Mass was said for his soul and the great deeds of his accomplishments read out with Donnina, her hair shorn for widowhood, and his children, in pride of place.

They buried his body in the sacristy but it did not long remain there, and was, after cremation, buried for eternity in the choir. After a period of mourning the time came for the city to look to the needs of his dependants, complicated by the fact that the hero of Florence had not executed a last will and testament.

This left Donnina at the mercy of people quick to either forget or repudiate their obligations. Perhaps because she was a Visconti there was haggling over what she could be paid of the agreed pensions, which found her dealing with a very different Florence to that which had so richly and recently interred her husband at great expense.

Hawkwood had the right of it about peace. The Viper of Milan, no Count of Virtue now, did not stay content for long; Giangaleazzo still hankered after Florence and a crown and was outside its walls within five years, preparing to declare himself king, when the fever struck him as had been prophesied. Taken back to Lombardy he died and as he did so all that he had built up collapsed, almost as if his old enemy had come back to haunt him and his ambitions.

It took many years before Hawkwood was properly commemorated in a way that would speak to coming generations – some forty years later when Florence had just ended a war with Lucca and the original fresco to honour him was much faded. The artist chosen was Paolo Uccello and if you visit the Duomo of Florence today it is there for all to see, for if he lived a life of questionable behaviour, he is still a hero to the city he saved.

To discover more great books and to
place an order visit our website at
allisonandbusby.com

Don't forget to sign up to our free newsletter at
allisonandbusby.com/newsletter
for latest releases, events and exclusive offers

Allison & Busby Books
@AllisonandBusby

You can also call us on
020 7580 1080
for orders, queries
and reading recommendations